The Irrationalist

The Tragic Murder of René Descartes

Andrew Pessin

Published by Open Books

ISBN-10: 0998427446/ISBN-13: 978-0998427447

PROLOGUE

NOVEMBER 10, 1619 (JULIAN)
ULM-JUNGINGEN

*I*t was the eve of St. Martin's Day. Everybody in the village was at home that cold late afternoon making costumes and paper lanterns for the children, slaughtering geese for the communal feast, drinking apricot schnapps. There was thus no one around the house with the large wood-burning stove that Kaspar Rausche had recently built for his son and soon-to-be bride on the outskirts of the village. There was no one around to wonder why the plump young French gentleman who had leased the house was not inside enjoying that stove, given the freezing weather. Nor was there anyone around to follow the spidery footprints in the snow into the darkening woods, to hear the clanging rapiers, the booted feet stomping, and the deep throaty grunts of the two young men busily fighting each other to the death.

Stomps, and grunts, and plenty of swearing, the latter produced with the smallest of lisps and in various languages, for a gentleman must swear in many tongues—or so said the gentleman. There were impressive lunges, a

Coulé counterattack. The gentleman suddenly stepped over a fallen tree and executed a sharp Reprise, taking his opponent by surprise. The servant barely stepped to the side, but then swung his weapon around quickly, pointed it at his master's throat, and pressed it on his larynx.

For a moment the two men glared at each other, their breath steaming in the air. From the side, from a certain angle perhaps, they almost resembled each other, despite everything that separated them. Or maybe it was just the deepening twilight, that they were both rather short, that they shared that French black hair and those protruding lips—though only one of them had the plump body and flowing locks of a gentleman.

The servant dropped his blade to his side and stood there. The snow was falling more heavily, even through the thick branches above.

Words were exchanged, angry words in foggy breaths, words making demands, words rejecting demands, words of scorn, words weary of scorn.

Words perhaps threatening—

Without warning the gentleman switched his grip and executed a sharp Cut. It landed perfectly, slicing a long thin wound along his opponent's jaw that promptly began spurting blood. The servant groaned in pain as he grabbed his jaw and fell to his knee. He felt the warm blood dripping through his fingers, only then realizing how cold his hands were. Then he looked up to find his master's rapier pointing between his eyes and to see his own rapier several steps away.

More glaring, for a moment. Then more words, as the gentleman reached with his free hand into his cloak and withdrew a small leather purse, wiggled out a pair of ivory dice. The gentleman offered, the servant hissed in reply. The gentleman shrugged, cleared some snow from a rock with his boot. The dice were rolled, then rolled again. The gentleman whistled, and not without enthusiasm, then stepped to the side, picked up the dropped rapier, and tossed it to the other man.

The injured servant gazed up at his benefactor with cold eyes.

Then he took a deep breath, reached for his rapier, and returned to his feet. No longer noticing the pain from his bleeding jaw he advanced slowly and began speaking. As he spoke his rapier moved, with some technique and serious intention, toward his master's chest. There was a Circular Parry, some stomps, some grunts. An Extension, Saint Didier variation. And then the servant's blade came up high and sliced horizontally, inflicting a wound along his master's jaw similar to that he had himself just suffered moments before.

Another hand went to another jaw, felt goopy blood.

They stared at each other again. That same angle, that deepened dusk, those similar wounds; but the moment passed and the snow was falling more heavily and the rapiers were clanging and someone was running out of breath when one of the men unconventionally dropped and sliced low, slashing through the lined leather boot and the ligaments in his opponent's right ankle almost to the bone.

The man on the receiving end screamed and fell to the ground clutching his ankle. His opponent hesitated, then prodded him with his rapier until the inferior man was lying on his back, looking up at the sharp point of steel now poised directly over him.

There was a long moment in which they stared at each other.

A slightly cleft tongue licked some protruding lips.

The superior man said something, perhaps clever or witty, then hesitated briefly before thrusting his rapier into the chest of the other, for the moment unmoved by the shrill scream in the deserted November woods.

Slayer, he thought to himself, and of himself, then glanced down at the other man's body—*and slain*.

Then he tugged his rapier out of the fresh corpse, the

weapon making a *thwrup* sound as it departed from the leaking wound. Maybe it was that awful sound, or maybe the sight of that human body steaming in the snow, or maybe it was his returning to his senses, but at that moment his equanimity evaporated. He stumbled over the body, over the fallen branches, through the snow. He struggled through the snowy underbrush while he fingered the warm syrupy blood thickening on his jaw, felt the bitter cold enveloping him all over. He made his way back through the woods, back to the house leased from Kaspar Rausche, entering just as that snow was beginning its ascent to legendary status. He closed the door behind him, managed to rekindle that stove, and stood before the mirror.

He began to sob.

Shortly after midnight his fever spiked, and the man whose name would soon be known to the entire civilized world fell into three days of delirium, three days of strange and vivid dreams, three days that would change the course of modern intellectual history.

THE DEATH AND THE LIFE

1
MONDAY, FEBRUARY 11, 1650
(JULIAN)

*T*here was no escape.

The massive swells. The icy sea spray battering the decks, seeping through the planks and into the cramped cabins below. The frigid wet air penetrating wood and blanket and bones. The darkness of the endless nights and brief stormy days. The perpetual howl of the angry ocean. The bangs and crashes of blocks of ice against the vessel. The creaking ship was in constant violent motion, and neither rest nor respite was to be had.

In his airless cabin—his coffin, he called it—Adrien Baillet stood up from the pail into which he had just emptied his stomach and wiped his mouth on his sleeve. The men from the shipping firm had assured him the seasickness would last only a few days if he sucked the ginger root they gave him. They had also told him that the voyage on the trading fluit would only take three weeks, that his coffin would have air in it, and that the Baltic would be calmer than the North Sea. Baillet wiped the last drops of vomit from his chin as he reminded himself to be less credulous next time he contemplated sea travel.

Well, it was almost over. They had passed Dalarö two days before, and they were expected to arrive at last in Stockholm later that morning.

He paused to look at himself in the cracked mirror on the wall of his coffin, trying to breathe calmly in the small space. The dim light only accented the dark hollows in his cheeks and eyes caused by weeks of eating, and expelling, salted herring and mackerel. Nor was his appearance brightened by the thick black beard grown in the weeks since they'd departed. He was not so foolish as to take a razor to his throat on these inhospitable seas. He would groom himself when they made it to solid land—later that day, if the miracle was to be believed.

A wise decision, too, he thought again, to abandon the costume his superiors had given him to wear, as a gentleman and an ambassador, for what should have been a three-week journey. (And probably *would* have been, had he booked punctually on one of the sold-out passenger ships). He glanced at the single hook on the wall: the fine black silk robe, white cincture, black tuftless biretta, and the gorgeous black ferraiolo to drape over his shoulders on formal occasions. He looked back at the mirror, and pulled his thick black woolen cassock tighter around himself. It was warmer, more comfortable, and, with all the vomiting, easier to wash.

He poured himself some water from the flagon on the tiny table in the corner. Sipping, he grimaced, still not used to the sulphur keeping the water potable. He then withdrew from his inside pocket a small flask containing almost the last of the *jenever* he had discovered in Amsterdam and wisely stocked up on. Its anise flavor was more appealing than the sulphur, and its intoxicating effect an added bonus.

He took a sip, rinsed his mouth, swallowed.

It was time for breakfast.

He turned and squeezed himself out the door, into the

narrow dark hallway leading to the galley, toward the plate of mackerel that would temporarily refill his stomach.

That first afternoon at sea, four weeks earlier, had been a glorious one: a clear winter's day, the bright sun shining over calmer seas. Baillet had lingered on the rear of the ship in his costume, watching Amsterdam shrinking from view behind them. It was lovely, although he found himself wishing he were at the front of the ship and approaching the harbor instead, his mission completed, on his way back to his quiet room and life. "Sir," he had pleaded with the Père Supérieure weeks before, "I'll do whatever you want. I can assist in the kitchens. I'll help— the stable boy. Just don't make me go."

"You must go, Adrien," the Père Supérieure insisted. "It will be good for you. You have been here too long."

"But I'm—happy here."

"You aren't. You only think you are."

"But the Rector. He needs me."

"The Rector proposed you, Adrien. *Because* he believes it will be good for you."

Baillet sighed. Of course, he thought. Rector Charlet was in his nineties, blind, couldn't walk, could neither dress nor feed himself, but he would send away his live-in assistant in a heartbeat if he believed it were good for the younger man. "Yes, sir. I'll begin looking for my replacement, then."

"We'll take care of that, Adrien. You leave tomorrow."

"Tomorrow?"

"You'll spend a month in Amsterdam, training for your mission. But be sure to book your passage to Stockholm as soon as you arrive. The passenger ships are likely to sell out. And, Adrien, one more thing."

"Yes, sir?"

"The stable boy *could* use a little help before you go."

"Of course, sir," Baillet sighed.

As he gazed at the vanishing Amsterdam harbor that

first day he tried to get excited about the journey. He was in his early thirties—he didn't know exactly how old—and had lived nearly his whole life first under the care of, and now taking care of, Rector Charlet. The good man had tried to make something of him, without much success. Baillet failed to do much academically, unable to distinguish himself in any subject at the college except swordsmanship, and even there his distinction was merely being the only boy to serve as live target dummy for the fencing classes. He had worked as an errand boy for the administration, and then as the Rector's assistant when the old man finally retired. True, he was good with the Rector, making his nightly hot chocolate, fluffing his expensive pillows; but being a good nursemaid did not exactly count as being a success in life. And now after that whole life spent at La Flèche he was being given a mission, to represent his institution's Order to a foreign government—to the most powerful government in Europe. Shouldn't he be excited at this chance to travel, explore, make something of himself? But why, he thought as his stomach swelled with the ship's first swells, did he still feel like a target dummy?

He sighed for the first of many times on the voyage, and began making his way into the hold, in search of the galley. Supper was to be served at four o'clock, appetite or not.

The galley was a long narrow room lit only by three flickering candles, apparently as distressed by the airlessness of the chamber as Baillet immediately was. There were two longer tables for the crew, the first shift of whom were already gorging themselves and chattering in their native language. One crew member, a greasy fellow with a droopy left eye, was uncomfortably focusing that eye on him so Baillet looked away. At the other end of the room was a small table where the only other passenger, a skinny old man, was reading some papers under one of the candles, giving him just enough light.

"Monsieur," Baillet tipped his biretta as he took the seat opposite the old man, who glanced up, then returned to his reading.

Baillet sighed and looked down at the plate in front of him. It looked like herring; perhaps mackerel. Something scurried under the table, ran over his foot.

He decided not to look.

Baillet had reading material of his own, when he wasn't vomiting. His month in Amsterdam mostly cowering in his room had hardly repaired the preparatory deficit from years of mediocre academics. On calmer days that first week at sea he found a spot on the top deck, beneath the starboard gunwale, where he might enjoy some sun protected from wind and spray; if it wasn't exactly warm there in his greatcoat, in late January, at least there was fresh air and light. No, with his uneasy stomach it wasn't easy to concentrate on recent political and military events, obscure points of theological doctrine, some controversial writings about natural philosophy. But the fact was that there was nothing else to do and no one to talk to, so he might as well try to read.

Nor was it easy to concentrate given his ongoing ruminations over his fellow passenger. A full week in and the old fellow still hadn't spoken to him, and indeed after that first unfriendly glance didn't even bother looking up when Baillet joined him at the table.

Well, two can play at that game, Baillet thought, seated, silent, reading opposite the old man in the galley.

Though not perhaps equally well. Baillet occasionally stole glances at the man. A thin face, wrinkled skin, weary dark eyes staring at sheets filled with indecipherable symbols. At least seventy. Never mind Charlet's nineties, Baillet couldn't imagine even being seventy. One must be so *tired* at that age.

Baillet looked around the galley as the crew members were rotating the eating shift. Intimidating types were leaving their table and being replaced by even more intimidating types. Baillet kept catching that creepy Droopy Eye seeming to wink at him and then snorting.

Nights were the worst.

There was no way Baillet would go up on deck after dark. Just the thought of those vast, black, deep waters of the nocturnal North Sea made him ill. So after supper he slinked back to his coffin and hunkered down for the darkness. To mitigate the sensation that he was in a coffin he kept his door open a crack, but it didn't mitigate much: at night the whole dark ship felt like a coffin. Nor did it help that with the door open he kept imagining Droopy Eye creeping in on him and attempting—*something*. As he lay on his thin mattress on the floor, shivering under the useless blanket, he tried to focus on the sounds of little feet scurrying across the floor since that helped him not to focus on the roaring wind sounds from *out there*. When he did finally fall asleep he did his best not to dream about the vast black waters of the nocturnal North Sea swallowing him up.

It was a good thing for the *jenever*, he thought, lying awake now on the nineteenth night at sea, not thinking about the large chunks of sea ice lately smashing against the vessel. What if they were to smash a hole in the ship, he refused to wonder. What if the sea were to freeze over? No, there was nothing to worry about. The shipping agent had *sworn* the sea was safely passable this time of year ...

Still, another sip of *jenever* might be in order. Lying on his back on the mattress as another thump indicated another ice collision, he treated himself to a long draw from his flask. The only problem with the *jenever*, of course, was that he soon found himself badly needing to void his bladder, much to his dismay. If he were to retain any shred of his dignity—he was going to have to venture out to the *facilities* on the ship. (That's how the shipping agent referred to the bucket fastened by a long rope beneath the one porthole under deck.)

He grimaced, and slipped out unsteadily from his blanket and to his feet.

The narrow hallway was dark, of course; in his haste Baillet forgot to bring a candle. He felt his way along the wall, occasionally aware of something slinking over his feet. The ship was swaying, perhaps a squall was starting; or perhaps *he* was just swaying. There was the pitter-patter of little feet.

Then there was the pitter-patter of bigger feet.

Baillet felt rough hands grabbing him.

He attempted to protest, but no sound came out.

He heard a loud long sniff.

There were animal sounds as the hands pushed him, felt him. The ship surged and he lost his footing and stumbled. In the dark he fell against the opposite wall, hard. He fell to the floor, against the wall, found himself all wet, sweating profusely or—dear Mary no, had he released his bladder?

Something was poking him. The man was toeing him, laughing, if that's what those sounds were. The snorting and grunting changed in tone; it was no longer mocking, but—heavy strong hands were pulling at his cassock.

The man was climbing on top of him.

The smell of garlic and grease and sin.

"For the love of Mary," Baillet attempted to moan but no sound came out.

There was something pressing on him—

Then suddenly a match was struck.

A sharp glint of light. A man screamed.

Another match was struck and the solitary sconce on the wall was lit.

Droopy Eye was kneeling on the floor, screaming, holding his bloody hands over his groin. The rodents had already scattered. Standing over the screaming man, with a long bloodied knife in one hand and an equally bloody severed *something* in the other, was the old man.

"I thought you Jesuits could take care of yourselves," he said to Baillet in a German-accented and rather annoyed French, before disappearing back into his cabin.

It *was* just sweat, fortunately.

His heart still pounding Baillet watched Droopy Eye crawl away, blood trailing behind him. Realizing his bladder was still bursting he recovered himself and made his use of the "facilities." Then he came back to the old man's door and stood there, hesitating, still perspiring. He knocked once, to no reply. Then knocked again.

"Who is it?" the gruff voice responded.

Was that a—*joke*, Baillet wondered. "Please," he said in German, "I just want to—thank you."

The door opened a crack. The old man glared at him, looked him over. "You speak German?"

"*Ein bisschen*," Baillet answered modestly. In fact he spoke German well, almost naturally, for some reason, unlike every other foreign language he had attempted, and failed, to learn.

There was a long silence.

"Anyway," Baillet nervously pulled out his flask, "can I at least offer you a drink?"

The old man stared a moment longer, then opened the door. His cabin was larger than Baillet's, big enough for a desk on which a lantern was burning. He gestured to the mattress on the floor. Baillet sat down while the old man took the chair at the desk and accepted Baillet's flask. He took a generous swig then stared at Baillet before offering the flask back.

"I should probably introduce myself," Baillet said. "Adrien Baillet, of La Flèche."

"I know," the old man said.

"You do?"

"The crew has been talking about you interminably."

"You speak—Flemish?"

"Dutch, in this case. Yes."

"What have they been saying about me?"

"Less about you," the old man took the flask back from Baillet, "than about what they were planning to do to you."

Baillet grimaced. "He seemed to back off pretty quickly, though, all considered. Though I suppose it helped that—you cut off his ..."

The old man picked up the severed *something* from the desk and inspected it in the candlelight. "Relax, Père," he held it up, "just his pinky."

Baillet made a mental note to be *very* careful around this strange old man. "I suppose I should mention,'" he said quietly, "that I'm not *Père*, strictly speaking."

"No?"

"Perhaps if I had applied myself more seriously to—my studies."

"That explains it, then."

"What?"

"Your inability to defend yourself. Because Jesuits normally *can* take care of themselves."

"I'm not," Baillet answered, "your typical Jesuit." He accepted the flask back from the old man. "And what do you have against Jesuits?"

The old man stared at him.

Then he reached inside his cloak and withdrew the weapon that moments before had removed part of the sailor's digit. There was a long mother of pearl sheath with a black metal hinge at the end, fastened to a sharp and slightly curved blade that the old man now folded out from the sheath. "This is a folding gully. It's better suited to hacking than to stabbing. But one works with what one has."

"Why," Baillet asked apprehensively, "are you telling me this?"

The old man stared at him a moment longer.

"I took this," he answered, "from a Jesuit."

Some time later that night they became stuck in the ice.

It was sudden. Baillet was lying on his mattress trying not to reach for his *jenever*. He was also trying to decide what to think about this old man who had perhaps saved his life even despite his obvious antipathy toward Jesuits. Baillet had wisely decided not to pursue the anecdote about the folding gully. He also realized that he had neglected to ask for the old man's name. As he was pondering all this there was all the usual swaying, the loud bangs as mountains of ice hit the ship, and then, in an instant, all was still.

His first response was to wonder how a ship frozen in early February into the northern North Sea (or wherever they were) would ever become unfrozen.

His second response was to reach for the *jenever*.

At least the sea ice helped break the ice between the two passengers.

"I dabble in architecture," the old man revealed the next evening.

They were sitting at the small table where they took their meals. The light from the candle was just adequate to play backgammon on the old man's set. Droopy Eye had not shown up to supper.

"Architecture?" Baillet rolled the dice to start what would be a five-game losing streak.

"Some castles, fortresses, that sort of thing. A church or two."

"Anything I would have heard of?"

"Nothing significant. Just dabbling."

"Are *you* anyone I would have heard of?"

"No one significant," the old man said as he hit two of Baillet's blots.

"How do you—do that?"

"Just luck. Your turn."

Baillet rolled and brought one of his men back in. The old man promptly hit the man on his next roll and returned him to the bar.

Baillet sighed. "You're not worried?" he asked, failing to retrieve his man from the bar. "About the ice?"

"I don't worry," the old man shrugged as he started bearing off en route to a gammon.

"That isn't very helpful."

"Either is worrying. Roll."

"Your deal, Père," Benjamin Bramer said to him two nights later, their third night in the ice and twenty-second on the ship. They were at their table, playing Alouette. They were bundled into greatcoats, which neither took off anymore.

"Thank Mary," Baillet took the cards from him. His breath made puffs of smoke in the chilly air of the galley. "I don't believe I can afford any more of *your* dealing."

"You'll deal more quickly if you remove your limericks." Bramer was referring to Baillet's leather gloves, made in Limerick, Ireland; they weren't very warm but they were all the fashion in Paris, and the only part of Baillet's fancy costume that he continued to wear.

"I'll deal more slowly if my fingers fall off from frostbite."

"Fine. Ante."

Baillet placed two coins beside the two already there. "You're still not worried?"

The old man shrugged. "What's your play, Père?"

Alouette was not the most interesting game but it had the advantage, from Baillet's perspective, of being mostly a matter of chance, thus increasing his odds of occasionally winning. The first night's backgammon had quickly damaged his purse, and the second night's Landsknecht—a card game he'd learned at La Flèche—hadn't gone much better. Out of mercy, Bramer had suggested this evening they try Alouette.

"How do you do that?" Baillet sighed several moments later.

"Just luck, Père," Bramer answered, raking in yet

another pot.

But Baillet had already figured out that Bramer was disproportionately modest. During their three evenings in the ice he had managed to pry a little more information from him. "Dabbling" in architecture? The man was the official architect for the Landgrave of Hesse-Rotenburg.

"And how did Rotenburg make out during the ...?" Baillet asked tentatively as Bramer dealt another hand. He was referring of course to the "Thirty Years War" that had concluded a year before. There weren't many easy ways that a Jesuit, even if atypical, could mention to a German Lutheran the conflict in which Catholics and Protestants had so massively slaughtered each other. Especially to a German Lutheran who had at some point removed a folding gully from a now presumably dead Jesuit.

"Survived," Bramer answered, nodding to the card he'd just played. "You should take this trick."

"*Danke*," Baillet acknowledged, choosing not to.

Bramer's next play forced Baillet to take the Jack of Swords and lose the hand. "Listen, Père, shall we play something else instead?"

Baillet grit his teeth. "Another round," he said, simultaneously calling for more Alouette and more *jenever*. Three more rounds of each and they finally got around to the question of what each of them was doing on the ship in the first place.

"Representing the Landgrave," Bramer explained.

"That's it? It just seems a grueling journey for—such a short event." The Gala that Queen Christina was sponsoring—to celebrate the "Birth of Peace" in Europe—was only to last for several days. The proclaimed intention was to honor Sweden's great winter culture but it was obvious to all that the young Queen was flexing her muscles, so to speak, by deliberately throwing the event in winter in Stockholm. No one would risk offending her by not showing.

"I could say the same for you."

"Yes, but I am young," Baillet said. And—dispensable, he did not add.

"Well, the Queen also wants to build an addition or two."

"To Tre Kronor Castle?"

"And Riddarholm Church."

"Oh. I hadn't heard about that. Only that she—was to build a grand home for her new Academy."

Bramer didn't say anything.

"The Academy building too?" Baillet asked.

The old man shrugged.

"Next you'll tell me you're being inducted into the Academy as well. For dabbling in architecture."

"No," Bramer said after another swig of *jenever*. "I dabble in mathematics too."

Baillet sighed. "Pass the *jenever*, will you."

Bramer passed the *jenever* a lot over the next hands of Alouette as he tried to buoy his shipmate's spirits with spirits. "You're young," he said as Baillet finally won a hand, "you have time. And anyway, your presence here is a testament to your accomplishments. Surely your superiors wouldn't have sent you unless they believed you would represent them honorably?"

"How well do you know the Jesuits?"

"Fairly well," Bramer patted the folded gully in his cloak.

"Let me put it this way. My superiors think as—highly of my ability to represent them as you do of my ability at cards."

Bramer winced. "So, what, sending you was their way of getting rid of you?"

"They have powers, Herr Bramer. This ice is probably their doing. May I?" Baillet took a long draft of the *jenever*. He chose not to mention that when he'd asked his superiors about his return passage they had suggested they play it by ear.

Bramer waited until Baillet finished. "And a subtle little

insult to Her Majesty while they're at it, I suppose. For lording her victory over the Catholics. Or most of them." For reasons not even the major players could understand, Lutheran Sweden had allied with Catholic France but against the Catholic Habsburgs.

Baillet nodded, possibly with a hint of tears in his eyes.

"But surely, Père, you have some talents? Aptitudes?"

"None they—recognize."

"So why do you stay with them?"

Baillet took a deep breath. "I have as much freedom to depart the Order as I do to depart this ship."

"Well then why are you with them in the first place?"

Baillet gazed at him. Then took another deep breath, expelled a steamy puff in the cold air. "You promise you're not—worried about the ice, Herr Bramer?"

The next day the sun was shining and it was warm.

Well, not *warm*. But warm*er*, and warm enough.

The ice was beginning to break. The ship was beginning to move.

"I could almost believe, Père," Bramer stood beside Baillet at the railing looking over the cracking ice, "that it is spring."

"A North Sea spring, perhaps," Baillet replied from beneath his beaver hat, feeling some renewed queasiness with the new motion. "If this is the North Sea."

"It isn't. This should be the Baltic."

"I suppose it's not spring either."

"Lost track of the days, again, eh?"

"You haven't?"

"No. But it helps that I keep a journal of my nightly winnings."

Baillet was not quite ready to smile. "What day *is* it?"

"That depends who you ask. The Dutch or the Swedes?"

"Let's go with the Dutch."

"Well, it's our twenty-third day at sea. That would make

it February 16."

"And for the Swedes?"

"February 6."

They stared out over the still mostly frozen waters of the southern Baltic, so calm and peaceful, unlike most of the uncivilized world over the past three decades. These waters just *were*, indifferent, neutral. They didn't care about calendars, about the refusal of several Protestant countries to adopt Pope Gregory's new calendar for fear of being somehow corrupted by the Catholics. Today was just today, whatever people wanted to call it.

"So we'll make it in time?" Baillet said.

"I hope. The Gala begins on the 12th. The Swedish 12th."

"You were cutting it close, weren't you? Considering that you are being inducted. Seems unlike you. You would think you'd have booked an earlier ship."

Bramer shrugged, gazing at the sea ice.

Baillet took the response as a suggestion to talk about something else. "You think it will last?"

"What? The warmth?"

"No, the peace. The new world order."

"Nothing lasts long, Père. Hopefully, especially, the ballet. 'The Birth of Peace' leads me to think we're in for a very peaceful evening of snoring." The Gala was to include a ballet that Queen Christina had specially commissioned for the event.

"Ah!" Baillet gasped, reminded. "Did you hear the rumor that the Queen got *Descartes* to write the—hey," he saw that Bramer's normally stoic expression had momentarily lapsed, "are you all right?"

"I'm fine," Bramer answered quickly. "The mathematician."

"One and the same. They say the Queen got *him* to compose the verses for the ballet."

"He is there? In Stockholm?"

"He is. The Queen brought him in."

"To write verses?"

"No, to—" Baillet stopped himself. "Do you know him? You who 'dabble' in mathematics?"

"No. Just his work. Some of it. But—*you* know him?"

"Of him. La Flèche. Most famous alumnus."

"Ah, he went there. You didn't know him there?"

"No, he was before my time. But that's why—" Baillet caught himself.

"What?"

"Nothing."

"Père, you were awfully talkative a moment ago. Suddenly, 'nothing'?"

Baillet hesitated. "There is also the other rumor. About the Queen."

"Which?" Bramer asked lightly. "I know of two. One about her religion and one about his sex."

They shared a laugh. It had long been speculated across Europe that Christina was in fact a man. Something to do with her masculine build, the way her voice would drop an octave and stay there, and her frequent sexual relations with young women.

"So now tell me, Père," Bramer continued, "what have you heard about the religion?"

Just then the ship lurched as it broke free of some ice. With the violent motion Baillet's face turned green. He waved his hand in apology and leaned his head over the rail to commence vomiting.

Everything was back to normal.

Well, it was almost over.

Two days earlier they had passed Dalarö.

And now Stockholm itself could be seen approaching across the brassy winter water.

The giant cluster of black-timbered buildings composed an outline jagged with steeples. The late morning light produced a shimmering palate of yellows and browns and grays, accented by the crisp white sails of the ships scattered throughout the harbor. But most of all, standing out even more proudly than the enormous spire of Riddarholm Church, was the stunning Tre Kronor Castle. Even from the distance you could see its great central tower topped by the Three Crowns, rising from the ancient stone fort below. You could make out the massive castellated walls surrounding it, the copper-roofed turrets of its many subsidiary structures. From the distance you might know nothing of the deceased King Adolphus, who had transformed Stockholm from a sleepy hamlet of four hundred people into the resplendent and powerful capital now home to forty thousand. But even from this distance you could see the awesome thing he had brought into being.

"Magnificent," Baillet stood at the gunwale huddled into his greatcoat. Beneath it he had returned to his costume, the black silk robe, the white cincture, and the black ferraiolo. The biretta would return later, once he was indoors and could remove his beaver hat.

Bramer stood silent beside him.

It was a gray, cold and blustery morning, as you might expect on a mid-February approach to Stockholm harbor. But Baillet was barely feeling the chill, with the last of the *jenever* in his belly and with the great joy in his heart that the very last sea journey of his life was coming to an end. He would definitely take the overland route back, should his superiors ever send the return fare.

He would have to remember to get a new deck of cards before then, though, to replace the one he'd lost to Bramer after his cash ran out.

The two men stood side by side as the ship pulled into the harbor. Baillet felt nervous as he saw the hubbub going on around the harbor. He had been so busy rejoicing about disembarking that he had forgotten his anxiety about his mission, which was about to commence. His preparatory reading had not prepared him, not least, he thought, because he had given it up a week into the voyage. His stomach lurched a bit as he examined the crowd on the quay as the ship approached the dock. Stockholm was an important place, and about to host the most important event in modern European history. A three-day Gala celebrating European culture. Inauguration of the most important intellectual academy in Europe. The debut of the great ballet commissioned to celebrate the Birth of Peace throughout Europe.

And he hadn't done his reading.

He glanced over at the old man, whose eyes were fixed not on the harbor but on the towers of Tre Kronor Castle. Perhaps Bramer was thinking about his commission; or his induction into the Academy; or perhaps about their wager. A healthy sum on the question of whether Queen Christina would be a Catholic by year's end—by the Julian calendar, anyway, a concession Baillet made since Christina was monarch of a non-Gregorian country. Even so, Baillet thought his chances on the wager were good. Their man was tutoring the Queen, and having the First Ear must surely mean some influence. Her Majesty had him composing her ballet, hadn't she?

Baillet congratulated himself again on steering that earlier conversation away from Descartes after mistakenly bringing him up in the first place. Baillet's mission for his Order included facilitating in any way possible their man's influence on the Queen, and it was surely better to let Bramer believe that Descartes was only here as a mathematician and philosopher.

They were pulling into the dock now. Crew members were throwing ropes overboard, men on the dock were grabbing them, pulling the ship in, tying it. There were large carts parked nearby, teams of mules, ready for the offloading of whatever cargo the ship was carrying. After four weeks aboard Baillet had never thought to ask.

There also seemed to be a small crowd gathered on the dock to meet—*them*.

It was all rather a blur. The gangplank was laid down

and they were disembarking. Baillet had to assume someone was in charge of his trunk, would get it off the ship and to wherever he was going. In fact he had to assume someone was in charge of *him*, since it suddenly struck him that he had no idea where he was supposed to go. There was a swell of people coming up to them as their feet landed on—*land*, Baillet thought, feeling woozy. Most of the people swarmed Bramer and ferreted him quickly away, but Baillet was too disoriented to note who they were or where they were going. It only occurred to him later that he never bade farewell to the old man.

And then there was someone coming to meet *him*, thank Mary.

Someone official, apparently. Sharply dressed in an expensive greatcoat, wearing a fashionable Parisian top hat, sporting a dapper mustache and goatee. Round face, puffy cheeks, perhaps about fifty years old, with the air of a distinguished grandfather. Leaving behind a small entourage of assistants the man strode up to Baillet, looked him up and down, and asked, "You are with the *Societas Iesu*?"

"Adrien Baillet, at your service," he extended his limericked hand.

The man did not look happy and did not take Baillet's hand. "I assumed they would send someone I know."

"Alas, you have—me," Baillet answered, withdrawing his hand and placing it in his greatcoat pocket.

The man frowned. "Where do you come from?"

"La Flèche, sir."

"Your position?"

"I do—a little of this," Baillet said hesitantly, "and a little of that."

"This and that?"

"Basically I do whatever Rector Charlet asks me to do, sir."

At the mention of Rector Charlet the man's expression softened slightly. "Very well, then. I am afraid we have a situation on our hands."

"Sir?"

The man glanced around, then looked at Baillet. "Descartes," he said calmly but with an expression of discomfort, "is dead. Early this morning."

It took a moment for this information to register with Baillet. And then for it to register that as the official representative of La Flèche, and of the Jesuits, Baillet might be expected by this official—whoever he was—to play some role in whatever was supposed to happen next.

"Sir—" Baillet began.

The man waved him off.

"We cannot speak here. There is much to be done, and you are—" he paused briefly, tactfully, "in need of freshening up from your journey. My people shall remove you to my house for lunch. I shall meet you there shortly." He paused a moment, then added, as he turned to depart, "Oh, and welcome to Stockholm."

2

Someone shoved him into a coach and they were off into Stockholm. No one shared his concern for his trunk. The hooves clattering over snowy cobblestone were so loud he could barely think, could barely absorb the shocking news about Descartes, so he pulled back the curtain from the glass window to watch the passing view. They were moving through the narrow streets, past wooden carts hauling hay and wood and dung, past (and sometimes over, it seemed) the many pedestrians, soldiers, merchants, and thinly dressed children darting through the snow and traffic. Before Baillet knew it the coach door was being pulled open and he was climbing out.

An imposing four-story red-brick building, with sandstone cherubs and crests of many varieties, loomed before him. Two upright cannons stood on either side of the red front door. A few flakes of snow were falling as he gazed at the many bearded busts carved into the building's façade, glaring down on him. There was a man beside the front door wearing a thick greatcoat and fur hat into which the falling snowflakes immediately disappeared.

The doorman stepped forward to greet Baillet in French.

"No luggage, Monsieur?"

Baillet grimaced and shook his head. "Where am I? What is this place?"

"The Residence of Ambassador Hector-Pierre Chanut, of course. If you would step inside, the houseman will show you where you may *freshen up*." The doorman was frowning at him. "Dinner is served in twenty-five minutes."

Baillet looked around. The coach had clattered away. The snow was falling more heavily on the low buildings stretching down the street. He turned and looked across the river at the Tre Kronor Castle, the sharp spire of Riddarholm Church thrusting up to its west. The gray snow clouds were shifting there, darkening.

Twenty-three minutes later Baillet was washed, slightly fresher, and seated alone in the dining room before a platter of pickled herring when the Ambassador himself came rolling in.

"Good, they have taken care of you!" he exclaimed.

"Yes, thank you," Baillet answered politely. "This— herring is delicious."

"Herring? François gave you the herring? Ah! Even the beastly Swedes can do better than that." Chanut snapped his fingers for the attendant. "Bring our guest the pickled mackerel. *Tout de suite!*"

Baillet barely had time to react before Chanut was inspecting his glass. "At least they served the Bordeaux. Not that despicable Swedish schnapps." Chanut took a deep sip, swirled it in his mouth, his cheeks puffing. "Mm! Now, Père, you'll have to eat quickly. We're due at the Castle in under an hour."

Baillet was too flustered to ask why he would be accompanying the diplomat to the Castle. "I should mention, Ambassador, that I am not actually a *Père*."

"No?"

"Perhaps—if I had applied myself more seriously—"

"This won't do," Chanut shook his head. "It will go much better for us if you had some ... *standing*. Look, Père, let this be our secret. I would prefer you to be a Cardinal or a Bishop, but I don't think they would buy it."

"I am not sure I am comfortable—"

"Your comfort is of no concern to me," Chanut interrupted. "Although it *is* of concern to my wife, now that I think of it. She has reserved a decent flat for you in a nearby rooming house. Of course we assumed the Jesuits would send someone with more ... you know. But I suppose that's how it goes. We'll settle you in there later. After the Castle. You are sure you cannot pull off a Cardinal or Bishop?"

"Regretfully no, Ambassador."

"Too bad." Chanut shook his head. "This Descartes business. It is unbearable. Awkward."

"Awkward, sir?"

"Put yourself in my shoes, Père. Her Majesty's Chancellor asked me to bring the man here and I made it happen. I brought him here on a mission of great international significance. I put him up in my own guest house. And now weeks later he is dead. It is so— *uncomfortable*."

"May I ask how it happened? Sir?"

"He got sick. He died. Four o'clock this morning. That's the story."

"The 'story'?"

"You are a *Père* and France is happy to play second fiddle to Sweden in international affairs. Those are also the story."

"I'm not sure I understand, Ambassador."

"It is complicated, Père. You better finish your mackerel. How is it, by the way?"

"Delicious," Baillet forced another forkful into his mouth.

"My wife loves it too. But then again, what food doesn't that woman love?" Chanut took a deep breath.

"Can't stand it myself."

There was a short silence while Baillet worked on his mackerel and Chanut had the attendant refill Baillet's wine, which the Ambassador had drained.

"I would have liked to have known him," Baillet said, nearly finished. "My superiors—I was expecting to meet with him. If not for the ice—"

"'If not for the ice'! That is what they always say in this God-forsaken land. Our man called it the land of ice and bears."

"Descartes, sir? He wasn't—happy here?"

"He was certainly disappointed. He expected the Queen to be more eager about natural philosophy, but instead she only met with him a half-dozen times or so. And he certainly despised the awful weather here. Especially at five in the morning!"

Baillet looked at him, puzzled.

"That's when the Queen insisted they meet."

"Wasn't he famous for—"

"Insomnia, yes, and for lounging late in bed, writing. He did his best work in bed, he liked to say, so innocently it would have been endearing if it hadn't been so tragic. Eh, Père?" Chanut winked at Baillet, who had flushed as deeply as possible for someone who'd been eating only fish for weeks. "It was his valet's unpleasant responsibility to have him in the coach by 4:45 AM, for the trip to the Castle. It is hard to know who was unhappier, Descartes or Schlüter."

"It's a wonder he didn't fall ill sooner."

"He was fanatical about his health, you know," Chanut said after sipping Baillet's Bordeaux. "All the more tragic, I suppose."

Baillet looked down at his plate and drew the line at the mackerel heads. He put down his fork and looked up at the Ambassador, who was ruminating again with a troubled expression on his face. "Ambassador, am I right to infer—are you suspicious—do you think—"

"Out with it already, Père!"

"I am gathering—you suspect—Monsieur Descartes was—"

"*We* suspect nothing, Père. As I told you. Sick, died, boom." Chanut finished, snapped his fingers for a refill of the wine. "But there are rumors. Already! Of course. Descartes had no shortage of enemies, as you will see when you get to work. With his disdain for inferiors he managed to alienate every scholar the Queen assembled here. And that envious lot, they could not *stand* that he had been chosen to write the statutes for the Academy. A foreigner, no less! Not to mention the verses for that dreadful ballet. He had just delivered them, in fact, when he got sick, died, boom."

Things were happening too quickly for Baillet to ask what Chanut meant by his "getting to work." "So you believe some *scholars* might have—what?" He dropped his voice. "Poison?"

"He got sick, he died, *that* is what we believe. I am talking about the rumors, Père."

"The rumors, then, Ambassador?"

"Not just the scholars. There is also the religious angle, Père. Sweden speaks much of its religious tolerance, but there is no deficit of tension between their heresies and our true Catholic faith. Their clerics were not at all pleased that our man enjoyed private audiences with Her Majesty."

"So either a scholar or a cleric," Baillet murmured, "according to the rumors."

"Ah! And that's just a start. Even the Queen's physician is in question. The man had printed a paragraph or two against some of Descartes's medical theories, so Descartes considered him an enemy. Refused to be treated by the fellow, at least until the end. The man had done a smash-up job treating me just two weeks earlier."

"You were sick as well, sir?"

"Same thing, two weeks earlier. Descartes and I went out for a stroll, to take some measurements for his pal

Pascal. He got the measurements and I got the pleurisy."

"And the physician treated you?"

"Was good as new in a week. Then Descartes got it and was dead in a week. But you know," Chanut added reflectively, "Descartes wasn't entirely himself lately anyway. He seemed worried, nervous."

"How so, sir?"

"I can't explain, Père. But, you know, Stockholm was filling up for the Gala. Scholars arriving, diplomats, dignitaries. I don't think he liked all the activity. The attention. Something was bothering him. He had plenty of enemies from his earlier years. Some of them showed up too."

"That's a lot of possible suspects, Ambassador."

"*Rumored* suspects, Père. But to be honest I just don't see how it can be true. Foul play, I mean. His valet was with him all the time. There just would not have been the opportunity. For poison, say."

"So why are you so—concerned about it? About 'the story', I mean?"

"It is not reality that matters, Père, it's what people make of it. It is uncomfortable enough for me—for France—that Descartes dies of natural causes so soon after he is brought here. But if the murmurs of, well of *murder* damn it, take hold, we could have a major scandal on our hands. The leading mind of Catholic France, brought to Lutheran Sweden and murdered! Do you believe that our boy-King, not to mention First Minister Mazarin, would take that lightly?"

"But surely if these are just—rumors ...?"

"Are you sure you are with the Jesuits?"

Baillet shrugged.

"You, my young friend," Chanut continued with a suppressed belch, "are naive. Monarchs and ministers care nothing of the truth. They care only about the story, and *that* story could undo the entire Swedish-French alliance that finally ended the wars. It would not take ten minutes to unravel the Treaty of Westphalia and plunge Europe back into the mess."

"So what will you do, Ambassador?"

"Ah!" Chanut answered. "But first—"

He snapped his fingers for the attendant but instead a large matronly woman came into the room. As she came to the table Baillet couldn't help observing that she looked exactly like Chanut, round-faced and puffy-cheeked, only with a slightly fainter mustache.

"Marguerite, my dear!" Chanut exclaimed, "Come meet our guest, the distinguished Père Adrien Baillet. Père, my ravishing wife."

"A pleasure, Père," Madame Chanut offered her hand for Baillet to kiss. "Welcome."

"Thank you, Madame," Baillet answered, kissing it.

"I am sorry to interrupt, gentlemen, but my husband tends to lose track of wine and of time, and especially both together. Don't you have an appointment, dear?"

"Ah! Of course," Chanut glanced at his mantle clock and stood up. The Queen, on her collecting spree, had recently furnished all the embassies with their own "Nuremberg Eggs," as they were called. While Chanut missed the more accurate pendulum clock that once hung there, the Egg *was* lovely to look at, despite its inconstant relationship with the Riddarholm bells. "What would I do without you, my dear? Are you ready, Père?"

"Sir?" Baillet asked, standing, realizing that he'd forgotten to ask what it was the Ambassador wanted from him.

"It is time for us to go meet the Queen."

3

Baillet found himself next to the Ambassador in the coach as they raced down Fredsgatan on their way to Tre Kronor Castle.

Well, not racing.

"What are all these animals doing here?" Baillet asked, looking out the window through the snow. The street was lined with one magnificent residence after another, as most of the embassies were located here as well as the estates of the more prominent nobles. It was filled, meanwhile, with swarms of liveried knights on plumed horses, floats pulled by decorated mules, and streams of people carrying colorful banners.

"The Queen likes parades," Chanut explained in exasperation.

"Could those be—camels? Here, in Sweden?"

"Her Majesty has exotic tastes. Let me see if we can take another route."

The Ambassador pounded on the ceiling of the coach. It grounded to a halt from its previous creep. The driver climbed down and opened the door. "Sir?"

"Can't we avoid this—this *circus*, Mak?" Chanut demanded.

"I'm afraid not, sir. The Vasabron is closed. They're moving the lions and bears that way just now."

"Lions and bears?" Baillet asked as Mak returned to his perch.

"For the animal combat," Chanut muttered. "I only hope that the Chancellor does not throw us into the ring with them for being late."

The coach crept until they finally reached the end of Fredsgatan and turned off, away from a marching company of halberdiers and archers, onto the Norrbro. This gorgeous stone bridge was the main conduit across the Riddarfjärden to the small island on which the Castle and Riddarholm Church were built.

"And what is that?" Baillet asked, pointing below the bridge.

"Helgeandsholmen," Chanut leaned over to look at the islet under the bridge. "That's the parliament building at the other end there. And you see that building?"

"With all those—gargoyles?"

"Exactly! That's Her Majesty's new Museum of Curiosities. Every bizarre thing she ransacked from Europe is there. For the festivities they're keeping it open all day and night. You should visit. Ah, Père, here we are!"

They were pulling up before the main gate in the massive stone wall surrounding Tre Kronor Castle.

It wasn't every day you got to meet a Queen, and certainly not this famous twenty-three-year-old Queen. Her father had of course envisioned a male heir but realized soon after Christina's birth in 1626 that his crazy wife was not someone it was wise to sire more children by. So he raised his daughter to be a king instead. Even by age three the little princess loved the riding and hunting normally only for males, and had already developed her famous reputation for indifference to the cold, going bareheaded and often barefoot in the snow. By her early teens she could shoot a running rabbit in the head, from her horse, with a single bullet. She also scandalized everyone in the court by taking less than fifteen minutes to dress. This was helped by the fact that she kept her hair short and wore men's clothes. The rumors about her secretly being male were obviously fueled by these behaviors; as well as by the fact that the patriarchs of Europe were not thrilled that this "woman," after officially donning her deceased father's crown at the age of eighteen, promptly won the Thirty Years War and became the most powerful monarch in Europe.

His stomach in knots, Baillet glanced at the Ambassador as they waited to be shown into the Royal Chamber. The diplomat was calmly twirling the waxed tips of his mustache. A bell rang one o'clock as the Royal Guard beckoned them to enter.

"We're on—time?" Baillet whispered to Chanut with relief.

"I keep my Nuremberg Egg fifteen minutes fast," Chanut whispered back. "Diplomat's trick."

"Representing His Majesty King Louis XIV, Ambassador Hector-Pierre Chanut," the guard announced as they entered, "and—"

"You *sure* you can't do a Bishop?" Chanut whispered to Baillet, who shook his head.

"—and representing the *Societas Iesu*, of La Flèche, Père Adrien Baillet."

The two men were shown to the center of the room and bowed, long and deep.

Finally rising, the first thing Baillet noticed were the half-dozen burly uniformed guards around the room, bearing muskets and axes. The next thing he noticed were the bears—or rather heads of bears, of snarling bears mounted along every wall. The third thing he noticed were the two thrones, an enormous gilded throne on the right and an oversized gilded throne on the left. The right one was empty, but the one on the left contained a man with an impeccably groomed graying beard whose facial expression seemed to somehow simultaneously reflect both homicidal rage and profound despair.

Baillet and the Ambassador stood silently until the man finally noticed them. "So good of you to come, Ambassador Chanut," the man said slowly in a perfect French.

"Your Excellence, my Sovereign, His Majesty, expresses his deepest condolences to your Sovereign, Her Majesty, for her loss."

"And she," the man responded, "for yours."

"Your Excellence," Chanut continued with another bow, "on behalf of my Sovereign I was hoping to convey these condolences in person to Her Majesty."

"You shall have to settle for her Chancellor."

So this, Baillet realized as his stomach flipped again, must be the infamous Carolus Zolindius. The Chancellor was now boring his dark eyes directly into Baillet.

"And this is?" the Chancellor was asking.

"Mon—" Baillet began to say.

"Père Adrien Baillet," Chanut interrupted.

"At your service," Baillet finished with a bow, "Your Magnificence."

The Chancellor's eyes remained on him a moment then returned to the Ambassador. Baillet took the reprieve to steal a glance at the man and observe how pale he looked, even for a Swede in the middle of winter. Sitting perfectly still, Zolindius addressed the Ambassador. "Well, then, Chanut. The details, if you will."

Chanut cleared his throat. "As Your Excellence knows, we thought he was improving. When I spoke to you early Saturday his lungs had cleared significantly and his fever had abated. He was well enough Saturday morning to receive communion. But then—"

"Yes?" Zolindius said quietly.

"Saturday night, suddenly, he took a turn for the worse."

"And Wullens?"

"Her Majesty's physician was present, of course. But with due respect, Your Excellence, the one point on which Wullens and Descartes could agree was that Descartes would die happier if Wullens were not involved in his care. Nevertheless, the good doctor did as Descartes requested."

"And that was?"

"Late Saturday night, as his condition worsened, Descartes requested some wine infused with tobacco. Wullens felt that what was needed instead was to purge the blood, as he had been insisting since the first day of the illness. But Descartes—"

"Yes?"

"He could be stubborn, Your Excellence. Wullens did what Descartes asked, rather than what he himself thought best."

"The wine sop did not work?"

Baillet permitted himself to steal another glance. The Chancellor sat utterly immobile. His sharp beard hugged his jaw in a manner that somehow felt threatening. His eyes stared intensely at Chanut and his lips strangely did not seem to move when he spoke.

"Not at all, Your Excellence," Chanut replied. "Descartes was soon beset with stomach convulsions. As his fever resumed climbing overnight he finally relented to the purging, and by morning gestured to Wullens to proceed. I suspected, then, that Descartes believed that the end was near, for he had long objected to bloodletting. My suspicion was confirmed when Descartes waved me over and whispered the name of his confessor. When I returned an hour later with Père Viogué the bloodletting was done. The blood was like oil, thick, and yellow."

Chanut paused. Zolindius stared, motionless, waiting.

"Descartes fell into a deeper delirium," Chanut resumed softly, "and did not, or could not, say another word. He remained wordless for the remainder, finally passing from this world into the far better one at about four o'clock this morning. Your Excellence."

There was a long silence. The Chancellor seemed lost—somewhere.

Finally Chanut cleared his throat. "You don't seem quite yourself today, Chancellor."

Zolindius returned his gaze to Chanut. He spoke with a voice that was deep and deliberate and devoid of affect. "And the cause of death, Ambassador?"

"Inflammation of the lung, Your Excellence. Of course."

There was another prolonged silence. Once again the Chancellor seemed distracted, until the Ambassador cleared his throat.

Zolindius glanced up and spoke. "Very well, Ambassador. Her Majesty has composed a letter expressing her condolences to your Sovereign. If you will accompany me to my chamber I shall give it to you."

The Chancellor rose and the guards snapped to attention. He stepped down from his throne and moved toward a door in the rear. Chanut paused a respectful moment and followed suit. Baillet, unsure what he was supposed to do, remained standing.

Zolindius turned and stared directly at him. "Won't our Jesuit friend join us?"

Zolindius strode ahead of them at a measured but strong pace, even with his limp. Chanut strode two steps behind him struggling to keep up. Baillet followed a step further back, wondering how a limp could seem so intimidating. The Chancellor led them down a long narrow hall whose windows on either side revealed how dark it already was outside, and that it was still snowing. Between the windows were sconces and more decapitated snarling bears.

"The Queen likes to hunt," Chanut whispered back to Baillet.

They fell into silence as they turned down another hallway that was wider, before at last stopping in front of a large plain wooden door. The soldier guarding it bowed as Zolindius removed a ring of iron keys and opened the door. The Chancellor entered but the guard stopped Chanut and Baillet. A moment later a bell was rung inside and the guard waved them in.

Another spacious room, with three windows behind the massive desk in the center letting in the afternoon darkness. Lit sconces on the walls. And absolutely nothing else before them but for the Chancellor seated in a throne of a chair behind the desk and staring at them as they entered. With no place to sit in the empty office, Chanut and Baillet stood in front of the desk.

"Those were mine, Ambassador," Zolindius said in his deep voice.

"Your Excellence?" Chanut asked.

"The mounted beasts you just passed."

"Ah! Impressive shooting, Chancellor! I have been down that hall a dozen times and you never mentioned."

"As are those."

Zolindius gestured to the wall behind Chanut and Baillet. They turned around to discover four human heads stuck on spikes, mounted on the wall.

"Heresy, disloyalty, begging, that sort of thing," Zolindius explained. "Normally we display them on the Norrbro, but with the festivities—you understand."

"Of course," Chanut bowed.

"Do you hunt, Père Baillet?" Zolindius said.

Baillet was feeling sick, his heart pounding.

The Chancellor sat absolutely still. He was actually small yet seemed to tower over them, even seated. He was not handsome, with rough features and that sculpted graying beard, yet he was compelling to look at. In his fifties perhaps, he emanated the vigor of a younger man. His flawless French bore no hint of a Swedish accent. His nearly immobile lips formed each word deliberately. And his eyes continued to bore into Baillet.

"No, sir, Your—Excellence," Baillet stammered. "I'm

not very comfortable with—firearms."

"What? They didn't train you at—was it La Flèche, did you say? My understanding was that they pride themselves on producing soldiers for their savior."

"Perhaps if I had applied myself—"

"No matter," Zolindius interrupted. "Chanut, your letter." He opened a drawer and withdrew a parchment. "Her Majesty wishes to arrange for—" Zolindius hesitated then said the word with noticeable care—"Descartes's interment with highest honor. A full state funeral, at Riddarholm Church."

Chanut accepted the parchment. "A wonderful honor, indeed, Chancellor. Riddarholm is the resting place of King Adolphus himself, is it not?"

"And of all the Swedish monarchs preceding him."

Chanut cleared his throat. "I do wonder, naturally, whether His Highness, my Sovereign, might prefer to repatriate the remains."

"His Majesty may always bring that up with Her Majesty at some later time."

"Of course. But still I wonder if the wishes of Monsieur Descartes himself—"

"Her Majesty's wishes perhaps trump those of Monsieur Descartes."

"Of course, Your Excellence," Chanut bowed. "And yet, sir—are you not concerned that, perhaps, such a *conspicuous* event might overshadow the celebrations?"

"To the contrary. Her Majesty believes it would be a fitting prelude. The Gala commemorates the new era in Europe, of peace across borders, of religious toleration. That your great Frenchman would serve in the Swedish Court, and die in this Court, is a symbol of that new era."

"And yet, Chancellor," Chanut persisted bravely, "with all due respect, to bury our most prominent Catholic in the most prominent Lutheran Church in the world. And particularly with the rumors—"

"Ambassador," Zolindius held up his left hand.

Chanut fell silent. Zolindius stared at him in silence. Baillet stood watching, perspiring, feeling those awful heads on spikes behind him staring at him the way the Chancellor was staring at Chanut.

"In any court," Zolindius said calmly, "there is no shortage of rumors. May I ask to which particular rumors you refer?"

The Ambassador took a deep breath. "That the death of Monsieur Descartes was not natural, Your Excellence. That he was poisoned. Perhaps for religious ..." His voice trailed off.

Zolindius sat silent and still, though Baillet thought he saw the smallest flinch in his face. "You and I both understand, Ambassador, that that is nonsense—but dangerous nonsense. And that interment in Riddarholm would only inflame that nonsense. But you may relax, Chanut. I have ordered an official medical report to quell the rumors. And there will be no state funeral."

"Sir? You said that Her Majesty insists on—"

"You and I both also know, Ambassador, that Her Majesty insists on many things. She has grand ideas and wonderful intentions. Indeed she was even prone to pardon—" Here the Chancellor nodded toward the heads on the wall behind them, though neither Baillet nor Chanut turned around. "In any case, we shall assemble something discreet for your man. The details will be sent to you later today."

Chanut bowed. "On behalf of my Sovereign, Chancellor, I thank you for your understanding."

Baillet too bowed, and turned with Chanut to go when the Chancellor stopped him.

"Oh, and Père," Zolindius said, his eyes burning into Baillet, "you might consider some shooting lessons while you are here."

"Your Excellence?" Baillet asked, unable to meet the gaze.

"Sweden has come far, but Stockholm, I am afraid,"

Zolindius stared at him, "still has the occasional hungry bear stalking its streets."

4
TUESDAY, FEBRUARY 12, 1650

*F*our in the morning is a heavy time even when you *aren't* in the middle of the Swedish winter. Except for their tiny lanterns the night was pitch dark, and even with the wool cloak Chanut had lent him beneath his greatcoat, Baillet had never been so cold in his life. With the sounds only of crunching boots and gusts of wind the four men carried the coffin to the open grave somehow dug earlier that day in the frozen ground. Baillet glanced around, saw the many small wood crosses, topped by snow. His lantern allowed him to read some of the names, the birth and death dates separated by such depressingly short distances. Well, Baillet thought, shivering, if Descartes was to suffer the indignity of being buried here, in a graveyard for unbaptized infants, he would at least be attended by the leading members of his faith in the vicinity. The Ambassador bore the leading edge of the coffin, his son the other front corner; the Ambassador's secretary took the next corner around. And then there was Adrien Baillet, just eighteen hours off the ship, so numb that he barely listened to the Latin words muttered by Père Viogué, barely noticed that these weren't the ordinary words—but then again, there was nothing ordinary about this Catholic man being buried on a frozen night in a non-Catholic land.

What, Baillet was thinking, am I doing here?

"I have a job for you, my friend," Chanut had said earlier over their after-supper Burgundy. His wife had poured their glasses and withdrawn. "One that requires tact, discretion, and a Jesuit's penetrating intelligence."

"I thought you said it was for me," Baillet answered.

"Père," Chanut ignored him, "Listen. The Chancellor has made it quite clear that Descartes died of natural causes. But the situation is delicate. The whisperings must be contained."

"But surely, Ambassador, a little whispering is harmless?"

"Père, is it possible you are unaware of the temperament of our Sovereign?"

"Frankly, Ambassador, I didn't get out of La Flèche much."

"Most eleven-year-old boys enjoy pulling the legs off insects for sport, Père. Our Sovereign prefers to do so with people. Which I naturally say with all due respect to the Crown. Shall we toast His Majesty's Health?"

They clinked their Burgundys, and the Ambassador continued.

"I have a larger mission here, Père. To keep the peace. And to do that I need to keep His Majesty satisfied. The moment he hears of Descartes's death *he* will start whispering, and whispering is the first step toward dismembering. It is my mission to nip his whispering in the bud."

"And this is where—"

"Yes. You, Père."

"But how?"

"An investigation."

"But—didn't the Chancellor already say he had ordered

a medical report? Wouldn't that suffice?"

"Obviously that report will conclude the death was by natural causes. And just as obviously that report is useless."

"But why?"

"Are you *sure* you are a Jesuit?"

"Perhaps if I had—"

"Fine, fine. Look, if His Majesty suspects that someone in Sweden murdered the greatest French philosopher, the Court's official medical report claiming natural causes will only convince him that the conspiracy goes all the way up to the Crown. He is already ill-disposed toward Her Majesty because she is older than he, more powerful than he, not to mention more manly than he. He needs little excuse to start dismembering Swedes, and that would be the end of everything we have worked for."

"So what could I do?"

"An investigation, Père. Of the circumstances surrounding Descartes's illness and passing. One that will conclusively demonstrate that this was indeed a life that God Himself chose to remove, for reasons unknown, at this time and in these circumstances."

"But I—have no experience in such matters, Ambassador."

"A perfect time to acquire some."

"There must be someone else you could turn to."

"For this to assuage His Royal Temper, it must be from us. And a Jesuit might be the only person he would trust here. Even one such as yourself, Père. Frankly, Père, you're the best thing we've got."

"I am not sure I am suited to—international intrigues, Ambassador."

"You are also the *only* thing we've got."

God save us all, then, Baillet thought to himself, mentally crossing himself.

"Indeed," Chanut agreed, actually crossing himself.

"Did I say that aloud?"

"Listen, Père, there is a lot to do. We've got to get you moved into your flat. The place is just around the corner, but in this weather you'll want the houseman to help you. I've got to think about how best to get the Chancellor on board with our investigation. We'll need his authority. And do try to get a little rest. My man will be there to wake you at 2:30 AM sharp. Marguerite installed our old clock there but you might have some trouble figuring out the alarm mechanism."

"2:30 AM?"

"We're meeting at the morgue at 3 AM to convey the body to the graveyard. We wanted discretion, and we got discretion. Oh, and Père?"

"Yes, Ambassador?"

"You're not inclined to believe this nonsense about a murder, are you?"

But at the moment it didn't matter to Baillet what the truth was, beyond the truth of the bitter cold, the dark night, and the human body inside that plain wooden box now being lowered into that lonely hole. There was a body in that box, that small closed box now being dropped into the frozen ground. A body that couldn't feel the stinging wind or see the swirling snow, that couldn't hear the dirt being shoveled upon its box, nor the unusual words being mumbled over it.

Baillet was so busy thinking about all this that he did not notice a heavily cloaked figure standing some distance away. Obscured by some trees, not quite within earshot, but present, watching the men assembled before the open grave taking turns with the shovel. The figure—surely a man, for no woman would be out at this hour and in this place—watched a few minutes longer, then turned and slipped away.

5
1596-97
LA HAYE, FRANCE

*E*arly Sunday morning, March 31, 1596, Jeanne Descartes
began the one-league trek to her parents' house just
outside the small town of La Haye on the Creuse River in
Touraine, France. This was not a good idea, bundling her
very pregnant body and her two small children into their
winter gear in order to attend church and have Sunday
dinner with her family; but the alternative, with Joachim
away serving his annual term in the Parliament in Rennes,
was sitting home all day alone with her children, and that
seemed worse.

"Mama!" her six-year-old daughter (also Jeanne) cried
as her brother pushed her into a puddle.

"She started it!" five-year-old Pierre exclaimed.

"Pierre, please," Jeanne (the mother) sighed. It surely
would have been easier if they could go to the church of
their own parish, near their home in town. But that church
had been given to the Protestants when La Haye was
declared free for Protestant worship back in '89.

47

"Pierre, please," she repeated when her son pulled out a vine from the garden they were just passing and began trying to tangle her legs in it.

"Mama!" young Jeanne cried when Pierre instead started tangling her.

"Pierre, that's enough!" the mother said sharply.

And indeed that *was* enough, not to stop Pierre but to start something else a few moments later. Jeanne felt an excruciating pain in her abdomen and realized then just how bad an idea this really was.

"Pierre," Jeanne said now urgently, "run for Grandmère."

The boy for once listened, and ran off. The child Jeanne began crying when her mother did, as the grown-up slowly rested her heavy body into the wet drainage ditch alongside the road. Seven minutes later, too soon for help to arrive, there was a load groan and a splursh and then the delicate sound of a little tiny cry.

René Descartes had slipped into the world slightly prematurely, his lungs not quite ready nor perhaps the rest of his body, all five pounds and six ounces of it.

"Too much atrabile," said the local Catholic physician.

"Too little," said the local Protestant physician.

"Atrabile, bah!" scoffed Grandpère Brochard, himself a physician but skeptical of all things atrabile. "It's clearly the poor ratio between the blood and phlegm."

Fearful of losing the frail new child Jeanne insisted on hearing every medical opinion, religious considerations aside. Little René's pale complexion looked like that of a corpse, and the only thing worse than the persistent cough, she thought, was his not coughing: for then he became quiet and still and *really* looked like a corpse. At least when he coughed she could know he was alive.

"Send him to that wet nurse," Joachim suggested a few weeks later, reluctantly returned from Rennes because of the baby's poor health. "She'll take care of him."

Jeanne hesitated before disagreeing with her husband. "That's what I'm afraid of," she said softly, cradling the sleeping baby. It wasn't that Mme Bettremieu's moral reputation was sketchy (although it was). It was her *other* reputation, as a wet nurse, for it was also widely known that for the right fee she might accidentally leave your unwelcome little one alone in the bath or out in the snow.

"You're not worried about that—thing?" Joachim looked at her skeptically. The baby had been born with a mildly cleft tongue that had the superstitious townspeople talking.

"No," Jeanne answered firmly.

"Then send him to that one we used for Pierre. The fat one in Saint-Rémy. She did fine with him."

And look at how Pierre is turning out, Jeanne thought. "This child needs its mother," she insisted instead, poking the baby to make sure he was still breathing.

Joachim didn't pursue the matter, happily. He was instead focused on his business dealings—he had lately begun acquiring properties around Touraine—and on his desire to produce another son. (He thought it unlikely the baby would survive infancy and wanted a more reliable back-up heir to Pierre.) Indeed within five months after sickly René's birth Joachim had acquired two small farms outside Poitiers and gotten Jeanne pregnant again.

Jeanne dedicated what energy she had to the care of her infant son. This wasn't much, with taking care of two older children and dealing with her difficult new pregnancy. Nor did it help that daughter Jeanne had developed a little girl crush on the stableman's teenaged son, a situation which Joachim's palm made clear to both Jeannes could not stand. Meanwhile the grown-up Jeanne was busy vomiting half the day and suffering from debilitating cramps the rest.

Thank goodness for Jeanne's mother, also named Jeanne but called simply Grandmère.

"Joachim still wants to give him to Mme Bettremieu,"

Jeanne whispered to Grandmère.

"That woman," Grandmère muttered, "deserves every disease inside her body." These would include one or two that Grandpère Brochard had himself brought home from her in recent years.

"So what do I do?"

"You don't listen to your husband. You listen to me."

Listening to Grandmère when it came to child-rearing amounted to listening to centuries worth of Catholic teaching on the subject. Childhood was basically the most abject state a human being could be in, a kind of mortal illness that only determined vigilance could eventually cure. The first step was to get that little invalid into a swaddle to curb his vile body's natural tendencies to deformity and let it know who was boss. Grandmère's famous swaddle was pulled so tightly that those little arms and legs would have no choice but to grow in straight. Always practical, Grandmère wove a curved hook into the swaddle too so that the neatly packaged child might be hung on the wall while Jeanne tried to teach the poor cook how to prepare Joachim's supper in a way that might allow her to retain her job.

The little child didn't cry much, either because he was comforted by the restraint or because he simply couldn't breathe in it. Nor did he cry when he was dosed with a sweet syrup of horehound and maidenhair, which Grandmère insisted would help him put on some weight. When that failed, Grandmère imposed a regimen of fresh donkey milk to supplement his mother's milk. This did initially add some ounces to that undersized body but then took them off (and then some) with the extended diarrhea. The combination of tight swaddling and loose bowels was difficult on everyone but especially on the infant, whose ghost-white skin turned a blistered swollen red around the buttocks and groin. The situation was so serious that Joachim actually got involved: after suggesting Mme Bettremieu one more time, without success, he ordered at great expense the new skin cream developed by the Count of Saint Germain to be delivered straight from Paris.

The stuff was awful.

"Please, stop, Mother!" Jeanne pleaded each time Grandmère applied it to the baby, four times daily for the next four days.

"Be strong, Jeanne," Grandmère replied sternly. "It must be done."

It must have stung the poor little boy terribly, the way he cried, and cried, and cried.

"Give him to me!" Jeanne exclaimed the moment each application was over.

His mother, exhausted from her responsibilities, in pain from her pregnancy, lay down with him and cuddled with him and cried with him. Only this could comfort him and only this could comfort her. This poor little creature *needed* her, she realized, and she needed *him*. Oddly these were almost happy moments as mother and son suffered together, and Jeanne found herself almost disappointed when they were over. The stuff was awful but it worked. By the fourth day René's skin was nearly back to its normal abnormal pale, his bowel movements back to their normal inconsistency, and Grandmère back to trying to cure him from his infancy.

At the end of March, 1597 a miracle occurred: the baby survived his first year.

That was more than could be said for the domestic staff. The cook, the stableman, and the gardener had all been fired in the past year, and replaced. While he was at it Joachim had also hired a nanny over the winter, over Jeanne's objections.

"But I want to take care of the children myself," Jeanne had protested.

"The wife of Jacques Marcel has a nanny. The wife of André Gauthier has a nanny. The wife of Joachim Descartes needs a nanny."

"Why can't my mother—" Jeanne saw Joachim's eyes narrow, indicating that this was a good time for her to capitulate.

But the nanny turned out to be a wonderful addition. The young woman, Ayala, was from a good Catholic family, with a Dutch father, a Spanish mother, and excellent French. Warm, cheerful, happy to run all of Grandmère's errands to the apothecary—the old woman had not yet given up attempting to make baby René strong—she soon proved herself to be as indispensable as she was delightful, especially once Jeanne's pregnancy became problematic.

"But, Madame, I will take care of everything," Ayala insisted.

Jeanne, exhausted in bed with the almost one-year-old René asleep on her breast, gazed at her nanny's youthful face. Back in January Joachim had grumbled off to Nantes to protest His Majesty's apparent intention to improve life for the Protestants. A few weeks later the older children were removed to their grandparents' house outside town, as all (except for Jeanne) agreed that that would be best for her complicated pregnancy. For the past few weeks it had just been her miserable self, now confined to bed, her almost-one-year-old baby René, and her wonderful nanny, the latter insisting on celebrating the upcoming milestone birthday.

"Cook will make a pepper cake," Ayala was saying enthusiastically. "I'll decorate the parlor myself. I'll go get the older children, so that Madame and Monsieur Brochard might travel in their carriage. Shall I engage someone to play the shawm?"

Jeanne was about to protest when the gentle suction on her breast drew her attention, as René had awoken and begun nursing. She gazed down at him peacefully. Not really "the baby" anymore, at almost one and with his successor just a few weeks away. To think that he had made it this far, this skinny little thing with his nearly translucent skin and little bones, those weak lungs and lingering cough; how she loved him, despite or because of those infirmities, as he suckled grasping for every ounce of fluid, still trying to gain every ounce of weight. They'd spent many sleepless nights together, she and he, this sweet little vulnerable thing; and she realized that she was going to miss him, and those nights together, when the new baby finally arrived.

And he, she thought sadly, would miss her.

"You're right, Ayala," she said, half-smiling despite her exhaustion, "we must celebrate. Perhaps you might bring me some paper and a quill, my dear—so that I may attempt to convince the Monsieur to come home for the occasion?"

Joachim was too busy zealously pursuing Catholic interests to return to La Haye for his son's first birthday. In fact he was so busy trying to stop the Protestants from receiving the military stronghold of La Rochelle that he didn't respond to his wife's letter urging him home. He continued to be too busy in the following weeks even to bother opening Ayala's concerned letter about the deteriorating state of her mistress's health. And finally he was so busy trying to prevent what would become His Majesty's Protestant-loving Edict of Nantes that he neglected to open any of the letters arriving from his wife's irritating mother.

It was Thursday afternoon, the 15th of May, 1597. In Nantes the weather was unseasonably warm, which suited Monsieur Joachim Descartes just fine as he strolled down the Rue Henri IV, deciding which tavern to celebrate in. He had just met with the more conservative of His Majesty's representatives and been offered, in recognition of his efforts against the Edict, the position of Deputy Counsel to the Royal Exchequer. This combined with the estate he had recently acquired in Orvault meant that he had officially become a wealthy and important man. True, the Exchequer position required him to spend more time in Nantes, so he would have to consider moving here. But that decision could wait until his belly was full of wine.

Full of these happy thoughts Joachim walked right past his hotel, and thus right past the urgent letter that had been delivered for him by an exhausted courier not thirty minutes earlier. Three buildings down he stopped at the Jolly Miller, a tavern classier inside than its name suggested.

The perfect place to fill his belly.

Things were less jolly back in La Haye, seventy-two hours earlier. But at least since Jeanne was bedridden there was no danger of finding herself in a ditch this time.

"Ayala!" she screamed, late that Monday afternoon, when the fluids began gushing from between her legs.

"Madame!" Ayala ran in with the salve Grandmère had prepared and which Ayala had been applying regularly to treat her mistress's continuous abominable pain.

"Send for my mother! And—the midwife!"

There was a moment's hesitation, Ayala understanding what a poor combination that might be. But Jeanne saw her expression and nodded, and Ayala dropped the now useless salve and departed. Jeanne, gritting her teeth from pain, curled on her side to comfort thirteen-month-old René snuggled in bed with her, who had woken from her scream and begun screaming himself.

Madame Pasquier was considered by many a miracle worker, and even Grandmère acknowledged on arriving that a miracle was going to be necessary here. Grandmère rushed into the house with a satchel of her own preparations: tinctures of myrrh, aloe and aluwe for cataplasms and laves, saffron and aniseed waters for sedatives, and soft cheese and chamomile-steeped wine to keep up the mother's strength during the delivery. The first thing she saw was Ayala outside the closed bedroom door, sobbing as she rocked little René in her arms; she had had to pry him from his mother's arms, but was in her own agony from being away from her mistress's side. Grandmère pushed past her and opened the door.

There was blood everywhere.

Madame Pasquier had managed to sit the poor mother up in the bed and was now working between her legs, leaning over her and rubbing her abdomen with her own analgesic preparation while her other hand was feeling around inside, attempting to coax the stubborn newborn along its destined path.

"My daughter!" Grandmère exclaimed.

Jeanne, pale from loss of blood, only semi-conscious, barely turned her head.

Madame Pasquier remained focused. "Melt some butter," the midwife instructed Grandmère without looking at her.

"But why—" Grandmère glared at the woman between her daughter's legs.

"Now! We must lubricate *immediately!*"

Grandmère hesitated, but when Jeanne screamed in agony she did as she was told.

It was a very long night.

The room was sweltering, claustrophobic. Jeanne faded in and out of consciousness as the blood streamed continuously from her. Madame Pasquier remained calm but was concerned. At regular intervals she lubricated her hand and attempted to manipulate the stubborn baby within. Ayala had moved René's crib into another room and put him down to sleep, and since then had been holding Jeanne's hand next to the bed, except when she ran out to melt some more butter for the next attempt to liberate the infant. Some hours earlier Grandmère had become quiet and compliant, and was now silently praying and softly weeping in the corner of the bedroom.

At around 3:15 AM Madame Pasquier whispered, "Mademoiselle, boil some water."

Ayala nodded and dropped her mistress's hand to

attend to the task.

Grandmère crossed herself and resumed praying.

"Madame," Madame Pasquier said gently to Grandmère when Ayala returned with the hot water, "your saffron and aniseed, please."

Grandmère broke off her praying and obliged.

"Mademoiselle," Madame Pasquier said, "*mon couteau.*"

Ayala, weeping, removed the sharpened blade from the midwife's bag and submerged it in the hot water, as she had been instructed earlier. The midwife was applying Grandmère's analgesics to the mother's genital area. Fortunately, all were thinking, Jeanne was unconscious.

"Now," the midwife said quietly.

Ayala handed her the blade.

Kneeling between the mother's legs the midwife made several sharp incisions on the labia majora.

Jeanne shot awake and screamed.

"The wine!" the midwife commanded.

Ayala attempted to bring the cup to Jeanne's lips but her mistress was thrashing wildly. "Drink, Madame," Ayala sobbed, "please drink!"

"Restrain her!" the midwife shouted when Jeanne knocked the cup from Ayala's hand. She herself leaned on Jeanne's legs as she inserted her blade further inside the labia and made several additional incisions.

Somehow neither Ayala nor Grandmère would later remember the screams punctuating that sweltering late night in May. What they would remember was the remarkably calm way Madame Pasquier maintained her hold on Jeanne; the remarkably calm manner in which she now slid her hand up the much widened birth canal and gripped one of that awful baby's limbs; and then that remarkably enormous gush of blood and fluids when out came that soggy wet mass which seemed awfully small in comparison with the amount of agony it was responsible for inflicting.

And then the silence.

And then its tiny little cry.

"Madame," Madame Pasquier said gently, holding the bloodied creature. "It is a boy."

"My daughter!" Grandmère let go of Jeanne's arm and began wiping her daughter's sweaty pale forehead with a damp cloth.

Jeanne was breathing shallowly, sweating, aching in every particle of her body. "My baby," she whispered weakly, nearly inaudibly.

The midwife brought the new little thing to the side of the bed.

"René," Jeanne shook her head, whispered.

Ayala ran out to retrieve René from his crib, returned a moment later with the groggy thirteen-month-old.

"My baby," Jeanne weakly received him.

She pulled him close with what strength was left.

"Who is going to love you?" she exhaled weakly, weeping, holding him and closing her eyes.

Neither Ayala nor Grandmère would forget the image of mother and son curled up together in that bed of birth and death, the one as ghostly pale as the other.

Adjacent to them stood the midwife, holding the newborn as it recommenced its very little cry.

6
1605-06
LA FLÈCHE, FRANCE

Several days' ride southwest from Paris, the town of La Flèche sat inside a large valley surrounded by rolling hills, broad forests, and shimmering lakes, enjoying the clean waters of the Loir running through its center. Its inhabitants were genial and happy, appropriate for a place famous for its succulent black chickens, its sparkling wines, and its dark-chocolate-dipped pralines. It was the perfect place to set up an oversized manor, an opulent estate, a Royal Château, or all three in one, as King Henri of Navarre's parents had done years before. It was this château that Henri, now King Henri IV of France, donated to the Jesuits after they finally promised to stop trying to assassinate him.

Inspired by classical architecture and mathematics, the estate consisted of five connected buildings, each an enormous rectangle around a perfectly symmetric courtyard. Dominating the central rectangle was the Church of Saint Louis, whose splendor was best summarized by stating that it simply could not be summarized. Zealous Catholic boys now spent long hours praying here, at least when they weren't studying or doing vigorous physical exercises on the expertly manicured lawns now the rage among the elite.

In the spring of 1606 *Le Collège Royal Henri-le-Grand* was already the most prestigious school in France. It was home to fourteen hundred sons of barons and dukes, counts and viscounts, princes and lords, as well as to the first son of the now third-largest landholder in Touraine. As the fancy coach with the glass windows approached, it was about to become home to the second.

The long ride from La Haye had been unpleasant. The first son had been sent to retrieve him during the Easter vacation at the end of March, and took advantage of the two days' confinement to cycle through his familiar monologue: berating him for being a rat, for being a runt, for being a secret Protestant rat and runt, reminding him that La Flèche was *his* school, predicting that he would come to nothing, would disappoint their father even more than he already had. "And you will learn to act like a gentleman's son here if I have to beat it into you myself," Pierre concluded before returning to berating him for being a rat and a runt.

"*Dupek*," René finally muttered in Polish.

"What was that, runt?" Pierre hissed, his hand poised to slap, when the coachman banged on the roof of the coach.

"In sight, gents," he yelled out.

René turned away to look out the window, barely listening to Pierre's continued rant. Some small buildings stood straight ahead, where the cobblestones began: the beginning of the town itself, its central square bustling with merchants and peddlers and well-dressed people. Just beyond that was the beautiful Loir, and the gargoyled bridge carrying the cobblestoned road across it. Across that bridge, overlooking an enormous square, were the most enormous buildings the ten-year-old had ever seen. Smack in the center was The Church, topped by the tallest imaginable cross rising as its spire.

"And you will probably get whipped—" Pierre was saying.

"What are they doing? Over there?" René ignored him as their carriage was trotted over the bridge. It being the last day of the vacation the square was filled with well-to-do young men doing all sorts of well-to-do things. They were all dressed alike: breeches with pom-pom fastenings, fancy black blouse with large-puffed sleeves, floppy felt hat. Long curly locks hung beneath every floppy hat.

In one unpaved corner of the square was a net strung between two small trees. On each side of the net were young men, who were batting a ball back and forth across the net with gloved hands.

"*Jeu de paume*," Pierre answered.

"That looks like fun."

"It is. But not for you."

"Why not?"

"You need to be able to breathe without coughing. Here, this might be a little more your speed." Their coach had pulled up before the main gate in front of The Church. Groups of young men sat around small tables, rolling dice and moving pieces around a board.

"Trictrac," René observed.

"Not for money though. They whip you if they catch you."

"If they catch you," René echoed.

The coachman pulled open the door for them.

The fifteen-year-old brother preceded the ten-year-old out of the coach. Though René found the air chilly it was good to stretch his limbs. The coachman unloaded their luggage, tipped his hat and led the coach away. Several young men came over to greet Pierre, who did not bother to introduce his younger brother standing behind him until one of them finally asked, "Hey, who is the little guy?"

"My valet," Pierre jabbed his elbow into René's thin chest.

"I hope you don't pay him much," another said, poking René's skinny legs through the boy's baggy trousers. "He looks like he's worth *merde*."

"He smells like *merde* too," the biggest of the young men boomed, leaning in as if to sniff. "I guess he's not big on the bath either. Is this the one you told us about, Descartes, with the freakish tongue? Come on, *merde*-boy, let's have a look."

The large young man demanding this was not only the biggest but also one of the richest: his father was the Duke of Sully, whose influence on the King, as Royal Minister of Finance, was said to be such that he could start a war just by being in a bad mood.

"*Pisvleck*," the younger Descartes said quietly but firmly, his slightly cleft tongue briefly darting out.

"What?" Master Sully said, startled, unaccustomed to anyone speaking back to him.

"He curses in foreign languages," Pierre explained, eager to goad Sully on. Several more young men had gathered around.

"Tough guy, huh?" Sully snorted as he pushed the smaller boy lightly.

"*Nique ta mère,*" René said in French so that Sully might understand.

"He didn't mean that!" Pierre exclaimed, surprising himself.

"He didn't have to mean it," Sully answered, rolling up his puffy black sleeves so as not to crease them. This took a moment because he first had to undo the gold buttons at the cuffs, being one of the only young men at the school to use buttons rather than lace or string.

"But I did mean it," René clarified.

Sully was stunned at the disrespect just long enough for René to get in one congested breath of air while still upright. But then it was over. The dozen young men who'd circled around were disappointed how quickly the little guy was gasping for breath on his stomach, on the cold hard cobblestone, with the bigger guy's booted foot pressing on his upper back.

"Finish him, Sully!" Sully's lackeys chanted, including Pierre.

"Oh, I will," Sully said. "I'm just trying to decide exactly how. Ah—I've got it." Without removing his foot from the younger boy's back he began to unbutton his blouse, always hating to soil it.

But all good things come to an end.

"Mersenne!" someone hissed.

The surrounding young men scattered.

"What is going on here, Descartes?"

Like Pierre, Marin Mersenne had been at La Flèche since its founding two years earlier. But at eighteen he was older than Pierre and was widely recognized as the most brilliant student there. Or rather part student, part teacher: he was already assisting with classes, having shown particular aptitude in mathematics and natural philosophy. He also was religiously fastidious and had taken on the role of a House Master, keeping his keen eye on the often unruly young men who lived in the dormitory.

"Some playful sparring, sir," Pierre responded quickly.

"The boot on the neck suggests otherwise," Mersenne observed.

Sully's boot had slipped upward. Sully removed his foot.

"You are dismissed, Master Sully," Mersenne said.

Sully nodded vaguely respectfully, then carefully rebuttoned his blouse, rolled his sleeves back down, gave his curly locks a shake and rejoined the game of checkers his classmates always allowed him to win.

Mersenne watched the Finance Minister's son walk away. Then he turned and extended a hand to the ten-year-old catching his breath on the ground. "You must be the new Descartes?"

René nodded as he was pulled to his feet.

Mersenne barely glanced at the little fellow who with his rumpled clothes, pale skin, and bleeding nose looked like he had no chance at all in this place. This was to be the only direct interaction the little fellow would have at La Flèche with the man who many years later would become one of René Descartes's closest friends, correspondents, and primary conduit to the world at large.

"God, no! Not Sully!" Joachim Descartes groaned two days later on reading the letter from Mersenne.

Joachim was in Paris attempting to obtain an audience with the Royal Minister of Finance himself. As the third-largest landholder in Touraine, Joachim wanted to direct some of the Minister's public works funds toward his own province. He wanted this so badly that he was willing to overcome his aversion to the Protestant Huguenots and make nice to the Minister. The last thing he needed was for his worthless second son to go provoking fights with the Minister's son.

But what should he do? If anything was to become of the boy then La Flèche was the only place for him to be. But if he was to stay there he would have to be kept out of trouble, particularly with the future Duke of Sully.

He briefly wondered what the boy's mother would have done, but then dismissed the thought as quickly as he would have dismissed *her* thoughts.

"Father says you are to live with Père Charlet," Pierre shook René out of bed three days later. The bed was a scattering of straw on the floor of a small room in the rear of The Church. This was where Mersenne had deposited René while he waited to hear back from the boy's father. "Come on, you lazy scum! The day is half over."

"What time is it?" René groaned.

"After seven."

"Why are you waking me?"

"You've got to get fitted for your uniform. Then get

your stuff moved over to Charlet's house. Then get ready for Mass. And anyway," Pierre clapped him on the head, "you should get your lazy arse out of bed before sundown. I swear, I sometimes wonder why he got rid of the other one, instead of you."

Here Pierre was referring, as he was wont to do, to Joachim's decision to give away the infant whose birth had taken the life of their mother a year after René's—which he had, with the appropriate fee, to the infamous Mme Bettremieu.

"Who is Père Charlet?" René grumbled as Pierre dragged him to the tailor's.

"Some distant cousin of Grandmère's. He's a teacher here. Grammar and rhetoric. Very boring."

"Why am I going to live with him? Why not the dormitory?"

"Ask him. I'm sure he'll give you a very boring explanation."

"What about you?"

Pierre glared at him. Père Charlet may have been boring but he was also loaded and lived in a lovely private home just outside the West Gate, with his own staff. He was also to become Rector at the College the following year. René would have a comfortable life in that house.

"You couldn't pay me enough to live with him. I'll stay in the dorm, thank you. Look, here's the tailor." They had stopped in front of a shop inside the Second Quadrangle. "You better be at Mass at ten sharp or you'll have me to answer to."

"Just look at you," Père Charlet said, concern in his eyes when his houseman showed the younger Descartes into his study. Looking at *him* René assumed that he was dressed up for some occasion: the crisp black cossack covered by a spotless white surplice, the gold cope draped over his shoulders with a matching zucheto atop his bald pate, the long finely-patterned stole around his neck. It would take several days before René understood that this was how he always dressed. "How are you feeling, my poor child? Sit down this instant, before you catch pneumonia."

René obliged, dropping into the plush armchair.

"I'm afraid there's no time for tea," Père Charlet continued, "though there is time to change those dreadful clothes before Mass. Valois!" He rang a hand bell beside him and the houseman reappeared. He pointed to the boy with his index finger then pointed upstairs with his thumb, signals sufficiently clear to the houseman that he departed. "Now, how is my dear cousin Jeanne? And why didn't your father write me sooner about your condition? Your poor lungs. Ah! There's no time now to talk. We'll get you dressed and off to Mass, and we'll talk later."

The good Father had plenty of time to talk later, after Mass. But René didn't mind. He had fallen out of the habit of speaking much during the last few years on his own, mostly secluding himself in the ancient tunnels beneath La Haye with his father away permanently on business, his older brother away at school, and with Grandmère barely emerging from her room after Grandpère passed. Anyway his host was charming enough, and soon after Mass René had learned (among other things) that his absent father Joachim was desperately concerned for his second son's fragile health, and that the money Joachim offered Père Charlet for his son's room and board would conveniently pay for the diamond cuff buttons that the good Father had recently bought in a fit of decadence.

"Alas, taste," Père Charlet sighed with sincere regret, "is my primary vice."

René would also soon learn that the man had many virtues to balance that vice. Great kindness and generosity were among them, as manifest in what turned out to be his habit of taking in the unfortunate and unwanted.

"Ah, but listen to me prattle on," Père Charlet prattled on. "You must be exhausted, you poor thing. Finish your *sabayon* and we'll get you straight to bed."

"But it is not yet three o'clock," René protested.

"A boy in your condition must not overexert himself, my dear child. My cook will put some meat on those bones of yours while we build up your strength to attend a class or two. But we must not rush things. Now you wrap yourself in this cloak while I have the boy prepare your room."

Père Charlet was surely right about this: René would need his strength if he were to participate in the academic life at La Flèche.

The day began at 5:00 AM sharp. The young men were roused from their beds by a loud bell and would be whipped if they weren't washed and uniformed for morning prayers at 5:15 AM. From 5:45 to 7:15 AM they did their individual work, followed by a simple breakfast of gruel. Classes were from 7:30 until 9:55 AM, then Mass at 10:00 AM sharp. After Mass was dinner, also gruel. Then an hour for recreation, then afternoon classes from 1:30 to 4:30 PM in winter (5:30 PM in summer), after which they were free for their supper (some fruit in their gruel) and to do whatever they wanted until 8:45 PM sharp—when they would be whipped if they weren't washed and in dressing gowns for the evening's spiritual lecture. 9:00 PM sharp was whipping time for those not in bed.

Well not *whatever* they wanted in the evenings: they were allowed to play with dice and cards and to mingle with females in town, but in neither case was money to be involved. To encourage obedience the King himself had dictated that neither gambling nor prostitutes were allowed within four leagues of town, on penalty of death.

A mere eight years of this routine, it was thought, and these boys would be *men*: gentlemanly men ready to slash their way around the world, conquering hearts and minds and assets enough to ensure that every human soul achieved eternal salvation through the Roman Catholic Church.

A mere eight years of grammar and rhetoric and classical literature and poetry. Of Latin, and Greek and French; and since conquering Europe would be facilitated by multilingualism there were courses on other modern languages. There was religious instruction and theology. Philosophy, which meant mostly Aristotle. There was mathematics, which meant mostly Euclid, Pythagoras, and Archimedes, for all you ever needed to do, after all, could be done with just a compass and straightedge.

"This looks impossible," René sighed the next evening, reading through the curriculum.

"You will get the hang of it, sir," the boy answered. They were in the comfortable bedroom assigned to René on the second floor of the house. The houseboy, an urchin of a fellow about René's age and just about as slight, had been assigned to help him settle in.

René turned to him. "What's your name?"

"It does not matter, sir."

"What does that mean?"

"I am the houseboy."

"Well then what shall I call you?"

"'Boy' would be sufficient, sir."

Of course, René thought to himself, remembering Pierre calling the servants 'boy' when he returned to Grandmère's on school breaks; even the adult servants. Well he was here to learn how to be a gentleman's son. He might as well get started.

"Very well, 'boy,'" he said with a sigh. "How old are you?"

The boy did not meet his gaze. "Nine, sir."

"And what do you do here?"

"I help in the kitchen, sir. Run errands. Whatever's necessary, sir."

"You live here? In the house, I mean?"

"In the rear wing, sir."

"No parents?"

"No, sir."

There was a long silence while Renè thought about living alone in a tunnel and living alone in somebody else's house.

"One more thing, if I may, sir," the boy addressed him.

"Yes—'boy'?"

"You should know that I am not supposed to address you without your addressing me first."

René gazed at him. "All right, then, boy. Thank you."

"You will get the hang of it, sir," the boy returned to putting the clothes away.

"You go back to bed, now, child," Père Charlet said as they were finishing dinner the next day. "You need your rest."

"But it's only half-past twelve!" René objected.

"Did you not notice the pillows on your bed? From Beauvais. Lyon silk. Gobelin dyes. Those pillows are for sleeping, my dear child, and sleep you shall."

"But I need to pick up my uniform. The tailor said it would be ready today."

"The boy can get that for you."

"He said there would be some final fitting. I have to go myself."

"Dear Mary! It will be the death of you. And then of me."

"So may I go?"

Père Charlet nodded unhappily, his hand on the cross on his chest.

René hesitated. "How do I—summon the boy? To show me the way."

Père Charlet reached for the bell on the oak buffet next to the dining table. "All right, young master, but remember: straight to bed when you come back."

Bundled against the early April overcast chill, young master and servant set out for the tailor shop. The master walked two steps ahead and granted the servant permission to address him whenever it was time to make a turn. René felt conspicuous as they walked. The grounds were mostly deserted since the young men were in class, but he felt dozens of eyes on him as he walked past the long rows of windows in his oversized greatcoat with the boy trailing behind him. It was a relief to find the tailor shop and step inside.

The uniform was ready. The tailor made a few final adjustments while he waited. When they were done René admired himself in the mirror.

"Now, young master," the tailor interrupted him, "for your cuff strings?"

René looked at him blankly.

"That's the only part of the uniform at the student's discretion," the tailor explained. "You get to pick your color."

"What are my choices?"

"Dark black, medium black, or light black."

René sighed. He found himself unable to decide. Too much to think about lately, really. Then he remembered the dice he had slipped into his greatcoat pocket when getting ready to go out. He withdrew them and rolled several times. "Light black, then."

The tailor stared at him as he removed a small package from a drawer. "A word of advice to you, young master: you might want to keep those in your pocket around here."

The sun was out and it had warmed up when he stepped outside. He took off his coat and gave it to the boy to carry, and they set out for home. But René hadn't even made it halfway to the gate of the quadrangle before a voice boomed from behind him.

"Well don't you look pretty in your little uniform. How's that death wish of yours?"

René turned to face the future Duke of Sully. The boy—René's boy—scurried around to remain behind his master.

"Shouldn't you be in class, *dum arse?*" René answered quietly, his death wish apparently alive and well.

"This," Sully answered, beginning to unbutton his

sleeves, "will be worth the whipping."

"Why don't you pick on people your own size?" René said, aware of the boy shuffling behind him.

"I do that too. Now listen," Sully began rolling up his sleeves, "this might hurt a bit."

By the time Mersenne arrived it was all over. The future Duke of Sully was already back at his dorm presenting himself for a whipping. The ten-year-old boy who had been battered on the ground, for some reason not crying, had already been helped to his feet by the younger boy serving him, and the young master and servant were already back at the tailor shop for a new fitting. There was no trace of the altercation at the now deserted spot in the quadrangle, other than the torn and bloodied black blouse with the light black cuff strings crumpled in the mud.

René's academic career was having trouble getting started.

Père Charlet confined him to a week of bed until his bruises healed and he was convinced that René's persistent cough was not pleurisy. On the plus side, however, the good Father did let him have several looks at the new diamond cuff buttons that were so beautiful that Père Charlet couldn't even bring himself to wear them. "From India," he whispered to his invalid, his eyes moist as he showed them off. René's eyes too shined as he gazed at the jewels: the way the faces were so precisely shaped, the interlocking patterns, the three-dimensional versions of two-dimensional shapes. They weren't merely beautiful but—fascinating. He sorely wished that Père Charlet would let him see them more often, study them, without standing there to chaperone.

On the minus side, Pierre dropped by to inform him that since his scuffle had occurred in the middle of the quadrangle, most of the student body had enjoyed watching it. "It's too bad you haven't begun to fence," Pierre said encouragingly. "Then you could challenge him to a duel and get skewered."

"When does fencing start?" René asked from bed.

"Any time. But it's too late for you. Sully is leaving at the end of term." Sully was moving on to wherever it was they taught dukes' sons how to be dukes. "You'll probably have to wait a few years to get skewered by him."

Or perhaps not, for no more than an hour after Pierre departed with a clap to René's head, René's bedroom door flew open and Sully himself burst in waving a sword.

"*Söt Jesus!*" René exclaimed, jumping out of bed.

"Relax, runt," Sully shook out his ringlets. "I'm not going to kill you. At least not now."

"Then why the sword?" René licked his lips, drenched in sweat.

"Just came from fencing practice. Hey, for a sick kid you move pretty fast."

René didn't respond. The bell for the boy was out of reach, and he was still breathing too hard to try yelling for help. "Where is Valois? And Père Charlet?"

"How should I know? I knocked. No one answered. I came in. I wandered around until I found your room." Sully looked closely at him. "What's wrong with you?"

René's complexion had just returned from its sudden red burst to its ordinary pale. "What do you want?"

"What I *want* is to run you through," Sully raised his sword as René turned red again. "Relax, runt! I said I wasn't going to. Mersenne said I have to apologize or he will cancel my diploma. So," Sully paused, "I apologize."

"You...do?"

"Yeah. For not hurting you more. For allowing you to live. For making you wait until you are eighteen before I kill you."

René stared uncomprehendingly.

"Mersenne didn't specify what I had to apologize for," Sully explained. "And eighteen is the legal age for dueling. How old are you now?"

"Ten," René answered softly.

"See you in eight years, runt," Sully swirled back out of the room.

When the houseboy found his master shivering in bed a half-hour later he ran off for Père Charlet, who promptly prescribed another week of bedrest. On the minus side Père Charlet was going to be mostly absent for the next week administering exams, thus wouldn't be able to bring René the diamond cuff buttons to contemplate.

But on the plus side his absence meant that René could just take care of that himself.

"Boy," René said when the boy answered his ring.

"Sir?"

"Please fetch me Père Charlet's new cuff buttons."

The boy didn't move.

"Boy?"

"Sir," the boy said nervously, "A servant is forbidden to touch the master's things."

"Fine. Then just tell me where he keeps them."

The boy made no response.

"Boy!"

"Third drawer, sir," the boy said quietly. "His largest bureau."

"You're dismissed," René waved him away.

When the boy was gone René got out of bed and opened his bedroom door. It was a Thursday: the housekeeper was off today and Père Charlet had given Valois and the cook the day off as well, since he would be out. Still, René crept stealthily down the hallway, turned at the end and crept down another long hallway, before coming to Père Charlet's rooms. There were three closed doors here, his sitting room, his bedroom, his dressing room. All three were locked but René was prepared: his brother had long ago taught him how to pick the simple locks in these old houses and he had brought along a pin for just this purpose.

Several jiggles later and he was in the dressing room.

René approached the largest bureau and felt his heart

pounding as he opened the third drawer, carefully moved around the crisply folded maniples. After a moment he found the small carved jewelry box buried in the back. He was just going to look, he was thinking, as he placed the box on the floor, opened it. He was just going to look, he was thinking, as he saw those sparkling gems with their multi-faceted cuts and thought his heart was going to pop out of his chest.

Was that a creak of a floorboard, outside the door?

He froze, his heart thumping.

No, it was nothing.

This was foolish. It was foolish to sneak into these rooms, to go through this every time he wanted a glance at these gems. Père Charlet was busy with exams, he would barely be home this week. He wouldn't miss them if René were to take them to his own room for a little while. He would return them in a day or two, before Père Charlet returned to his routine. This way René could study them as much as he wanted. He'd have to find a good hiding spot in his room of course, but that shouldn't be hard. There were niches in the walls inside one of his closets, where he occasionally secluded himself when he was missing his tunnels.

Yes, that was a good idea, René thought, looking at the glittering things in his slightly sweaty palms.

And anyway, if anyone were to claim they had been stolen he could always just blame it on the boy.

"I'm afraid it is too late to join most of the classes," Père Charlet explained, delicately chewing the succulent capon his cook had prepared. He had popped in for an early dinner before his afternoon exams, and had clearly not yet noticed the missing buttons. "It is already May, my dear child, and the term ends first of July."

"Should I just go home?" René asked apprehensively.

"Nonsense. We shall find something for you to do." Père Charlet thumbed through the class schedule. "You say you have a facility for languages? Let me see—what do you say to Italian?"

"*Eccellente.*"

"You speak it already?"

"Just the word *eccellente.*"

"Then Italian it shall be! Oh, dear Mary—"

"What?"

"It meets before Mass. Out of the question. You need your rest."

René knew better than to argue with his benefactor, and anyway he had a better idea. "I would like to study mathematics, Père."

"But surely—"

"With Père François," René insisted. "The course in geometry." He left out that he had become fixated on the three-dimensional geometrical structure of the diamond cuff buttons.

"But that course is not for first-year students."

"I have studied some already, Père. On my own. And I am a quick learner."

"Very well," Père Charlet wiped his glistening lips on some fine Parisian linen. "I shall speak with François at Vespers. Meanwhile, you, dear child, straight back to bed."

It turned out that Père François was willing to allow the young master to sit in the back of the classroom without speaking. It also turned out that the young master's education was simply not to get started that year. It was Sunday evening, the night before his first class, his new uniform was ready and the boy had acquired the notebooks and quills for his master when the news came that Grandmère had passed away.

"My poor dear cousin," Père Charlet dabbed his eyes with his Parisian linen upon delivering the sad news. René watched the man's cassock trembling and felt very sad. The old woman had been good to him, raising him in his mother's and father's respective absences. And she was all he—had left, he realized, beginning to tremble himself.

The next morning René rode alone as the carriage bumped its way back across the bridge he had crossed not five weeks earlier. It never occurred to him to wonder why Pierre didn't come. Five days later he was also alone as the carriage bumped back again, feeling surprisingly bereft considering that he was now considerably richer than when he left. The Brochard estate was to come entirely to him upon reaching his majority at age twenty-five.

That was an eternity away, but Pierre was not going to be happy about it now. And by "now" he meant *now*, because there was Pierre out on the main square before The Church, playing cards with some curly-haired young men. René's carriage pulled up and he got out, reluctantly.

Pierre barely looked up from his game. "How was the trip home, runt? The old lady's funeral go all right?"

René was struck by the word "home." With Grandmére gone, home could only be La Flèche for him from this point on.

"I have some news," he said with a lick of his lips, figuring he might as well get it over with.

"That's all right," Pierre said unexpectedly after hearing about Grandmère's estate.

"It's all right?"

"Yeah. By my calculations you'll be dead seven years by then. To the day, if you show up to your duel with Sully on time."

But there was no point dwelling on this thought, because worse was waiting when he got—home—to the house of Père Charlet.

The first clue that something was terribly wrong was that Père Charlet was home when René arrived, instead of out boring his students. The second clue was the look on the good Father's face, the phrase *murderous rage* coming to René's mind. And the third clue was the way he glared at his young charge and said, slowly, "Something is terribly wrong."

"Père?" René's stomach sank as the footman dropped his luggage behind him and wisely left.

"Where are they?"

"What?"

"Do not play innocent with me, young man. My cuff buttons. Where are they?"

"But Père. I have been away. Grandmère—"

"I have not seen them since before you left. I saw the way you looked at them, child."

"But—the servants. The—"

"Nonsense. They have been with me for years. But you," Père Charlet's eyes narrowed as René's heart moved into his throat. The man suddenly seemed less like an eccentric aesthete and more like a—Jesuit, "*You* just arrived."

René's mind was racing, but in circles.

"We shall fetch Valois, then," Père Charlet said. "And search your room."

He had never noticed just how strong Valois was, René was thinking as he followed the Père and the houseman up the stairs. But now he could see how the houseman's muscles rippled through his uniform, imagine the strength those arms would bring to any beating they might be ordered to administer.

They stood before René's closed bedroom door.

"Your key," Père Charlet said without turning around.

René felt sick as he handed it over.

"Would you care to spare us the trouble of searching?" Père Charlet said evenly.

The ten-year-old was adept at calculating probabilities in cards and dice but far less so in calculating risks. Should he just confess and get it over with, or take his chances?

Feeling faint he just shook his head.

Père Charlet stood in the doorway, René outside, while Valois began to search the room. The houseman moved furniture, looked behind things, opened drawers. He pulled back the covers from the bed and ran his fingers under the silk quilt, along the mattress, behind it. René didn't understand how his heart could pound so without simply bursting in his chest.

"Nothing, sir," Valois said, pushing the bed back against the wall. "I've looked everywhere."

The good Father was stroking his chin. René, not much inclined to attend church, found himself contemplating doing so given his luck that they had overlooked the closet. "Perhaps ... the boy," he ventured softly, hating himself for saying it but having calculated that the distraction was his best chance to extend his luck.

"Where *is* the boy?" Père Charlet asked.

"Haven't seen him since this morning, sir," Valois said.

"It doesn't seem possible. He has been with me—since his mother died. Valois?"

"He is a good boy, sir."

Père Charlet cast a last glance at the room. "I suppose we shall have to search his room as well. Valois, please come with me. You, young man," he took a long last look at his charge, "shall stay here."

"Yes, sir," René said looking down. The sense of reprieve he felt was brief however, for Valois suddenly said, "The closet, sir! Shouldn't take a moment."

René closed his eyes as Valois opened the closet door. It didn't take a prodigy to calculate that the odds had just shifted against him.

Valois shuffled around in there, rummaging through the pockets of the hanging trousers and vest jackets. "Nothing in the clothing, sir." He then began running his hands up and down the walls of the closet, so it was indeed but a moment before he announced, "There's a small hole up here, sir. I think I can squeeze my fingers in."

"A hole?" Père Charlet stepped closer to the closet.

"Seems to be empty, sir. Let me just check the rest of the wall."

He would become a perfect Catholic, René was

thinking, if only the Lord would protect him here.

"There's another hole down here, sir," Valois discovered the lower niche.

Or a Protestant if that were His preference, René was thinking.

"Empty too, sir," Valois announced.

A Hindoo maybe, René was thinking before he realized what Valois had said.

Empty?

"That's it, sir," Valois emerged from the closet. "Now we *have* searched everywhere."

"Very well," Père Charlet said softly. "Let us go look for the boy. Child, you stay here."

When they were gone René closed the door and went into the closet. Feeling in the little niche near the floor he confirmed that it was empty.

The boy, indeed.

The boy was nowhere to be found. Neither were the diamond buttons. René could hear sounds coming from other parts of the house, raised voices, things being moved, but nothing suggesting the discovery either of the boy or the gems.

It wasn't until late in the afternoon that the boy appeared.

René crept out into the hallway to hear what was being said downstairs.

"And you have been where all afternoon, boy?" Valois was interrogating. René could visualize Père Charlet standing to the side, observing.

"My errands, sir," the boy answered nervously.

"You have been to the laundry," Valois said.

"Yes, sir. It's Monday, sir."

"That took all afternoon?"

"No, sir. I picked up some papers from Père François, as Père Charlet instructed. For Master Descartes, sir, when he returns from La Haye. And I went out to the stables too, sir, to look in on the new stable boy. As you asked me to, sir."

"I did, didn't I. How is he faring?"

"Well, sir."

"Boy," Père Charlet's voice joined in, "Do you know anything about my new buttons?"

It just doesn't matter, René found himself thinking at this moment. Nothing really matters.

Then came the boy's reply. "Just that they are from India, sir."

There was a short silence before Père Charlet spoke. "Very well, then. Run off to the kitchen, child. Cook will need your assistance."

René crept back to his room to think. The boy had obviously stolen the cuff buttons but what could he have done with them? The search of his room had turned up nothing, so he must have hidden them somewhere. But he had been out all day, so that could be anywhere. And anyway René had to tread carefully here, since exposing the boy would expose himself. But then again, who would take the word of a servant over that of his master? But then again, again, Père Charlet had a soft spot for the boy. You could tell by the gentle way he had spoken, how easily he had been satisfied by the boy's response.

Was René feeling—jealous?

René shook off these thoughts. Nevertheless he had to recognize that the servant's word might prevail over his own. He would have to do simply nothing at all and just be grateful that the boy's being a thief had saved himself from being exposed as one.

There was a very quiet supper *chez* Charlet that evening.

Père Charlet barely smacked his lips over the jellied pork stew the cook had seasoned so perfectly, while René sat at the far end of the table, the silver candelabra burning between them, his eyes on the floor.

Forty-two hours later René finally set out to attend his first class at La Flèche.

There were only a few weeks left in the term, but better late than never. With enthusiasm he had read the papers Père François had sent, and was pleased to see how quickly the material came to him. With excitement he had dressed himself in the uniform, having left a note for the boy that his services would not be necessary until further notice. When he ran the light black string through his cuffs he thought of those diamond buttons. Let the boy have them, then. René had memorized their shapes and was ready to learn the mathematics necessary for understanding them. Half an hour later René had swallowed some dinner and was on his way to the Third Quadrangle.

He never made it to the classroom.

There was chaos everywhere. The quadrangle was swarming, everybody talking excitedly. René couldn't find anyone he knew since he had spent almost all his time there in quarantine at Père Charlet's. Finally he approached a cluster of younger boys who seemed less intimidating.

"What is going on?" he asked.

"You haven't heard?" one exclaimed.

René shook his head.

"For the love of God, man!" another interrupted. "Sully has been arrested!"

"What?"

"Stealing!" another shouted. "It's fantastic! Some kind of miracle. Christ is risen and Sully is fallen!"

They clambered away. The party atmosphere was all over campus. René could barely piece together the story by acquiring snippets here and there. Sully had either been arrested or merely interrogated, or possibly decapitated. This was because he had either assaulted a classmate, dishonored a woman, or stolen something. Classes at La Flèche were cancelled for the day, for the week, or for the term. But whatever exactly happened the one certain thing was that it was wonderful news for the many young men who had been living in terror of the future Duke.

It wasn't until later that René made it to the dorm and tracked down Pierre, who was miserable.

"What happened?" René trusted his brother, as Sully's lieutenant, to have reliable information.

"What happened," Pierre muttered angrily, "is that that weasel Melun found some stolen jewelry in Sully's trousers."

"Who is Melun?"

"A weasel son of a weasel Viscount. A frame job, obviously. Everybody knows that the Viscount of Melun is trying to weasel his way into the Royal Treasury. What better way than to sully the reputation of a Sully?"

"Father," René realized, "is not going to be happy. Wasn't he trying to do the same thing?"

"You idiot! You already ruined that for him."

"What?"

"That's right. Thanks to me the Sully and Descartes names were becoming close. Why do you think Father was in Paris?"

"I don't know."

"Securing a place for me at the Treasury after I get out of here. Until you ruined everything by pissing Sully off."

"But I didn't do anything. He attacked *me*."

"What difference does that make? A Duke doesn't need a reason to dislike you. Father is already very disappointed in you." Pierre paused to glower at his brother. "Anyway the Duke had already dismissed Father thanks to you. Father is back in Rennes now, fuming at you."

"So," René said after a long moment, "the College shuts down, just because Sully steals something?"

"Is *framed* for stealing."

"Framed. But still. To close it down?"

"Who said they're closing it down?"

"One or two of the students."

Pierre scoffed. "I doubt it. They just couldn't get anyone to go to class today once the word got out. But the Pères will be back to whipping truants by tomorrow morning. Hey," Pierre was staring intently at René. "Did *you* frame him?"

"What?"

"You have the most to gain. Sully would have made your life miserable at least the rest of this term. And then of course the stolen jewelry—"

"What does that have to do with me?"

"It was *your* patron's jewelry. Some gold or silver cuff buttons, I think. Charlet is probably whipping Sully personally right now."

René turned white, even for him. "Diamond cuff buttons, you mean."

"Yeah, you see? You know all about them. You had access to them. You had a motive." Pierre was peering *very* closely at him.

The boy, indeed.

"Why didn't you tell me, boy?"

They were in René's room. It was two days later and everything had returned to normal at Père Charlet's since the cherished gems had come home. Sully had been expelled and the diploma he was just weeks from earning in that early summer of 1606 had been cancelled. Two dozen young men had been whipped the morning before for missing classes, but only two that morning.

Meanwhile the younger Descartes had made out all right. His nemesis was gone, and the fact that he himself had stolen those cuff buttons was known by only one person, and that person seemed unlikely to say anything, given the circumstances.

"You forbade me from speaking to you, sir," the boy gazed at the floor, shuffling his feet.

"But you told me to. As you told me to call you 'boy.' And walk in front of you. And start growing out my hair."

"Yes, sir," the boy answered without looking up.

"And how did you—in his pocket?"

"The College laundry, sir. I know the girls who work there."

"And," René added softly, "why?"

The boy's brow was furrowed, but he made no response.

"Answer me, boy," René said more forcefully.

"You had not quite got the hang of it yet," the boy answered, adding for emphasis, "sir."

7
TUESDAY, FEBRUARY 12, 1650
STOCKHOLM, SWEDEN

A loud *thwump* against the shutter.

Baillet opened his eyes but he may as well have kept them closed. The room was pitch black. The shutter was apparently impermeable to light. Unless it were still before dawn. Baillet rubbed his eyes, stretched, having no idea if he had slept twenty minutes or twenty hours. His stomach rumbled, suggesting hunger, but that was no clue to the time since he had barely touched his sardine supper the evening before. He pulled back his quilt and swung his legs out to sit on the side of the bed, was surprised to discover he was already dressed.

Right. The funeral last night. The deserted cemetery. That awful long walk back through the lonely streets. Parting ways with Chanut at the corner near his rooming house. Ah, and right. Baillet was an investigator now. Had a notebook and everything. He was to begin this morning by inventorying the deceased man's possessions, and interviewing his valet.

This morning. If it *was* morning.

He stood up and stretched. No longer under the goose down quilt he realized the bedroom was freezing. The shutter clearly was not impermeable to the cold. He would have to figure out how to work the stove in the sitting room. The thought of the shutter reminded him that he needed to see if it was daylight yet and gauge the approximate time. That in turn reminded him that he'd also have to ask the Ambassador how to work the pendulum clock on the mantle.

That then reminded him of the *thwump* that had awoken him.

He stepped over to the window. It took a few minutes to figure out how to move the sash, a few more to unfasten the shutter. But finally he swung the shutter open over Jakobsgatan a story below. It was dark outside too, with thick dark clouds overhead; he could tell it was after sunrise but had no precise idea what time it was. As he went to close the shutter he glimpsed something on the snowy street directly beneath him.

The thick frozen body of a pigeon.

He looked up at the sky—dark, overcast—and back down at the pigeon. Then he shivered and closed the shutter. As he turned back into his darkened room to search for a candle he heard bells striking in the distance. These would be the peals of Riddarholm Church, carrying over the Riddarfjärden.

Baillet counted the eleven bells.

Day one, and already he was late.

There was no time for breakfast.

Back into his greatcoat Baillet let himself out the front door of the building, locking it behind him, stepped gingerly over the dead pigeon and went in search of the Ambassador's Guest House. He knew it couldn't be too far. Last night, led by the houseman, it had only taken maybe ten minutes to walk from the Ambassador's Residence to Baillet's flat, and the Guest House was attached to the Residence even if it had a separate street entrance. In the distance somewhere Baillet could hear the sounds of parades. Shouts and murmurs, musical instruments, marching. Animal sounds, roars and snarls. Chanut had said something about animal combat, awful. Baillet turned down an alley, then retreated and turned down the next alley. He listened to his boots crunching in the snow. Off in the distance, somewhere, he smelled meat roasting. His stomach rumbled.

Flakes of snow began falling.

He was lost.

Just then he heard a commotion coming from down the street. Screaming, arguing, heavy whacks of something beating something. Baillet followed the sounds, around a gentle curve.

"I've told you, you puking pumpion, to keep your stink away from here! You come by again I'll rip your arse out through your rotting teeth!"

A man in a neatly pressed uniform was saying these words in a German-accented French at the door of a pleasant little house. The decrepit old vagabond to whom they were addressed might have minded them less if they weren't accompanied by the whacks of a plank against his head and back. At least those on his head had some cushion, since the man sported mounds of clotted gray hair; the tattered rags he wore were as inadequate for cushion as they were for the Swedish winter. As Baillet came around the turn the man administering the beating saw him and stopped. The vagabond looked up, directed a bulbous red nose in Baillet's direction, then scampered off the other way.

The remaining man smoothed his uniform, and turned toward Baillet a rough face that didn't quite match his fine attire. "*Vänligen?*" he said as he casually stashed his plank inside the door of the house.

"*Främmande-gatan*?" Baillet proffered his version of the name of the street he was seeking.

"You are Père Baillet," the man answered in French.

"Well—yes," Baillet responded naturally in German. "How—did you know?"

"*Bitte*, come in."

Baillet stood in the deliciously warm foyer. The man turned around, brushed the snow off Baillet's greatcoat, gestured for the coat itself. "May I, Père?"

"Thank you. So this, then, is the Ambassador's Guest House?"

"Yes, sir. I was expecting you at eleven."

"My apologies, I got a bit lost. You are Herr Schlüter? Monsieur Descartes's valet?" Uniform aside, the man just didn't look the gentleman's valet type: too rough, unfinished, beater of vagabonds.

"'Schlüter' will do, sir. May I get you a warm drink, sir? Some *Glögg*, perhaps?"

"And what is that, my good man?"

"A kind of *Glühwein*, sir."

"Ah! That would be lovely. But wait—how did you know I was coming?"

"A messenger from the Chancellor's office arrived earlier. Now if you'll excuse me a moment, sir, please make yourself comfortable."

Well that was fast, Baillet thought as he settled into the deliciously warm drawing room with the blazing fireplace. Between late last night and this morning the Ambassador must have communicated with the Chancellor and the Chancellor with the valet.

A few minutes later Schlüter returned with the beverage and served it to Baillet, who had nearly fallen asleep by the fire. "*Bitte*," Baillet pointed to another chair, "join me."

Schlüter hesitated, then, visibly ill at ease, took the other chair.

There was a long silence.

"How may I be of service to you, sir?" Schlüter finally asked.

"Right," Baillet thought a moment. "Well, I—have been charged to take an inventory of the Monsieur's possessions, as well as to—well, ask you some questions. About the—illness. If, of course, you don't mind."

"Not at all, sir."

"All right then." Baillet hesitated, wondering what the first question of his new career ought to be. "Mmm—does—or I suppose did—all this belong to the Monsieur?" he indicated the furnishings.

"No, sir. To the Ambassador."

"Well, then, I imagine that will make the packing easier for you." Chanut had said that Schlüter was to prepare Descartes's possessions for their repatriation, with or without his body.

"Yes, sir."

"Have you—yourself any plans, now?"

"Yes, sir. My master is back in Amsterdam."

"Your master?"

"I was merely on loan to Monsieur Descartes, sir."

"I didn't know that."

"No one did, sir. The Monsieur preferred people to believe he had his own valet."

"But why didn't he?"

Schlüter rubbed his fingers together.

"Ah," Baillet said, uncomfortable with the coarse gesture. "So who—provided—your wages?"

"I assume the Ambassador, sir. My wages here are paid through his office."

"And you—are obviously German?"

"*Sicher.* And you, sir? Your German is good."

"A fluke," Baillet shook his head, contemplated a moment. "The Monsieur. Was he—good to you, his personal finances notwithstanding?"

"Yes, sir. He left me half his estate, modest as it was."

"Half?"

"The other half provided the funeral, sir."

"Mmm," Baillet paused to sip his *Glögg*. "All right. Now, perhaps we might—I might ask you a few questions. About the—final days. You were present throughout?"

"Yes, sir."

"When did the Monsieur first complain of his illness?"

"Let me think a moment, sir. It was Sunday, a little after four in the morning. I was helping him to dress. To meet the Queen. He complained of the chill. I urged him to return to bed but he argued with me. As was his way. But by the time he got outside for the coach he realized that I was right. I helped him back inside, and to undress, and to return to bed. That was his first complaint, sir, I think."

"This would be Sunday, February..."

"February the third, I believe, sir."

"What, specifically, were his symptoms at that time?"

"Let me think, sir. He felt cold, but of course, sir, he often complained of that. He said something about a headache, as well. About having phlegm on the stomach."

"Did he take nothing?"

"I offered to make a parsnip soup. His favorite, sir, with prunes. But he declined, asking, instead for three or four sips of *brännvin*."

"Is that—*Branntwein*? Was that usual? At that hour?"

"Not at all, sir. The Monsieur rarely drank."

"But you had it in the house?"

"*I* had it in the house, sir. An occasional privilege. I did not know that the Monsieur knew of it."

"And then?"

"He slept, sir."

"He slept? Is that worth noting?"

"For two days he slept."

"Ah, I see. And then?"

"Let me think a moment, sir. He must have woken up on Tuesday. He was not at all well. He complained of severe heat and pain in his side. That increased with each

89

passing day. He had trouble breathing. And his waters—"

"His waters?"

"They were a strange color. Brownish."

Baillet's brow furrowed. "The Queen's physician was present, of course, by then?"

"Herr Wullens, sir. Of course."

"And his opinion?"

"That it was necessary to let blood."

"And did he?"

"The Monsieur was not keen for his blood to be spilled. He did not believe in it. Nor—"

"What?"

"Nor was he keen on the physician."

"Right," Baillet nodded, suddenly aware of his stomach rumbling. He took a moment to scribble in his notebook. "Did—did the Monsieur eat anything? It is Tuesday, now, am I right? The—fifth?"

"Yes, sir. But almost nothing, for some days. Perhaps a bite of bread. I think on Friday he took some parsnip soup. He was afraid his bowels were retracting. From the lack of nourishment."

"He—spoke?"

"On Friday, yes, sir."

"And before? During the week?"

"Not much, sir. He was often quite delirious. He couldn't speak. He did not seem to understand what we were saying to him. The physician tried to take advantage of this and let his blood without his will. But I stopped him."

"Admirable loyalty, my good man."

Schlüter remained silent. For a man who had just administered a beating worthy of a seasoned street thug, Baillet thought, the valet's expression seemed almost tender.

"You said 'not much,'" Baillet continued. "What—did he say?"

"He might mutter strange things, sir. Once or twice he

denied he was ill. He denied he had a fever, even as he was burning up. And his eyes. They became wide, and wild. I thought even bloody at one point. The physician dismissed it but I saw what I saw." Schlüter dropped his voice. "And he spoke, once or twice, about confessing, I believe."

"You believe?"

"The Monsieur muttered in Latin. Alas, my school days did not introduce me to that tongue."

"Then what makes you think he was talking about confessing?"

"Your Père Viogué was good enough to translate."

"Ah, Père Viogué. Of course. He was here regularly, then?"

"Several times, sir."

"The Monsieur's desire to confess—do you take that as a sign of his awareness of his condition?"

"I suppose that is a natural thought, sir."

"I suppose," Baillet repeated softly. "But now by Friday the Monsieur was speaking, requesting food. Was the delirium—diminished?"

"It was, for a time. Père Viogué was especially pleased. He was afraid the Monsieur would not be fit for a final repentance. He took the opportunity to insist upon the Monsieur's confession, and to offer him communion one last time."

"Friday evening?"

"No, sir. The next morning. But I am sure Père Viogué was glad he acted swiftly. The Monsieur soon after took a turn for the worse. And at that point I believe he knew the end was coming."

"And why is that?"

"That evening—"

"This is Saturday evening? The—ninth?" Baillet scribbled.

"I think so, sir."

"Right. The parsnip soup on Friday, the communion on Saturday."

"Yes, sir."

"And then you were saying, about Saturday evening?"

"The Monsieur began complaining of his bowel, sir. And he had—a fit of sobbing, sir."

"Sobbing?"

"Blubbering, sir. Like a baby."

"I don't suppose that was—normal?"

"It was not entirely abnormal either, sir."

"How so?"

"The Monsieur indulged in some bawling, now and again," Schlüter said softly. "One hears things, through these walls. A howl, now and again."

Baillet felt a wave of sadness. "Did the Monsieur say—why he was sobbing? Was it—the pain?"

"I don't know, sir. But then something else unusual occurred. He requested a wine sop."

"Wine and—tobacco," Baillet remembered Chanut mentioning this.

"Wine infused with tobacco pulp, yes, sir."

"Why is that odd?"

"I am no physician, sir. But I had heard the Monsieur criticize that as an old wives' remedy. And the physician. He strongly advised against it. He felt it might kill the Monsieur. In his weakened condition."

"And?"

"The Monsieur insisted. And the physician, I suppose, was right. Sir."

Baillet thought a moment. "But this is Saturday evening. Still a day and more before he passed."

"Yes, but the Monsieur declined after this. He was awake all that night. With fever. Vomiting. His eyes all wild again. And in the morning he finally relented to being bled. If indeed he knew what he was doing at all."

"Sunday morning?"

"Yes, sir."

"Herr Wullens must have been pleased."

The rough contours of Schlüter's face softened. "Even

I could see that the end was near."

"How so?"

"The blood was yellow."

Baillet grimaced as he had when Chanut made the same observation. "Who else was present then?"

"The Ambassador was here, sir. Père Viogué. Myself, sir. And the physician."

"And then?"

"Little else to report, sir. The Monsieur no longer spoke to us. Late that night, about four o'clock the next morning, he died. His eyes were closed. They did not re-open."

There was a long silence, punctuated only by the crackling flames in the fireplace.

After a while Schlüter said, rising, "Shall I show you to his rooms, sir?"

8

Baillet followed Schlüter down a hallway first to the Monsieur's bedroom, where the body had lain just twenty-four hours before. There was no reason to linger here, as the room contained only the small freshly made bed. The valet then led him to the Monsieur's dressing room, furnished with a chair, a stool, a dresser, and a mirror.

Descartes indeed did not have many possessions. There were three suits hanging on the pole, all of green taffeta, only one in decent condition. Baillet entered this information into his notebook. Also entered were the two wigs on their stands, both with gray hairs woven in. Baillet briefly rummaged through the dresser drawers, through stretched hose, worn gloves, underthings; uncomfortable, embarrassed. He was about to close the last drawer when something caught his eye. Delicately lifting a garment he discovered a small, bright yellow band, a sort of child's toy, he thought, buried beneath. It was unusual, stiff yet bendable, bent into a loop. An odd thing for a man of such seriousness as Descartes.

He turned to ask Schlüter about it but the valet had disappeared. So he turned to enter it in his notebook, then realized his quill had cracked. Well, he thought, he was done with this room anyway, so he slipped the band into his pocket and went to look for the valet. He promptly collided with him in the hall.

"Ah—Schlüter," Baillet said, stepping back.

"Apologies, sir, but I saw that you needed this." Schlüter offered a sharpened quill.

"That is—impressive."

"A valet's job, sir. I imagine you are ready for the Monsieur's study?"

There was another corridor, leading to a wooden door. The valet unlocked it and swung it open.

"I shall leave you, sir," Schlüter bowed slightly, "to examine the room at your leisure."

"Is there a clock somewhere, by any chance?"

"In the drawing room, sir."

"Would you kindly let me know when it is 3 o'clock?" The Gala's Opening Banquet was set for 6:00 PM, and Baillet wanted to leave time to find his way back to his flat to wash up and change.

"Of course, sir," Schlüter answered, then disappeared down the darkened hall.

This was the largest of the three rooms, and the only one with a window. The gray overcast light from outside, along with the candles Schlüter had thoughtfully lit, allowed Baillet to work. The size of the room, however, only emphasized how spare it was. There were but two paintings on the walls, of a style he recognized from La Flèche: voluptuous lines and colors, famous French painters certainly, surely belonging to the Ambassador. As for furniture there was only an almost empty bookcase, a long table along the wall opposite the window, a simple wooden chair at the table and another chair in the opposite corner.

Baillet's eye first fell on the bookcase. Descartes had only two books: the Bible and the first volume of Aquinas's *Summa Theologica*. Baillet pulled the Bible off the shelf. He wasn't sure why he did this. Maybe he just wanted to hold a volume that Descartes himself had held. Inside the front cover he saw the seal: *ex libris* P. F. Viogué. He opened the Aquinas volume to find the seal of the Royal Library. For some reason Baillet found this information—sad.

He next turned to the table, where Descartes clearly did his work. There were papers scattered, messy stacks of papers, loose sheets scribbled with ink, with cross-outs, the margins filled and arrows connecting marginalia to where they were to be inserted. Looking closer Baillet could see the nearly illegible handwriting, pick out French and Latin, mathematical symbols. Randomly he picked one up: it was a record of measurements Descartes was keeping for that Pascal fellow in Paris the Ambassador had mentioned, studying air pressure and latitude. A few other papers, on quick perusal, seemed to involve financial matters.

Suddenly Baillet was gripped by the feeling that someone was watching him.

He turned around, looked at the doorway, which was empty.

Strange.

He sighed and sat down at the table to work through the papers. The goal was just an inventory, a list, so he skimmed through them, to categorize them: mathematics, natural philosophy, medicine, correspondence, financial. These he sorted into piles to be shipped back to Paris, for the long-term management of Descartes's intellectual legacy. If his own investigation required him to read anything carefully, well, that could be done afterward.

It seemed just a short while later that he heard, in the distance, the first bell of Riddarholm Church ringing, followed by the second bell and a knock on the doorframe, and then the third bell.

"3 o'clock, sir," Schlüter announced from the door.

"That is—impressive," Baillet acknowledged, startled.

"It is the valet's job to be punctual, sir."

"I'll just be a few more minutes. Would you mind coming back in a bit, if I get—distracted?"

"Very good, sir," Schlüter disappeared.

Baillet knew he should finish, get going. But he didn't want to, just yet. Something about this room was— something. He sat in the chair and looked over the table, its papers in piles. He looked around the room, at the bookcase, wondering about Descartes's borrowing *those* volumes, from Père Viogué and the Royal Library respectively. He looked again at the two paintings. He should have been able to identify them. The Rector had wanted to educate him, to instill *something* in him; or he had until he had realized his was a lost cause. Well he could at least see these were important paintings. When he had some time maybe he would learn something about art.

As if he had anything but time, in his apparent exile to this land of ice and bears.

He was about to stand when his eye was caught by the painting over the table. Two young men, soldiers, and perhaps three young women (the sexes of two weren't clear), standing around a table playing dice by the light of a candle itself obscured by one of the gambler's arms. On the left was an older gentleman smoking a pipe who seemed to be stealing another gambler's purse. Baillet was drawn to the detail, the light and shadow, the way the figures' hands were drawn so perfectly: tossing the dice, resting on the table, knuckles bent. He was drawn to the faces, young, at ease, at play. He leaned closer, and in the dim candlelight could make out the initials in the corner: G. de la T.

As he pulled back he also noticed that the painting was not hung perfectly straight. Instinctively he leaned over the table to straighten it. But as he did so the wire holding it slipped and the painting fell, and he was just able to catch it before it hit the table.

There was a small rectangular opening in the wall behind the painting.

Baillet placed the painting on the floor, against the bookcase. He pulled the table from the wall a bit and looked more closely.

There was something inside there.

A notebook of some sort. A bound set of vellum sheets, Baillet saw as he removed it. A few sheets were loose, stuck in. On its worn cover were several strange symbols and, in careful block letters, the word *Olympica*. Beneath that was written, in Latin, *Mathematical Treasure of Polybius the Cosmopolitan*, whoever that was. Beneath that in turn were neat small letters: *The true means of resolving all the difficulties of this science*. Finally, at the bottom, was a dedication: *Offered afresh to learned men throughout the world and especially to G. F. R. C.*

Well *this* just got interesting, Baillet thought as he sat down at the table with the notebook.

Why would Descartes have this? Why would he have hidden it? Who was Polybius the Cosmopolitan? And who was this G. F. R. C.? Inside the cover were two epigrams: *To love truth more than beauty* on top, *Who lives well hidden, lives well* on bottom. The first few pages were in a neat, legible hand, mostly Latin with some French, the faded ink suggesting they had been written long ago. Skimming, Baillet could see the writing changing, become smaller, more frenetic, more marginalia with arrows and cross-outs, the author cramming as much as he could onto each page as if he were running out of time and space. Oddly throughout there were many meticulously drawn sketches of—*bugs*. Baillet shuddered. He tried without success to decipher the little annotations near the sketches composed in some abbreviated Latin. By the last few sheets— clearly recent, in vibrant ink—there was almost no blank space left. There was plenty of mathematics too, lots of symbols he did not recognize, and on some sheets there were long sequences of numbers meaning nothing to him. But there also were some dated entries, he saw, remarks perhaps constituting some kind of personal journal.

When he realized this he went back to the first page. There, in small letters at the top, was the date, "February, 1623." Immediately below was written in Latin:

> In November 1619 I had a dream of the Seventh Ode of Ausonius, which begins: "Which path in life shall I follow?"

Then there was a space, beneath which was written:

> In the year 1620 I began to grasp the fundamental principles of a miraculous discovery.

And then:

> Masked, I advance.

The candles were nearly spent, Baillet realized; he was exhausted from his journey, from the early morning funeral, and he had to get ready for the Gala. There would be time for study of the notebook later but he couldn't help himself. He skimmed through again quickly, picking out dates, realizing that it progressed from 1620 through the next decades. He discovered toward the end some dates in the late 1640s, scrawled amidst mathematics, and then one in 1649. His heart moved into his throat as he began to grasp who Polybius the Cosmopolitan must be. Indeed his heart was right there in his mouth when he turned to the last page of the notebook and saw in ink newly dried, in a tense, trembling hand, the very last entry along with its date:

> Friday, 1ˢᵗ February, 1650
> *He* is here.

Just then there was a sharp knock on the doorframe.

"Half past three, sir," Schlüter's voice came from the door.

"Just a minute!" Baillet, startled, jumped up from the table.

"Sir? Are you quite all right?"

"Fine," Baillet stammered. "I got—distracted."

"I have your greatcoat, sir. I imagine you will be eager to get going."

"Thank you, I—am."

"Did you find everything you needed?"

"Yes, yes, thank you. I might, ah—"

"Sir?"

"I might need some directions to get back to my flat."

A few moments later Baillet was back outside trying to find his way through the streets to his rooms. He was feeling proud of himself, for having accomplished his inventory. But more importantly he was proud that he'd so quickly stuffed the mysterious notebook under his cassock before turning toward the valet. Whatever exactly this notebook was, it was clear it was important—for understanding Descartes, his life, his work, and now, likely, his murder.

"*He* is here," Descartes had written.

Baillet stopped in his tracks. He felt a cold chill through his bones, different from those he had been feeling since arriving in this frozen place. The thought of Descartes writing that line in his notebook. Just a day or two before somebody—killed him.

Well, Baillet thought as he resumed walking, Investigator Baillet is on the case.

What he wasn't thinking was that he had neglected to return the painting of the dice players to its spot on the wall.

9

The fireworks exploding outside were barely audible above the murmuring crowds in the Grand Foyer adjoining the Great Hall of the Castle.

"Ah! The spectacle!" the man with the delicate spectacles was saying in Italian-accented French to the man with an even more delicate monocle. "First they put the lion in the ring with the buffalo. But the buffalo only lay down for a nap while the lion wandered around sniffing the walls. I thought it was going to be dreadful."

"The lion? The one from Prague?"

"Precisely." The solitary lion Queen Christina had captured from the halls of Hradčany Castle had finally found its place, as an animal gladiator.

"So what happened?" the monocled man inquired.

"They replaced the buffalo with a bear. That got the lion interested. They reared at each other, then went after each other. Bit each other's limbs off, practically. At the end the soldiers went in with swords and slaughtered them both mercilessly. It was *spectacular!*"

Baillet's stomach turned as he listened in on this conversation. For once in his life he had arrived somewhere on time and he was now seriously wishing he hadn't. After having gotten lost on his way back to his flat he had quickly washed and changed and managed to make the half-hour walk toward Tre Kronor Castle without incident. He was soon enough crossing the wind-whipped Norrbro over Helgeandsholmen, with the torch-illuminated towers of the Castle rising up before him. It was quite the sight as he approached, an important sight, he found himself thinking: he'd spent much time himself wondering what path in life he should follow—the thought of Descartes's notebook entry chilled him again—and now here he was about to participate in something undeniably important.

But then he was jostled along forward. The street was crowded with people in elegant greatcoats and fur hats bearing him up the steep path to the Great Hall, somehow clear despite the afternoon's snow. At the door a burly soldier in a blue and gold uniform stopped him to ask who he was.

"Adrien Baillet," he answered, feeling the enormity of the moment.

"I have a Bishop Baillet?"

"Yes," Baillet sighed, deciding not to explain.

"Welcome, Bishop. Catholics enter the Grand Foyer through the left. You'll find your seating assignment on the table at the far end. Next?"

Baillet entered, checked his greatcoat, found the seating assignments. He milled about the Grand Foyer for a while listening to the conversations around him. His stomach was just recovering from the thoughts of slaughter when a loud gong was rung.

The Opening Banquet was to begin.

The vaulted ceilings. The massive stained glass windows letting in flashes of light from the fireworks exploding outside. Innumerable elaborate sconces bearing long brightly burning candles, competing with candelabras hanging heavily from those vaulted ceilings. Beneath those lights the Great Hall was filled to the brim, with dozens of round tables. At the far end on an elevated dais was the Royal Table, with its extravagant décor.

"Must this hall be so drafty?" complained a man in Scandinavian-accented French, pushing past him wearing the widest reticella collar Baillet had ever seen.

"Who cares?" his female attachment answered as her cartwheel farthingale cleared a wide berth through the crowd. She was pointing at a large round fountain with multiple spigots, from which flowed *akvavits* of many colors and flavors. "This party may be bearable after all!"

Baillet peered at the table placards, numbered above 100 at this end of the hall. Moving through the crowd he followed the declining numbers, catching snatches of conversation as people began taking their seats. On the far side of the hall—the *non*-Catholic entrance—he thought he saw Bramer from the ship, found himself longing to speak with him. But the crowd was too thick, and the time was too short as the fireworks outside became louder. Toward the front near the dais he found his table, and was soon happy to see Ambassador Chanut with his round Marguerite streaming through the crowd greeting people, nodding, shaking hands.

"Baillet! You rascal! Not arrested yet, eh?" Chanut exclaimed with a wink as he arrived at the table. He was somehow carrying three goblets of different *akvavits*, the gold and ruby goblets as deep red as his puffed cheeks.

"Hector!" Marguerite's faint mustache twitched in disapproval. She turned to Baillet, who had risen to greet them. "He is *impossible* when he drinks."

"But I always drink, darling," Chanut winked.

"Exactly," it twitched.

"Ambassador—" Baillet began to say when there was an enormous explosion of fireworks outside the stained glass windows.

"Ah!" Chanut exclaimed, taking his seat. "That's the

signal for Her Majesty's entrance."

"But—why are you sitting?"

"The signal for her entrance generally precedes her actual entrance by an hour. But look, Père, it *is* time to start the benedictions, not to mention the drinking."

The Ambassador downed his first goblet while the Queen's Lutheran minister took the podium on the dais and began praising God, Jesus Christ, and Her Majesty. Then in the spirit of religious tolerance, the highest ranking Catholic priest in Stockholm, Père Viogué, followed him by adding some praise for the Virgin as well. Père Viogué then asked for quiet to make an important announcement.

"My fellow—seekers," he said solemnly, his strong voice resonating beneath the vaulted ceilings. "Her Majesty has gathered us in her beautiful city to celebrate the birth of peace across Europe. To celebrate the inauguration of the most prestigious scholarly academy in the world. And to lead this new academy Her Majesty selected the greatest mind of our generation, of our century." Père Viogué paused dramatically. "It is my sad duty to report that yesterday morning Monsieur René Descartes passed from this life as the result of an illness contracted a fortnight before."

There was a loud collective gasp. Père Viogué soaked it in, and continued.

"Her Majesty, in her own great wisdom, however, has decreed that we shall not let this sad event cast its pall over the festivities. To the contrary we shall *double* our joy in honor of God and Jesus Christ—and *Mary*—in the celebration of peace, in celebration of the Royal Academy, and now in celebration of the First Philosopher of Europe." Père Viogué concluded with some vigorous self-crossing, then retreated as the first course was served.

Despite the news the overall mood in the Great Hall was positive. How could it not be? Assembled in this beautiful hall were the greatest minds of Europe along with dignitaries and representatives from every civilized nation and institution. The death of Descartes was unfortunate, but he was just one man; learning and knowledge would go on without him. And anyway, wasn't this eelpout-anchovy appetizer delicious, with the slightly fermented lingonberry sauce?

Baillet did not share the general ebullience; and exhausted from his journey and the sad news, and eager to return to his rooms to look at Descartes's notebook and then sleep, he found it impossible to pay attention to the speeches. Happily, Ambassador Chanut was also eager to learn how things had gone that afternoon.

"Dear," he said to his wife, who had just finished his appetizer after eating her own. "I am sure they will give you the recipe if you ask in the kitchen. And on the way back ...?"

He held out his three empty goblets.

Marguerite frowned and stood up, taking them.

"What's the news, Père?" Chanut turned to Baillet.

Baillet hesitated, decided to be—cautious. "Nothing, sir."

"You spoke to the valet?"

"I did. But—"

"What?"

"So far, it seems, Descartes simply got sick, died," Baillet added, "boom."

"Well, then, it's off to a good start! The Chancellor will be pleased."

"You—spoke to—the Chancellor?"

"Of course. Nothing goes on here without his permission."

"And he approves of the investigation?"

"Presuming it concurs with the official medical report, yes. The one that will conclude that Descartes got sick and died. Now, as long as I have you here, let me point out some people to you."

Over there was the Queen's Librarian, Freinsheimus, a

doddering old fool but useful to know, since he was in charge of resources Baillet might need; plus, as a gossipmonger, he knew every scholar in town and their business. He could help with translations as well, since he had served as the Queen's language tutor before Zolindius—then a soldier—returned from the wars a hero and took over the job as he began his political ascent.

"You are really concerned about the scholars?"

"Everybody, Père. As I told you, they were bitterly envious of him."

"But—grammarians, mathematicians ...?"

"The worst!" Chanut paused to drink Baillet's *akvavit*. "Speaking of, see that man over there? Toward the side wall, maybe ten tables over?"

Baillet could make out a very tall, thin, large-headed man in a shabby suit who stood out for those four reasons. "Who is he?"

"Roberval. They say he may be the world's greatest mathematician now."

"Now?"

"With Descartes out of the way."

"Who says that?"

"Well, actually, he did. He arrived in town a couple of weeks ago and came to me. He wanted to see Descartes, who was refusing to see him, and he thought that I could help."

"And why did he want to see Descartes?"

"That's what I asked. He said that the world's two greatest mathematicians had private business to discuss but that our friend was being pig-headed." Chanut belched quietly. "There was some bad blood between them years ago. Ah! Speaking of suspects, look there."

Two tables over, directly before the dais where the Queen's seat still stood empty, was seated a man who was neither tall, thin, large-headed, nor dressed shabbily.

"Wullens, the Queen's physician. Bad blood there, too, between him and our man, as I told you. And of course he

was the one attending to him all week. And there ..."
Baillet followed the Ambassador's rearward gaze.
"Depressed looking man, long stern nose, upturned
nostril? Sorry, in the Calvinist section in back?"

"I see."

"Gisbertus Voetius. *Fantastic* scandal between him and
our man in the United Provinces a couple of years ago. I
personally had to rescue Descartes from his clutches."

"But who is he?"

"A nasty *predikant*, basically. We had him knocked
down a few pegs. Only made him nastier. He, too, arrived
a couple of weeks ago and has been irritating people all
over town."

"And what he is doing here?"

"Representing somebody or something for the Gala.
The Queen insisted on being inclusive. Her heart was big
enough to make some room in the rear for the Calvinists,"
Chanut chortled.

"So, Ambassador, that is quite a few suspects."

"Ah!" Chanut slapped his forehead. "I forgot
someone!" Chanut gestured around the room. "Every
Protestant in this room, and every one outside. Don't
forget the rumors. The religious ones."

"Descartes's—influence. On the Queen."

"Exactly."

"So, Ambassador, everyone is a suspect."

"Exactly, Père."

"Even you?" Baillet arched his brow. "Imagine if
Descartes—succeeded. *You* bring him here, and he
promptly topples the Swedish hierarchy by converting the
Queen. Hardly good for France's international reputation,
I would imagine. And disastrous for yours. And possible
grounds for—murder."

Chanut had stopped chortling and was staring at
Baillet.

"Not bad, Père," a smile slowly formed on his face.
"Ah, they're finally serving something other than fish. This

dish is in honor of the Chancellor. Oxen stuffed with turkey stuffed with goose."

"Sounds—delicious," Baillet said as the waiter delivered their plates.

"Zolindius likes meat. I suggest we get started on it before the next speech."

But it was too late. Already His Excellence Carolus Zolindius was being introduced and limping heavily toward the podium. An equally heavy silence fell upon the vaulted room. Zolindius stood at the podium, gazing out at the audience, staring at them, remaining absolutely, perfectly still.

10

*F*ive tomorrow morning!

Well, Baillet thought as he huddled across the Norrbro, nobody said the investigator's life was an easy one.

The snow was coming down on the mostly deserted streets. He was feeling on edge, from the desolation. He held his lantern out, lighting the way as best he could. Perhaps he should not have left the Opening Banquet so early, but he couldn't tolerate the prospect of hours more speeches about tolerance. Shortly after the Chancellor's speech—some pleasantries about the many nations whose citizens his army had just finished slaughtering—Baillet had made his excuses to the Chanuts, reclaimed his greatcoat, and was standing at the main door watching the snow when something pulled at his elbow.

Baillet turned to look.

"Down here," a scratchy voice said in German.

Just above his elbow was the head of the Queen's Librarian.

"Don't underestimate me because I am small!" Freinsheimus scolded.

"Of course not," Baillet stammered, in German.

Freinsheimus stared at him from beneath bushy white eyebrows. "So you are the Jesuit."

"The Jesuit?"

"Investigating the murder."

"The murder?"

"It was obviously a murder."

"Obviously?"

Freinsheimus rolled his eyes. "You must be new at this."

"My first day."

"I can help you," Freinsheimus lowered his voice. "Come to my library."

"Now?" Baillet asked, dropping his voice to a whisper to match the Librarian's.

"Of course not now! Too many people up and about, snooping around. You will come tomorrow morning, before the library opens."

"What—time?"

"Five bells, Jesuit!"

"But it will be—freezing at that hour."

"Take a tunnel, for God's sake! Now disappear before anyone sees us talking. And remember."

The Librarian whispered something.

"I'm sorry?" Baillet leaned down closer.

"I said *trust no one*! Now go!"

Five in the morning! Baillet wasn't sure what time it was as he turned down Jakobsgatan, but he was sure that it wasn't enough hours before five in the morning. And a tunnel? Whatever that meant, he was also sure he wouldn't be climbing down into any tight spaces beneath the earth any time soon, even if they were warmer. The thought of warmth made him think of the warm quilt at his flat, a fire in the stove, sleep. Perhaps Descartes's notebook wouldn't have much to offer and he'd be able to get to sleep sooner rather than later. With the wind the drifts were accumulating quite high, unpleasantly so as he trudged. In fact a particularly high pile of snow seemed to have collected directly before the front door of his rooming house.

But then he saw it wasn't snow at all.

There was a man lying there.

"Wake up, man!" Baillet shook him, brushing the snow from him. Baillet's own fingers were frozen just in the thirty-minute walk from the Castle. He couldn't imagine how the man was still alive, in rags, half-buried in snow. Or was he—alive?

The man slowly came to. He shook his head, scattering the snow from his long ragged gray hair and beard. His clothes were as ragged as his hair and he smelled of wine.

It was the vagabond Schlüter had beaten away earlier.

And he spoke a perfect French.

"Unhand me, you beast!" he exclaimed.

"I'm sorry?" Baillet complied.

"Do you have any idea who I am?"

"I'm sorry, I don't."

"Oh, but you will. You will!" With those words the man got to his feet, brushed the snow off his shoulders, and stomped away through the drifts. Baillet could see that he was missing one of his shoes. Baillet also saw him suddenly disappear as if into a hole in the ground.

A tunnel entrance? Baillet wondered.

Too frozen even to contemplate pursuit Baillet fumbled inside his greatcoat pocket for his keys. He found what he thought was the key to the front door, slipped it in, but it wouldn't budge. He fumbled for his other key and it turned easily. But when he tried the door he found it locked. That was odd; his turning the key must have locked it. Perhaps another tenant had left it unlocked. Baillet turned the key again, re-unlocking it, and entered the long dark hall. He felt his way the ten paces down the hall to the stairs, and went up. He was standing just outside the door to his flat, looking for his first key, when he realized there were voices within.

Inside his rooms.

His heart skipped a beat.

Sweet Mother, he thought, petrified. There seemed to be two voices, a lower one and a thin high one. They were arguing, although he was unable to make out what it was about. Go wake the landlady, he thought, that would be a good idea. She was a tough character, as broad as she was tall and hardened by these Swedish winters. The only problem was that waking her meant going back outside, since her flat was around the corner. And anyway, what was he thinking, running to the woman of the house? Was he not a man—a timid man prone to weeping, but nevertheless a man? And if he was serious about—being an investigator—of a *murder*—shouldn't he learn to take care of situations like this himself?

His heart in his throat, refusing to let himself weep, Baillet leaned against the door, took a deep breath, and burst into his sitting room.

The flat was a mess. The furniture had been overturned. The desk had been emptied of its drawers. The several paintings had been knifed down the middle. Baillet could see all this because whoever had been ransacking had lit a candle to ransack by.

The voices, coming from his bedroom, had silenced.

Sweet Mother, Baillet thought again, again contemplating going for the landlady. Wasn't bursting into his own flat enough for tonight? Couldn't he just ease into this—*man* business? Must he actually burst into the bedroom as well?

One more deep breath and he stepped down the hallway toward his bedroom.

Just then the door swung open and a tall man in a long cloak sprang out and pushed past him into the sitting room. But before Baillet could react a second man sprang out of the room, a shorter, stockier man, aiming to push past him as well but failing to anticipate that Baillet, in his terror, would collapse onto the floor. The second man stumbled over him, falling on top of him.

"Murder!" Baillet squeaked in his panic, praying the landlady might hear him.

The man was trying to stand up and was as astonished as Baillet that the Jesuit was holding on to his legs.

The man grunted, and kicked. Baillet hung on.

The man dragged him into the sitting room. Baillet hung on.

"Murder!" Baillet exclaimed again, only this time slightly audibly, causing the man to take notice.

"Calm down, you fool! Let go of me!"

"You've broken into my rooms," Baillet croaked, trembling. "And you tell me to calm down?"

"Listen," the man said, himself calming down. "Just let go."

"What are you doing here? And who was that other man?"

"Let go and I'll explain."

"Explain," Baillet said, just now realizing he was still holding on, "and I'll let go."

"Fine. My name is Descartes."

"I'm sorry? He's—dead."

"No, no," the man shook his head in irritation.

"But he is."

"No, you fool. Pierre. That one's brother."

11

*T*hey were in the sitting room, in matching re-overturned chairs. Baillet was catching his breath as he looked at the man across from him. Descartes's brother! Or so he claimed. (*Trust no one!* Freinsheimus's voice echoed in his ear.) When Baillet expressed his skepticism the man had shown him the ring on his finger with the family arms, the name "Descartes" distinctly visible. That would have to do for now, Baillet thought, looking at him. He was small, as the philosopher had famously been, although you could see through his thin jacket that he was built like a—Swede.

"Aren't you going to offer me a drink, Père?" Pierre said gruffly.

"Absolutely not," Baillet retorted sharply, making a mental note to stock himself up on whisky. "And certainly not before your explanation, Monsieur—Descartes."

How strange it felt to say *that*.

"What's to explain, Père? The runt squandered our family fortune. Or his portion of it, anyway. I was here to get it back."

"In my flat?"

"Not *here*. Here. In Stockholm."

"I don't understand. If it's squandered, then what is there to get back?"

"I assume he still had his share. And then some."

"But then why did you say squandered?"

"Look, Père. The runt inherited money from our grandmother. And stole money from our father. And all he did was write books and pretend he was the Lord's gift to humanity. He couldn't possibly have spent it all."

"Apparently he did, you know."

"What makes you say that?"

"There wasn't much left at the end. What little there was went to his valet. And his funeral." As Baillet said this, it occurred to him that a good investigator probably doesn't share his information with—his suspects.

Pierre huffed. "Damn him! Once a pile of *merde*, always one."

"But—what, exactly, were you hoping for? In coming here?"

"I told you. To talk to the runt."

"No, *here*." Baillet gestured to his rooms.

"I heard you had collected his papers. I was hoping to find financial records, bank accounts, anything to help me recover some of those assets."

"But how did you hear I had collected his papers?"

"I heard, that's all. Well, do you? Have any of his financial records?"

"I beg your pardon! I certainly wouldn't tell you, if I did. And anyway, why didn't you just ask your brother, whom you traveled all this distance to see?" Baillet peered closely. "Allegedly?"

"He wouldn't see me."

"But why on earth not?"

"I don't know, Père. Maybe it was on account of the letters."

"What letters?"

"The threatening ones I sent once I found out he was here."

"Yes," Baillet scratched his chin. "I imagine that could do it."

"You would write nasty letters too, Père, if you were me. I have been chasing him for years. Every time I found out where he was he would move. He was always a coward, always running away. And then when my circumstances ... changed—"

"Your circumstances?"

"I lost a bundle in the *Fronde*. In '48. You know how that was."

Baillet nodded, pretending he did.

"Well, imagine how it felt to lose everything and then learn that your scoundrel brother, who stole what was rightfully yours, was becoming the Royal Philosopher of Sweden. I got here as soon as I could. Then the runt wouldn't see me. His man threatened to beat me with a plank. I've been sleeping in these goddamn tunnels for two weeks now."

Two weeks, Baillet thought.

He is here.

"You don't give him much credit, Monsieur," Baillet said carefully.

"He doesn't deserve any."

"He *was* a genius, you know."

"Ha!"

"What does that mean?"

"He was lazy, a cheat, a gambler. A wastrel. Always was."

"But—even at La Flèche he was legendary for mathematics."

Pierre scoffed. "He was a fraud. There was this—" He stopped. "You don't know anything about your man, do you, Pére?"

"Maybe," Baillet answered, since, of course, he didn't.

"Aren't you supposed to be the investigator?"

"Yes, but—first day, you know."

"Well, your man was not what he appeared to be, Père.

Everyone revered him. Or this image they had of him. They don't know who he really was."

"And who was that?"

"Once a runt, always a runt."

"That isn't very helpful."

"Maybe, but it's the truth, Père."

"*You* didn't murder him, did you?" Baillet asked, spontaneously deciding to try the direct approach.

"I should murder *you*," Pierre muttered, glaring angrily at Baillet.

Baillet made another mental note not to try the direct approach again. Then it finally occurred to him to ask the most obvious question. "Who was the other man?"

"What?"

"The other man with you. When I arrived."

"How should I know?"

"You were ransacking the place together."

"We were not," Pierre said indignantly.

"But—"

"He was here when I got here. He'd already wrecked the place."

"But—"

"I told you. I don't know who he was. I'm just furious he got here before me." Pierre hesitated. "Listen, Père."

"What?" Baillet's mind was spinning.

"You don't have any money you can lend me, do you?"

"I'm sorry?"

"I don't even have enough to get back to France."

Baillet was just trying to decide whether to be outraged at Pierre's request for money or feel sorry for him when the door swung open. Two large Swedish police officers burst in, followed by the even larger landlady in her nightdress waving a rolling pin and screaming in Swedish. Before Baillet knew what was happening the two officers had grabbed Pierre by the underarms and were dragging him out the door—followed by the landlady still screaming, though now apparently at the police officers.

Baillet found himself alone in his suddenly quiet sitting room.

Should he have helped Pierre? But then again, good investigators probably resist feeling sympathy toward possible suspects.

And surely Pierre was a suspect.

A long-term grudge against his brother? Clearly a man with an anger issue, who had traveled great distances to confront his brother, only to be turned away? Who seemed the sort not to mind a little—physical violence?

Who had arrived in town right before his frightened brother wrote those cryptic words in his notebook?

In all the excitement Baillet had completely forgotten about his primary reason for leaving the Opening Banquet early. He jumped up from the chair and rushed into his bedroom.

The notebook, left on the table beside his bed, was gone.

12
1606-19
LA FLÈCHE, FRANCE
BAVARIA, GERMANY

*T*raffic in Paris on that Friday, May 14, 1610, was awful.

All the fancy people in their fancy carriages were sloshing through the mud in their attempt to escape the early summer heat. The Rue de la Ferronnerie was a notorious spot of congestion on days such as these, since it led directly to the docks on the Seine, where a few coins put a fancy person on a boat to one of the shaded parks outside the city. It was there that a thirty-one-year-old man with severe eyes and voices in his head lay in wait. This François Ravaillac waited beside a fruit stall he was pretty sure was selling Protestant produce; "Where were you baptized?" he whispered suspiciously at one point to an adjacent pear. When the Royal Carriage entered the intersection from St Honoré, sure enough, it was halted by traffic, stuck between carts of wine bottles and hay. Ravaillac had time enough to climb onto the carriage and stick eight of his dagger's nine inches between that

Protestant-loving King Henri's second and third ribs.

Which leads to the heart of the story, literally.

"I have a big heart," Henri would say after various fantastic actions aimed to endear him to people. Well this turned out to be true, as was soon discovered, for the gallant King had stipulated in his will that his oversized heart be entombed in the Church of Saint Louis in La Flèche. Two weeks after the assassination, thousands crowded the main square as a privileged few were admitted into The Church for the final ceremony. These included local nobility, town authorities, faculty of the College, and a select group of twenty-three students dressed in their finest mourning. Torches were lit and a somber herald was sounded as the King's heart, on a green silk pillow, was carried to a large scaffold, held high for all to see. Then it was gently slipped into the small urn where it was to remain forever.

Twenty-three students were there, but there should have been twenty-four.

For twenty-four had been informed, three days earlier, that due to their rank, wealth, or academic achievements they were to represent the College. As the Royal Heart was lifted high, Rector Charlet's heart was sinking, for he was looking at the four rows of seats set up for the students, and noticing that in the first row sat only five young men.

One young man was missing.

The young man who had won the mathematics competition just a few weeks earlier. The young man who was recognized for his mathematical prowess even if he couldn't be bothered to develop it properly. The young man who had ridden his horse four leagues last night with his curly locks bouncing on his back, done his business at Luché-Pringé, and returned just before dawn. The young man who after long nights like that couldn't really resist when his body made certain demands on him.

At the very moment that the Royal Heart was being slipped into its eternal urn, fourteen-year-old René was slipping into the deepest part of his sleep.

Four years had passed since the future Duke of Sully's expulsion from La Flèche. Two years had passed since Pierre's graduation. The older brother administered an impressive farewell beating upon his younger brother, then set off to extend their father's real estate empire southward since the advance toward Paris was stalled by the Sully episode.

"Quite an achievement," twelve-year-old René had observed to his father on the hot, sunny day of Pierre's graduation, at the beginning of July, 1608.

"Something to emulate perhaps," Joachim stared ahead, refusing eye contact with his second son.

"I meant that he made it through here without being arrested."

Joachim's temple tightened as it did whenever someone brought up the episode in nearby Le Mans. (Two young Protestant boys had been beaten senseless there the year before, one of whom died from his injuries.) "You will not speak, child, when you have nothing meaningful to say."

Obliging, René remained silent the rest of the day. During their post-ceremony dinner he barely touched his fried lamb livers, instead moving them around his plate in mathematical patterns. Nor did he speak when his father climbed into his carriage without looking at him, nor when Pierre climbed in behind him doing the same.

It was never discussed. René simply stayed on with Père—now Rector—Charlet the entire eleven years he was to be at La Flèche.

It didn't need discussion. Rector Charlet appreciated the extra income. Joachim barely noticed the expense, and anyway was embarrassed enough about his second son to keep him separated from the general population. As for René, well, the place was comfortable, the cook had a way with meats, no one ever looked for him when he didn't show up for classes or Masses, and when the other young men got angry with him for taking their money over cards or dice he had a safe place to hide away until things cooled down.

The only classes that interested him were in mathematics. In René's first full year at La Flèche, Père François taught him algebra and some new methods of calculating probabilities. Over his first and second years, Père de Fontenay taught him proportional analysis and how to represent quantities as lines and curves; with these techniques René began to glimpse that algebraic problems could be approached geometrically and vice versa—and that life just might be worth living. Not that he stood out in his coursework: there was that "lack of industriousness" his father always complained about. He loved learning the material, he loved making steps toward solving the problems. But since his day didn't get started until after dinner, by the time he'd scribbled some equations down his afternoon nap would already be overdue.

But then in his fourth year there was Père Clavius.

"Ze seventh digit, Master Descartes?" Clavius growled in his thickly German-accented French in response to René's raised left hand. There were only six students remaining in the class that had started with thirteen. The missing seven had been directed to the door in turn by Clavius's fierce glare, for various offenses ranging from incorrect answers to speaking out of turn.

"A three, sir," René answered effortlessly then added, "and the eighth is a six."

Clavius glowered, which was his way of smiling. Never had he come across a young man with such natural aptitude. When Clavius had taught the class about his work on the astrolabe, Master Descartes was one of only five students remaining at the end. And when they had covered the problem of calendar reform that several decades earlier had made Clavius's reputation? Halfway through the lecture Master Descartes sat alone in the classroom.

"But ven ve employ ze modern method," Clavius had explained drawing some diagrams on the slate, "ze period between ze vernal equinox comes out not to 365.25 days but to—"

"365.2425 days," René blurted out

Clavius glared at his speaking out of turn, but then realized that banishing him would leave him lecturing to an empty room. "Correct. Und ven zis seemingly small error accumulates over ze course of twelve centuries, it yields a differential of—"

"About ten days," René answered immediately.

This then explained why by the mid-sixteenth century people were celebrating the spring festival of Easter practically in winter. The ten-day misalignment could best be corrected, Clavius had explained to Pope Gregory XIII back in 1579, by moving directly from Thursday October 4, 1582, to Friday October 15, 1582 and simply skipping all the dates in between. Thus was born the Gregorian calendar, at least in the Catholic countries that listened to the Pope. The Protestant nations were slower to adopt it, convinced it was a scheme to convert them, though for the life of them they couldn't figure out how.

It was Clavius who taught René geometry as if from the lips of Euclid himself, though with the German accent. It was Clavius who gave him the books on the medieval astronomer Sacrobosco; it was Clavius who taught him what was in these books when he didn't quite get around to reading them. It was also Clavius who got him thinking about multi-dimensional mathematics and who thus first got him thinking that the problem inspired by Père Charlet's beautiful cuff buttons, the analysis of three-dimensional figures, might be solvable.

And it was Clavius who came right out one day and growled bluntly, "You are von fobbing, fen-sucked fustilarian, boy." René had no idea what this meant but got the drift. He had once again shown up to class without having done the assigned work. Clavius was clearly concurring with his father's opinion of him: whatever natural talents he might have had, René Descartes was one lazy, unmotivated fustilarian.

What René could do easily he did brilliantly. But anything else he just didn't do at all.

And so it was that in the late fall of 1609, during René's fourth year at La Flèche, Père Clavius, who had applied mathematics to the heavens and reformed the international calendar, set himself the far more difficult problem of how to inspire the thirteen-year-old young man who had the raw talent, but not the perseverance, to become his personal protégé.

Perhaps, Clavius thought, a little competition.

"You had not quite got the hang of it yet," the boy had said to René three-plus years earlier, throwing in the word "sir" as if to obscure his extremely inappropriately behavior. To have taken it upon himself to remove the cuff buttons from René's room and transfer them to Sully's trousers. To have entered René's room without permission. A mere servant boy destroying the reputation of a gentleman, a future Duke, even one as objectionable as Sully.

Not to mention implying that his master was incapable of handling his own affairs.

René had just stared at the boy a long time before dismissing him with a wave of his hand. René *was* capable of perseverance when it came to harboring grudges, at least, and he knew he was supposed to feel a grudge at the boy's—well, *insolence.* For rather a long time he barked his commands to the boy to run his errands, to make his appointments at the tailor and hairdresser. To carry René's dinners to his room, to leave the tray with the tasty roast hare or pheasant outside his door and then remove the greasy dishes after. But his heart was not in it. Although (or maybe because) the Sully episode was never mentioned, over several months his tone softened. In time

René started almost asking politely when he sent the boy
to pick up his class assignments, or to the printer's shop—
not the one in town but the more interesting one outside
Le Mans, a half-day's ride away, where one might find
something other than dour Jesuit tracts. In René's
adolescent noble mind, ineluctably influenced by the airy
world of gentlemen's sons around him, tasks such as these
were actually helping the boy, giving him useful
experience, maybe helping him to make something of
himself one day.

Perhaps it was such largesse that invited the next act
of—well, insolence.

One day early in that fourth year at the Collège René
sent the boy to pick up assignments from Pères Visdelou
and Bouvet. René had missed several classes of each, still
officially "sickly" despite the weight he had gained from
the cook's meats. And so it was not unusual that the boy
might be found bearing a satchel of papers en route from
some quadrangle to the Château Charlet, or seen entering
the Rector's home by the rear servants' entrance, carrying
the satchel through the long hallway leading into the
residential portion of the house. But what was unusual was
what René saw when he made his way to the secondary
pantry, down the hall from the main kitchen. He had heard
that some recently arrived green cheese from Gouda was
stored there, and thought that on the off chance he might
decide to do Père Visdelou's logarithms assignment later
he might as well do so on a belly full of that cheese.

The room was small but well lit by its large window.
On each of its walls were shelves packed with jars of
delectable things. The smell of deliciously stinky green
cheese filled his nostrils.

"What are you doing?" René asked, startled.

The boy was crouched on the floor and looking
through some papers. He looked up, shut his eyes and
released the papers, and dropped his head back down.

René picked up one of the sheets.

Père Visdelou's impeccable handwriting and lines of equations filled with logarithms.

"The boy must be whipped, Rector," René demanded that evening at the heavy oak supper table, having asked himself what his father would demand in this situation.

The Rector's face showed concern. "Now, child, one need not be hasty here."

"That's fine. It can wait until tomorrow."

"I mean with our judgment, child."

"But sir. The boy took liberties with my things."

"Surely there is no harm—"

"It was not his place."

"Perhaps. But it is hardly catastrophic."

"But it is. He cannot be trusted. He must be punished. For his own benefit."

"His own benefit?"

"He must learn his place." René felt a small burst of pride on thinking of this, remembering all the times his brother had reminded *him* of "his place."

The Rector contemplated, his face tense. "All right," he said softly.

"Very well, sir. Tomorrow, then?"

"Dear Mary, no! I did not agree to a whipping, dear child."

"But you said 'all right.'"

"To the punishment. Not to a whipping."

René might have put up more of a fight, but in fact he was more interested in enjoying these cold slices of goose with apple paste, which he now set about to do. In fact he had forgotten what they were talking about by the time the Rector resumed the conversation.

"My child," the Rector said, pushing his plate away and wiping his lips with the linen napkin. "There is another way to proceed here. You say you are concerned for his benefit, am I right?"

René looked up, nodded.

"Well, then, you might begin by asking why he was so interested in your mathematics. Perhaps the boy has an aptitude that might be worth developing. For his benefit, as you say."

René had been so startled at the boy's—the word *insolence* kept coming to him—that it hadn't even occurred to him to be surprised at what the boy had been looking at. "May I ask, sir, how the boy came to be in your charge in the first place?"

"After three years you ask me this?"

"I hadn't thought to before."

"And why now?"

"I am curious why you are so eager to defend him."

"I may as well ask, child, why you are so eager to attack him."

"I am not, really. It is—the principle of the thing."

"And what principle is that?"

René reflected. "To each," he answered, "his life."

"Wise words for a thirteen-year-old," the Rector said, gazing at him not unkindly. "Now perhaps you should find out a little more about the life of that boy. In the meanwhile I shall give some thought to his punishment."

"Yes, sir?" the boy said nervously and out of breath. When his master had rung the bell after supper he had run as quickly as he could to his master's room. He now stood, waiting, his eyes on the floor.

"How long have you been here, boy?" René asked. "With the Rector, I mean?"

"About eight years, sir."

"And—*why* did you come here?"

"My mama died, sir."

"So why here?"

"The Rector took me in, sir."

"What about your father?"

"I don't know, sir."

"And why the Rector?"

"He does that, sir."

"Does what?"

"Takes people in, sir."

"There have been others?"

"Yes, sir. Valois says the Rector has often cared for—orphans. Sir."

René watched the boy shuffle his feet. "Are you from here? La Flèche."

"No, sir."

"Then where?"

"Most recently Luché-Pringé, sir."

That was the village just outside the proscription against prostitutes, and thus well-known among the students for its plentiful supply of them.

"'Most recently'?" René asked more softly.

"My mama moved a lot, sir."

There was a moment's silence.

"To the matter at hand, then, boy," René said slowly. "My papers."

The boy lifted his head and, with his eyes closed, offered his right cheek.

"What are you doing, boy?" René asked.

"I assume you will be slapping me, sir."

René cringed. "Tell me where—how you learned mathematics."

"From your papers, sir."

"How long have you been looking through them?"

"Maybe—three years, sir."

"Three years?!"

"Since you moved in, sir."

The boy lifted his head once more and offered his cheek.

The boy could do mathematics.

It was astonishing, René thought the next afternoon. For three years the boy had been looking through his mathematics, learning what his master was learning. All on his own. He was now adept at arithmetic and geometry. He had mastered Père Visdelou's logarithms before René even bothered to look at them. And that copy of Père Clavius's book on Sacrobosco's *Tractatus*, which the boy had picked up for René after René slept through three classes in a row? The reason some of the pages were smudged was that the boy had read it before delivering it to him. Not to mention that the Rector had taught the servant Latin so he could read the book in the first place.

It was really rather outrageous, René knew he should be thinking. The boy needed to learn his place. For his own benefit.

René had an idea.

"So," he said, the boy standing before him, eyes to the floor, "you want to learn some mathematics?"

That was how the boy started doing René's homework for him.

It began small, with René assigning the boy a problem or two to work on. But then René began giving him more problems. And when it became clear that the boy was *really* competent René began offering him some instruction now and then, saving him the effort of reading through René's papers on his own. Helping the boy this way helped René to begin thinking of himself as the boy's generous benefactor. The fact that René himself was benefiting— less schoolwork for him to do—was just the apple paste on the goose.

Now if only he could figure out a way to have the boy attend classes for him.

"Impossible," Rector Charlet said flatly when René raised the idea.

"But, sir. My health."

René added a hearty cough for emphasis. Though his cough had lingered his health had much improved since his early childhood: he had gained weight, his skin had gained color, and his hair had grown long enough for curls. The only person not to notice this change was, fortunately, the Rector, who was still convinced that his charge was one scrape away from an early demise and who therefore soon relented.

Young René did love mathematics. But even more he loved relaxing at home, trying out new feathers on his hats, gazing into the Rector's many jeweled mirrors and admiring how handsome a gentleman he was becoming. Most of all he loved sleeping—sleeping in, sleeping until dinner, sleeping after dinner. Indeed sleeping was what he was doing that afternoon in the winter of that fourth year while the boy sat in the rear of Père Clavius's classroom, when Père Clavius suddenly stopped his lecture on Ptolemaic orbits, looked at the four students still remaining in the class, then fixed his gaze on the boy.

"A competition, sir," the boy informed René later that afternoon.

"A competition?" René asked groggily.

"The winner is to receive 500 livres tournois, sir. And furthermore, sir."

"What, boy?"

"The winner will accompany Père Clavius to Italy in the summer, to meet with Galileo."

René was quite awake now.

"Tell me, boy," he sat up in bed. "What do we have to do?"

The problem concerned music. Referring to some recent work in Germany on the ancient concept of the *musica universalis*, or music of the heavenly spheres, the challenge was to develop a theory explaining the mathematical ratios of the harmonic vibrations of strings. But René instantly saw the deeper implication, that mathematical concepts applicable to mundane phenomena such as music might also be applicable to cosmology.

The most elegant successful solution received before the Easter break would be the winner.

"We shall start," René said, falling back into bed, "after supper."

By "we" René sincerely included himself, and he sincerely intended to work after that delicious venison supper. But the problem was large and the venison even larger, and after supper he decided a good night's rest would be more productive than actually being productive. Something similar occurred after the next night's marrowbone stew, and the night after that. More than a week had passed before he'd had any promising ideas, enough to set the boy to some calculations. Of course he could have done the calculations himself. But it didn't seem efficient to spend his time on details when he could be focusing on the general strategy. And anyway the boy could use the practice.

"You must have made an error," René scolded him some nights later. René had taken several nights off to celebrate his fourteenth birthday and was now ready to resume work. "These coefficients should be proportional."

"I don't know, sir," the boy said, shuffling his feet next to René's desk, his eyes averted.

"Rework them. I want the answers I expect by tomorrow night."

"You must have made an error," René said again the next night when the boy returned a fresh stack of papers leading to the very same conclusion. He turned and looked at the boy. "Stop that."

The boy was offering his right cheek. He dropped his gaze to the floor.

René was silent a moment. "There is a week left, yes?"

"I believe so, sir."

There was a long silence.

"What would you recommend here?" René asked softly.

"Sir?"

"You heard me."

"You might try," the boy offered tentatively, "focusing

on the geometry, sir."

"Not the algebra?"

"The polyhedra, sir."

"This way?" René sketched a diagram along with a couple of equations.

The boy nodded.

"Very well," René waved his hand, dismissing him.

Two nights later René gave the boy some more calculations to do. The next night the boy returned them, confirming that the geometric approach was the right one. René stared at the results, not sure what to do next. The boy stood beside his desk, silent, shuffling.

"You might try graphing the results," the boy finally spit out unsolicited.

René looked up at him hotly.

The boy flinched.

But then René's expression softened. "This way?"

He began to draw. The boy nodded.

The next night the boy did more calculations for his master as suggested by the graphs, and the problem was solved. The solution was original, it was elegant, and it would surely win the competition. René was going to enjoy those 500 livres tournois, and he was going to enjoy being the greatest student of mathematics at La Flèche. And along the way he had generously helped the boy improve his own skills, educated him, raised him a bit.

"So, boy," René turned toward his servant, "you say you are from Luché-Pringé?"

In the late spring of 1610 the *Compendium Musicae*, René's solution, won him Clavius's esteem, the prize money, and one of the twenty-four student places at the entombment of King Henri IV's heart. It didn't win him the trip to Italy however, since the College revoked the trip after his disgraceful no-show at the entombment ceremony.

"I shall just meet Signore Galileo some other time," René answered philosophically when Rector Charlet told him the news.

Their attention was caught by the boy, who was clearing the braised boar remains from the table and suddenly flushed bright red.

"My boy!" the Rector exclaimed. "Are you all right?"

The boy nodded and quickly left the room.

"At least this way," René continued, a little flustered, "when I do meet him I shall be able to speak with him in Italian."

At the end of summer the faculty was to welcome two Italian Jesuits to the College's fencing program. Still smarting from Sully, René had begun fencing his first full year at the College, eager to acquire some competence with a weapon to supplement his small size. But fencing turned out to be hard work, what with all that moving and poking and grunting. He found he was more interested in its theory than its practice. In fact the famous 1573 treatise on fencing by Henry de Saint Didier, the father of modern French fencing, was really quite fascinating: there was plenty of mathematics in it and the diagrams were marvels of geometric representation.

But René's fifth year was about to get underway. He was in much better physical condition than upon his arrival back in 1606, and now with that prize money he found himself thinking about some private fencing lessons with the new instructors.

The Italian would be a bonus, in case he ever did get around to meeting Galileo.

René thought he would enjoy being the greatest student of mathematics at La Flèche.

He was wrong.

"To Germany, sir?" René gasped to Père Clavius.

"*Und* Holland," Clavius added beneath those bushy gray eyebrows. "*Und* Bohemia."

Since Clavius had shipped it out, René's little compendium was making quite the splash around Europe.

Some of its mathematics had been truly original, it seemed, and provocative too: its application of polyhedra even supported some of the controversial conclusions of that Protestant Kepler's *Mysterium Cosmographicum*.

"Zey invite you to shpeak in Prague," Clavius added, holding up the letter he had just received.

"Prague?" René repeated as the mathematics crown on his head felt suddenly heavy indeed. The thought of facing these men, the world's greatest mathematicians, was dizzying.

"It is just too risky, Rector," René explained at the supper table that evening, generating an impressive cough. "My health."

There was a loud clatter as the boy dropped the bloodied silver press that had just crushed the two ducks the Rector and his charge were soon to consume, in honor of René's approaching fifteenth birthday.

"My boy!" the Rector exclaimed to the boy. "Are you all right?"

The boy nodded and quickly left the room.

"The poor lad seems uneasy lately, does he not?" the Rector asked René.

But if anyone was uneasy, it was René. The international threat to his crown was perhaps avoidable but there was trouble enough here at La Flèche. The problem was that he now walked around with a target on his back. Every young buck with a smattering of mathematics would challenge him. Do a hard calculation on the spot. Work out some algebraic solution. Hey, is this number a prime? To what angle should you elevate this cannon to clear a city wall half a league away?

Thank Mary that René was quick, almost always able to generate the answer on the spot. But the pressure was enormous. Any day, any moment, he felt, he would be defeated, dethroned.

Maybe even today, he thought nervously as he excused himself after devouring that delectably bloody duck supper. That afternoon an older student named Desargues had confronted him with an engineering problem. The fellow was always blathering about projective geometry. Well now he had posed René a problem about how to take the plane sections of cones, curious whether the "greatest student of mathematics" could solve it as he himself had.

Thank Mary that René was clever. Now if only Mary would give him even the slightest idea how to approach the problem.

For that he might need to thank someone else.

René went in search of the boy's quarters.

The Rector directed him to Valois. Valois directed him to the cook. The cook directed him down the long hallway past the kitchen and the secondary pantry. The light from René's candle barely penetrated the gloom of the hallway. But there it was. A sliver of light seeped from the partly open door, near the rear door of the house that led out to the stables.

René crept close and peered through the open crack.

In the dimness he could barely make out the long rows of little jars on the shelves along the side of the room. When he squinted he could see them: bugs. Squirming bugs. The boy had jars of squirming bugs in his room.

René pushed open the door.

When it creaked the boy jumped from the straw mattress on the floor. René could see that in the light of the single candle he had been writing something on a sheet of paper.

"Boy," René said, entering.

"Sir," the boy dropped his eyes.

"What are these for?" René stepped over to the shelves, reached into a jar and pulled out a caterpillar.

"I like caterpillars, sir."

René gazed at the caterpillar sniffing around his palm, remembered his earlier life, his lonely days in Grandmère's gardens. After a moment he dropped it back into the jar.

"And what's that?" René's eyes wandered to the stack of papers on the mattress.

"My papers, sir."

"I can see that, boy. What are you—working on?"

The boy shuffled his feet. "This and that, sir."

"This and that?"

"I draw them, sir."

"The caterpillars?"

"Yes, sir."

"Give them here."

The boy hesitated, then reached down and handed two sheets to his master.

"These aren't bad," René said after a few moments glancing through them. In fact they were remarkable, detailed, precise—*mathematical*. Intriguing. Still for some reason he found himself feeling uneasy, ill at ease. Sad, maybe. After another long look he dropped the sheets back onto the mattress. "I think I will go to Luché-Pringé this evening. My horse should be ready at nine."

The boy nodded.

"While I am gone you may work on a little exercise. It involves some of the—projective geometry I have taught you."

The boy looked up at him but then dropped his eyes.

René felt uneasy but continued. "Let me describe the exercise to you. You begin with a set of cones—"

"May I get some paper, sir?" As the boy said this he reached down to find a sheet from the stack on the mattress.

René saw there were already some figures on the sheet. "You write down mathematics on these papers?"

"Sometimes, sir."

"Let me see."

The boy looked down, did not answer.

"Give it here, boy," René said with a lick of his lips, feeling suddenly anxious.

The boy looked at him. "Those are my papers, sir."

René hesitated. He didn't really care what was on those papers. But there was a principle here. He could almost hear his father's voice in his head, stating so firmly that you wanted to fold up and die, *this will not stand*; but since he could barely remember his father's voice it was more likely Pierre's voice he was hearing.

No, he didn't really care, in fact he didn't care at all, and yet he found himself saying, "You hand me those papers now, boy, or I shall have you replaced. One word from me to the Rector and you are back in the gutter. Orphaned and alone."

The boy was staring back at him.

"What was that you needed help with, sir? Projective geometry?"

René felt himself flush. He stared at the boy, who held his gaze for a long moment and then very slowly dropped his eyes again.

"What is it you want?" René asked quietly, it being all he could do not to whisper *I'm sorry*.

"The next time Sir has the opportunity to meet Galileo perhaps he might take it."

"Galileo? Are you serious?"

"Are you?" the boy said tersely.

"Ah, there will be other opportunities, boy."

"For you perhaps."

René was keenly aware of the absence of "sir" in the boy's reply. "What is it you want now?"

The boy reflected. "Teach me to fence, sir."

"To fence? But that's—a gentleman's sport."

The boy made no response.

It struck René just then that the caterpillar drawings had involved a very creative use of projective geometry. And then it struck him that teaching the boy some fencing might not be so impossible. In his lessons with the Italian fathers over the past year he'd gotten quite proficient with the rapier, and there were spare rooms in the Château Charlet in which to practice. The boy was short just like

René, too; maybe sparring with him would benefit René. And it would be good for the boy too, helping to improve his station in life. Maybe even raise him to the point where he might come along one day on a trip to meet Galileo. At any rate it would be pleasant enough having the chance to stick the boy with a sword now and then.

"Have my horse ready at nine," René said quietly, nodding, then turned and left the caterpillars and the papers and that boy behind to make the long journey back to the civilized part of the house.

By early 1616 Joachim Descartes had resumed working his way toward Paris. This northward advance was aided by the fall of the Duke of Sully, whose recalcitrant Protestantism didn't fit well with the homicidal anti-Protestantism of King Henri's widow, reigning Regent Marie de Medici. By the time René entered what *finally* would be his last year at La Flèche, Joachim had acquired some fertile tracts near the capital city itself. It was all the *good* son Pierre could do to manage these estates. Between all his obligations the twenty-four-year-old made it home only once or twice a year, to keep his wife pregnant.

Master and servant were sparring in a spare room, the furniture against the walls to make room. The fire had dwindled, but its warmth was unnecessary given their vigorous physical activity. Or at least it felt vigorous to almost twenty-year-old René, whose plump physique made almost any activity feel vigorous.

"Stand down!" he barked, out of breath and relieved that he hadn't let the boy remove the cork from his rapier tip. "Shall we have us a cool drink?"

"I shall fetch some water."

"Even better, the Rector has some new Bordeaux in the cellar."

The boy nodded and departed. Fifteen minutes later the master had refreshed himself with some wine, the servant with some water, and they had resumed the sparring.

"Prepare to suffer," René said with a smirk and a lunge.

"How so, sir?" the boy parried with a Quinte. "Were you planning to tell me more about *Amadis de Gaul*?"

With its exotic tales of giants, monsters, whores, and knights, this popular many-volume work had been consuming René for most of the past year. This was no simple feat since the work was banned at La Flèche; the Jesuits were not pleased with its incest, extramarital sex, and occasional show-mercy-to-your-enemies thing. The boy had made many trips to Le Mans to obtain the Portuguese editions, and René had learned the language just to read the books.

"Your place!" René snapped.

The boy stepped back. "And yours, sir. It is not here."

"Again with that. There is no rush. Look what your feet are doing."

The boy was too familiar with René's ruses to fall for this: a glance down and the master would have pointed him. Instead he parried with something resembling a Quarte. "What is this called, sir?"

"Read my treatise and you shall know."

"Finish your treatise and I shall."

"Only seven volumes of Amadis left," René stepped aside deftly for a gentleman with a plumpness problem. "Then I shall get right on it."

The "it" here was the manuscript on fencing that René had been fiddling with for two years. There was a void in the literature on fencing both as, and against, a shorter gentleman, and René's volume aimed to fill that void.

"Before or after you finish your *responsa* to the queries from Prague, sir? On our *Compendium*?"

"Ours?" René executed an elegant *Croisé*, adapted for the left hand.

"Yours, sir."

"What does it matter? They are too busy over there

fulminating about the Emperor's successor to care much about those *responsa*."

"After four years it is more likely they have forgotten about them, sir."

"Stand down," René answered sharply. When he had recovered his breath he added, "You tire me, boy."

The boy looked back at him. "To the contrary, sir, you tire yourself. If you were not at Luché-Pringé so often you might not be so exhausted right now."

"So what? What does it matter?"

"Your *responsa* and your treatise are why it matters, sir."

"And why do *they* matter?"

"I speak out of concern for you, sir."

"You? Concerned for me?"

"Yes, sir. Sir, you are becoming careless with the gambling."

René's ability to track cards and probabilities had long made him the king of games of chance on campus, even as his reign as king of mathematics had waned from his failure to complete most of his assignments.

"Hardly," René answered. "There is no risk of my losing."

"The risk of getting caught. You have become more brazen."

"The Fourth Quadrangle is deserted on Tuesday evenings."

"You mean 'Tuesday Night Club'? They now put up posters on campus announcing it."

"At any rate," René waved his hand, "I like a little risk. That is the whole point of gambling."

The boy sighed. "Also the—women."

René had been using his winnings to support two or three of his favorites at Luché-Pringé. "I told you I like to gamble. It keeps all this—" he gestured widely, "interesting."

"But it is your future life you are risking."

"It keeps that interesting too."

"And mine," the boy added quietly.

There was a long moment of silence as master and servant stared at each other.

"Sir," the boy said. "You say you are a gambling man?"

"I am, boy."

"Then why not let me remove my cork?"

Fulmination became defenestration.

Europe was about to explode with fantastic violence.

First, things were simmering at home in France. In early 1617 rumbles of revolt were stirring among some Huguenot Dukes, a problem that sixteen-year-old boy-King Louis XIII solved by removing their heads. This was not received well by the remaining French Huguenots.

Things were warming up to the northeast as well. Unused to the quiet of the Twelve Year Truce with Catholic Spain, Dutch Protestants started bickering among themselves. Liberal Calvinists had some beefs with Orthodox Calvinists who then had some beefs with those beefs. Hoping to be made King by the Orthodox, Prince Maurice of Nassau, of the famous bright orange scarves, generously murdered Liberal Dutch leader Johan van Oldenbarnevelt for them. When the Orthodox didn't make him King after all, he assembled an army instead. A national Synod was called to settle the matter but it soon became clear that bringing together large groups of armed men to resolve bitter religious and political disputes was not such a good idea.

Speaking of good ideas, Holy Roman Emperor-elect Ferdinand of Austria thought at this time to prepare his new Protestant subjects for his forthcoming succession by forcefully rededicating every Protestant church in the Empire back to Catholicism. Yet another good idea was to send representatives to the Protestant Bohemian capital to tell them about his first good idea. The noble citizens of Prague promptly threw these representatives out the third floor window. If the poor fellows hadn't landed in a heap of dung on that fateful day in May of 1618 their fall would have been the end of them. One thing was certain, though: the Holy Roman Empire would not allow this smelly offense to remain unanswered. Protestant rulers everywhere quickly began assembling their armies in preparation for the Empire's answer.

The Thirty Years War was begun.

But first a remarkable thing occurred: René finally completed his studies at La Flèche.

It was a perfect La Flèche day, back at the start of July, 1617, when the long journey begun eleven years earlier came to an end.

"Have another," René said.

He and the boy were seated in René's room, the candlelight casting shadows. René had had the boy bring up some cognac to enjoy while they talked about bugs for a while, which had also become an interest for René.

"Sorry about the Finé prize," René said suddenly.

This prize was awarded to the graduating student judged most accomplished in mathematics. Had René graduated by his eighth or ninth year he (or perhaps they) might have had that prize.

"There will be other opportunities," the boy softly echoed one of his master's favorite expressions.

"I knew you'd come around. You see, there are more important things in life than 'achievements.'"

"Like what?"

René gestured around the room. "I don't know. This."

The gesture seemed to include the boy.

There was a moment of silence.

A sip of cognac.

"At least he sent a representative," the boy said.

René shrugged. The boy was referring to the man Joachim had sent to attend the graduation ceremony.

There was another moment of silence.

"I don't understand," René said, "why they hate me so much."

"They just do not understand you."

"What isn't to understand?"

"They want you to be them. And you are not."

"But it goes back—further. Ever since my mother died—"

"Sir?"

René shook his head. "It doesn't matter. Listen. Boy."

The boy looked at him.

"What next?" René asked.

"Aren't you going to Luché-Pringé tonight?"

"I mean after. Tomorrow. The day after tomorrow."

René had steadfastly refused to discuss the issue but at last it was unavoidable.

"You are not just staying on here?" the boy asked.

"Joachim is cutting off the rent. The Rector is very depressed."

"So," the boy said, "what are the options?"

"Joachim wants me to go to law school. At Poitiers. But I was thinking about the army."

"The army?"

"Do you see me in law school?"

The boy did not smile. "But the army?"

"It will be an adventure. New places. People. Maybe even a risk or two, if I play my cards right."

"But which army? There are so many."

"What does it matter?"

"Some might think it matters."

René sighed. "Fine. As I see it there are several main contenders. There is the Royal Army. Advantage: prestige. Disadvantage: France. And I—know a few Huguenots who really aren't so awful. Then there is the Imperial Army, or maybe the Catholic League. I rather like Maximilian, but then you have to admire the Bohemians' standing up to the Emperor. Advantages either way: get out of France. Disadvantage: the Holy Roman Empire is not the best hound to bet on these days. And then there are the Calvinist armies in the Provinces. I would probably side with Maurice. He's building a military academy in Breda so I could do some mathematics, and he's got those great scarves. And from what I hear about the women of Amsterdam—"

"Disadvantages?" the boy interrupted.

"Joachim might disown me."

"But you'd be fighting against Protestants."

"Also with Protestants. And anyway all of them are opposed to Spain, and the Habsburgs, and the Pope. There will be war."

"So," the boy asked, "what do you do?"

"That is why I have these."

He withdrew a pair of carved ivory dice.

Several sips of cognac and throws of the dice later René said quietly, "So where can a gentleman get a nice orange scarf around here?"

"So when," the boy said hesitatingly, "will you leave?"

"You mean when do *we* leave."

"What?"

"I have spoken to the Rector."

"I do not understand."

"I'm taking you with me. A gentleman soldier needs a valet, doesn't he?"

"The Rector is permitting this?"

"The thousand livres tournois went a long way toward relieving his depression."

The boy stared at the floor.

"Think of it as a chance to learn something about Dutch bugs," René added.

"But I do not know how to be a valet," the boy finally said.

"Someone who could understand those queries from Prague can figure out how to be a valet."

The boy was silent, then glanced at the clock. "I better get your horse ready. It is after nine."

"No, wait," René reached out to touch the boy's arm. "I have changed my mind."

"Sir?"

"I would rather stay home tonight."

"All right, sir."

"Why don't you," René said, returning to his seat, "go fetch another bottle?"

The morning after graduation the twenty-one-year-old wrote to his father accepting his proposal to study the law at Poitiers. Joachim, briefly fantasizing that something might come of this offspring, wrote back that he'd arranged for René to meet a distant relative who conveniently was the mayor of Poitiers. That man would provide the monies for all expenses. The Rector was sad to see René go but openly wept when he embraced the boy, and stood at the main door of Château Charlet watching gentleman and valet drive away. Two days with the mayor of Poitiers was enough for René to make small talk about distant relations, accept Joachim's monies, then announce that he had found lodgings in town and would drop by to visit occasionally.

Then gentleman and valet set off for some adventure.

To avoid anyone associated with his father René set off toward the east. They got as far as Geneva before turning northward. There was good wine to be consumed throughout eastern France, René discovered; and as long as you remained packed for quick departures there was good money to be made at cards and dice at all the taverns serving that wine. The boy was proving his worth as well, as he could pack their carriage almost as quickly as he did mathematics. True, it was irritating that he often wanted to stay longer in the places and work on the mathematics, but he could be quieted by the reminders that they were heading to Prince Maurice's military college and that were René ever to drop him the boy would have absolutely no future of his own whatever.

In February of 1618 they arrived in Breda, a bustling town thirty-five leagues south of Amsterdam. There was no military college there after all, nor Prince Maurice. But no matter. René found it a pleasant enough place to entertain himself. He immediately picked up Flemish for talking to all those healthy, big-boned Dutch girls who seemed to have a thing for diminutive plump French gentlemen with flowing curls. He also spent some time in the fencing salons there as well. He didn't like how many scratches he was lately receiving from that aggressive valet of his during their frequent sparring. He should never have allowed the boy to remove that cork.

Indeed to placate the increasingly irritating fellow René also spent some time meeting other worthwhile gentlemen around town. He answered several mathematical challenges posted in Breda, including one that led to some productive conversations before René tired of relaying them afterward to his valet. He acquiesced when the valet insisted on their attending some lectures in nearby Dordrecht on the medieval mystic Ramon Lulle. A few words were also said there about some secret society forming in Germany, but by then René's attention had wandered to the healthy Dutch girl serving them beer.

By the spring of 1619 René had grown weary of drinking and whoring in Breda. It was time for drinking and whoring elsewhere.

"So," the valet said with the scowl he no longer attempted to hide, "what are the options?"

"Something Bohemian, maybe?" René suggested.

"But which side?"

"What does it matter?"

The valet just stared.

"It might be interesting to visit Prague," René said, increasingly weary of his servant's scorn. "The defenestration thing. And you would probably like it. Boy."

Prague had become a center for secret methods of wisdom: alchemy, astrology, numerology, and so on.

Although the valet preferred traditional mathematics and natural philosophy, he was open to the idea that these alternative methods might be useful. Unlike his master, he had been intrigued by the talk about that secret society in Germany.

"But they will surely be crushed," the valet answered. The Imperial Army and the Catholic League of Maximilian the Bavarian were already mobilizing to advance on Prague.

"True. But then that might be interesting to watch. Fetch the dice, would you?"

The valet obliged, scowling even more than usual at the master's preferred technique for making major life decisions.

Two rolls of the dice, and the matter was settled.

"We join the Bavarian," René announced. "We switch sides for now. My father would be pleased."

As he said this he picked up the letter that had arrived the day before. It had taken Joachim a year and a half to discover their location and the letter began with some unpleasant remarks about René's little ruse back in Poitiers.

He now held the letter gently, slipping its corner into the tip of the candle, dropping it to the ground when it burst into flame.

Gentleman and valet were going to Germany.

The valet scowled.

A few days in Amsterdam before leaving for Copenhagen. A couple of weeks there, then a tour through Denmark, then eastward to Danzig, through Poland, Hungary. From there due west, arriving in Frankfurt mid-July of 1619, for the coronation of Holy Roman Emperor Ferdinand II. Making himself conspicuous there was wise, to assuage those suspicious of his Catholic loyalties. Anyway, who would object to seven weeks in the city with the best *Glühwein* in Germany? Other than that sour, sullen valet of his, of course. The twenty-three-year-old René was sorry when he woke early afternoon on the day after the ceremonies concluded to find that the valet already had their carriage packed and the coach waiting outside.

They headed south through Heidelberg and Stuttgart, traveling along the northeast rim of the great Black Forest. René mostly ignored the valet's relentless haranguing about drinking and gambling in the taverns along the way. Already many of these villages had experienced pillaging and plundering at the hands of roaming armies, and they were not benevolently inclined toward foreigners passing through, particularly of the Catholic persuasion. More than once the valet's quick thinking, and packing, got them out of drinking and gambling induced scrapes.

By late October they had arrived in Ulm, where Maximilian's forces were settling in for the winter. Due to the tardy arrival of the gentleman and his constantly complaining valet, all of the decent lodgings in town had already been relieved of their proper owners. The gentleman chose to lease a house from a farmer in the village of Ulm-Junginen, a short distance from town. A decent house it was, too, with a large wood-burning stove. A comfortable place to spend the winter bickering about who should get credit for what, and who depended on whom, and all the wasted opportunities.

It was early November of 1619.

The Thirty Years War was about to get serious.

St. Martin's Day was approaching and so was the coldest winter this region had ever known.

A gentleman and a valet went into the woods and began to argue.

13
WEDNESDAY,
FEBRUARY 13, 1650
STOCKHOLM, SWEDEN

*T*he sharp clangs penetrated the darkness like nails being driven into his brain. Baillet shot awake, opened his eyes, to blackness. Sweden, Stockholm, his rooms, his bedroom. The pendulum clock in the sitting room had just rung four horrible times. Chanut had boasted of it, a prototype, he said, made by the great Huygens himself. Assuming it *was* accurate it had taken Baillet almost thirty minutes the night before to figure out how to set the alarm. As far as he could see, it could only be set to ring on the hour. Since he was due at the Royal Library at five bells he'd had to set it for four. And so here he was, in the dark, in the cold, at four in the morning, about to set off—or so he thought before falling back asleep.

The next thing he knew it was forty-five minutes later and he was racing through the flurries once more across the wind-whipped Norrbro. There were some lights on Helgeandsholmen below. Her Majesty's Museum of

Curiosities was down there, he recalled, open all hours. He wondered how the Swedes had already managed to clear the snow from the night before. He remembered that in his haste he had forgotten to look for the hole, the tunnel, that the vagabond had disappeared into.

Men ransacking his rooms! he was thinking as he reached the end of the bridge. A mysterious tall stranger. Descartes's brother. Whisked away by policemen. He couldn't believe that he hadn't thought to search Pierre before he was taken away. To think, he might have escaped with the notebook!

Or maybe it was the other man, the one in the cloak who had slipped away.

Baillet stood on—Slottskajen, the street in front of the Castle, he recalled from the map Chanut had shown him. He was fairly sure the Royal Library was up the road to his left, attached to the Castle. He set out along the stone wall surrounding the Castle, the thick wall to his right and the black river to his left.

As the fifth Riddarholm bell was clanging down the street he took a deep breath, exhaled some foggy breath, and knocked on the hard oak door of the Royal Library.

Nothing happened.

He knocked again, waited.

Nothing.

Then he knocked as hard and loud as he could. The door opened.

No one was there.

"Down here!" a voice hissed in German.

It was the old man, Librarian Freinsheimus.

"*Guten Morgen*," Baillet began. "I—"

"Shh! Quiet, for the love of God! Now come inside, quick!"

The old man led him—slowly—down a dark hallway into a large room whose main feature, besides the many candelabras, were the thousands of books and manuscripts on display. The old man led him—slowly—into the center of the room, then stopped, turned around, and waved his little arms grandly.

"Welcome to my library!" he exclaimed.

"You mean Her Majesty's Library," Baillet said, perhaps attempting to be amusing.

Freinsheimus glared at him from beneath his bushy white eyebrows. "You may hang your greatcoat over there, Jesuit. Try not to drip on anything, if you please."

Baillet obeyed, then awaited further instruction.

"We begin with a tour," Freinsheimus said.

It was indeed magnificent, despite the painfully slow pace at which the old man walked. Freinsheimus had been collecting these works for Her Majesty for some years (he explained), thanks to the just concluded wars in which Sweden captured whole libraries at a time. "You know," he added with a smirk, "your man was really just an afterthought."

"You mean—Descartes? An afterthought?"

"We were sending the Admiral to The Hague anyway, to pick up Heinsius's library when the old goat finally retired. So why not pick up a philosopher too." The bushy white eyebrows suddenly furrowed. "Shh!"

"I'm sorry?"

"I thought I heard something."

"What?"

"Shh!"

They stood in silence, the old man's eyes darting around.

"May I take it, then," Baillet said wearily, after a moment, "that you were not fond of Monsieur Descartes?"

"I've never met any man I liked half so well as a book. And, you know, *that* man didn't have many good things to say about books. He said that people spent far too much time reading books. Not thinking for themselves. That sort of thing."

"He told you that?"

"I heard him tell Her Majesty. I chaperoned their

meetings, you know."

"I had heard."

"You heard that I chaperoned?"

"That the meetings occurred in the library."

"Yes, in *my* library. You can understand why the scholars here might take offense. Oh, they despised him all right."

"Were there any scholars who were—particularly offended?"

"No, your man was fair. He offended all of them equally."

"I suppose it didn't help," Baillet gestured to a case displaying the Queen's personal copy of *The Passions of the Soul*, with its dedication to Her Majesty, "that his own works received such prominent placement."

Freinsheimus scowled. "The Chancellor should have listened to me about him."

"He consulted with you?"

"I offered my advice, yes, when I bumped into His Excellence at a state dinner."

"Oh. And what did he say?"

"He said watch where you are going, you old fool!" the old man answered humorlessly. "And that your man was the world's greatest philosopher. That it would be a jewel in Her Majesty's crown, so to speak, to have him here. You know," the eyebrows arched, "I used to be the Queen's language tutor. Before *he* came along."

"He?"

Freinsheimus lowered his voice. "I speak of the Chancellor, of course."

"Why are you lowering your voice?" Baillet lowered his own instinctively.

"Around here you always lower your voice when you speak of the Chancellor."

Baillet sighed. "Herr Freinsheimus. You said you might be able to help my investigation."

"Shh!"

"But—there's no one here."

"No one you can *see*. Now come this way."

The old man led him down a narrow dark hall hidden behind some bookshelves. At the end of the hall was an ornately carved wooden door. Freinsheimus withdrew a key, slipped it into the lock, then pulled with all his strength to open the door. He beckoned Baillet to follow him.

"The Queen's Study," he announced.

The room was spacious and beautifully appointed. In the center was an oak desk, behind which was a large cushioned chair and before which was a smaller wooden chair. Behind the desk blue linen drapes were drawn over presumably a window. The walls were lined with shelves, overflowing with books and manuscripts and papers. But as they stepped into the room the first thing that struck Baillet was the burst of cold air.

"Is there no stove in here?" Baillet asked.

"Her Majesty does not care for heat."

"And this is where they met? At five in the morning?"

"Ah, yes. Your man would sit there," Freinsheimus, smirking, gestured to the wooden chair, "bundled in his coat, wearing his boots and gauntlets, and that ridiculous wig. He seemed more like a semi-articulate bear than a person."

"Semi-articulate?"

"He had this strange manner of speaking. Stiff. Rolled his r's."

"And you—observed their meetings?" Baillet felt a wave of sadness.

"I was in the vicinity."

"Herr Freinsheimus," Baillet sighed, "you said you might be able to help me."

"Fine. Sit."

Baillet sat in—Descartes's chair. Freinsheimus glanced around then seated himself behind the desk. The old man stared at him. "Now listen carefully. You are familiar with—" his voice dropped to a whisper, "*the Brethren?*"

"I'm sorry? I can't hear you."

"The Brethren, Jesuit, the Brethren!"

"Which—Brethren?"

Freinsheimus looked around, then pulled out some paper and a quill and scribbled something. He passed it over to Baillet.

It was a sketch of a Rosy Cross.

"The Rosicrucians?" Baillet asked incredulously.

"Shh!"

"But they've been extinct for decades! Since—White Mountain, I believe."

"That's just what they want you to believe."

"But they haven't been heard from. Since then."

"That is why they are a *secret* society, Jesuit."

"That's if they ever even existed at all. I was under the impression they were a hoax, a Protestant—plot, of some sort."

"Exactly. They can be more effective if people believe they don't exist."

"Effective at what? Have they ever actually done anything?"

"What haven't they done! The wars. Westphalia. The rise of your man Richelieu. The English civil wars. The crowning and then beheading of King Charles. The Dutch tulips. The plague in Seville. Her Majesty." Freinsheimus's voice dropped again. "The Chancellor."

"What?"

"His Majesty Gustavus Adolphus—"

"Speak up!"

"Fine. His Majesty 'happens' to die mysteriously in battle. 1632. A hitherto unknown soldier 'happens' to be there to retrieve the body, under enemy fire. On returning to Sweden this heroism is rewarded by appointing him language tutor to the girl Queen." Freinsheimus glared. "Before long the young girl assumes sovereignty, and he becomes Chancellor. Your man arrives and then dies. And here you are."

"I don't understand. You are simply naming everything that has ever happened."

"Exactly."

"But you are—contradicting yourself! They are responsible for the war, and for the peace! They crown a King, then behead him!"

"You are catching on, Jesuit."

"So—they bring Descartes here. And then murder him."

"Apparently."

"Unless," Baillet suggested for him, "Descartes was one of them?"

"Yes, of course," Freinsheimus answered excitedly.

"But which is it? Was Descartes a Rosicrucian? Or was he murdered by the Rosicrucians?"

"How should I know?"

"But this is your theory!"

"They are a *secret* society, Jesuit. They are very good at what they do. It's remarkable that I know as much as I do. I cannot be expected to unravel all the details."

"Next you'll be telling me that you are one."

Freinsheimus's eyes lit up beneath his brows. "Oh! They are *good*."

"All right," Baillet said, rising, "I appreciate your—help, sir. But I really must—"

"Sit down!"

Baillet complied.

"Listen to me. You *must* understand, Jesuit. I don't know the details. But the Brethren are *everywhere*." Freinsheimus suddenly looked nervous. "Even here, in Stockholm. Especially here. And they are watching."

"And you believe they are responsible for Descartes's death."

The old man was glancing around, perspiring. "I cannot say more here. It's too dangerous. Just remember one thing," Freinsheimus dropped his voice.

"What?"

"*Trust no one*," Freinsheimus whispered urgently, then his eyes lit up again. "Not even me."

Just then the Riddarholm bells could be heard ringing outside.

"Seven!" the old man stood abruptly. "I've got work to do. You may show yourself out."

As Baillet exited the Study he glanced back and saw that Freinsheimus was dusting the Queen's books.

Baillet sighed as he made his way down the dark hall, found his way back to the entrance of the library and retrieved his greatcoat. Pulling open the front door he set out down the path then out, once more, into the pre-dawn darkness of Slottskajen. As he walked he found himself alternating between being annoyed at the man's buffoonery and feeling alarmed at what he had been saying. The Brethren of the Rosy Cross. The legends about them had been powerful. But they were just that—legends. Unless they weren't? Would they have wanted to murder Descartes? Some sort of Protestant plot—to prevent Descartes from converting the Queen to Catholicism, as the rumor mill had it? But then there was the other famous rumor, about Descartes himself being a Rosicrucian. But then what would that do to the whole theory of a murder in the first place?

Still, Baillet was thinking as he stepped onto the Norrbro, the idea was chilling. Members of a secret society, invisibly stalking the streets, aiming for—what? Resorting to murder. And anybody or everybody could be one.

Feeling nervous fear washing over him he sensed someone behind him. Footsteps in the snow. Following him. His heart in his throat, taking a deep breath he turned.

There *was* a man rapidly approaching him down the street.

Benjamin Bramer.

14

"What are you doing here, Bramer?" Baillet asked in German as they embraced. Startled as he was by the sudden appearance it was a relief to see his former shipmate.

"Just taking a little walk, Père," the architect replied.

"At seven in the morning? In the dark? In this weather?"

"I like the empty streets. At my age you don't sleep much anyway. And in any case," Bramer added, "I could ask *you* the same thing."

"I had an appointment with the Royal Librarian."

"At seven in the morning?"

"No," Baillet smiled. "At five. I've gotten myself appointed as—investigator."

"I know."

"You know?"

"Everyone knows. Word travels as fast as the flu in this town."

"I hardly imagine that that will help my cause. How do you track down a murderer if everyone knows that's what you're doing?"

"You think it was a murder, then," Bramer asked quietly.

"I don't honestly know what I think."

"Listen, Père. Maybe I can help. I don't have any experience investigating murders. But I do have experience constructing theories. I could be someone to bounce ideas off of."

Baillet hesitated. *Trust no one* rang in his ears. But five minutes outside the Royal Library and already he was frozen to the bone. He also realized that he was starving.

"All right," he said tentatively. "I think I need some— breakfast."

"Perfect. There's a tavern near my rooms, behind the Castle. We can talk there. Come. It's a ten-minute crawl through the tunnel."

He was pointing to a small round opening next to the street covered with a stone, cleared of snow. Baillet hadn't noticed it previously.

"'Crawl'?" he asked apprehensively.

"They're small. But they're often direct. This one cuts under the Castle."

Baillet remembered his coffin on the ship, his chest tightening. "Perhaps we could walk? In the air?"

Bramer acquiesced, and Baillet followed him on the walk around the Castle, then through the maze of narrow streets as dawn arrived. At one point he thought he recognized the morgue from the burial night—just over twenty-four hours earlier!—though he couldn't be sure, since it had been three in the morning and pitch dark then. Nor did it help that all the buildings back here looked the same, these low wooden dwellings with red-timbered roofs. Finally they came upon a small tavern, outside of which hung a sign depicting a rooster with a distended red wattle holding a mallet and playing paille-maille with some blue and yellow balls.

"That's where they've lodged me," Bramer pointed two doors down. "I've got the whole second floor."

"Looks nice."

"It would be, if it weren't in Stockholm. Now come along."

It was a greasy unappealing place, but at least it was warm and the smell resembling that of food was not unwelcome. Bramer led him to a table in the rear. Within moments Bramer had muttered some Swedish words to the thick-armed man at the counter and they now had some half-edible meat and half-potable liquid on the table between them. At tables around them were other men who looked rather the sort who regularly consumed this fare.

"What—is this?" Baillet poked at the meat with his fork.

"It's either chicken kidneys," Bramer sampled a mouthful, "or rooster testicles. I'm not sure."

"You're not sure?"

"My Swedish isn't great. So, Père. What have we learned so far?"

Baillet hesitated—over the food and over speaking—but decided to answer. "Well, I've spoken to Descartes's valet. Schlüter. On loan, apparently, from someone in Amsterdam. He gave me an account of the illness. And the death."

"On loan from whom?"

"I—didn't ask."

"All right. What did he say?"

"Descartes fell ill, then died."

"You're not a physician, is that it?"

"Exactly. I don't know what I'm looking for."

"You'll speak to the physician in charge?"

"Wullens. I shall try. I am sure he's busy with the official medical report."

"There's to be an official report?"

Baillet dropped his voice. "The Chancellor demanded one."

"Why are you whispering?"

Baillet sighed. "Never mind."

"Well, then, did anything particularly strike you about the valet's report?"

"That Descartes's waters were a strange color. That his eyes were wild. And that he generally—sobbed a lot." A man after my own heart, Baillet thought, then noticed Bramer's grimace. "Something was bothering him."

"Why do you say that?"

"The Ambassador said that in recent weeks he was very uneasy. People arriving in Stockholm, perhaps, enemies. Something weighing heavily on him."

Bramer was silent a moment, lips pursed. "What else, Père? Have you had a chance, yet, to look through his papers?"

"What made you ask that?"

"Ask what?"

"About his papers."

"It's a natural question."

"Is it?"

"For the world's greatest mathematician, yes, Père. You have just suggested something was weighing on him. His papers might offer a clue. You have found them, I presume?"

"It's—funny you should mention the papers. I had a visitor last night. Descartes's brother."

"His *brother*?"

Baillet noticed Bramer's strange expression. "Pierre Descartes. You—know him? Or of him?"

"No, no. I didn't know. Just surprised. What is he doing here?"

"He was also interested in his brother's papers. Looking for money."

"Money? Was there any?"

"Not as far as I could see."

"And was there anything else? In his papers?"

"You are very keen on the papers."

Bramer seemed to be studying Baillet's face. "I am curious about what Descartes was working on.

Professionally, I mean. But I suppose that can wait. But you do have them, don't you?"

Baillet contemplated telling him about the notebook, but in light of its current status—namely, embarrassingly, missing—decided not to. Besides, he reminded himself (now half an hour into talking openly), an investigator should play his cards closely, particularly with someone like Bramer who had won Baillet's cards, and much of his money, at sea. "As far as I can tell they suggest nothing. For the investigation. So I—"

"What?"

"I have no idea what to do next."

"Père," Bramer said with now a small smile, "must I do all your thinking for you?"

"Yes, please."

"All right, then. You will speak to the physician later, hopefully. Wullens."

Baillet nodded.

"And there is a priest involved, I assume?"

"How did you know?"

"There always is. Viogué, I'm guessing? From the way he spoke at the Banquet last night?"

"Was it that obvious?"

"It was. Talk to him. He'll know something."

"And how do you know *that*?"

"Because they always do." Bramer sipped his oily brown beverage. "And my further advice, Père. Watch out for Zolindius. The second in command is always dangerous, even more so than the priest. I cannot imagine that he truly supports your investigation."

"To the contrary he does, assuming I conclude there was no foul play. Apparently one always has to agree with him around here."

"Of course. You don't get into his position without the ability to control others. Not to mention hurt them. Now if you'll excuse me, Père," Bramer stood and grabbed his greatcoat, "I have an appointment."

"At this hour?"

"It was the only time the Librarian would meet me."

"You're meeting with Freinsheimus too?"

Bramer nodded. "I'm giving a talk Thursday and I need to check some references. But listen, Père. The priest and the physician. Your next stops. And keep me posted."

With that the architect departed, just as the Riddarholm bells began chiming eight somewhere outside. The ringing reminded Baillet that there was a Mass scheduled now at the Catholic chapel back near the Ambassador's Residence. The uneasy thought of speaking with Père Viogué weighing on him, he returned his attention to his plate, picked up his fork, and resumed praying these were chicken kidneys.

15

Follow the sounds, Baillet told himself, working his way back through the warren of streets. More parades were underway nearby, whose music and marching sounds were a useful way to stay oriented. It helped too that it was lighter now, with the morning skies just mildly overcast. Before long he was crossing the Norrbro, pausing to watch the floats below on Helgeandsholmen. They seemed to be representing military victories, displaying large Swedish men spearing, chopping, or disemboweling smaller men, women, and children of various other nationalities. Baillet pulled his greatcoat tighter, continued on to the Ambassador's Residence and then to the tiny Catholic chapel around the corner.

The service was ending. At the head of the room Père François Viogué was wrapping up. He was brilliantly attired in his vestments, which Baillet began silently to recite in order: the Amice, the Alb, the Cincture ...You cannot have lived with Rector Charlet for thirty years, he thought with sad nostalgia, without picking up a thing or two about priestly fashion. Some of the maybe two dozen men in attendance looked familiar, from the Banquet. To the side, by himself, his large head hanging low, was Roberval, the mathematician. A few minutes later the congregants rose for the final blessing, were dismissed, and began leaving.

"Ah!" Père Viogué exclaimed on seeing Baillet. "My distinguished colleague at last! A shame you could not make it for the Mass. I was expecting you."

Baillet gazed at the senior cleric, admiring the older man's strong rugged nose. It reminded him of an eagle's beak, as the man's intense round eyes staring at him reminded him of an eagle's eyes. The only thing missing, Baillet thought, were the claws.

"My apologies, Père," Baillet answered uncomfortably. "I got a little lost."

"Not a worry—Adrien, is it? But even so I was expecting you earlier."

"You were?"

"Yes. A messenger from the Chancellor's office said you would be here by 7:30. You had an appointment at the Library, I believe?"

Baillet's stomach tightened. "Why, yes."

"Well, no matter. Come join me for a hot chocolate."

"Thank you—François."

The nose pointed directly between Baillet's eyes. "Please, call me Père."

The priest led him back to his modest study, with just a small desk, two chairs, and a single particularly disturbing crucifix over the door. "The Queen herself tolerates our faith," Viogué explained after the servant had delivered the beverage, "but most of her clergy and nobility despise us. They compromise by charging us exorbitant rent for this little shack. Now," Viogué peered at him, "catch me up, won't you, on the gossip back home?"

They made some small talk, discussing who had been appointed where and instead of whom, who was embroiled in what scandal and so on. All of this information was conveyed by Viogué, who didn't bother hiding his disappointment as it became obvious that Baillet knew no one and *was* no one. Baillet certainly was unlike François Viogué, who had risen ambitiously through the clerical ranks to his current position, as the Apostolic Emissary to the Northern Lands.

"A half-dozen men conveniently had to die for me to receive this post," Viogué explained almost with the pride, it seemed to Baillet, of an unrepentant murderer. "But enough about me. I understand that you are preparing a report for the Ambassador, about our poor friend. How can I help you?"

"Yes, thank you—Père," Baillet took a deep breath. "Perhaps—you can tell me, how well did you know Monsieur Descartes?"

"Well, naturally. As the senior Catholic here I tend to all the Catholic souls."

"How did he seem to you? I mean, in the days before he—fell ill?"

"Before he fell ill? Why, fine. Or as fine as could be expected."

"I'm sorry?"

"He was not very happy here. He complained about the weather. About being away from France. From other Catholics, of course. But nothing in particular, in the days before."

"You visited regularly during the course of his illness?"

"Every day, of course. It was my duty to be available to him. This despite my other obligations. Tending to the others of our faith who have been arriving for Her Majesty's Gala. You understand."

"I do," Baillet nodded, his brow slightly furrowed. "Can you tell me about Descartes's illness, then, as you observed it?"

"But Adrien—I am a doctor to the soul, not to the body. Why ask me this?"

"Yes. Père. Still, there might be details you observed

that others didn't. Not necessarily—medical details. Anything, really, that might help me understand Descartes—himself."

"But why?"

"There are rumors, Père," Baillet said slowly, "that he was murdered."

"That is preposterous, of course!"

"I believe so as well, but—"

"But what?"

"It might be good to rule it out absolutely."

"Very well, Adrien. But I truly have nothing to tell you about the illness."

"I understand, Père," Baillet continued tentatively. "All right then. So you were present—daily during the illness."

"As I said."

"When exactly did he fall ill, do you recall?"

Viogué thought it over. "Well, he arrived for Candlemas celebrations looking rather pasty. So I suppose that may have been the first day of his illness."

"I'm sorry. That would have been—Saturday? The 2nd?"

"Yes."

"And you are sure he was already unwell."

"I am."

"The valet, Schlüter, said he became ill the next morning."

"The valet is mistaken," Viogué said sharply. "The Monsieur was definitely unwell when he arrived here. He came late, having overslept, as was his habit. And I distinctly recall noticing his appearance when I gave him communion. Indeed he looked just as pasty when I gave him communion again the following week. Only then he appeared to be on the mend. His condition had improved enough for him to call for me. Naturally I came immediately."

"He called for you? For communion?" Hadn't Schlüter also said that—Viogué initiated the sacrament?

"Yes. And to confess. Perhaps he understood—"

"What?"

"That the end was approaching."

Baillet took the last swig of his chocolate and swirled it around his mouth. "Was there anything—did you notice anything—during the week? Between the two communions?"

"Nothing, Adrien. The Monsieur was either asleep or raving when I was there. My function was to tend to his soul, when the opportunity was available. But it generally was not."

Baillet thought a moment. "The second communion—that was on Saturday? The—9th? Do you recall what time?"

"It was morning."

"You can't be more precise?"

Viogué shrugged. "I left immediately afterward. I had other business to attend to. I returned the next day. The Monsieur had taken a turn for the worse. The end indeed was near."

"What did you do?"

"The Monsieur was very weak, as the physician had just bled him. He motioned for me to come near. He whispered that he desired to speak to me, in private. To confess. Again. And so I cleared the room and heard his last confession."

There was a momentary pause.

"You will not even consider that question," Viogué pointed his beak between Baillet's eyes.

"Of course not," Baillet nodded. "After the confession?"

"We spoke for some hours in private, of matters of religion, of salvation, of courage."

"He was coherent?"

"Adequately."

"The valet," Baillet offered hesitantly, "said that Descartes could no longer speak. After the bleeding, I mean."

"That was true, as of some hours later. At the very end."

"I think he said immediately thereafter."

"Then the man is again mistaken." Color rose to Viogué's face.

Baillet moved on. "And then?"

"In his last moments of clarity, he announced that it was his time to depart. That his soul was now at last to escape its imprisonment in the body. That he would meet this temporary disunion, till resurrection, with joy and courage." Viogué paused. "He said something about returning to France. And then requested the last rites, which I naturally obliged."

"Returning to France?"

Viogué shrugged.

"And that was it?"

"A few minutes later the others returned to the room. I offered some moral encouragement, but by then the Monsieur could no longer speak. He simply tilted his head and raised his eyes to heaven. And then his soul was freed." Viogué hesitated. "His pure Catholic soul. Adrien?"

"I'm sorry?"

"You seem distracted."

"I'm sorry. That—happens." Baillet had been trying to organize his thoughts. The valet and the priest had several differences between their accounts: about when Descartes fell ill, how often the priest was there, who initiated the second communion. Probably nothing, he thought, but these struck Baillet as his first—leads. "You said that—a pure Catholic soul?"

"Indeed."

"Père, were you familiar with Descartes's writings? His work?"

"Alas, no. I read only theological materials, naturally."

"But were you—are you familiar with his— reputation?"

"Which reputation would that be?"

"Some say that his works support—skepticism. About the faith. About God. That Descartes was not as steady in his own belief as—one might like."

Viogué's stared at him. "Adrien, allow me to offer some advice. As one who enjoys hearing some gossip now and again, I assure you: very little of what people say about others is true. I saw no reason to be concerned about the Monsieur's faith."

"Thank you, Père. That is reassuring. But speaking of gossip—there are some rumors. Two in particular, about which I would be curious to—hear your opinion."

"Those being?"

"Well, first, that—unlike Monsieur Descartes—Her Highness is not—all that steady in her own faith."

Viogué hesitated, then leaned forward. "Adrien. Obviously it would be wonderful were Her Majesty to find her way to the true faith. And were Her Majesty to request resources toward this end, I would be happy to provide them."

"And would—Descartes have any role to play in this?"

"Our man was a good Catholic, Adrien. And I was enthusiastic when I heard the Queen was to bring him here. But beyond that I cannot say more. Now, Adrien," Viogué eyed Baillet's mug, "can I have the boy get you some more chocolate? You sit. I won't be a minute."

Baillet had barely processed the priest's response to the rumor when he returned with a fresh mug.

"There was some still warm," Viogué proclaimed on re-entering. "Now I am afraid I have only a few more minutes, Adrien. You said there was a second rumor?"

"Yes," Baillet answered, his stomach churning as he embarked on the next line of thought. "The murder."

"I have already given you my opinion on that!"

"You have. And I share it. But still."

"Still what, Adrien?"

"Well, Père, Descartes did have—a strong reputation. Many people had strong feelings about him apparently.

And you were one of the few people present throughout his illness. Physically, in the room. Indeed no one was closer."

"Are you accusing me of something, Adrien?"

"Of course not, Père. I just want to—the question whether you saw anything—unusual. That struck you as odd. Anything."

Viogué closed his eyes for a moment. "There was perhaps one thing. I am sure it is nothing."

"It probably is. But still."

"All right, then. The manservant—this Schlüter. He prepared the Monsieur a broth one evening, a day or two before the end. The day before the communion. So it must have been Friday."

"A broth? A parsnip soup, perhaps?"

"Perhaps."

"But why was that unusual?"

"Well, you see, the ingredients were delivered that afternoon. Out of the blue. And the Monsieur happened to be fastidious about his food, and insisted on inspecting everything he consumed. I do not know if you were aware of that."

"So—what are you proposing, Père? Someone sent—poison—and Schlüter just cooked it up?"

"You asked if anything struck me. It is your job to make any sense of it."

"You're right. I'm sorry, Père. But Schlüter? What could be his—motive? I understand that he was quite a loyal servant."

"Must I do all your theorizing for you, Adrien?" Viogué looked irritated. "Very well, then. Among the rumors reaching my own ears were those about the Monsieur's financial straits. Perhaps he was not paying his servant well enough. The criminal element often has money as its motivation, you know."

"So you think Schlüter was—paid. To poison."

"I merely offer you information, Adrien. You will

please cast your own aspersions."

"You're right. Of course, Père. But as long as you're doing some—theorizing—for me, Père—who might be the one paying the criminal element here. Just hypothetically?"

A hint of a smile crossed Viogué's face. "You are in the gossip business now, my friend. The Monsieur, now, was not exactly warmly received by any of the Queen's intellectual sycophants in the court. You have spoken to Freinsheimus, the old Librarian. Go back to him on that subject. He seems to know everybody's business. And then there are all the foreigners arriving ..."

"For the Gala?"

"Exactly. You asked how the Monsieur seemed before he fell ill. Now that I think of it I do believe he seemed uneasy, perhaps. Distracted. Like yourself." Viogué's smile gradually became a stare. "Perhaps even afraid."

Baillet's stomach tightened again. "Afraid?"

"You spoke of his reputation. Of rumors. Would you not be uneasy, if perhaps your enemies were arriving in your city, rather *en masse*?"

Baillet again recalled with a shiver: "*He* is here." "Was there anyone in particular?"

"You mentioned the rumor that Descartes was attempting to, shall we say, influence the Queen's faith."

"Yes."

"Someone, then, who might be opposed to that possibility."

"Yes, but I understand that that would apply to almost everyone in Stock—"

"Someone who knew Descartes personally. And despised him. Who perhaps suffered some injury at Descartes's hands. And someone known to be committed to extreme heretical views."

"Please, Père, who?"

"Far be it from me to cast aspersions."

"Please, Père. You obviously have a knack for this."

Viogué smiled that dark smile. "I affirm nothing, Adrien. I am merely doing your theorizing for you, my son, when I mention the name of Voetius."

"The *predikant*?"

"Former *predikant*. Former Rector at Utrecht. Former Chief Pastor as well. You are familiar with that affair in the United Provinces?"

"Only—vaguely."

"Descartes destroyed him professionally, Adrien. Had him removed from his posts, replaced with that drunken boor Swartenius, who is now the highest-ranking heretic in that God-forsaken land."

"And Voetius—*he* is here," Baillet said slowly. "In what capacity?"

"As secretary."

"To—Swartenius?"

"Even better, Adrien."

"How do you mean, Père?"

Viogué's powerful nose didn't quiver as the smile grew beneath. "To Swartenius's secretary."

16

A gloomy morning. Overcast, dark, flurries. In Stockholm the weather was easy to predict. Three possibilities: cold, bitter cold, and deadly bitter cold. The recent cold was now yielding to the bitter cold. Filthy pigeons dropping frozen from the sky. Long black nights split by brief dark days. And snow that never stopped.

This was a lousy business, the man thought, bundled in his greatcoat as he kept his eye on the crappy little chapel. He wasn't paid enough for this. Even with the extra income he was generating for himself. He couldn't wait to get out of this. He stepped back into the doorway, protection from the bitter blasts of wind. He could still keep his eye on the chapel from here.

A few minutes later the silly priest finally stepped out of the chapel door, made an effort to bundle up, and began walking up the street.

Why would that fool be heading north? thought the man. There was nothing that way, some houses then snow-filled fields. After the priest had walked up the street a bit the man stepped out from his doorway and began to follow. But no sooner had he done that then the priest halted, and turned around. The man just had time to duck into another doorway before the priest came back down the street. The fool walked right past him, too distracted to notice him. When the priest had walked far enough down the street again, southward, the man stepped out of the doorway and resumed his tracking.

Ah! The priest stopped again, at the corner, to look around and scratch his chin. The man dropped into a doorway and waited, fingering the sheath in his pocket. He pulled off his glove and felt the smooth wood handle. He had just had the blade professionally sharpened three days ago. At his employer's expense, naturally. He was wondering if he would use it soon. Another billable item.

The damn priest apparently made up his mind, and turned left.

The man stepped out from the doorway.

At the same time, about fifty paces behind the man, a second man was groaning, bundling his greatcoat, stepping out of a doorway, and going in pursuit. This man, too, had passed the brief delay by slipping his hand into his pocket and touching the weapon there. But unlike the first man he was not wondering whether he would have to use it.

The only question for him was on whom.

But there was no time to think about that. The man he was following had just turned the corner down the street. It was not easy following someone in this absurd city, with its twisted, narrow streets, its crowds and snow. Not to mention all these doorways and tunnels your target could disappear into in a blink of an eye.

Speaking of which, it was time to pick up the pace lest he lose him.

Where the hell, exactly, were they going?

Where the hell, exactly, is he going? That is what the first man was thinking about twenty-five minutes later when his own target made a sudden turn into the streets behind Tre Kronor Castle.

Where the hell, exactly, am I going? Baillet was thinking at the same time.

He was frozen to the bone. He shouldn't have lingered over the Norrbro, with its icy winds. But the frozen Riddarfjärden stretching out from there, the gray ice merging at the horizon with the gray skies under the swirling snow—beautiful, in its mournful way. Anyway as long as his body could endure it the walk would do him some good. He had too much on his mind to worry about the weather, much less notice the intrigue going on behind him. The Voetius angle. And of course the valet. Although he couldn't help but recoil from the scorn in Viogué's voice about the valet; the kind of scorn with which Baillet was familiar from La Flèche, the scorn the haves felt toward the have-nots, the have-mores felt toward the have-less, and all seemed to feel toward—him.

But still, a good investigator *should* wonder about the valet. Not to mention a valet who took liberties with the truth. Was he lying about when Descartes fell ill? And he suspiciously left out the groceries, the broth. Baillet would have to talk to Schlüter again. But he should probably talk to Voetius too, first. Gather as much information as he could, conflicting information, before returning for second interviews and clarifications.

Baillet paused to get his bearings. He looked around behind him, at all the people in the streets, and then turned back. These awful gloomy Stockholm streets were *very* difficult to navigate. He had mastered the routes between the Ambassador's Residence, his own rooms, and the Castle. But now he was heading behind the Castle and the familiar unfamiliarity was settling upon him. And it was so crowded, these tough Swedes with their mules pushing through the snow. Most of them didn't bother with head coverings. Their thick mops of blond hair were apparently enough to keep them warm.

Ah—this seemed to be the street leading to the morgue.

Now where was he—in his thoughts, that is?

The inconsistencies between Viogué and the valet.

But who said that it was the servant who was misrepresenting the facts?

Viogué, of course; and he was a priest, a—colleague, sort of—but Baillet wasn't sure if that was in favor of Viogué's credibility or against. But still, it was absurd to imagine Viogué having anything to do with Descartes's death. Not when the conversion to Catholicism of the most powerful European monarch was at stake.

Voetius was a far more likely suspect.

And the valet.

Or the brother. Pierre. He had a motive. Descartes would surely have been shocked to learn that "*he* is here." Perhaps Pierre was working with the valet. Both motivated by the money. Although Descartes didn't have any money. *Apparently* didn't, at least.

And then there was the missing notebook.

Wait, where was he, Baillet interrupted himself. The corner did look familiar, but all the corners looked the same. He turned around again. The streets were so crowded; he thought he saw someone jostled into a doorway some paces back. Suddenly he had the sense that the man being jostled into the doorway was also familiar.

Was he being—*followed?*

No, that was ridiculous. He was letting the weather—the mood—get to him.

Then the memory of the assault on the ship came to mind. Droopy Eye threatening to—whatever. And of the girlish squeaks he had emitted when stumbling upon Pierre in his flat. And of the way he had trembled before the Chancellor, feeling fear even of the man's facial hair, of all things. This would not—do. Baillet took a deep breath and made himself return down the street. He approached the doorway into which he thought he'd seen the man disappear.

There *was* someone there.

"You!" Baillet shook the man half-buried in snow.

"Unhand me, you beast!" the vagabond exclaimed, rising to his feet.

"Are you following me?" Baillet demanded.

"Are you following *me*?"

"That is absurd!"

"Absurd is being shaken awake by a lunatic! Can't a man be left alone in this murderous shithole of a city? First Descartes, then me?" With those words the man stomped away through the snow. Baillet could see that he was still missing one of his shoes—the *other* one than was missing last time.

Had he said *Descartes*?

Baillet went in pursuit. The vagabond was fast despite the snow and lack of shoe. But Baillet, breathing hard, was just a bit faster. The vagabond turned the corner, Baillet reached it a moment after, saw him stomping up the street. Baillet gained, his chest pounding, the street twisted, Baillet got to the bend in time to see the vagabond turn the next corner. The frigid air burning his lungs Baillet pushed faster, got to the corner, the vagabond was just ahead of him, then—

He was gone.

Disappeared.

As if into a hole in the ground.

Baillet approached the spot.

It was indeed the entrance to a tunnel. A sheltered small opening on the side of the street, with a ladder leading down into darkness. Baillet's heart pounded even faster even though he was no longer running. The man had said *Descartes*.

Baillet had to—pursue.

Taking a *very* deep breath he turned around, put his boot on the first rung. He hesitated. He lowered his second boot onto the first rung, then the first boot onto the second rung. Another deep breath, another rung. Three rungs, four. Then a fifth and sixth step and Baillet's foot reached bottom. He was standing in a dark narrow cylinder, the ladder leading up to the small opening above through which a sliver of gray light shone. At about his waist he could feel the horizontal opening, the tunnel itself, leading into pitch darkness.

A vertical coffin leading to a horizontal one.

The air no longer seared his lungs but that was because he couldn't breathe at all.

It no longer mattered to him in the slightest what the vagabond had said.

An instant later Baillet was back up on the street, welcoming the snow and bitter cold and most of all the air, which he was sucking in greedily. As he hyperventilated he noticed just another twenty paces down the street three burly blond bare-headed Swedes removing a wooden coffin from a small building and loading it onto a cart attached to a mule.

The morgue.

Ah! All right then, this was the street. As he recovered he headed that way, passed the morgue, and continued further. There was the building he was looking for. As small and old as every other building back here, behind the Castle, it housed the municipal jail which, Freinsheimus had told him, didn't need to be large. "The Chancellor," he'd explained, "likes to execute quick."

"There is a—matter," Baillet soon found himself explaining to the policeman on duty who, he was relieved, could speak French. "A man was arrested late last night. In my rooms. On Jakobsgatan. Would he have been brought here?"

"Indeed, sir."

"Might I be permitted to speak with him?"

"You would, sir."

"That is wonderful, thank you."

The policeman did not move.

"May I—speak with him?" Baillet asked, confused.

"Ah! I'm afraid that isn't possible, sir. He isn't here."

"I'm sorry? You just said that he was."

"I said he was *brought* here, sir. But he is no longer here."

"Oh! Then where is he?"

"I wouldn't know, sir. His Excellence did not share that information with me."

"His Excellence? The Chancellor took him away?"

"Not personally, sir. He sent a soldier with orders. To take the prisoner."

"When was this?"

"Not even an hour ago, sir."

Baillet stared at the policeman, at a loss. "My good fellow, I need to find this man. Where might he have been taken?"

"You could ask *him*. That's who took him."

Walking in the door was a Swedish soldier in uniform. He must have been over a *toise* tall, Baillet thought. He shook his bare blond head, shedding thick flakes of snow.

"Père Adrien Baillet," he growled in French. "His Excellence requests the pleasure of your company."

17

The three windows revealed the darkness outside as the Riddarholm bells chimed noon. The subsequent silence was long and suffocating. In the unbearable vacuum Baillet found himself wondering which was more remarkable: the way the Chancellor's limp exuded strength or the way the Chancellor's immobility just crushed him. Zolindius sat there not speaking, his dark eyes boring into Baillet's soul until he could stand it no longer.

"Thank you for seeing me, Your Excellence," Baillet exclaimed, painfully aware that his remark made no sense since Zolindius had sent for *him*.

Zolindius stared at him unblinking.

"As you are—aware," Baillet stammered, "I am undertaking an investigation. And—I am beginning to make some progress."

Zolindius seemed to be looking—through him, past him. Baillet ventured a glance behind him.

Those four heads on spikes on the wall.

They were *different* heads from last time.

"Silence, Père," Zolindius said in that deep soft voice.

Baillet complied.

"I am aware of your investigation. I authorized it in the

interest of Her Majesty, of course. To that end, I trust you have so far met with cooperation? From the Royal Librarian? From our distinguished Emissary from Rome? From the valet of Monsieur—" Zolindius hesitated, "Descartes?"

"Yes—sir."

"Very good. You will find that ours can be a most hospitable town."

"Yes, sir. Speaking of hospitality, sir. Last night I received an unexpected visitor. The brother of the— victim. Who apparently arrived here to—"

"I am fully aware of what transpires here, Père. And may I also remind you—what I thought had been made clear—that there was no 'victim,' to use your word."

Baillet swallowed, visualizing his own head on one of the spikes behind him. "Sir?"

"If there was no murder, Père, there could be no victim."

"Of course, but, sir—"

"Allow me also to remind you, Père, that it is only for the sake of the continued good relations between our great nations that I have authorized your investigation. That I have ensured cooperation. This despite the fact that you will with perfect certainty conclude that there was no murder. For there is to be no scandal here. And so there cannot have been a murder. That stands to reason, does it not?"

"Of course, sir."

"And do you believe that arresting a French citizen, in the middle of our celebration, is likely to increase or decrease the possibility of a scandal?"

"Sir, if I may, the deceased man's brother—"

"I care as little about his family tree as I do about those of the men on the wall behind you."

"But sir," Baillet took a deep breath, "you said you were authorizing me—"

"To satisfy the Ambassador's needs. To maintain the

Peace of Westphalia. Not to go around arresting people at all hours of the night. Calling attention to yourself. Disrupting Her Majesty's festivities."

Baillet had gleaned enough not to point out that *he* hadn't had anyone arrested. That all he wanted to do, the reason he had gone to the jail, was to speak with Pierre again. "I understand, Your Excellence. Still—"

"There is no 'still.' You have been indiscreet, Père. And I will not have it. Indeed the last three men who defied our authority are on the wall behind you."

"But there are four—"

"One for good luck."

Zolindius fell into a silence that was crushing. Baillet averted his eyes so he could concentrate on the pounding of his heart. As the moments went on Baillet found himself both unable to speak and wanting to divulge everything he knew about anything.

Finally Zolindius spoke.

"Of course, I understand," he added more lightly now with a strange almost half-smile, "that you are new at this sort of thing."

"Yes, sir," Baillet whispered, "I have much to learn."

"Well, Père, perhaps I might be of some assistance as you learn your trade. You will feel free to report to me daily on your progress."

Zolindius's tone made it clear that Baillet should not feel free *not* to. But before he could respond there was a knock at the door.

"The courier, sir," the soldier announced, entering.

"Speaking of our investigation, Père," Zolindius said a moment later, after the terrified young courier had backed out of the room, "it seems the physician has completed his official report. I am sure it would be useful for you to know of its contents."

"Yes, sir," Baillet whispered.

The Chancellor's lips shifted into that strange half-smile.

"Well, then, Père, you'll be wanting to find your way to the good doctor's home then."

18

"*D*escartes was a nasty little prick who deserved what he got," Wullens said. "Not that he got anything other than a nasty case of pleurisy, combined with some terminal mule-headedness."

"You were not—fond of the man, then," Baillet said evenly.

"His being dead doesn't change the facts, Père. Now, then. How precisely I might help you?"

They were in the beautiful sitting room of the Doctor's house at the most beautiful end of the boulevard Österlånggatan. Fortunately for Baillet this street, home to gentry and senior courtiers, began just behind the rear wall of the Castle. Even Baillet—once he had calmed down from Zolindius's stare—was able to navigate down the boulevard to the Royal Physician's mansion.

A servant had opened the door and said, strangely coldly, "The Doctor is expecting you, sir." Baillet had marveled again at the Chancellor's ability for rapid communication.

"Perhaps we might begin, Doctor," Baillet now ventured, "with your medical report. May I see it?"

"No."

"I'm sorry?"

"That would require the Chancellor's approval."

"But His Excellence just sent me to you himself."

"Sorry, Pére, but without the Chancellor's seal my hands are tied. I'm sure you understand."

"I am beginning to, Doctor. In that case, would you perhaps be able to share your impressions with me? Verbally?"

"The Chancellor has also informed me that I must."

"Thank you, then. So," Baillet said slowly, "you were no friend of the deceased. May I inquire?"

"You may, Père. Your man fancied himself a physician. But his medical opinions were absurd, and I did not mind publishing a word or two explaining why. The man did not take kindly to criticism, as I'm sure you know. He in turn published an offensive thing or two in response. When we finally met at Her Majesty's court, the little bastard refused to shake my hand. So be it."

Baillet nodded. "Perhaps then, speaking of medical opinions—you might help me understand—his passing."

"Inflammation of the lung, Père."

"Plus mule-headedness."

"Exactly. The little man refused to be bled."

"He had medical objections to bleeding?"

"He did. But even stronger personal objections to *my* bleeding him. 'Spare this French blood!' he cried out in that dramatic way of his. Please. It is a shame, really. Had he relented earlier, he might have been spared."

"You think so?"

"Bleeding is the most effective way to relieve a fever."

"Again, Descartes did not share the view?"

"Again, he did not. But then again, he also insisted he did not have a fever."

"But was that not undeniable?"

"Did I mention the mule-headedness?"

Baillet nodded. "So you let it go, then?"

Wullens shrugged.

"But you kept returning?"

"His Excellence insisted."

"He knew of your—mutual disregard—with the patient?"

"He knows everything."

"So the Chancellor was personally concerned with Descartes's care?"

"The Chancellor is the Queen's agent in everything. She rides horses and dallies with Greek inflections while His Excellence handles all state matters. And your man's welfare was a state matter. The Chancellor insisted I monitor his progress daily. And report back to him." Wullens gave a meaningful glance to Baillet. "I gather you discern the general pattern here?"

Baillet nodded again. "But now, did you consider simply bleeding him while he was—delirious? Early on? Particularly in light of the Chancellor's concern?"

"I did consider it. But did not."

"Respecting, again, the patient's own philosophy?"

"Respecting, rather, the manservant's philosophy. Have you noticed the man's muscles?"

"Who, Schlüter? The valet?"

"Yes, the valet. You'd sooner expect to find him at Långholmen than attending a gentleman. After I saw him beat a vagrant away with a plank I was hardly going to cross him. He too objected to the bleeding."

Baillet grimaced at the mention of the infamously inhospitable prison the Ambassador had told him about. "But—the Chancellor was concerned ..."

"Ah, very good, Père. There *was* more to my decision. I did not press the case at the beginning because there was no need to. It already seemed clear that he would die soon, even if we bled."

"But—isn't delirium caused by fever? And didn't you say that bloodletting relieves fevers?"

Wullens's expression hardened. "The Chancellor has

explained to you, I am sure, that the cause of death was inflammation of the lung. Certain questions, may I suggest, just might upset His Excellence. And in this town it is rarely a good idea to upset His Excellence."

Baillet felt his stomach tighten, decided to change the subject. "The parsnip soup."

"The what?"

"You were first called in—Tuesday, am I right, Doctor? February 5th?"

"That is correct."

"The valet prepared parsnip soup. On Friday, the 8th, in the evening. So that was several days after you first saw— the patient. And then the patient improved, the next day."

"Perhaps I should ask what was in that soup?"

"But why," Baillet persisted, "might he have improved, Doctor, if he had refused to let blood?"

"Your little man had his own ideas about that, Père. Something about his blood circulation theory. Absurd!"

"This was when, exactly?"

"Saturday, in the morning. The patient was almost himself around that time. As offensive as ever."

"And your own understanding would be?"

"Sometimes God does mysterious things, Pére."

"Are you, then, a man of faith, Doctor?"

"Not according to your superiors, Père. But no worse off in their eyes, I suppose, than your man."

"How do you mean?"

The doctor hesitated. "When your man seemed to improve, that morning, your colleague—"

"Pére Viogué?"

"Yes, of course. He rushed over to perform your— before the patient could slip away again. As if he were afraid that the little man was in danger of perdition unless he saved him quickly."

"My understanding is that he came at Descartes's own request?"

"It is hard to see how. The man was out of his mind

most of the week."

"But didn't Descartes himself request the—communion—on feeling better that Saturday morning?"

"Not at all. I was there when he woke up and began spewing verbal bile about the doctrine of humors, and then your colleague was suddenly there doing his thing." Wullens paused. "A lot of good it did, medically speaking. By that night he was violently ill again. Spewing *real* bile."

"He requested the wine sop that evening, did he not?"

"An old wives' remedy. I told him it would be probably be harmful. Not that I take pleasure in being correct, in this instance." Wullens took a deep breath. "I cannot explain why he briefly seemed to improve on Saturday, Père. But as I told you, without bloodletting the man was doomed."

"But you did finally bleed him the next day? The last day?"

"Indeed. He requested it. Demanded it, in fact."

"But that makes no sense. You yourself said he was opposed to it."

"He bloody well was. But who could tell what he was thinking by that time? And far be it from me to deny a dying man's requests, no matter how mad he was. I almost felt bad for the little bastard by that point, after watching him suffer all week long."

"Ah, that reminds me." Baillet's mind was working fast. "Would you know when, precisely, Descartes fell ill, Doctor?"

"I would. I believe it was some time on Friday."

"*Friday*? The 1st?"

"I was with Her Majesty at the Castle that morning. When I left her chambers I chanced upon your man in the hallway."

"He was delivering the statutes for the Academy, I believe. And the ballet verses."

"I would not know. He refused to greet me. But I did observe that he looked terrible. As white as a Swedish winter, as they say."

Well, Baillet thought, that would fit with Père Viogué's claim that he was unwell by the next morning, on Candlemas. But then what about Schlüter's claim that he didn't fall ill until Sunday? "All right, then. The last day. How long after the bloodletting did Père Viogué perform the last rites?"

"I don't believe he performed them at all."

"I'm sorry?"

"In fact he seemed opposed to the idea. I suggested myself that he do it. That the end was near. And he looked annoyed with me for doing so."

"That is rather surprising."

"I thought so. But then what do I know about you people?"

Baillet frowned. "Did he—say anything? Explain?"

"No holy oil, I think."

"But there must have been some nearby. In the Ambassador's Residence. Or—the chapel."

"Again, what do I know?"

"Was Descartes able to—speak—at the end?"

"Not much. He had little energy left after the bloodletting. Your colleague spent some private time with him, toward the end. But I cannot imagine much was said. Then the rest of us rejoined them. Your man briefly opened his eyes. They rolled up in his head. And he was gone."

There was a long silence.

"Doctor," Baillet finally asked cautiously. "Am I right to understand—"

There was a loud crash as the door of the Doctor's home burst open, then an instant later a soldier barged into the sitting room. "Doctor, you are to come immediately."

"What is it?" Wullens rose.

"I am authorized only to escort you. Not to inform."

Wullens glanced at Baillet as he grabbed his greatcoat.

"Why don't you come along, Père? There's a good chance this will be interesting."

They followed the soldier out the door and into a carriage. Minutes later they pulled up to a familiar building. As they arrived, three burly bare-headed Swedes were removing another wooden coffin from the building and loading it onto a mule-drawn cart.

"The morgue," Baillet said.

"Usually is," Wullens answered.

But as they exited the carriage the soldier directed them to the narrow alley beside the building. "You're wanted in the rear, sir."

Baillet followed the physician through the alley, to another alley behind the building.

There were two soldiers standing there, smoking.

At their feet was a—body.

Or more precisely, the remnants thereof. It had been carved into several pieces. All the snow within fifteen paces of the pile was red with blood.

But that wasn't the worst of it, Baillet thought as he heaved the contents of his stomach onto the already soiled ground. He had gotten a glimpse of the victim's face—or remnants thereof. Despite the fact that it was badly slashed and missing one eyeball, he had recognized it.

It was the face of Pierre Descartes.

19
1620-26
KASSEL, GERMANY

*T*hough in the heart of the Catholic Roman Empire, the central German town of Kassel was not a bad place to be a Protestant in 1620. Behind its high walls, guard turrets, and surrounding moat its Calvinist leader, Landgraf Maurice the Learned, had created an oasis of culture. There were parks, and gardens, a theater, an astronomical observatory, and the town was a mecca for those producing scientific instruments such as clocks and watches.

And tucked away, there was also something else.

On this evening, in a small house on a quiet street, something was taking place. From the outside you would not know it since the windows were shuttered and dark. Nor were there any horses tied out front since everyone had arrived separately, by foot, and entered through a small door behind the house. It was only through that rear door that they could make their way down to the second cellar, the secret one. Though reasonably ventilated it could get steamy down there, with all the sconces burning fat scented candles. And then there were those long gowns the members wore, the masks of flax and pitch, the thick woolen hats adopted because someone believed such hats had been worn by members of some earlier secret society.

Tonight, the 18th of November, 1620, was an important night.

Or rather it was one week after an important night.

For November 11 was a critical date in modern astronomy's attempt to divorce itself from the Catholic Church. On that date in 1572 Brahe had observed the new star bursting into being in the sky, the first new heavenly object in five centuries. On that date in 1618 Kepler had observed the great comet that led to his third law of planetary motion, which refuted the ancient Ptolemaic belief that all heavenly bodies revolve around the earth. It was thus an appropriate night for some enlightened men using secret names to don robes and masks and chant some chants. They just had to do it in the secret cellar, and without inadvertently inviting any spies from the Catholic Inquisition. And if their leader hadn't been out of town until today they would have done all this, the week before.

They had just reached a fever pitch of incantation when there came a loud rapping on the back door. They all stopped chanting.

It was the secret knock.

"But everyone is here," one masked person said.

"Obviously not," said another. "Open the slide."

The first man stepped to the door, slid open the view slide. "Password."

Two penetrating eyes stared through the open slit.

"*Cogitamus*," the voice outside said slowly, "*ergo sumus*."

The first man hesitated, then pulled open the door.

Accompanied by a burst of cold air a serious-looking young man entered the cellar. In his early twenties perhaps, he was disheveled, his long black hair unkempt, his thin cloak tattered over his diminutive body. His gauntness suggested some harrowing recent history. His eyes were as dark as the deep rings circling them, the open pustule on his unshaven cheek looked painful, and the jagged scar along his jaw indicated he had traveled a not very easy way.

"I come with news," he said with a slight French accent. "I must speak with B—"

"No names!" the masked man who had opened the door interrupted. "Who—"

"Who are you?" the second masked man interrupted. "And how did you acquire the knock? And the password?"

"A man in Dordrecht told me of Ramon Lulle. Lulle referred me to—"

"You come with news?" Another man with a mask of finer flax emerged from the far end of the cellar where he had been seated at a table.

"You must be—?" the young man stared at the man's eyes through the mask.

The man nodded.

"Prague has fallen to Tilly," the young man said quickly. "A massacre on White Mountain. The King has fled. I have—"

He pointed behind him.

On his horse were a small boy and girl wearing too-thin cloaks. The girl was asleep, leaning forward holding the horse's neck; the boy was leaning forward, covering her with his body, watching, shivering.

"Bring the children in immediately," the man with the mask instructed the man who had opened the door. "Take them upstairs." He returned his gaze to the visitor, the pain in his eyes visible through the mask's eyeholes. "And who are *you*?"

There was a silence.

"My name," the young man said, "is René Descartes."

There was no reason these Brothers of the Rosy Cross should have heard of him. His mathematical notoriety was back at a Catholic school far away in France, and already well eclipsed by the lack of accomplishment since. Throw in the disgraceful fact that he had deserted an army post and spent the past year traipsing who knew where and there was no reason to expect that anyone there should pay any attention to him beyond the astonishingly awful news he'd brought.

"The *Compendium Musicae*?" the man with the fine flax mask asked.

Descartes nodded.

"Brothers," the man said to the assembled, "continue the ceremony. I will meet with tactics in ninety minutes to discuss Prague. You," he turned to Descartes, "come with me."

The man led Descartes up a narrow wooden staircase into the house. He lit a candle and seated Descartes in the small kitchen. From somewhere in the house came the sounds of a female voice singing quietly to comfort whimpering children.

"You must be exhausted," the man said. He removed his mask, revealing the face of a man of perhaps forty, with a neatly cropped beard and gentle sad eyes. "And famished."

"I am all right," Descartes answered.

"Well, have something."

The man brought out some black bread, hard cheese, beer. Descartes took a little, to be polite. When the man saw that Descartes was not going to eat much he continued.

"You may call me Eudoxus. I have very many questions to ask you. First, the children's parents ...?"

Descartes looked down and shook his head.

Eudoxus swallowed. From elsewhere in the house the soft female singing continued but the whimpering had quieted. "All right, then. About the *Compendium* ..."

Eudoxus began with questions about the ratios and proportions required for the analysis of musical harmony. But within just minutes his questions were about some ancient mathematical problems that had resisted solution for centuries: the squaring of the circle, the trisection of an angle. After several more minutes they were about the use of the compass and the straightedge in constructing geometrical figures, and then, as the forty-five minutes that he had allotted came to an end, they were about the entire concept of the rational mind grasping the order of nature.

Then he turned to what had just happened at Prague.

The recently crowned Catholic Emperor Ferdinand II had had his revenge on those Protestant Bohemians who, after defenestrating his representatives in 1618, had boldly declared they could choose their own King. The Imperial Army, led by General Tilly, had arrived at White Mountain just ten days earlier and slaughtered the hapless Bohemians. The very briefly reigning Bohemian King Frederick was able to escape, but in his haste he forgot his garter, to the delight of the pamphleteers—who would make merciless fun of the "Winter King" and his pathetic flight from the Catholics with his stockings around his ankles.

Prague, which stood at the head of the new sciences, of man's enlightened quest to grasp the secrets of nature, had fallen back under the axe of those medieval Catholics.

"You saw this?" Eudoxus said tensely after Descartes gave some details about White Mountain.

Descartes nodded.

"You were fighting?"

"Observing."

"Why were you in Prague?"

"I was studying."

"With whom?"

"De Boodt. The disciples of the Maharal. And of course Bürgi."

They fell silent at the mention of Jost Bürgi— mathematician, master maker of clocks and astronomical instruments, sometimes collaborator of Eudoxus, and father of the two children who were at last sleeping peacefully somewhere in the house. Eudoxus would only ask later about the specific fate of Brother Diophantus and his lovely wife Hypatia, the only female "Brother." The savagery of soldiers was well-known and he had no stomach for it at the moment.

"You must have had an introduction," Eudoxus said. "Bürgi is—was—discriminating."

"I was previously in Ulm."

"With Eratosthenes."

"Yes," Descartes affirmed the Brethren name for the great German mathematician Faulhaber.

"Then you are Polybius."

"I am," Descartes dropped his eyes.

Eratosthenes had written Eudoxus the winter before about the young man who showed up at his door disheveled and distraught, badly injured, and needing to leave Ulm as quickly as possible. Eratosthenes was closing the door on him when the young man began reciting the Ludolphine number, the constant π as computed by Dutch mathematician Ludolph van Ceulen. By the time he reached the twenty-first digit Eratosthenes had him seated in the kitchen with food and beer.

Eratosthenes hid the young man for several days. That was long enough to confirm his great, but underdeveloped, mathematical aptitude, but not long enough to pry from him what terrible thing had happened and why he needed to disappear from Ulm. Eratosthenes sent the young man on to Prague with letters of introduction, and the new name of Polybius. Let the brilliant young man settle somewhere, recover, and get properly trained, Eratosthenes thought. Whatever secrets he was hiding could be extracted from him later, like the twenty-second digit of π.

Eudoxus studied the young man before him, the odd growth on his cheek. "The Brotherhood involves serious commitments. Starting with sustained and continuous study."

"I am ready to work," Descartes answered firmly.

"There is a long probation period. A full year."

"I have time."

"There is danger. The Inquisition considers us to be heretics. You cannot trust anyone, even here in Kassel. Some of our own members might be spies. If you are found out—"

"I am not afraid."

"The Brotherhood considers human life to be the highest value, and demands the highest moral standards of its members. Perhaps you might tell me how you came by....?" Eudoxus gestured to the scar along Descartes's jaw.

An uneasy expression crossed Descartes's face. "Perfectly justly, I assure you."

Well, Eudoxus thought, this would be a good place to stop. If this young man could write the *Compendium Musicae*, if he had even a fraction of the talent that Eratosthenes thought, then maybe it was better not to ask too many questions about just what he was running from.

There were more important matters to tend to now. Polybius had just passed the first test for membership: the attempt to dissuade him from joining had failed.

"I should ask," Eudoxus said, "whether you have any questions for me?"

A tender look came across Descartes's eyes. "The children?"

"They'll be looked after. We'll take care of them."

Descartes nodded. "I am ready, Eudoxus."

"All right then, Polybius. We begin tomorrow."

Whatever it was, it must have been bad.

Eudoxus couldn't help himself. Over the next few months he extracted bits of the young man's story from him, the prominent Catholic father, the antagonistic brother, both of whom despised him; the years at La Flèche. Other details took more work: his attendance at the Emperor's coronation, the brief stay in Maximilian's army. But the rest—just why he had deserted the army, fled from Ulm, just where he had been during his long journey to Prague—not a word. He surely was no longer the frivolous boy he described himself as having been. His mood was dark, dour. His oddly formal manner of speaking only emphasized that.

If he had been through Germany and Bohemia in the past year, Eudoxus also knew, then he had seen the results of war. Marauding soldiers killing and being killed, their bodies left for the crows. When they weren't killing each other they were killing all the peasants along the way and leaving *their* bodies for the crows. If whatever had happened to Polybius in Ulm hadn't made him more serious, then whatever he had seen since then had done the trick.

He was good with the children, though. He was gentle with them, easy, his mood would lighten, his eyes would soften. And he was good *for* them. The younger sister, who at three lacked any understanding of the situation, giggled when he played with them, taught them to count with dice, made funny sketches of people and animals. The four-year-old brother was tougher, crying often and asking after his mother. Only Eudoxus's sixteen-year-old daughter Kunigunda could consistently comfort him, by snuggling and singing lullabies. But even he might seem almost happy when Descartes would draw some of the bugs he said they would go dig up after the weather warmed.

"Fellow orphans, I suppose," Descartes explained after Eudoxus complimented his way with the children.

It was late February. Eudoxus was chatting with the initiate at the latter's early afternoon job, which consisted of digging a pit in a half-frozen field near the house. This was hard, unpleasant, and pointless labor given that his late afternoon job was filling the pit back in again.

Eudoxus sighed. "Perhaps you should let your father know you are alive, at least."

Descartes, digging, shook his head. "He might be happier believing that I am not."

"Is it not cruel to leave him in the dark?"

"By now he has told enough people that I died defending the faith that he himself believes it. It would be more cruel to remove this delusion."

But no matter how tired Descartes was from his day labor he always had energy for the night labor. A few conversations had shown Eudoxus that the initiate was unquestionably brilliant and had been exposed to many important things, without having mastered them. Eudoxus thus constructed a course of evening study to bring him up to speed, and they were now examining the work Eudoxus had done with the children's parents toward the construction of a new kind of compass. It also helped Descartes's evening energy that he had been recovering the weight lost during the past difficult year. The Brethren believed that a healthy diet should be free of flesh and full of roots, vegetables, and dairy, so that's what Kunigunda prepared.

"Would Herr Polybius care for some more tuber pudding?" the girl offered another ladle one noontime in late March, serving his breakfast. Descartes's insomnia since fleeing Ulm meant that he usually got only a few desperate hours of sleep, from dawn until late morning.

"*Nein, danke, fraülein,*" Descartes answered, a bowl of the thick pudding already inside him.

The girl bowed without speaking and left the room.

"She's upset about the children," Eudoxus explained his daughter's uncustomary lack of cheer.

The day before they had been shipped off to a safer house outside town. The children would stay there until an adoptive family could be found, probably to the south.

Descartes and Eudoxus sat in silence for a few moments.

"I have been teaching her geometry, you know," Eudoxus said.

"You did not tell me that you were at The Wedding," Descartes changed the subject. He was referring to the fabled nuptials of Frederick and Elisabeth back in 1613, seven years before the Winter King would flee Prague with his stockings down. "And?"

Descartes was asking after the famous fountains at the Heidelberg Castle, built with a system of mechanical statues that could move, and even be made to talk through hidden speaking tubes. Thus when you entered the garden you might glimpse the naked Diana bathing; but when you approached you would trigger her protective father Jupiter to rush at you with a thunderbolt. What he was asking was whether the doctrine of mechanism that he and Eudoxus had been discussing—the idea that living creatures were only complex machines without an immaterial soul—was supported by the fountains.

"It is uncanny," Eudoxus nodded. The statues were so lifelike yet were just machines of relatively primitive engineering. Imagine what nature could do in assembling the machines that were actual living bodies! "The Book describes it perfectly."

The Book was *The Chymical Wedding of Christian Rosenkreutz.* Appearing in 1616 it told of a couple who lived in an enchanted castle surrounded by gardens full of wonders. Replete with allegories and mystical symbols it allegedly contained secret information; read by those capable it showed the way for seekers of truth and wisdom, for those understanding the relation between religion and science, for those, in short, who were Brothers of the Rosy Cross. These Brethren were allegedly creating a great encyclopedia containing the collected wisdom of humankind. Their goal was to attain perfect knowledge of *everything,* for the benefit of humankind: to promote health and happiness; to cure disease and increase longevity; to replace dark medieval humanity with an improved species of mild and beneficent beings. To accomplish all this it was necessary to apply mathematics to nature and develop scientific instruments for measuring it. It was apparently also necessary to say some nasty things about the Pope and occasionally also Luther and Calvin. That was why joining the Brotherhood required you to be discreet, to use a secret name, and purchase the hoods and masks. If they were not quite "The Invisibles" they were sometimes said to be, they were at least "The Incognitos."

The men fell silent as Kunigunda returned to clear the dishes.

"Well, Polybius," Eudoxus said when she had left, "are you ready to get to work?"

"I will go get the shovel."

"No."

Descartes looked at him confused.

"Enough digging. We'll do some mathematics in the afternoons."

Polybius had passed the second test for membership: persevering through months of meaningless physical labor.

Just one more test to go.

Over the next month or so they made great progress.

They studied the new discoveries on polynomials by their Brother Eratosthenes in Ulm. They did a close reading of Kepler's recent *Harmonices Mundi*, emphasizing his analysis of the five Platonic solids. But most rewarding of all was the work done by Brothers Diophantus and Hypatia just prior to their deaths in Prague five months earlier. Descartes was amazed by their astronomical clock, by their mechanized globe that charted the motion of the heavenly bodies across the night sky. In fact after studying their prototypes, and with some engineering suggestions from Eudoxus, Descartes himself constructed the first of what would eventually be four new kinds of compasses.

"Eudoxus." Descartes's voice trembled as he emerged just before noon, carrying some papers.

"Again?" Eudoxus asked. The rings under Descartes's eyes revealed yet another sleepless night as his protégé collapsed into the sitting room chair.

"It does not matter. I have done it."

"What?"

"The trisection."

Eudoxus's eyes widened. "With the new compass?"

Descartes nodded.

The silence that lingered marked the significance of the event. Descartes had just solved a two-thousand-year-old problem.

"Polybius. You must publish."

"Not yet."

"You'll use the pseudonym."

"He will find me."

"That is incredibly unlikely."

"So was trisecting the angle."

Eratosthenes had written Eudoxus that agents for Joachim Descartes had come to his door in Ulm, aiming to bring to justice the worthless second son who had treasonably deserted the Catholic League army. If Joachim could track Descartes to Eratosthenes, he could track him further.

"All right," Eudoxus sighed. "Let's get you some breakfast. And then we'll talk."

What Eudoxus wanted to say did not concern geometry, or Descartes's father, or the inability of organized religions to recognize the priority of human reason. Rather it was about the plague that had decimated Kassel a decade before, that had taken the lives of sixty percent both of the town's residents and of Eudoxus's family, his darling wife, his older daughter, and his only son. The pain from that loss was indescribable.

"Why," Descartes asked quietly, "are you telling me this?"

"Polybius, our work is important. But we are human beings, and our work is about human beings. Ultimately, anyway."

His protégé looked at him searchingly.

"You have a great future ahead of you. You will solve problems in mathematics and you will advance our understanding of nature. You will improve the health and longevity of the human being. But," his voice softened, "to what end? What is the value of a healthy and long life, if that life is not itself something valuable?"

"You are sounding like a priest."

"No, René. We have our reason but we also have our heart. And in one beat of that human heart I would trade your trisected angle for just one more day with my wife and children. You may not understand this now, but you will in time."

"So why," Descartes asked again respectfully, "are you telling me this?"

"Because I am presuming to offer you advice."

"Specifically?"

"Theoretical, and practical. The theoretical is that you should consider, perhaps soon, taking a—wife. Mathematics may be a tempting mistress to one as talented as you, but a human life is not complete without—family."

"Is this about your daughter?" Descartes asked, again respectfully.

"Her happiness is more important to me than my own. And were you—and she to—well that would solve two problems at once. But at the moment my concern is with you. And—your father."

"Joachim?"

"You cannot run from him forever."

"But I can, Eudoxus. Nay, I think I must."

"As a father I can understand what he must be feeling, about your disappearance."

"Yes. It is called 'relief.'"

"But then he would not seek you so. With such diligence, and expense."

"That would be his rage, in addition to his relief."

"A father has a greater capacity to forgive than you realize, René."

"My 'father' is not like you."

There was a long silence.

"Tell me what you are running from, René," Eudoxus said gently, staring at his protégé's scar. "What happened in Ulm?"

"Everything."

"Everything?"

"I was—reborn. *Re-né.*"

"Yes, but how?"

"Why are you asking me again now? After all these months?"

"Why aren't you telling me now? After all these months?"

Descartes dropped his eyes to the uneaten turnip bread that Kunigunda had made especially for him. "Eudoxus. You said you had some practical advice as well."

Eudoxus sighed again. "All right, then, Polybius. The practical. You have a great future ahead of you, whether you take my theoretical advice or not. But there is much work ahead and important men you must meet." Here he was referring to Galileo in Italy, with whom there had recently been some correspondence. "For all this you shall need funds. Funds for research, to construct prototypes, to publish. Funds for travel. More funds than the Brotherhood has at its disposal. And to obtain these funds—"

"Joachim."

"One way or the other."

"But what about 'The Invisibles'? 'Who lives well hidden, lives well?' 'Advance masked'?"

"As a Brother, yes. But not as a son."

"Joachim would never release funds to me voluntarily."

Eudoxus made no answer.

"You are suggesting something involuntary? But what about the Brotherhood's—moral standards?"

"Your father's assets have been generated through the corrupt practices and false beliefs of his King and his Church. To liberate those assets toward the acquisition of true knowledge," Eudoxus suggested gingerly, "would be to purify them."

Now Descartes made no answer.

"And while you are contemplating that, Polybius, will you also give some thought to the other things I said? When you're taking a break from solving—" he pointed to the papers on the table—"other impossible problems?"

Descartes nodded. He reached out and took a bite of the turnip bread.

That Kunigunda *could* do some pretty immodest things with those modest little turnips.

Maybe it was the money. Or maybe it was the offer to cut open his belly, remove his stomach, and feed it back to him. Whatever it was, the Inquisition successfully converted a Brother into a mole and the awful had happened: the safe house with the children had been raided. If not for the mother's having ferreted the children away just in time to an even safer house, they would have been lost.

"Just a week," Eudoxus said. "We found a family down south. They'll be fine."

Kunigunda dried her tears. She knew enough not to ask for details. But she was deeply worried. Wherever they were going the journey would be dangerous. There were spies and marauders everywhere, not to mention the rumors that the evil Jesuits were kidnapping Protestant children and raising them Catholic.

"But why must you go too?" her voice trembled.

"I'll be fine too. Don't worry." What he didn't say was that the reason he was going was *because* the journey would be dangerous, and he had heard those same rumors.

What a long night it was in the empty house after Eudoxus's departure.

Besides accompanying the children to their adoptive family, Eudoxus had one other purpose for the journey. In his satchel was a letter apologizing for that business at Poitiers, and promising to explain his disappearance and subsequent three-year silence; but adding that he was soon to journey to France to do this in person. But meanwhile there was a matter of immediate urgency ... Thus began Descartes's first letter to Joachim since disappearing from Poitiers in the fall of 1617. The letter was dated May 21, 1621, and would be posted from Munich, the home of Maximilian, Duke of Bavaria, in whose army Descartes had been serving. This would lend the story Descartes told in this letter an air of plausibility. It needed this because, of course, almost nothing in it was true.

"No luck?" Kunigunda asked, concerned, when Descartes appeared at the kitchen table in the middle of night, several nights after Eudoxus's departure.

Descartes shook his head, the rings under his eyes even darker from the candle's shadows.

"I knew my father was wrong. Valerian tisanes are too weak. I'll prepare something tomorrow. I'll include some poppy in the infusion."

"Thank you." Descartes glanced at the papers on the table, could see by the flickering light that the seventeen-year-old had been practicing geometric constructions with his newest compass. "I will not disturb you then—"

"No, please. Wait. You must be hungry. There's earthnut stew in the cold room. Let me get you some. Please."

"All right. Thank you."

A few minutes later she had had him seated at the table. They sat in silence while he sipped his stew.

"Oh. The bread," Kunigunda suddenly said, rising.

"No, let me get it. It's that cabinet, am I right?"

"*Ja*," she gazed at him, taking her seat.

"I am sorry," Descartes grimaced a moment later, flushing. He was pointing to the top shelf which, alas, was out of his reach.

The lanky young woman sprang up. "My father is always ..."

Her complaint about her father's storing things on high

shelves trailed off because she stumbled as she got up and immediately found herself pressed against their house guest. Surely it was not intentional that her firm young breasts, under her linen nightdress, were pressed against him.

Their faces, Descartes was rapidly calculating, were only about three *pouce* apart.

Her lips were threatening an advance upon his.

"Excuse me—" he gasped again, just pulling his body from hers.

"Don't you—like me?"

He looked at her from a safer distance and dropped his eyes. There was the possibility she was about to cry and that was something he was not at all prepared to deal with.

"Of course I do," he stammered. "It is only that—"

"What?"

"We are pledged to celibacy."

"You can't," she said as the first drops came, "do better than that?"

"It's just—that I—" Descartes said, still inching away.

"What?"

"I love truth more than I love beauty."

"I don't believe you."

"You don't believe me?"

"You may love the truth but I don't believe you are telling it. There's something else."

"Kunigunda," he protested.

"Why does it weigh so heavily on you, René? Tell me. Let me share it with you."

She was looking at him gently. Lovingly.

As a mother might gaze upon her hurting child, he thought.

But then—what would he know about that?

"Kunigunda," he said awkwardly, incapably, backing away.

A few days later Eudoxus returned. There had been some trouble after all, he admitted as Kunigunda tended to him. He was scratched and bruised, suffering from a mild limp; but everything had turned out all right, he insisted. The children were fine, in their new home, and would be well looked after. Kunigunda knew better than to ask questions. Even about the unfamiliar bloodied knife she found when unpacking her father's things after he had gone to bed.

Two mornings later Eudoxus informed Descartes that he was waiving the normal full-year probation period and making his protégé a full-fledged Brother. The young man's remarkable prospects, it was clear, merited the exception. That and the fact that, though Eudoxus was disappointed for his daughter's sake, the young man had passed the third test. "To love truth more than beauty" might well become their new motto, Eudoxus thought; even if loving truth sometimes meant concealing it.

Descartes's letter addressed to Joachim's estate outside Nantes arrived ten weeks later. But Joachim was not there. Several unexpected beheadings had again stalled his advance on Paris, and his new interest in cognac production had led him back south, to Limoges. But by the time the letter arrived in Limoges Joachim had left to oversee the cognac supply to the Royal Generals leading His Majesty's siege of the Huguenot city of Montauban. When Joachim finally did receive the letter, though, he was in a good mood indeed, having made a handsome profit despite, or because of, the thousands of Royal troops dying of petechial fever all around him.

So he lives, Joachim thought to himself.

He began to read.

An apology for that "misunderstanding" about law school in Poitiers. Some story about being attacked in Ulm by another soldier and needing to flee. (Someone he'd cheated in gambling, Joachim presumed.) But now he was ready to become serious, to advance his studies. (More studies? Eleven years at La Flèche had produced nothing!)

And since in March he had reached his majority age of twenty-five he could now receive his inheritance from Grandmère Brochard, which was substantial: the house in La Haye, another house in Poitiers, several small farms near Châtellerault. Once liquidated these properties would support his endeavors over the coming years. But these properties, not liquidated, were all the way back in France. And he was currently cash-poor, lacking the funds to journey home to claim them. And so might his father advance some cash so that his son might return home, reunite with the family, and then liquidate the estate and so reimburse his father?

Joachim shook his head.

He would instruct Pierre, the *good* son, to advance the monies to the Munich address. And then to advance an agent to track the money and obtain the location of the other son. And have that agent also find out what had become of that houseboy the other son had absconded with. Charlet was driving him crazy with his anguished letters on the subject.

It wasn't until after the siege at Montauban ended— unsuccessfully, when the Royal Generals ran out of both cognac and living troops—that Joachim realized that that other son had not explained where he had been for the past year and a half.

Descartes's next letter was dated January 17, 1622, posted from Frankfurt. It requested a thousand pardons from Joachim for his inexcusable silence. When his father heard of his difficulties, he would surely understand. These were "terrible times" across Europe ... No, Descartes wrote, he could not make it home as intended. The money Joachim sent had never arrived. Some man had been seen rifling through the envelope, but in any case Descartes thanked his father for the permission implicit in the letter itself to sell the inherited properties. In fact he now planned to return home by summer; and he could do this because with his father's implicit permission he had managed to sell the La Haye property via proxy. But now there was a small matter delaying the liquidation of the other properties, so would his father please sign some documents so that Descartes might quickly take care of the business on his return?

Joachim stared angrily at the letter in his hands. So his lesser son had evaded the agent in Munich, claimed the money never arrived; very clever. Even more clever, he had sold the Brochards's house by proxy; he must have some local connections. But now disposing of the other properties required Joachim's cooperation, and he was not going to provide that until he had the lesser son seated before him.

When Joachim calmed down he instructed his good son to write back that he would be happy to help the lesser son obtain the remaining properties, once he returned home. And oh, would he *please* inform them what had become of the Rector's houseboy before Joachim had to use his influence to instigate an official investigation?

"You absolutely will not," Joachim said to Pierre when the older son informed his father of his intention to accompany the letter personally.

"But you don't trust the little runt, Father, do you?"

"I do not."

"So let me go. I am sure I can convince him to come back to France."

"That is just what I am afraid of." Joachim had bailed the older son out of enough scrapes—including those *totally* trumped up homicide charges—not to recognize that look in his eyes. "You will remain here."

As much as Pierre would have enjoyed going to Germany to confront his worthless brother he would have to pass. With much regret he sent his father's letter on its way to the specified Frankfurt address, this time with two agents to accompany it.

Joachim Descartes was savvy but the people he was dealing with were savvier. This was not surprising, given that they were code-named after brilliant ancient Greek mathematicians.

"It helps to be invisible," Eudoxus smiled a year later as their machinations proceeded exactly as planned. By some careful editing of Joachim's last letter, and with the aid of Brothers well-placed in legal and financial institutions, they had just concluded liquidating the properties bequeathed to Descartes.

Kunigunda frowned. The now nineteen-year-old had mostly recovered from her romantic disappointment nearly two years before, and now enjoyed an intimate relationship with her father's protégé. Or at least as intimate as you could have with a man who preferred truth to beauty and was inclined to keep secrets.

"What is it?" Descartes noticed her frown.

"Are you sure you are comfortable with this, René?"

"It *is* my inheritance. Even if acquiring it has involved some small deceits."

"And remember, my daughter," Eudoxus weighed in, "we are uncorrupting—"

"I know, I know, you're purifying the assets. But what about those two men? Was that justified too?"

"They weren't badly hurt," Eudoxus answered. "Only their dignity."

The three Brothers sent to retrieve Joachim's letter in Frankfurt had lured the two agents accompanying the letter to an abandoned building, then tossed them from a third story window into a mound of dung. Ever since the Bohemian defenestration such gestures had become the trademark of rebels everywhere.

And indeed the world had been busy in the five years since that 1618 defenestration. Tilly's Catholic Imperial Army had taken Protestant Heidelberg south of Kassel. The Catholic Spanish and the Protestant Dutch had resumed their own hostilities after their Twelve Year Truce. The French Catholic King Louis XIII had moved on from Montauban to besieging Huguenot Montpellier; and while both sieges failed to capture the cities, they succeeded in inflicting slow painful deaths upon the besieged. In the midst of all this suffering, what could the soft landing of Joachim's men in a pile of donkey manure really matter?

Oh, and things were simmering in Kassel as well. The Landgraf and the Inquisition had been assassinating each other's moles, taking breaks only to combine forces against their mutual enemy, the Brotherhood. There had been two raids in the past month alone. Things were getting dangerous at home.

Fortunately the twenty-seven-year-old now had enough money to live on for many years ahead, because by the early spring of 1623 it was time for him to go.

"Paris, my son," Eudoxus said with some regret.

The protégé grimaced. "You believe I am ready?"

"You now have the foundations. To grow from you here you need better mathematicians than I."

"I would rather stay."

"Your father and brother are in the south now. There is no danger of meeting them in Paris."

"I would just rather—stay."

"You must go, Polybius. You will have Brothers everywhere to help you, should you need it."

There was a moment of silence.

"If I must go," Descartes said, "then I shall go to Italy."

Descartes had told his mentor that when his life was transformed back in those woods in 1619—however that had happened—he had had several days of vivid, portentous dreams. These had convinced him to make a pilgrimage to the famous Our Lady of Loreto shrine, should it ever prove feasible. The legend was that that was the very house in which the Virgin Mother had birthed her Divine Infant, though how it had made its way from the

Holy Land to the little Adriatic village no one could explain.

"You know that's all nonsense," Eudoxus responded with some annoyance.

Descartes shrugged.

"Fine. If you must go to Italy then we should arrange for you to meet with Galileo too."

A pained expression crossed Descartes's face.

"What is it?" Eudoxus asked.

Descartes shook his head, recovering. "So when do I leave?"

A quiet farewell.

Eudoxus and Descartes spent most of the final night reviewing their best work in the twenty-seven months since Polybius had arrived. By the time the candle started flickering around 3:30 AM they were discussing military applications of their new compasses. Eudoxus retired soon after, leaving Descartes alone at the table admiring the beautiful notebook of bound vellum that Eudoxus had given him as a parting gift. The cover had been left blank, Eudoxus explained, for Descartes to fill in should he ever want to title his work. But on the inside cover Eudoxus had printed two mottos: at the top *To love truth more than beauty*, and at the bottom, *Who lives well hidden, lives well.*

"I made you this," Kunigunda suddenly said, appearing from the larder with a large dish. She was wearing that linen nightdress. "Your favorite."

She placed the rutabaga casserole on the table.

The young man and younger woman looked at each other in the soft dawn light filtering in through the window.

"Also this." She dropped onto the table some pages sewn into a booklet. "Your favorites."

"Recipes," he said, looking at it.

"In case you find someone to cook for you."

Maybe it was the soft light, maybe it was the exhaustion

of all the sleepless nights, but for a moment the young man was not so sure of the distinction between truth and beauty.

"Kunigunda," he said, gazing at her, long.

"Just come back," she said.

Nothing quite works as planned.

The newly hatched protégé made stops in Nuremberg and Munich to meet some Brothers who turned out not to be there. He detoured to Basel and Zurich to meet other Brothers, who also turned out not to be there; crossed the Alps thinking about meteorology instead of which way he was going and got frighteningly lost; in late March 1623 crossed the border into Italy; spent a day at the Our Lady of Loreto shrine, mostly wondering why anyone paid any attention to their dreams.

Then in mid-July of 1623 he set off to find Galileo.

But Galileo was not at his villa in Florence but in Rome, as the rumors had it that his friend and supporter Cardinal Barberini was about to be named the new pope. Galileo may have been there, but so were thousands of others when the white smoke rose from the chimney of the papal conclave inthe Piazza San Pietro. Nor did the great man return to Florence afterward, according to the ornery caretaker who informed Descartes that the master was more likely to return to Positano, an idyllic little village down the Amalfi coast where he kept a vacation home. Two weeks later Descartes had been told by a half-dozen Positanese, several rudely, that they'd never heard of the man and he surely possessed no property there.

Figuring that he might as well stay awhile—having nowhere else to go—Descartes rented a villa on the hillside overlooking the blue Tyrrhenian Sea. The beautiful sea visible from his desk would have distracted a lesser man, but not him: on waking around noon and settling down at his desk he might not look up again until supper time.

The weeks passed as he delved into sixteenth-century Italian algebra, reading about the great Tartaglia, his methods on cubic equations. His applied work on military architecture. His difficult life. At age thirteen Tartaglia—the nickname of Niccolò Fontana, meaning "The Stammerer"—had nearly been killed by French soldiers invading Venice. One cruel soldier had sliced the boy's jaw and palate with his saber, for sport, hence the stammering. In later life he never spoke of the event, grew a beard to hide his facial scars. On reading this, Descartes fingered the long scar along his own jawline. The same soldier had then raped the boy's mother and murdered her right in front of him.

Descartes thought of the horrible events in Prague.

He thought of his own absent mother.

Of absence in general.

Of being alone.

A year and a half later Descartes was back in Rome. When word came during February of 1625 that the aggressive French First Minister Richelieu had arrived in Turin for a siege on the town of Gavi, Descartes, curious about the siege machinery, thought he should go have a look. He arrived there in late April 1625, after the town's fall. He got a small glimpse of the siege machinery and a larger glimpse of the suffering and death that that machinery had inflicted.

A few days alone in the remains of Gavi and Descartes started to feel sick.

He sat in his room at the empty inn looking out the window. Some unpalatable cold rutabaga casserole was on the desk before him. He appreciated the innkeeper's willingness to try Kunigunda's recipe but could not bring himself to appreciate the result.

Maybe Eudoxus was right, after all. Mathematics suddenly felt alien to him, he thought, as he gazed out at the town that had been devastated by the applications of that mathematics.

Some palatable rutabaga casserole would be pleasant right now.

Time to go home.

On a warm evening at the end of July 1625 a solitary rider clattered up an otherwise quiet street in Kassel, Germany. Two saddlebags attached to his animal bulged with papers as he directed it to a small shuttered house at the end of the street. The man dismounted and tied the animal to the nearby pole, then brushed off the green taffeta suit he had put on for the last short leg of his long journey. Normally he didn't care much about his appearance, but he found himself wanting to look his best as he strode up to the front door of the darkened house.

"I came back," he whispered before the door.

He knocked, and waited.

He straightened the plume on his hat, then knocked again.

The door swung open.

Thin, pale, with deep lines on his face, the suddenly much older man stood before him.

He was wearing a tattered black mourning gown.

"I buried her two days ago," he whispered on seeing his protégé again.

They were at the familiar kitchen table, the candle casting strange shadows between them. It was just like old times except that it was nothing like old times.

They sat, silent.

"René," Eudoxus finally said. "I have taught you what I can. Now I am empty."

Descartes gazed at him.

"You *must* go to Paris."

"But what about you?"

"I will carry on. Here."

"But—Joachim. And Pierre."

216

"Still in the south. I had some Brothers confirm."

"I do not know anyone in Paris."

"There are men for you to meet. Desargues. Mersenne. Others."

Descartes hesitated. "I—knew Desargues. And Mersenne, briefly. At La Flèche."

"That is good, yes?"

"I am not likely to be well-received by them."

"Everything is different now. You are not the same person. You will have letters of introduction. And your work."

Eudoxus pointed at the notebook he had given Descartes, on the table.

"But—what about this?" Descartes picked up the notebook and opened to the inside cover: *Who lives well hidden, lives well.*

"My son, it is time," Eudoxus said, his voice breaking, "for the world's greatest mathematician to be known."

20
WEDNESDAY,
FEBRUARY 13, 1650
STOCKHOLM, SWEDEN

Baillet had not been much of—a student. Rector Charlet had tried, but eventually allowed him just to do what he did best: assist around the Rector's home and spend long hours in his room in melancholy reflection about the hand he had been dealt in life.

For that hand was much less than those of the *real* students at La Flèche. They lived in the dormitories while Baillet lived in a little room back of the Rector's kitchen. They had futures and prospects, while Baillet's future prospects were to continue spending long melancholy hours in his room. They also had pasts, with siblings, parents, people who could tell stories about their childhoods including such interesting information as when and where they had been born. Baillet only had Rector Charlet, who—kind and generous as he was—could only tell him that he had arrived one night when he was small,

218

that he didn't speak for the longest time, and that the Rector gladly accepted his Christian duty of caring for the boy and making an effort, however futile, to educate him.

But it *was* futile. It wasn't because the young Baillet wasn't bright. He simply couldn't see the point of someone like him learning Latin declensions, and mathematics, and how to be a gentleman. In fact he couldn't see the point of doing anything, really. Thinking such thoughts as these was what he was typically doing, during those student years, instead of listening to some instructor drone on about declensions and mathematics. And now once more he was in a lecture hall, toward the back, and once more someone was droning on, and once more he was not listening.

This time the subject was the arts, and some scholar was dissecting some painting of the dissection of some executed criminal. It was the second evening of the Gala, featuring lectures on the main themes to be celebrated that week. After the arts lecture was one on mathematics, and then one on religion. The Queen officially believed in tolerating all religions, meaning thereby Lutheranism, Calvinism, and Catholicism. To that end she had imported the German theologian Calixtus to share the podium with Sweden's own Bishop of Strängnäs, Matthiae, and together they were to present their doctrine that all Christians should unite around the only belief truly shared by all: that Jews must be relentlessly persecuted. Baillet intended to pay as little attention to that lecture as to the other two.

He had other things to think about.

What he had seen.

The image of that single open eye staring at him, its terror inspiring his own.

The word "dissection" from the podium again penetrated his reverie. Baillet glanced around the lecture hall. Everyone else appeared to be paying attention. But then again they were either extremely smart (the inaugural members of the Academy) or good at pretending to be smart (the diplomats), and were all blissfully ignorant of what he had seen some five hours before. A soldier from the Castle had arrived just as Wullens and Baillet started retching, who didn't bother to wait for them to stop before informing them, "Not one word of this will disturb this evening's events."

Baillet could hear Zolindius's deep voice saying those words.

"It's a robbery, that's all," the soldier indicated the body. Pierre's pockets were pulled inside-out. It didn't take an investigator to understand that no possessions would be found on the corpse.

"But—the butchery," Baillet began, ignoring Wullens' elbowing him.

"Not unusual in this part of town," the soldier answered. "Especially when you—" he looked down at the pile, "resist." He then turned to Baillet and added, somewhere between advice and a threat, "You might want to be careful yourself around here, Père."

Something the lecturer said caught Baillet's attention. For some reason he was comparing the Portuguese word *barroco* with the classical form of syllogism named *Baroco*. But Baillet didn't buy it. Not the lecturer's point but the Chancellor's soldier. A robbery? Why would a robber do that to a body? Most of the knife wounds, the—carving—must have occurred after Pierre was dead. Not to mention the coincidence of it all. Pierre, of all people?

Zolindius himself was the most obvious suspect. It was he who had taken Pierre from jail just hours earlier. And he was obviously a—dangerous man. But what could have been his motive? His insistence that Descartes's death was natural, that the investigation be discreet, aimed to avoid attention. But it would hardly help that cause to viciously murder Pierre, whatever role he might have had in the death of his brother, if any.

But then Baillet thought about—the vagabond. The one whom Schlüter had beaten away yesterday morning.

Who had then been in Baillet's own doorway last night, right before Baillet discovered Pierre in his rooms. Who had shown up again near the jail where Pierre had been held, near where the body had been found. Baillet couldn't begin to speculate about motives here either. But the coincidence again. It seemed impossible that this was just—chance.

Baillet sighed. He should probably talk to Bramer again. He looked around the lecture hall. Bramer should be here, somewhere. Probably the sort to sit toward the front. He would have to look for him at one of the breaks, then.

A few minutes later the first lecture came to an end. Baillet became aware of its ending by the applause that interrupted his thoughts, which by that point had moved from reflections on Descartes's brother to reflections on Descartes, then to man's nastiness toward man, then to human suffering, then to the question of who his own parents might have been and what had happened to them and what his life might have been like had they lived. He was about to go in search of Bramer when a soft-spoken scholarly type appeared at the podium to make an announcement. Baillet could barely hear because some of the distinguished audience members near him were getting worked up about some juicy gossip.

"I for one approve," one pronounced. "Her *organs* are truly marvelous."

"You must be talking about Ebba Sparre?" another enthusiastically joined in.

"Yes, but Her Majesty calls her *Belle*."

"Her or them?" one snickered.

"I heard that she and the Queen sleep together."

"I heard they bathe together."

"Naked!" someone else exclaimed.

"Shh!" Baillet hushed them, ignoring their annoyed looks.

"...we will therefore skip the planned break," the scholar was saying at the podium, "and go directly to the next lecture." Baillet groaned to himself. The mathematics lecture. Originally to be presented by Descartes, now to be given by some other luminary. "And so I am pleased to present to you member-elect of the Swedish Royal Academy, Professor Gilles Personne de Roberval!"

There was modest applause as a tall, thin man with a large round head stood up in the front and ascended the stage. He began with some kind words about Descartes. Baillet found his attention divided, between gazing at how, well, *enormous* the man's head was and listening to the gossip going on around him. The gentlemen had moved on from the Queen's lesbian paramour to Roberval and Descartes. The debate was now about whether Roberval was a hypocrite or a gentleman in saying nice things about a man everyone knew he despised.

"Shh!" Baillet hushed them. He was tempted to remark that hypocrite and gentleman were hardly exclusive categories. And he'd have to ask Bramer about this business between Roberval and Descartes.

He turned his attention back to the stage. Roberval had begun his lecture. Something about new results in his geometric research that had important practical applications. Something about compasses with military applications, that had been indispensable in the recent wars, the end of which this very Gala was celebrating. Wasn't this what Bramer had talked about on the ship, what Bramer had worked on too? Yes, it did sound familiar, but not merely, Baillet realized, because of what the man was saying but because of his voice, a voice as high-pitched and thin as the man was tall and thin himself.

He knew that voice from somewhere.

He leaned forward, to get a closer look at the man.

And then it hit him.

Last night in his rooms Baillet had stumbled upon Pierre arguing with a second man. A man Pierre claimed had ransacked the place before Pierre got there. Who had raced out of the flat before Baillet could get a look at him.

Who might have stolen Descartes's notebook.

Who might later have been responsible for Pierre's murder.

It was his voice.

21

Roberval was done before Baillet knew it. Baillet hardly heard anything he said, could hardly think, as Roberval was packing up his papers, slipping away. A plan, Baillet thought urgently, he needed a plan. Well, at least pursuit. He got up from his seat at the rear, slid through the row, went for his greatcoat and went after the mathematician.

The man was fast.

It wasn't fair, really, Baillet thought, racing after the man's long cloak into the evening. The man's long legs gave him an advantage. Plus the man could use his lantern to light his way while to remain discreet Baillet carried his own lantern unlit, following the light bobbing in the darkness up ahead.

Where the hell was Roberval going? he thought as the man disappeared into the streets behind the Castle. Baillet picked up his pace, pounding loudly in the snow. Up ahead Roberval stopped, hearing the sound, and turned around. Baillet, his heart throbbing, slipped into a doorway until Roberval again took off. Baillet popped out, continued his pursuit, gave up all hope of discretion. He needed to stay close lest he also give up all hope of finding his way out of this warren. Once more Roberval stopped ahead, peered back into the darkness, then turned and broke into a gallop. Baillet—running now, trying not to slip, or trip, or bump, or fall—followed him around a corner, down another street, then saw him disappear into a doorway.

When the wars were beginning to wind down, around 1645, and it was clear that Sweden would be the major victor, Chancellor Zolindius began whispering into the Queen's ear the idea of a gala to celebrate "The Birth of Peace." Over the next year he also began whispering the idea of the Swedish Royal Academy. Shortly after that, he whispered the name *Descartes* into the Queen's ear. Contrary to the rumors, though, the Chancellor did not decide *everything* in Sweden: whispering into Her Majesty's other ear was her companion Ebba Sparre, who, as *doué* as she was *belle*, had a brain almost as marvelous as her "organs." It was she who whispered that if you wanted scholars to stay in a land where it snowed 275 days a year, you would need a comfortable place where they could relax, talk, and most of all consume plenty of *brännvin* and *glögg*. Done whispering this into the Queen's ear, Ebba Sparre resumed tonguing it. Neither paid any attention as the Chancellor uncomfortably removed himself from the room.

Less than a week later renovations were underway on the old *Råttahål*. Tucked into an obscure alley, this broken building had a century earlier housed prisoners during the brief interval between their being accused as heretics or witches and their being fed, alive, to the famous Swedish rats. It was here, now, in this pleasant spot, that many scholars would assemble after the lectures to continue their debates, or just get drunk. Soft candles, dark wood paneling, snug booths, the fire in the hearth, the nearly limitless supply of *brännvin* and *glögg*—and all absurdly inexpensive thanks to the subsidies from the limitless

Royal Treasury.

Outside the snow was falling but inside, warm and cozy in a booth at the rear, Baillet was silently congratulating himself. He had pushed himself through the snow, to the door, made himself enter, made himself do it. And now here he was, in this booth at the rear, an investigator. A small candle on the table cast shadows on the face of the famous scholar seated across from him. Baillet was nervously sipping his *brännvin* while the large-headed member-elect even more nervously was ignoring his *glögg*.

"I appreciate, Professor," Baillet was saying, "your willingness to speak with me."

Roberval looked pale in the candlelight. He looked up briefly, offered a shrug, then looked back down.

"All right, then," Baillet began, hesitantly, "perhaps I might start by asking whether it was indeed—you whom I found in my rooms last night?"

Roberval looked up, then nodded.

"May I ask what—"

"Descartes was a fraud," Roberval spluttered in a thin whispery voice. "I have been trying to prove that for years and was finally close. He cheated me by dying first."

"I'm sorry?"

"Let's not waste each other's time, Père. Everyone's mathematical genius. Except that his greatest work was not actually his. It was mine."

"Please, explain, Professor."

"In the 1620s he showed up in Paris, yes?"

"I'm aware, in broad outlines, of his biography," Baillet answered, having heard about Descartes's early years from Rector Charlet and having been filled in about his later years by the Ambassador.

"I'll stay to the point, Père. The man showed up in Paris around 1626 or so. Right at the time of the Rosicrucian scare, yes? No one knew where he came from, who he was. A mystery man, out of the blue, but allegedly the world's greatest genius. What was his training? Where did a man like that come from?"

"You may be aware of his schooling at my own institution, La Flèche," Baillet said with an unexpected sense of indignation.

"Please, Père," Roberval waved his hand so forcefully that the candle flickered. "You're talking about a school for training boys to be gentlemen rather than for preparing world-class mathematicians. And in any case, I did my own investigations."

Baillet was about to object, except that Roberval was quite correct. "Yes?"

"Your man was a mediocre student at La Flèche. Lazy, good-for-nothing, useless, from what I heard. A true gentleman, yes?"

Baillet nodded. The man had a point.

"And then he disappeared for half a decade, Père, then makes his debut in Paris. You don't find that a little strange?"

"Perhaps he—matured. He served as a soldier, I believe, at the start of the wars. He no doubt saw terrible things. Perhaps that experience could convert even a gentleman into—"

"A man?"

Baillet shrugged.

Roberval gazed at him, his eyes marbles in that round head. "Listen, Père, I do not deny that your man had talent. But there is a great gap between talent and genius." He grimaced as he said this. "I believe that something happened in the wars but I do not believe it could account for *that*."

"Please, Professor?"

"There was a boy," Roberval said softly. "His servant. Descartes left La Flèche with him, joined the army, brought him to the south of Germany in late 1619—and the boy was never heard from again. When Descartes arrived in Paris he had a long scar on his jaw. You do the math."

"Are you suggesting ...?" Baillet asked, not being one for math.

"Look, *something* happened around 1619, Père. And yes, I think he—murdered that boy. To say it bluntly. And perhaps that experience 'matured' him, as you put it. Perhaps."

"And you think, somehow—" Baillet pieced it together, "the boy helped him. With mathematics. At La Flèche."

"So go the rumors, Père."

"But—why would he murder the boy? If the boy did his work?"

"How should I know? Perhaps the boy was a threat to him. A liability. Maybe the boy threatened to expose him, yes? As a fraud. As I told you."

Baillet's mind was racing, remembering that Pierre had said something about Descartes's being a fraud as well. "But wait. Professor. If he—eliminated the boy, as you say. And the boy was responsible for his mathematics. You yourself just said that even—murder couldn't transform him into a genius ..."

"Exactly, Père." Roberval's marble eyes were glassy, feverish. "Descartes showed up in Paris just as I was developing some very important results. In geometry."

"Compasses," Baillet offered, having snatched a word or two from Roberval's lecture earlier.

"Far more fundamental. The work on compasses was based on my earlier work. Work that never got published." He hesitated. "Under my name, anyway."

"What does that mean?"

"I had my results in a notebook, Père. All my work from 1625 and 1626. Shortly after Descartes's arrival in Paris that notebook went missing. A short while later word reached me that Descartes was discussing some of my equations."

"Descartes stole your notebook," Baillet said, instinctively reaching into his cassock pocket to feel his own investigator notebook.

"I did not have absolute proof, unfortunately. Not until about ten years later."

"What happened then?"

"Père, surely the year 1637 means something to you, yes?"

"Of course." The year 1637 meant nothing to Baillet.

"Your man published his *Discourse on Method*. The one everyone raves about. The one that cemented his reputation as a genius. Along with his essay on geometry."

"You mean your essay."

"Exactly."

"But why the ten-year delay? On his part?"

"He added some things. Reformulated the work to fit his so-called method a little more clearly."

"But ten years! Why didn't *you* publish in the meanwhile?"

Roberval dropped his gaze to the candle again. "I—I couldn't re-create the work. I spent several years trying. But nothing."

Baillet grimaced sympathetically.

"And further," Roberval continued, "I was busy trying to get a job. Your man wasn't content to steal my work. He also sabotaged my prospects. In the early 1630s I was about to be offered the Ramus Chair ..." The expression on Roberval's face indicated that while the event was two decades past, the pain of it was not. "My sources tell me that damaging letters were received at the last minute. The Chair went to someone else."

"But you—landed on your feet, so to speak."

"Saint-Gervais is adequately prestigious, yes. But it took a long time to get here. And along the way I had my life's most important work stolen from me. By your man."

There was a long silence as the candle flickered out. After another moment Roberval called for the wench to refill Baillet's *brännvin* and bring a new candle.

"Père," Roberval now said. "You'll be wanting to ask me, next, what I was doing in your room, yes?"

"Of course," Baillet returned from his distraction. "But I think I can guess."

"Yes?"

"Looking for your notebook."

Roberval nodded. "It had been decades since I was this close to Descartes. When I was elected to the Academy I knew this would be my only chance to confront him. But he refused to see me. His man threatened me with a plank. Next thing I hear he is deathly ill. And then he's dead and some priest has collected his papers."

"How did you know—about me?"

"Everyone knows. So, Père, I must ask: do you have the notebook?"

"I was going to ask you the same thing."

"Please, Père, this is no time for joking."

"I assure you I am not. What did it look like?"

"I don't know. A sheath of papers. Loosely bound. A lot of mathematics in it. I haven't seen it in twenty-five years."

"But couldn't that—equally well describe Descartes's own notebooks, Professor?"

"I must see that notebook," Roberval insisted urgently, angrily.

"Professor, I am of the belief that you yourself have it."

"What?"

"You were in my rooms, you disappeared, as did the notebook. The conclusion is clear."

"You had it? Agh. You fool! I was not the only person in your rooms!"

"I am quite aware of that, Professor. But the man you were with did not have it." Baillet said this forcefully even though he had no idea whether Pierre had taken it.

"You fool. I was not with that man. He barged in on me when I was searching your rooms."

"But—that confirms he didn't have the notebook then!"

"Exactly."

"So you must!"

Roberval shook his head, then softened. "Père, if you are to be an investigator then you need to think more methodically, yes?"

Baillet suddenly understood. "You mean—"

"Exactly. Someone else was there before me. Your rooms were a mess when I arrived."

Baillet was too stunned to speak.

"Père, the man who barged in on me. Who was he?"

"'Was' is right," Baillet whispered, aware that a good investigator would not divulge what he was about to. "It was Descartes's brother. And he was murdered this afternoon."

You rarely get to see a face so large dramatically lose every hint of its color.

"Excuse me," the mathematician said suddenly. "I'm going to the toilet."

Baillet remained at the table, slowly calming down. When fifteen minutes had passed and Roberval had not returned, Baillet got up and went to look for him. He quickly discovered two things. First, the *Råttahål* had no toilet. Second, at the hooks near the front entrance, Roberval's cloak was gone.

22

Baillet's mind was on fire. The notebook. Another person in his rooms. Yet another—suspect. Or rather two. Roberval clearly despised Descartes as much as Pierre did. As much as the local scholars did. And of course there was the *predikant*, Voetius, not yet spoken to. "*He* is here": all of them, recent arrivals in Stockholm. And Schlüter, mustn't forget him either, who might have had his own motives. And then the vagabond, who spoke perfect French, had said Descartes's name. But wait—why had Roberval run out on him like that?

It was all Baillet could do to stay focused pushing through the swirling snow. Keeping the illuminated Castle in front of him he guided himself north, then circled around the wall to Slottskajen. The streetlamps were lit here, despite the wind, thanks to the innovative glass casings; much better than his inadequate lantern. From here he could find the Norrbro, cross the Riddarfjärden.

He was so preoccupied—with his investigation and his growing navigational confidence—that he could not be aware that about fifty paces behind him was another man, bundled into another greatcoat, also concentrating on his task. This task was easier than Baillet's, though; it didn't involve figuring out where to go, only waiting for the man in front of him to do so.

As the storm picked up Baillet arrived at his flat, glad to see no vagabond awaiting him. The Riddarholm bells were chiming eleven in the distance as he made his way inside without incident. How delicious it was to undress, slip under the goose down quilt, how utterly exhausted he was. He had been up since four this morning, on the move, battling the snow, battling suspects, battling—murderers. Sixty seconds under the quilt and he was getting drowsy, trying not to think about that bloody pile of body parts, the missing eyeball, or worse, the remaining one, not to think about whoever did that, could do that, carrying a knife, a hatchet, slicing, carving ...

He heard a noise out front.

He shot awake.

There was a distinct creak, he could hear it despite the wind. The creak on the steps leading up to his flat. Leading to his door.

The door that was now jiggling quietly.

Baillet's heart was pounding as he shot back down in the bed. Pulled the covers over his head. That lump in his throat was either his heart or an enormous sob of fear waiting to burst out.

Walking, creaking, softly, quietly.

Someone was inside his flat.

Then silence.

It made no sense. Ten, fifteen minutes, maybe more. Silence. Had he—made it up? Had he fallen asleep, dreamed it? He lay under the covers trying to decide what to do. The need to weep had passed, at least for the moment, thankfully.

Would someone break into his flat and then—just sit there, in the sitting room?

Maybe the person didn't realize Baillet was home, in his

bedroom, under the covers, cowering. Maybe the person was waiting for Baillet to come home, to murder him. Maybe the person was about to come to the bedroom door, try the knob. Find the cowerer under the covers and do to him what he had done to Pierre Descartes. Baillet imagined a blade slipping around behind his eyeball and cutting it loose. Where the hell was that huge landlady of his when he needed her?

All right.

Calm down, he told himself.

The element of surprise. That was his only advantage. His size, inexperience, cowardice, and inclination to weep were definitely disadvantages. He had survived that unbearable sea journey. He had survived whatever it was that had taken the lives of his parents. He had survived already two encounters with the terrifying Chancellor. Perhaps he would survive this too.

His heart bouncing between his throat and his chest he quietly slipped out from the quilt. Willing the floorboards not to creak he stepped first to the dresser where, in the dark, he felt around for his tinder and flint, a candle. Then he gingerly stepped over to his bedroom door.

He listened, waited, listened.

Silence.

He put his hand on the doorknob.

Listened, waited.

Then he began to turn.

"Murder!" he squeaked, plunging into the room and simultaneously lighting a candle, managing not to trip over himself as he did so.

In the flickering shadows was a small boy standing inside his front door, drenched from head to foot from the snow that had melted on him while he waited. He seemed not at all disturbed by Baillet's cry of murder, perhaps because Baillet had not actually succeeded in emitting any sound.

"Who the devil are you?!" Baillet exclaimed.

"I have a message for you, sir." He withdrew a slip of paper from his pocket and offered it to Baillet.

"But who—"

Too late. The boy had already slipped out the door and Baillet could hear his little steps going down the stairs. A moment later he heard the front door to the building slam.

Calm down, Baillet told himself.

He looked at the slip of paper in his hand. He sat down in the comfortable chair in the sitting room, beside the table on which he now rested his candle. He took a breath and in the dim light he unfolded the damp note.

You are in great danger, it began in a scraggly scrawl.

Urgent. Important information. Be here five bells sharp.

Then below that, *Tell no one!*

Then the signature: *Freinsheimus.*

Then: *P.S. Destroy this note immediately!*

Really, Baillet thought in the stillness of the room. People just barging in there; he would have to speak to the landlady about a more secure lock. And five bells again! He glanced at the pendulum clock on the shelf, groaned. Despite the late hour he sat there a good long while, finally leaning over and touching the edge of the Librarian's note to the dying flame of the candle.

23
THURSDAY,
FEBRUARY 14, 1650

*D*ark. Frozen. Snow. How *predictable*, Baillet muttered, trudging through the drifts. He was just thinking he was lost when something pulled at his ankle.

He looked down.

A hand had shot out from a hole in the ground, half buried by snow, a tunnel. A ragged half-gloved hand was grabbing his ankle, his leg, pulling him. He tried resisting, pulling back, but it was useless. A scream formed in his throat as the second hand shot from the tunnel, grabbed his other leg. They were pulling him, dragging him, down, into the tunnel. He was slipping, falling, into the darkness, the coffin, outside, above, he heard something, voices, a woman's voice, screaming, muffled, screaming, he tried clawing back up but he was falling ...

The sharp clangs penetrated the darkness again. Baillet awoke, opened his eyes, to the blackness. Stockholm, his rooms, his bedroom, right. Four AM. He dragged himself out from the quilt, freezing, into his cassock. Lighting a candle he found some stale bread in the cooking area near the sitting room. He forced some down, bundled into his greatcoat, headed down the stairs. Outside a sliver of moonlight poked through the cloudy skies. Adjusting his fur hat he stepped onto something hard and heard a squeal. Recoiling, his eyes adjusting, he could just make it out.

The hard thing was a frozen pigeon carcass.

The squealing thing was the rat that had been gnawing on it.

Baillet inched away and began the now familiar journey toward the Castle.

Riddarholm was just ringing five as Baillet knocked on the door.

Nothing happened.

He knocked again, waited.

Nothing.

Then he knocked as hard and loud as he could. The door swung open.

"Shh!" Librarian Freinsheimus said, his white eyebrows shaking. "For the love of God! Now come inside before anyone sees you!"

Baillet, too cold to complain about being kept waiting, pushed inside. "So you have some information for me, Herr Freinsheimus?" he asked impatiently, following the old man with small steps to match the slow pace.

"Patience, Jesuit." Freinsheimus shuffled into the large central room, then turned and waved his arms. "Welcome to my library!"

"*Ja, ja,* magnificent. The information, Herr Freinsheimus?"

Freinsheimus scowled. "Fine. Come this way."

"You can't just tell me here?"

"Are you mad, Jesuit? It's far too sensitive."

"But there's no one here!"

Freinsheimus glared at him then strode off. Baillet

trodded behind the old man down the dark narrow hall, retracing their steps from last time. A few moments later they were back in their respective seats in the Queen's unheated Study.

"And?" Baillet finally exclaimed.

"Your man—" Freinsheimus glanced around the room, then whispered, "*He was one.*"

"One what?"

"A member. Of the Brethren."

"The Rosicrucians again?"

"Of course, Jesuit! Who else?"

"But," Baillet sputtered, "I—I said that to *you*. Yesterday."

"You may have mentioned something," Freinsheimus huffed. "But I confirmed it. Yesterday afternoon. After we spoke."

"Get to the point, then, please! What is your information?"

"That your man was a Rosicrucian isn't enough?"

"Your confirmation!"

Freinsheimus huffed again. "Don't you see, Jesuit? It fits. If your man was a Brother, then the Brethren would send someone to eliminate him. Under cover of the Gala, when foreigners were arriving in town anyway. Someone he trusts, you understand. Who would have access to him. It fits beautifully!"

"But why—eliminate him?"

"Must I do all your thinking for you, Jesuit? They must eliminate him because he is about to betray them. He is attempting to—" he dropped again to a whisper, "convert the Queen to Catholicism!"

"But that's common knowledge already. And—this doesn't make sense. The Rosicrucians were—are Protestants, are they not? Why would Descartes bother belonging to them, yet seek to convert the Queen to Catholicism?"

"They were Protestant, all right, when it was

convenient for them."

"So what—are they secretly Catholics, now?"

"Very possibly."

"But then—wouldn't they *seek* the Queen's conversion? Why would they eliminate their man?"

"Clearly he changed his mind. About their plan."

"So now he's *against* converting the Queen?"

Freinsheimus scowled at him. "I can't be expected to have all the answers."

"Right," Baillet stood up, having had pretty much enough.

"Wait!"

"What is it, old man?"

"How can you be sure," Freinsheimus said mysteriously, "it wasn't me?"

Baillet stared at him, and softened. "Indeed I cannot, sir. You are my primary suspect, of course. With your fierce intelligence, your vast knowledge of the Brethren. Not to mention your privileged access both to the Queen and Descartes."

"Exactly," Freinsheimus nodded with satisfaction.

"I have my work cut out for me, sir, do I not?"

"Yes, you do, Jesuit."

"It is an honor to have such an adversary, sir."

"At your service," the old man bowed slightly.

Baillet was at the door of the room. "I can show myself out, sir. But you can be as sure as the winter is long, I will be back."

As he glanced back he noticed that the old man was still sitting at the desk, lost in thought with a soft smile on his weathered face.

24

*B*aillet was being followed.

He could sense it.

He had scurried out the gate from the Library and unthinkingly turned right instead of left. There were footsteps behind him, he could hear them through the wind, he was sure of it. How hard it was to walk through this snow, in the dark! He was in such a rush to escape that he turned the corner onto Skeppsbron without noticing that this corner shouldn't have been here. It was only minutes later that he realized he didn't recognize this particular dark frozen portion of Stockholm. The wall of the Castle was to his right as he strode. There was water to his left with some dark land mass on the opposite bank. But it wasn't the—Riddarfjärden. There were no bridges. No Helgeandsholmen. Five minutes from the Library and he had no idea where he was.

He paused to get his bearings.

There were footsteps in the snow behind him.

Bearings later, he thought.

After many pounding heartbeats he came to the end of the Castle wall. Baillet turned right down the small alley alongside the Castle's rear wall. The first glimmer of dawn was slowly brightening the gray clouds, some minutes later, when things began to look familiar. The main gate on the rear wall. A sleepy soldier stood guard. Across from there was the boulevard—the physician's home, Wullens. If Baillet just followed this alley, along the wall, he could return to more comfortable ground. Slowing down, catching his breath, his panic subsided. Now he just had to find the Ecumenical Breakfast scheduled later this morning. Somewhere on Helgeandsholmen. Calming, he paused on the street, his thoughts lingering on the queer old Librarian.

Then for some reason he turned around.

At the end of the alley down which he had just come was the snow-covered vagabond, lumbering Baillet's way.

Carrying an axe.

Baillet started to run, through the snow. He stumbled along the Castle wall. Hugging it tightly he raced back to Slottskajen and the Castle's main front gate. People were out and about now, soldiers, carpenters, fishmongers. But Baillet found no comfort in the crowd, in the pealing Riddarholm bells indicating the day was underway. He kept going, dragging himself, across the Norrbro, breathing hard, puffs of foggy breath. On the way over he noticed four spikes on the side of the bridge. The ones normally sporting the heads of Zolindius's victims, now empty for the Gala. He then noticed the stairs descending from the side of the bridge to Helgeandsholmen below. Something was going on in the arena, even at this hour, he could hear throngs of people roaring. Easier to disappear, to escape, he thought. Without looking behind him he dashed down the stairs.

On the ground below he followed the flow of people toward the arena. Mostly locals, from the unfinished looks of them. Starting to feel calmer again he stopped two or three people to ask what was going on but was unable to make himself understood. He was just looking for the building for the Ecumenical Breakfast when he saw some dignitaries from the Opening Banquet.

"*Bonjour, Messieurs*," Baillet approached them. "Are you gentlemen here for the Ecumenical Breakfast?"

The man with the delicate spectacles guffawed while the monocle'd man snorted. "Ah, that's good," they both sighed.

Baillet was less amused. "Well, perhaps you might know where it is being held?"

"It is your lucky day, Père," the monocle chortled, and pointed to the gargoyled building toward the end of the field. "The Museum of Curiosities. I believe the program says your breakfast is behind it. There is an annex in the rear."

"Ourselves, we are just *dying* to see the shrunken heads," the spectacles said.

"Forget your breakfast, Père!" the monocle winked cheerfully at him. "Come with us to the arena. It's gladiator day!"

"Gladiator day?" Baillet asked.

"That magnificent Chancellor is clearing the prisons today," the spectacles explained. "They'll draw some lots or something. One out of five prisoners will be let free."

"And the others?"

"Bare-handed fight to the death!" the monocle said.

"It should be spectacular!" the spectacles said. "Coming?"

But Baillet had already bowed and pulled away. The Museum of Curiosities. He had to admit he was curious about it, shrunken heads notwithstanding. The snow was picking up again as he walked down the field, his thoughts swirling like the flurries. He was probably late for the breakfast, but no matter. Some food, some warmth, maybe a little—peace. The unity of religion, a lovely idea. Would be nice if some of these—fanatics might buy it. And of course that Voetius fellow should be there. The Calvinist *predikant* who could easily be his primary suspect if there weren't so many other strong candidates.

For a moment he stood beneath the massive gargoyles at the entrance to the Museum of Curiosities. Then he went around the side, in search of the annex. As he did so he glanced up, above, to the Norrbro crossing over the island.

The vagabond was at the center of the bridge, gazing down at him.

Chewing on something.

25

Baillet was sitting at the back of the lecture hall. This being "Mathematics and Natural Philosophy Day," the morning symposium was dedicated to Cartesian geometry and its applications. The discussion was way over Baillet's head. Even the diagrams on stage, vaguely recognizable as triangles, squares, were such advanced versions of these shapes as to be almost *un*recognizable. At one point it was said they were multi-dimensional, whatever that meant; *his* triangles were satisfied with two dimensions.

But it was just as well. He had plenty of other things to think about.

The vagabond. He had disappeared from the bridge by the time Baillet left the Ecumenical Breakfast, or the remnants thereof anyway. But the chewing. What was that? Like the rat on the pigeon. It was odd, Baillet thought again, that there weren't more around. Rats *and* vagabonds. Stockholm's ability to clear them all away, except for this one. Who seemed to be everywhere.

Or everywhere Baillet was.

Baillet shuddered, forced himself to think about something else. Roberval. The nervous mathematician who left him at the *Råttahål* last night had shown up for today's symposium. He was seated at the end of the long table on stage, pale and unsteady. Descartes was a cheat, a fraud, a murderer even; a stolen notebook. *The* stolen notebook. The man had bolted the moment he'd heard about Pierre's murder. Roberval also had the motive to murder Descartes. He, like almost everyone, could be the recently arrived "*He* is here." But—did he have the means, the access, to do the deed?

Unlike the *predikant* Voetius. It was a shame that the man had not shown up for the breakfast, Baillet thought, really needing now to speak with him. The idea of the breakfast had been splendid: per the Gala's theme, Her Majesty wanted to bring leading members of the different faiths together over a hearty Swedish breakfast. When word spread that Her Majesty would be delayed—some snit with Ebba Sparre—the pleasantries had devolved into debate about just which *really* was the single true faith. By the time it became clear that Her Majesty wasn't to show at all, the fisticuffs had begun. The young man cleaning up the mess had been kind enough to suggest that Baillet might find Voetius at the physician's house.

Because—it turned out—Voetius and Wullens had known each other years.

Their wives were sisters.

Together, then, Baillet realized, Voetius and Wullens had motive and means. Père Viogué had filled Baillet in about the mutual accusations between Voetius and Descartes back in the Provinces, the lawsuits. But then Descartes had become First Philosopher of Sweden while Voetius was demoted, humiliated, broken. If anyone had a motive to murder Descartes it would be Voetius. And of course the former *predikant* would object to the Catholic influence Descartes might have had on the Queen. He was also apparently spreading incredible slanders about Descartes having fathered children with a—Baillet couldn't even allow himself to think the word. And Voetius had arrived in Stockholm just before the philosopher fell ill ...

And had he avoided the breakfast—to avoid Baillet?

Someone was tapping him urgently on the shoulder.

"Bramer!" Baillet whispered with relief, turning.

Bramer tilted his head, proposing they leave.

"What's so important?" Baillet asked out in the foyer.

"Not here. Let's get our coats."

They headed out the Castle's main entrance, turned right, then turned the corner onto Skeppsbron.

"Where are we going?" Baillet asked as they walked. Remarkably, it wasn't snowing. Even more remarkably, the sun was shining. Though still freezing, the sharp clear air was almost pleasant.

"You've heard of the Vasa, of course?"

"Of course," Baillet lied, wishing he had paid more attention at school.

They had turned off Skeppsbron and followed a cleared path down to the bank of the frozen river. There was a small rounded building there, with many large windows overlooking the water.

"They built this to honor those who perished," Bramer explained as they entered. "But none of the locals come here, since they all want to forget it happened. And everyone else is busy with the Gala. So it's perfect for a private conversation." He pointed out the window down the bank to the left, where the corner of the Castle complex came nearly to the river. "That's where the ship left from." He then shifted his finger very slightly to the right. "That's where it went down."

Baillet remembered the story now. The most advanced warship of its time, the Vasa was built back in the 20s by the Queen's father. Years in the building, at enormous labor and expense, its maiden voyage was marked with national celebrations. Thousands came, noble and peasant alike, for a glimpse of the marvel. The more privileged fought for the privilege to be on board. On the day itself the weather was gorgeous, the mood wonderful, the fanfare tremendous. Thousands lined the banks weeping with joy and pride as bands played patriotic music and the ship pulled out. They were still weeping roughly seventy seconds later when the ship sank before their eyes. The whole episode was one great national shame. No wonder no one ever came to visit here.

"Speaking of military mathematics," Baillet interrupted Bramer, who was, in describing the Vasa's construction, "why weren't you up there participating in today's symposium?"

"I declined."

"You were asked?"

"I was."

"Why?"

"Because I'm the world's leading expert on the military applications of Cartesian geometry."

"No, why did you decline?" Baillet asked, though he felt some surprise at Bramer's answer. Hadn't Bramer downplayed his familiarity with Descartes's work on the ship?

"I wanted to be able to skip sessions, should the mood strike me. As it has struck. And anyway I'll be giving a talk tonight, which is plenty, if you ask me." Bramer fixed his eyes on Baillet. "And so, Père, tell me: how goes the investigation? Last we met, you had spoken to the valet and the brother."

"Ah, yes," Baillet answered, thinking how pleasant it was to see a friendly face, not to mention have some help with his impossible task. "Well, a few things have happened since." Baillet filled him in on his conversations with Viogué, Wullens, Roberval, Freinsheimus, and the information about Voetius.

Then, with a deep breath, Baillet told him about the murder of Pierre.

"I know," Bramer said anticlimactically, "it's terrible."

"You already know about it?"

"Everyone does."

"A lot of talking seems to go on around here when I'm not around."

"That's a good thing, Père. It may help us get information when we need it."

"I don't know. I already have more information than I can handle."

"Well that's why I'm here. To help you process it. Now," Bramer stared once more at Baillet, "have you had any chance to look through Descartes's papers more thoroughly?"

Baillet straightened up. "What is it with you and the papers?"

"I'm just asking, Père. With a man like Descartes there are going to be clues in his papers. A journal, a notebook maybe, are you sure?"

Baillet hesitated. "No, nothing. But I can't see why some notebook—even if there were one—would help determine who murdered him. If he even *was* murdered."

"Let me put it this way, Père," Bramer was studying Baillet closely. "To solve the mystery of the death of a Descartes you are going to have to solve the mystery of his life, so to speak."

"That's very poetic, Bramer. But what does it mean?"

"A common theme with almost everyone has been that Descartes was not all he appeared to be, am I right? There are questions about his religious commitments. Questions about his secret affiliation with the Rosicrucians. His brother claimed he was a liar and a cheat and a thief. And that minister claims he had a secret mistress and—family?"

"You forget Roberval. A plagiarist and murderer as well."

"Exactly! Although between you and me, Père, Roberval is a little off."

"You discount his claim?"

"I ... do. But still, it fits the theme."

"Descartes was not all he appeared."

"Right."

"And the Rosicrucians? The Librarian seems even less credible than Roberval."

"I agree. The Rosicrucian stuff is nonsense. People love to believe in secret cults that control the world. But there never was such a group, and if there were, Descartes would have had nothing to do with it."

"But then," Baillet realized, "you're dismissing much of the evidence that Descartes was not—how did you put it—everything that he appeared."

"What matters, Père, is that many people *believed* that he was not. So if we are to understand why someone might have murdered him, we must, ultimately, determine both how he appeared to people and who, in the end, he really was. So to speak."

Baillet digested this a moment, then said, softly, "And the business about—the boy? Who disappeared with Descartes? Even apart from the cheating aspect?"

"I don't know. There could have been such a boy. But you seem upset?"

"There *was* a boy."

"What?"

"Who left La Flèche with Descartes. Who lived with Rector Charlet. The Rector has a heart as large as his home. He regularly took in strays. And took care of them."

"And you know this how?"

"I am one."

There was a long silence, except for the gentle whushing outside of the same soft breeze that had sunk the Vasa a quarter-century earlier.

"You lived with Charlet?" Bramer asked.

Baillet nodded. "You know—him?"

"Of him, yes. I have heard of him. When ....?"

"Still. Until I came here. My parents—died when I was very young and—I was brought to him. He still loves to talk about Descartes, despite—"

"Despite what?"

"Despite—he couldn't understand why Descartes—cut

him off. He went to the army, he disappeared for a few years, then became famous years later. But he never came back to visit, even when he was living just in Paris. And he never wrote."

"And the boy?"

"Gone. Disappeared." Baillet suppressed some emotion. "Broke the Rector's heart."

"So, Père, what do *you* think?"

"I don't know about the cheating part. But everything else Roberval said seems to be true. Descartes had talent at school but—wasted it. He would gamble and drink. He took off around 1618 with the boy and when he turned up a few years later, in Paris, the boy was gone and Descartes had become serious. So—*something* happened. In the years between."

"To solve the mystery of his murder," Bramer repeated, "we must solve the mystery of his life."

"Are we even sure it was a murder, Bramer?"

"Adrien, listen to me." Bramer hesitated. "What—what have you got in your pocket?"

Baillet's hand had wandered into his cassock pocket and was fiddling with the yellow band still in there from the other day. "Nothing, I'm sorry. You were saying?"

"Listen. Adrien. It *was* a poisoning."

"How—do you know?"

"Let's just say my experiences are diverse." Bramer's expression made clear that no follow-up questions were invited. "The first clue is the change in waters that the valet mentioned. That indicates something in the system that doesn't belong there."

"The first clue?"

"There were other anomalous symptoms. The black bile and vomit. And the restless eyes. Lung inflammation can't account for that, I think. And then we must consider Descartes's own behavior. You said something was bothering him in the days before he fell ill. Perhaps he felt... threatened. And he thought himself a physician, did he not?"

"Yes. But how is that relevant?"

"Well, he resisted treatment for a few days. What would that suggest?"

"That he—didn't believe anything was wrong with him. Medically speaking."

"At first, exactly. And then what?"

Baillet thought it over. "The wine sop. He requested it. But isn't it an old wives' remedy? In fact harmful?"

"Says Wullens. But he was surely basing that opinion on Galenic principles."

"Meaning?"

"Humors, imbalances, that sort of thing. On those principles the wine sop might well be dangerous. But that's not the point."

"Because," Baillet worked it out, "if we are interpreting Descartes's behavior, we must know how *he* understood the wine sop."

"There's hope for you yet, Adrien! On Cartesian medical principles, a wine sop would probably serve as an emetic."

"'Emetic'?"

"Induces vomiting."

"And—"

"He was right," Bramer said somberly.

"And he would request an emetic because he believed—" suddenly it was obvious to Baillet, "he'd been poisoned."

Bramer gazed at him wordlessly.

After some contemplation Baillet said, "That would be some time on Saturday. February 9th."

"Perhaps even the evening before."

"The parsnip soup?"

"Perhaps."

"He had been feeling better before the soup."

Bramer nodded.

"But wait a moment," Baillet objected. "This is at the

end of the illness. What about its onset?"

"Ah, good, Adrien. So what are the possibilities?"

"All right. One is that it was just an—illness at first, but on the 8th or 9th day someone poisoned him. The other is that he was also poisoned initially. But didn't realize it, or else he would have taken preventive measures sooner."

"And the change of waters was when?"

"By Tuesday I think. Which—suggests he was poisoned initially as well."

"Exactly. So when did you say the illness actually began?"

"It's not entirely clear. Wullens says he saw Descartes at the Castle on Friday, the 1st, looking unwell. Père Viogué says he first saw Descartes ill the next day, Saturday the 2nd, the morning of Candlemas. And the valet—Schlüter said he first fell ill early Sunday morning."

"Well then," Bramer said, "I think the next two steps are clear."

"Resolve the question of the onset of the illness."

"Exactly. And?"

Baillet's fingers had returned to fiddling with the yellow band in his pocket. "One out of two isn't bad, Benjamin, is it—for a beginner?"

"Determine how the poison might have been delivered," Bramer answered gently, "at the end and—it seems—at the beginning. And Adrien."

"What?"

"Not bad at all."

It felt good to hear that, Baillet thought. "I'll head over to speak to Schlüter again. Any chance you might accompany me?"

"It is perhaps better that I don't. And besides, I agreed to meet with the panelists from this morning's symposium, to explain all their mistakes."

"But you weren't even there."

"I like a little challenge now and again," Bramer smiled.

It was quite the glorious day, Baillet thought as he

strolled across the Norrbro a few minutes later. All was quiet down on Helgeandsholmen. With the geographical confidence almost of a native he crossed the bridge. *Främmandegatan* he thought proudly to himself as he came to the desired street. Smiling, he turned right, down the street.

As soon as he did he saw the cart in front of the Ambassador's Guest House. A burly Swede with his uncovered blond hair and coatless body was loading a crate from the house onto the mule cart beside several other crates already there.

Somebody was moving out.

26

Baillet burst through the door.

The foyer was empty.

He strode down the hall and into the drawing room. No fire in the fireplace this time, but there was Schlüter, directing another burly Swede tying a rope around a crate. Otherwise the room was bare: no furniture, no rugs, no paintings.

"What is going on here?" Baillet exclaimed.

"Moving out, sir," Schlüter responded, nodding to the man to remove the crate.

"Already?"

"The ship departs tomorrow afternoon, sir."

Baillet was gripped by the sadness of it. These empty rooms, the man's valet and clothes and papers about to depart for good; the loss of the great philosopher.

"Can you perhaps spare a few minutes," Baillet said quietly, "my good man?"

The valet disappeared then returned with two low stools. After they were seated, uncomfortably, Baillet gestured to the same empty rooms. "I thought the furnishings did not belong to the Monsieur?"

"The Ambassador was planning to redecorate anyway, sir. He generously offered me the furnishings, sir,"

"Ah. And where ....?"

"I shall accompany the Monsieur's things to Amsterdam, where I shall return to my master. The Monsieur's things will continue on to Paris."

Baillet paused, realizing that the papers he had inventoried were leaving the country. Bramer would be disappointed. "All right then," he began cautiously, reviewing his notebook, "You said the Monsieur complained of feeling ill early Sunday morning. The 3rd. Is that right?"

"That seems right, sir."

"According to others, however, the Monsieur first felt unwell earlier than Sunday."

"Indeed, sir, the Monsieur *was* unwell earlier than Sunday."

"But—now you are contradicting yourself."

"No, sir. You asked me when the Monsieur first complained of the illness, sir. And that was on the Sunday morning, preparing to meet the Queen."

"So he was unwell earlier, but without complaint? You didn't think it relevant to mention that?"

"I answer the questions as I am asked, sir."

"Fine." Baillet reflected a moment and attempted to be as precise as possible. "So, then, when exactly did the Monsieur first become unwell?"

"The day before, sir. By the time we returned from the Candlemas ceremony he was in significant distress."

"What time was that?"

"Perhaps one o'clock, sir."

"That is quite late."

"Yes, sir. But the Monsieur was in the habit of arriving late."

"But—why is that relevant?"

Schlüter hesitated, looked at him. "Père Viogué kindly accommodated the Monsieur's tardiness. He would provide communion for the Monsieur after the Mass."

"Hence the delay."

"Exactly, sir."

Outside the window there were some loud noises, some cursing in Swedish, a whip cracking. Then the sound of the loaded mule cart moving down the street through the snow. Baillet felt another wave of sadness.

"And the day before," he continued after composing himself. "The Friday. The 1st. I was also told the Monsieur was unwell already that morning, as white as—a ghost?"

"Nothing out of the ordinary, sir."

"He was ordinarily white as a ghost?"

"Not at all, sir. He was perhaps out of sorts that morning, sir. But that was not entirely unusual when he first met important personages. He could become quite flustered."

"He met with the Chancellor that morning, isn't that right?"

"Yes, sir."

"And that was his first audience with His Excellence? Are you sure?"

"A valet is always sure of such matters," Schlüter said stiffly.

Baillet was surprised to hear this, in light of the Chancellor's zeal to bring Descartes there and place him at the center of the new Academy. But then again the Chancellor was busy and Descartes tended to the recluse, so it was not impossible. And that Descartes might emerge from his first encounter with His Terrifying Excellence looking pale—well *that* was understandable. Moreover, if Schlüter was right that the illness began Saturday afternoon, that would narrow down the window as to when—the poison might have been administered.

At least the first poisoning.

"All right, then," Baillet continued, "I have a question about the parsnip—"

Just then they heard the front door crash open. Baillet

and Schlüter both rose as the door to the drawing room in turn crashed open. In rushed a blast of cold air, followed by Ambassador Chanut. "Ah, Père! Thank God!"

"What? Did something happen?" Baillet's heart was pounding.

"No, but it will, if you don't get to the Castle immediately. You haven't forgotten your appointment with the Chancellor, have you?!"

Ah! Baillet recalled, he was supposed to check in with Zolindius. "But—how did you find me here?"

"The Chancellor said you were here. Now get in my carriage this instant!"

Baillet's stomach tightened at these words. He was too busy being aware of his discomfort to notice that the valet, Schlüter, was giving him a strange and intense look.

27

"How goes it, Père?" the Ambassador sat opposite him in the carriage as they bounced along.

"If not for the Monsieur's death and the weather here, then grand, I would say."

"Isn't that right," Chanut stroked his goatee.

"That Schlüter fellow is quite a—fellow. Have you noticed the arms on that man, Ambassador?"

"He's handy with a plank too, I hear. But a good man."

"Where did you find him, Ambassador?"

"Who says I found him?"

"I don't understand. Didn't you—your office—pay his wages?"

"Yes, yes. He was officially in our employ. But the Chancellor found the man. Someone owed him a favor in Amsterdam, I believe."

Just then the carriage swerved, tossing the men inside. They heard the driver cursing as they straightened out. Baillet, righting himself, glanced out the window and looked behind them.

The vagabond was standing in the street brushing himself off, staring at them.

"Ambassador! That man!"

"Who?" Chanut looked out the window on his side.

Too late. The vagabond had disappeared.

"There's a vagabond," Baillet turned to Chanut. "Long, filthy gray hair. I keep seeing him. It's very strange. He—"

"Speaks perfect French?"

"Yes!"

"One shoe?"

"Yes! How—do you know him?"

"Everyone knows him. He is the only vagabond in Stockholm."

"The only one? But how is that possible?"

"Zolindius does not tolerate begging. You have seen his collection of heads."

Baillet grimaced. "But who is he?"

"I don't know, but he is good with the tunnels. Quick, boom, gone! He showed up in town a few weeks ago. Claims he was once in line to become the Duke of Sully. That's rich!"

A few minutes later they were standing in the Chancellor's office, facing the man seated in his enormous chair behind his enormous desk. Baillet refused to let himself turn around and look at whatever heads might now be spiked onto the wall.

The Chancellor's eyes fastened onto Baillet. "So, Père. How is your investigation coming along?"

"Well enough, Your Excellence," Baillet managed to squeak out.

"Tell me, Père. What have you learned so far?"

Baillet took a deep breath and explained that he had spoken with all the relevant people and that, of course, the official story—inflammation of the lung—was increasingly confirmed. But then in the void of the Chancellor's crushing silence he could not entirely restrain himself.

"And so there remains the question," he heard himself saying, "of when the Monsieur fell ill. It was suggested as early as Friday, the 1st. After leaving—Your Excellence."

"Hogwash!" Chanut interjected, not liking the

mentioning of the illness and His Excellence in the same breath. "What matters is what the man died of, not when he fell ill."

"Who suggested that?" Zolindius asked.

"I cannot recall," Baillet quickly thought to lie. "I have talked to so many people, Your Excellence."

Zolindius remained motionless, silent.

"Do you recall, sir," Baillet for some reason found himself continuing, "how the Monsieur seemed that morning? Was he—out of sorts? Not himself?"

Zolindius stared at him, then answered slowly. "He had been working quite hard, I understand, on the statutes for Her Majesty's Academy. And of course the ballet. One might expect the Monsieur to be fatigued, Père, would one not?"

"Exactly right," Chanut insisted.

"But did he strike you, sir," Baillet surprised himself by persisting, "as more fatigued than *usual*, perhaps?"

"It was the first time I had met the man, Père. I cannot generalize about his state of fatigue."

"The first time, sir?"

"The Chancellor is a busy man," Chanut interrupted. "You cannot expect him to be meeting with everyone in the court."

The strange half-smile slowly appeared on Zolindius's face. "The Ambassador is quite correct, Père. Her Majesty brought the Monsieur here for her edification. As for myself, I have been too occupied with matters of state to have enjoyed the pleasure of his acquaintance any sooner. Though surely, Père, you did not come here to interrogate *me*?"

"Of course not," Chanut answered for him quickly. "Just to update you, Chancellor, as you requested. Which I trust he has done, sir, to your satisfaction?"

Zolindius's half-smile lingered, then dissolved. "Indeed. I imagine then, Père, that you are ready to wrap up? Perhaps draft a small report for your sovereign, and be done with it?"

"There is one further matter, sir," Baillet answered, ignoring the Ambassador's pained look.

"Oh?"

"The Monsieur's brother, Your Excellence. His— murder."

"A simple case of robbery, I am told, and the police are close to apprehending the perpetrator."

"But, sir, you do not find it strangely coincidental that—"

"He does not," Chanut placed his hand firmly on Baillet's arm. "And anyway, Père, we are *not* here to interrogate the Chancellor."

"Of course not," Baillet looked away from Zolindius's gaze. Inside, though, he felt some strange—lightness.

"Ambassador, Père," Zolindius rose to indicate the end of the interview. "Our work is done on the first matter. And we will let you know when we make an arrest in the second. Now, Père, may I recommend you take in this afternoon's entertainment perhaps, before you write your report?"

"Sir?"

"For today's theme of applied philosophy we're debuting a new state-of-the-art rack. Maximal stretching without severing. We are bringing to justice one witch, two traitors, and—" here he paused, "an apparent Rosicrucian. Or three of the above, at any rate. At the arena. Now, if you will excuse me, gentlemen."

"'Three of the above'?" Baillet asked the Ambassador on their way toward the Castle's rear exit.

"The Chancellor lets one prisoner go free. By a random lottery. Some say he is merciful that way."

"And others?"

"That he just likes the arbitrariness of it."

The soldier opened the door and shuffled them outside. The earlier clear weather had been replaced with thick dark clouds dropping heavy flakes of snow.

28

"Cornelis, let the young man in this instant," the grandmotherly woman demanded, "before he catches his death!"

The servant grudgingly stepped aside to allow Baillet to enter.

"Will you please take his coat and have it dried?" she added.

Cornelis disdainfully brushed the snow off Baillet's greatcoat and disappeared.

"Cornelis has been a little cross since we came here from the Provinces," the woman explained as she led Baillet down the main hall. "I don't think he's used to the weather yet."

"How long ago was that?"

"Ten years now," she sighed. "Ah, here we are, the sitting room. Please, Père, rest before the fire and we shall get you something warm to drink."

The Doctor was at the clinic, Vrouw Wullens explained. But he was due home soon for dinner, and if Baillet wouldn't think her too rude she would leave him to wait in this lovely warm room. She and her sister were

262

organizing a supper for the visiting Dutch physicians and clergy, you see, and absolutely everything was in chaos. So would he please accept her apologies for being such a poor hostess?

"To the contrary, Madame, you have been wonderful," Baillet bowed, finding himself wishing she were his grandmother.

In fact he was relieved to have some quiet time before a fire, with a warm drink. He had notes to review, things to think through. Descartes's illness began on Saturday, the 2nd, so the poisoning would have been either late Friday or early Saturday. Then some days of illness, then he began recovering. Then that parsnip soup on Friday the 8th, and by Saturday the 9th he was ill again, requesting the emetic. A likely second poisoning, perhaps with that soup, so he would have to track down its source; and that also meant one of the people attending Descartes was involved, for only they knew he was improving and thus in need of a second dose.

Two poisonings, Baillet thought; how awful.

It was with this thought that he fell asleep on the sofa.

There were soldiers, always soldiers. Muskets firing, cannonballs exploding, they were—at home—and there was a fire and screaming, someone pounding on their door. His father led his mother and him and—to a room, their bedroom maybe, into a small closet and then went back out, to the front, they were huddling within the clothes, thick heavy clothes, buried in the clothes, they weren't—alone in there—he heard the front door bashed open outside, more screaming, his mother hugging him or them so tight he couldn't breathe. And then—they heard the bedroom door thrown open, boots stomping, shouts outside the closet door, his mother covering his mouth to stop him from crying and he couldn't breathe and then the closet door was flung open and soldiers pulled his mother out, soldiers growling, laughing, one—kicked him and closed him into the closet, locked him in, he was curled up, on the floor, sobbing, alone, not alone, listening to screams, his mother's screams, and then—the smoke, smoke, fire—

"Wake up, man, wake up! Are you all right?"

The physician was shaking him.

Baillet blinked awake, sweating.

"Are you all right, man?" Wullens repeated.

"Fine, fine," Baillet murmured, lying.

"Are you sure?"

"No, but—there you have it, I suppose."

Wullens helped him sit up on the sofa. "What language was that?"

"I'm sorry?"

"You were muttering. Screaming. It wasn't French."

"I—don't know."

"What was the dream," Wullens asked gently, "if you don't mind my asking?"

"It's a long story, Doctor." Baillet, recovering, took a sip of his still warm drink. "I don't want to waste your time. I was just hoping to—follow up. On our earlier conversation."

Wullens's gaze was not unfriendly. "First you shall join me for dinner, and then we can talk. Let me tell Cornelis to set another place."

A short while later they were at table with two silver candlesticks illuminating the plates that Cornelis had dropped before them. Either Baillet was starving or the minced intestines were the most delicious thing he had ever eaten; and the wormwood beer immediately invigorated his liver and spleen, as Wullens promised.

Baillet was soon feeling better.

"I already told you Descartes was a nasty prick," Wullens was saying. "It wouldn't surprise me if someone wanted to murder him. *I* would have liked to, frankly."

"But your official report, I gather, does not—mention that possibility, Doctor."

"Tell me, Père," Wullens lowered his voice. "Have you

noticed the way that the Chancellor sits absolutely still and silent, with that strange half-smile, just staring at you?"

"I have."

"Would *your* official report have said anything different?"

Baillet almost smiled. "Unofficially, then, Doctor. I sensed—during our earlier conversation—you were not being honest with me."

"I spoke only the truth, Père."

"Candid, then, might be the better word. There was something—unclear. About your reluctance to bleed the patient while he was indisposed. You said—it was already apparent that he was going to die soon anyway. And another thing ..."

"Yes, Père?"

"The valet. Schlüter. He mentioned that Descartes's waters were a strange color. Already by Tuesday, when you first arrived."

"And what of it?"

"You did *not* mention it."

Now it was Wullens who half-smiled. "Not bad, Père. So what is your theory?"

"May I speak frankly?"

"I insist."

"That there was a poisoning. On that first Friday, or Saturday. And that—you were fully aware of it. At least by Tuesday."

"Let me check on Cornelis," Wullens said after a moment, then stood. "He has an unpleasant habit of listening in when we have visitors."

When Wullens returned he had a bottle of *brännvin* and two glasses. "You'll join me, Père? It's flavored with blackthorn. That will make sure those intestines don't give you dysentery."

They toasted the health of Her Majesty.

Then Wullens spoke firmly and quickly. "It was clearly a poisoning, Père. The urine was obvious. And his eyes, wandering, crazy. They even seemed bloody on Tuesday or Wednesday. The valet noticed but I dismissed it. The last thing anyone needed was for this to be a murder. As you understand."

"Of course. But why weren't you—more straightforward with me earlier?"

"Père, my job is to do what the Chancellor tells me. Which I generally do, because it allows me to keep my head attached to my shoulders. You think it wise that I should come right out and tell you what I think, when I barely know you?"

"But you are being more candid now. What is different?"

"Two things, Père. For one, you didn't betray me on a careless slip I made in our first conversation. For some reason I told you I saw Descartes looking unwell outside the Chancellor's office."

"That wasn't true?"

"It was perfectly true. But it is never advisable for one to say the Chancellor's name in relation to bad news."

"Well—how can you be sure I didn't betray you?"

Wullens pointed to his head. "Still attached."

Baillet was starting to like this man, despite the fact that he just might have murdered the world's greatest philosopher. "And the second thing?"

"The way you were screaming a few minutes ago, Père. In your sleep, on the sofa. Like a little boy, almost. My wife and I were never blessed with children and—well. Made me almost want to take care of you. I am sorry, Père. I see I have embarrassed you."

"No, no," Baillet felt his face flush.

"Please," Wullens said gently, "let's have another toast. The Chancellor's health. And then I shall answer your next question."

"My next question?" Baillet said after they had drained their glasses.

"Regrettably, I didn't do it, Père. It's the obvious next

question, isn't it? Your man was poisoned. And what better suspect than the physician? Who knows about poisons—arsenic, I believe—and who had access to the victim?"

"And who despised the nasty prick as well?"

"Exactly. If only. But alas."

"Alas, indeed, Doctor. But my next question was not actually about you."

"Oh?"

"It concerns an—acquaintance of yours. The Reverend. Voetius."

Wullens burst out laughing. "Really, Père, the death of the philosopher may be a tragedy. But you are turning it into a farce."

"I take it that would be a no?" Baillet flushed again.

"Gisbertus couldn't hurt a fly. Or rather, a fly is about the only thing he *could* hurt."

"But I understand he had a history with Descartes, Doctor. He was vocal and harsh in his criticisms of him, and apparently he went so far as to—the Monsieur's dog. Descartes ruined him, you know. And here he arrives in Stockholm just before our philosopher is murdered, and happens to know the physician in charge of the philosopher's care. You wouldn't find that a little—convenient?"

"Very convenient, my friend. But even so, Père."

"There's more. You are obviously aware of the rumors about Descartes. And Her Majesty. Your acquaintance's own strong religious convictions might also have provided some—motive for his crime."

"You mean in preventing Her Majesty's conversion to Catholicism?"

"Yes."

Wullens laughed again.

"I fail to see what is amusing," Baillet said with irritation.

"Forgive me, inspector. I have—let me see, four

corrections for you. First, I should have said that a dog is about the only thing that Gisbertus could hurt. He has this strange obsession with the beasts, some obscure Calvinist thing. Second, we are not merely acquaintances. He's staying with us here. My wife is—"

"His wife's sister."

"Exactly. I've enjoyed twenty-five years of marital bliss, except for being saddled with an ornery *predikant* brother-in-law with a strange aversion to dogs."

"But Doctor. These corrections both *support* my suggestion."

"Indeed, my friend. But now the third correction."

"Yes?"

"If Voetius is your man then he could only have done it through me. But I had nothing to do with poisoning your Monsieur."

"So you say."

"But you have no choice but to accept what I say. Only a few of us were ever present at the sick man's bed."

"But your access to him. As his physician. You were there daily. Especially the last few—" Baillet hesitated.

"What is it?" Wullens asked

"The parsnip soup. Friday night."

"That the valet prepared."

"Who provided the ingredients?"

"Is that it? A second poisoning, when I observe that the patient survives the first?"

"Perhaps."

"There's just one thing, Père. I was never alone with him when I was there. Ask the others." Wullens paused, then added gently, "Not to mention that I was only called in on Tuesday. *After* the first poisoning. I could not have done it."

Baillet was silent. "That *is* rather unfortunate."

"I feel for you Père, I do. But you are frisking the wrong Frisian here."

"I'm sorry?"

"It means you are on the wrong track."

"I don't suppose," Baillet answered after a moment, "you can suggest a better one?"

"Perhaps I might, Père, but I'm afraid it is rather delicate. May I propose another toast before we continue? To *our* health, in this horrible murderous land we find ourselves in." They drank, both heartily, then Wullens resumed. "All right. A lot of people despised your man, but only a few were in that room during the week."

"You, the Ambassador, Schlüter, Père Viogué."

"Exactly."

"The Ambassador is out of the question. As is Père Viogue. So it would be you or the valet."

"Well, that narrows it down, doesn't it?"

"So you think the loyal valet was not so loyal?"

"Could be. You know, he was awfully insistent on giving the patient that broth of his. The evening before the patient fell into the final stages of his illness."

"Or perhaps he was devoted to his master, and wanted to nourish him back to health. The patient seemed better for a while. The next morning at least."

"I *said*, could be. But you know my delicate suggestion was not about the valet."

"But you already eliminated yourself!"

"Ah, Père, must I do all your deducing for you?"

"Apparently."

"My money is on the priest."

"Père Viogué? But that is outrageous!"

"I *said* it was delicate."

"But how on earth could you suggest that?"

"Don't take offense, Père. But your Viogué gives me the creeps. He hovers, even more than your sort normally do. When he was at the sick bed he was, how shall I put it, in the way. Like he was trying to manage the whole affair."

"Perhaps he was, managing the spiritual affair."

"Please. You don't need to *hover* to do that."

"Is that the best you have?" Baillet asked.

"Unlike myself, he had time alone with the patient."

"He was hearing the Monsieur's confession. And offering him communion."

"Yes. And he insisted upon it. Saturday morning. After the soup. After the patient was feeling better. But before he deteriorated again and died."

The parallel suddenly struck Baillet. Descartes had first fallen unambiguously ill that Candlemas afternoon—after receiving communion from Père Viogué. And now after recovering to a degree he had fallen fatally ill the second Saturday afternoon—again after receiving communion from Père Viogué.

And then had requested an emetic from Wullens that evening.

"The last rites," Baillet said softly, referring to the physician's comment in their earlier interview.

"My next point exactly, Père. What kind of priest refuses the last rites for a dying congregant?"

And then tells me that he did perform them, Baillet thought. "You didn't believe his excuse? The lack of holy oil?"

"*You* didn't believe it," Wullens chuckled.

"But—what does that suggest?"

"You tell me, Père, what it means when a priest refuses to perform last rites."

"He believed that Descartes's spiritual condition was—compromised."

"Your man's reputation there *was* tarnished, was it not, Père?"

"But what does *that* suggest? What could possibly be Père Viogué's motive? For—murder?"

"Père," Wullens said, "I mentioned a fourth correction."

Baillet gazed at him silently.

"Gisbertus could not have been motivated by the desire to stop your philosopher from converting the Queen to Catholicism."

"And why is that?" Baillet asked, already gleaning the answer.

"According to him, your man was actually an atheist."

"Those accusations are hardly new."

"No, he was not in the least alone in making them. And, indeed, that is my point."

"Yes?"

"Your Père Viogué almost surely felt the same way."

29

*I*nfernal darkness. His lantern barely penetrated the snow falling around him. It was not even half past four and already it was middle-of-the-night dark. He looked up the street to the left, but in the snow and dark could see nothing. He looked up the street to the right, could see nothing. Well, the one way to ensure he would get nowhere would be just to stand here.

So—he chose left.

A visit to the Royal Library might prove actually useful this time, since he now had specific information to acquire. It seemed absurd that Père Viogué could be responsible for Descartes's death. Rome's Apostolic Emissary to the Northern Lands. Whose remarks about Descartes's Catholicism had been nothing but laudatory. Who was enthused about Descartes's influencing the Queen, toward conversion. And he had been quick to dismiss Descartes's alleged skepticism, atheism.

As the wind increased Baillet stopped, confused, at an intersection. The way *to* the physician's home had not involved any intersections, he thought. Unless he were confusing that earlier journey with one of his others around this confusing city. Well, going back would be an admission of defeat. So turning seemed to be the thing to do, and a right turn was as good as any other.

Where was he, in his thoughts, that is?

Père Viogué. Had he been *too* quick to dismiss Descartes's atheism? He said he had never read Descartes's works. His claims that Descartes called for communion, last rites, had been contested by the valet, and Wullens. Could Viogué perhaps have *doubted* Descartes's Catholicism? Might he have been concerned to *prevent* Descartes's influence on the Queen, rather than promote it? Viogué, who insisted that Descartes fell ill *before* the first communion on Candlemas, which Baillet no longer believed; who had also been quick to mention the mysterious parsnip soup, perhaps to distract attention from the second communion; who was equally quick to accuse Voetius, among his own most bitter religious rivals.

Two communions. Two poisonings. Could it be?

And the Sunday morning. The last morning. The Ambassador said that Descartes whispered Viogué's name to him. Thinking Descartes was calling for his confessor Chanut had gone for the priest. But what if Descartes had, instead—*been naming his murderer?*

Baillet shivered, from this thought and from the cold. It hardly seemed possible. But then again if he had been asked just several months ago whether he would ever leave the Rector's home, leave La Flèche, journey across the sea, investigate the murder of the world's most famous philosopher—well that hardly seemed possible either. But here he was, and as an investigator he needed to research his senior colleague Père Viogué. The only place to do that research would be the Royal Library.

Now if only he could remember how to get there.

He was standing at a three-way intersection. Dark snowy roads stretched out to the left, to the right, and straight ahead, equally bleak. A good investigator doesn't weep, he reminded himself. The rational thing to do, he decided, would be simply to stand there and wait for a reason to arrive to choose one direction over the other.

There was a footstep in the snow behind him.

That was his reason.

His heart pounded as he set off in some direction, too distracted to notice which.

But then he stopped, paused.

And for some reason made himself turn around.

"Adrien!" the voice called from down the street. "Is that you?"

Bramer?

That was odd. What was Bramer doing here? He had also shown up outside the Library yesterday morning as Baillet was leaving. This morning he had popped up at the lecture—and now here he was again.

Wherever this was.

Baillet shook himself. This investigator business was making him paranoid.

"How is it going, Adrien?" Bramer said, reaching him. "Any news?"

"I believe I am lost."

"No, *news*, my friend. Any developments?"

Baillet could tell Bramer was staring at him, through the dark. He found himself not wanting to share what he had learned, and hesitated.

"Did you speak with the valet again?"

"I did," Baillet answered slowly.

"And?"

Baillet hesitated. "The illness probably began Saturday. Schlüter—Schlüter was helpful."

"Adrien, is something wrong?"

"Of course not. But—Benjamin. I'm freezing. And I was hoping to get to the Library before Freinsheimus closes up. Perhaps we can meet later?"

"You're not following up that silly Rosicrucian thread, Adrien?"

"No, no, I just want to—check on a—few medical

details, as you suggested."

"All right, then," Bramer said after a moment. "I'll let you go."

"Um. Would you mind pointing me in the right direction?"

Bramer laughed. "Adrien, come this way."

He led Baillet back to the intersection and then down the street to the right. Through the snow and the dark he could make out some lanterns, ahead on the right. Just enough to illuminate the sign hanging there, depicting the paille-maille-playing rooster with the swollen wattle.

"By the way," Bramer said, pointing to the sign.

"What?"

"They *were* rooster testicles. Anyway it's easy to get to the Castle from here. I'll even escort you. But on one condition."

"Yes?"

"You will come to my talk this evening. The subject is most interesting."

"Let me guess: the military applications of Cartesian geometry?"

"Is there any other?"

Baillet arrived at the Royal Library just as Riddarholm was chiming five. Five at night, five in the morning, it all looked the same, Baillet was thinking as he knocked on the door. He did not really feel like dealing with the annoying Librarian at the moment. Nor, with his intestines still full of intestines from his meal with Wullens, did he feel like attending the Gala supper afterward. And the thought of being surrounded by all his suspects was overwhelming. Trust no one, he thought—starting with himself, with his own opinions, reasoning. Bramer was his friend, he was sure of it. He had to shake this sense of suspicion. His one certainty, after all, was that Bramer could not have been involved in the murder since he had arrived in town with Baillet, after Descartes's death.

While he waited his hand slipped into his greatcoat

pocket. His gloved fingers found the yellow band he had moved there.

Then he pulled his hand from his pocket and knocked—pounded—again.

30

*H*e was back there on the quad with the—real students—
they were playing *jeu de paume* in their school uniforms,
their puffy-sleeved black blouses, pom-pommed breeches.
Or rather the real students were playing and Baillet was
watching, loitering, hoping to be asked to join. He watched
for a long time then walked back alone to the Rector's
house. After finishing his chores he retired to his room
back of the kitchen, spent the evening on his mattress,
staring at the ceiling, wondering who his parents had been
and who *he* would have been had his parents—just been
there. And then he was back in that closet, the screams
outside, then silent, the smoke, the door flung open, the
man—it was not the closet, he was in a *coffin*, a real coffin,
he could not breathe and there was—*another body in there
with him*, he could feel it pressing against him and then—

A disturbance. Rustling, mutterings, a shout perhaps,
someone standing, sliding noisily through the row of
chairs, making everyone stand to let him out, making a
scene. In the lecture hall of Tre Kronor Castle, Baillet
realized, opening his eyes slowly, realizing his cheeks were
moist from tears. With a discreet wipe he dried them and

looked up. Bramer was at the podium, he'd been discussing universal laws of motion, or *the* universal law of motion, but now he was talking about compasses, Descartes's geometric principles, dissecting angles, constructing shapes. But more important, Baillet realized as he woke more fully, was the disturbance that woke him: the tall, thin man with the deathly white complexion who was making the noisy exit out the side entrance.

It took Baillet another moment to realize that the man storming out was Roberval.

And yet another to realize that as the lead investigator into the murder of the philosopher it was his obligation to follow.

31
1626-28
PARIS, FRANCE
LA ROCHELLE, FRANCE

*T*he chatter was as thick as the flies on the dung-filled streets of Paris in the late summer of 1626.

There was *so* much to talk about.

First Minister Richelieu, for example, was suffering from strangury. Urinating involved horrible pain up the shaft of his penis to the point where some bloody drops of urine squeezed out. The implications of this for national policy were enormous.

Then there was the treachery of the Comte de Chalais, former Head of Wardrobe to King Louis XIII. This juicy tale involved money, sex, and an attempted assassination, not to mention the infamous left nipple of Madame de Chevreuse. It culminated in a beheading requiring nearly forty whacks of a dull axe before Chalais's still conscious head was finally separated from his neck.

And then there were the Brethren of the Rosy Cross,

the Rosicrucians.

Everyone was one. Friends eyed friends, spouses eyed spouses, even cutthroats thought twice before cutting any particular throat.

"Thirty-three!" one fellow might swear to another in a tavern, referring to the number of deputies the Brethren had secretly dispatched across Europe. "A half-dozen, right here in Paris!"

"I've not seen 'em," his tavern mate would scoff.

"They're invisible, you turd."

"But how do you know he's a Brother?" the neighborhood gendarme might ask with irritation as yet another local Jacques was ratting out some other local Michel.

"I saw the way he spoke to Luc!" Jacques would exclaim.

"And what way was that?"

"With—*his mind!*"

For everyone knew that the Rosicrucians communicated by means of thought. They were not only invisible, then, but inaudible too.

"I know where they are hiding," the dung-cart driver said to his fellow driver on the bank of the Seine, as the two appreciated the clear waters of the great river before dumping their dung-carts into it.

"And where would that be?" his colleague asked.

"The Temple."

"In the Marais?"

The first man nodded, referring to the fortified medieval church built centuries earlier in a swampy bog (or *marais*). Since then the bog had been drained, and the area was now one of the most attractive districts in Paris.

"And how do you know the Rosicrucians are there?" the second driver asked.

"The shit is different. It sort of—shimmers. Look."

They glanced down at the river beneath them. It was undeniable.

At the very moment of this conversation First Minister Richelieu was bickering with Père Pierre de Bérulle yet again about the Treaty of Monzón signed with Spain earlier in the year. The King was not in any better mood either. Having been married eleven years to the sister of the King of Spain it was hard enough keeping his domestic problems separate from his foreign ones without having to listen to his First Minister and his pointy-chinned Ambassador to Spain arguing next door. Thank goodness for all the gossip about the Rosicrucians, just for the distraction.

At this moment, too, a man of about thirty was approaching on horseback the Saint-Antoine gate on the eastern side of the city. Now refreshed after stopping for several days, he had also changed from his travel clothes into a more appropriate costume: the fresh green suit of single taffeta with the plumed hat, scarf, and rapier of a gentleman. His hair was clean, and long.

He paused briefly outside the gate, and then went through.

"But that is absurd," he said with impressive aplomb considering that he was lying through his teeth.

"You've been in Germany."

"There are millions of people in Germany. Even still, with the wars."

"You are a mathematician and natural philosopher who has been in Germany."

"And a Catholic."

"This man you studied with. This—"

"A Calvinist, true," Descartes objected. "But a decent one, all the same. And not a Rosicrucian."

"It is said they have sent deputies to Paris. You arrived in Paris at the same time."

"Months later, Père!"

"Their ways are subtle. They deliberately misdirect."

"They are also supposed to be invisible. But I, as you

can plainly see," Descartes insisted, "can be plainly seen."

Père Marin Mersenne pulled back the hood of his cassock and fixed his gaze on the man seated before him, who just then began to perspire. Mersenne's eyes burned from his narrow face, from beneath his closely cropped and just graying hair, as they studied the man. "Yes. I suppose you can."

But the gaze did not yet release the man. It quickly skimmed over the small pustule on the cheek, then settled on the scar along the jaw.

"Do I know you?" Mersenne asked.

The stuffy humid chamber they were in suddenly felt like the late August in Paris that it was. "I was at La Flèche," Descartes said from beneath his sweaty brow.

"When?"

"I arrived in '06. At the end of the term."

"As I was leaving."

"I suppose."

"You had an older brother there?"

"Pierre."

Mersenne's gaze lingered, then broke away. "I do not suppose it matters much now. What matters is this."

He touched the letter of introduction Descartes had presented, now on the small table in the sparsely furnished room. This room was one of the many humble rooms in the monastery, as was fitting for the Minim order. It was here, in the monastery located near the Temple in the Marais, that Mersenne studied, worked on theology, mathematics, and natural philosophy, and prayed. It was from this room that Mersenne aimed to create a "republic of letters," a clearinghouse for the great minds of Europe, most of whom he knew personally.

"So tell me," Mersenne now said, "a little more about your work."

Descartes's timing was actually good, apart from the Rosicrucian business. In the early fall of 1626 Mersenne was launching a series of weekly symposia, Wednesday evenings in the monastery's meeting room, featuring the leading thinkers of the day. Mersenne only needed to skim Descartes's notebook to realize that this man would soon be a leading thinker. He invited Descartes to attend the symposia, then to participate in them, and soon to become their main attraction: each week a visiting thinker would sit in conversation with Descartes at the front of the room. For a man who had been hidden for almost a decade, he was now coming very much into the open. Within a few months his circle of acquaintances included many persons of distinction in the arts, sciences, and politics.

Including one M. Étienne de Villebressieu.

"Look at this!" Villebressieu exclaimed at the *soirée* where he first met this Descartes that people had been talking about. "The ball should fall off here, but it doesn't!" He was performing a trick in which he made a wooden ball go up and down between two sticks without the sticks moving.

"And how," Descartes tried to keep the tone serious, "does that prove your view of ballistic motion?"

"It doesn't. But it's a lot more interesting. And more importantly," Villebressieu chuckled, "it undermines your earlier point about refraction."

The physician, inventor, and engineer then presented some equations suggesting that the bending of light follows principles similar to those of the ball moving up those sticks. It was quite the *tour de force*, until Descartes followed it with an even greater *tour de force*.

"...and that is why," Descartes concluded, "the arc of the rainbow requires equations of a higher order from yours. Your account of refraction cannot be correct."

Villebressieu accepted this refutation with his usual good cheer, not least because it was purely theoretical while his concerns were far more with the practical. In fact he made his living performing chemical, mechanical, and optical illusions at salons and taverns, being equally comfortable in both. He also designed such military devices as hand clamps and toe springs, tools most practical for scaling parapets while boiling oil is poured on your head. He had also designed portable bridges, wheeled-stretchers, and several siege engines which, he boasted, greatly improved on the traditional siege strategy of tossing corpses over a town's walls to spread disease inside. Just that week he had been asked by Richelieu's office to consult on an exciting new siege the Crown was preparing for the coming season.

As their differing orientations complemented each other, so too, Mersenne hoped, would their differing personalities.

"He is not too solemn for you?" Mersenne asked Villebressieu several days after the *soirée*.

"Not at all, Père. In fact, I found him rather affable."

"Affable? Really? Not—awkward?"

"A little, yes. But no trace, Père, of the somber guardedness you warned me about. Just some stiff formality, I think. Those rolled r's."

Mersenne nodded. His goal was to make just the right connections between thinkers to stimulate scientific and religious progress. He hoped Villebressieu would provide that for Descartes.

Unfortunately not all of Mersenne's matchmaking worked out so well.

Watching the fancy carriages being drawn outside the monastery window Mersenne had observed that a point on a moving wheel would trace an interesting curve, which he coined *une roulette*. Even more interesting was the problem of finding the area of such a curve. Hoping to generate some mathematical sparks, Mersenne paired Descartes with a younger mathematician named M. Gilles Personne de Roberval for a late November *soirée*. Posters announcing the event were plastered all over the city. Though Descartes was mildly annoyed to be paired with the younger man (at twenty-four Roberval was half-a-decade younger than he), he was interested to learn more about Roberval's work on surface areas and volumes.

"Quiet, everyone! Please take your seats!" Mersenne exclaimed at the front of the room, now packed with some of the greatest minds of Paris. "You are all familiar with the problem. M. Roberval will present his solution, then M. Descartes will present his. Then after some discussion between the two we shall open the floor to general discussion. And then the audience shall vote to determine which of our two guests has the superior position. Let us begin! M. Roberval?"

The large-headed young man with the powdered wig stood before the room. "Thank you, Père Mersenne. Allow me now to introduce my Method of Indivisibles." He went on to detail a procedure the cleverness of which was why he was already being considered for academic chairs in town. "And there," he concluded twenty minutes later with a toss of his oversized head, "is the area of the curve *de la roulette!*"

All eyes turned to Descartes, who had sat the entire time looking at the floor, listening without any visible response. In fact he was impressed with the younger man's approach to the problem. But rather than present his own solution—which was not as elegant—he did what Mersenne had hoped he would do: he offered a spontaneous critique of Roberval's.

"There is much to admire," he began, "but much, also, to question." The Method of Indivisibles, he explained, solved the problem Mersenne posed but it was limited in its generalizability. Moreover it generated some new problems, indeed worse problems than the original one, including the one about how to construct tangents to the curve described by that moving point.

A hush filled the room as the destructiveness of this critique sunk in.

Roberval's round face had turned red as Descartes's

critique went on. But again, there was a reason he was a contender for prestigious chairs. By the end of Descartes's remarks he had collected himself, and then set about doing what Mersenne also hoped for: he offered a point-by-point response, culminating in a spontaneous solution to the problem of constructing tangents that Descartes had just surprised upon him the moment before. "And that," he concluded with a flourish, "now proves that my method of solving the original problem in fact is a success."

Another hush, all eyes slowing turning to Descartes.

The tension was as thick as the Brie de Meaux on the refreshment table.

Expressionless, Descartes began to speak. "Once more," he started slowly, "my colleague has overlooked the question of generalizability." He showed how Roberval's solution to the tangents problem was applicable only to the particular curves Mersenne had discovered. But with such limits it could not offer any genuine understanding; it was hardly more than a lucky guess. What was required instead was a *general* procedure for the construction of tangents, one applicable to any kind of curve whatsoever.

"And this," he concluded, "is what I shall now provide."

It must have been a set-up, people said for days afterward.

It simply wasn't possible. Descartes could not have spontaneously constructed that general solution to the tangents problem—when he had himself generated that problem only in response to Roberval's solution to Mersenne's problem, which he had just heard for the first time that evening!

Were they all in on it? Roberval too? No, not Roberval, given his humiliation at the end. The way that round face turned red, the sweat dripped from under his wig, the way he stormed out while Mersenne tried in vain to stop the crowd, led by Villebressieu, from hooting and hollering. So it must have been Mersenne. Indeed in years to come he would develop the reputation of a troublemaker. The best way to advance science, he would say, was to get two great minds into serious dispute, preferably one with personal overtones.

Descartes always insisted that the result had come about as naturally as it appeared. It was only as things began to deteriorate between them that he might reveal just what had motivated him to humiliate the younger man so thoroughly: something about that oversized head, he would say, just really made him crazy.

"Père, I think I will take a little trip."

They were in Mersenne's cell, a single candle burning on the table. "But whatever for?"

"I could use a break."

"Now? But we have just gotten started."

"To gather energy, then. For the coming—storm."

"To where?"

"I have not quite decided." Descartes sat with his hand on his notebook, on the table, his eyes down. "I am sorry that I will miss Desargues."

The pioneer of projective geometry was due shortly in Paris, having accepted Mersenne's invitation to participate in a *soirée*.

"Desargues?" Mersenne asked.

"Didn't you say he was to arrive this week?"

"Oh, that. I've had a letter. His plans have changed. His father has taken ill."

They sat in silence a moment.

"Perhaps," Mersenne suggested, gazing kindly, "you might consider a visit to *your* father? As long as you are traveling? Perhaps it is time?"

Descartes did not look up.

At this same moment, at a safe distance from the monastery, another young mathematician with a heart as heavy as his head had lost track of his ales and was about to lose track of his wallet as well. The underdressed tart gently rubbing his leg underneath the tavern table knew nothing of mathematics or of this man of cards, this *des cartes*, but knew enough about men and ale to know that one more ale would get this man into a room upstairs and apart from his purse.

No, Roberval did not appreciate his drubbing by the man of cards.

He began badmouthing Descartes to anyone who would listen. "He is a showman," Roberval would rant, "but he has never published anything. And why is that? Because his ideas are like Emmental cheese."

"What?" his confused interlocutor might ask.

"Full of holes!" Roberval would exclaim, and then lay into everything that Descartes had said. Descartes understood nothing about indivisibles; nor about the quadrature of surfaces; and while that general solution to drawing tangents was impressive, he, Roberval, had since worked out methods of deriving curves from each other, by means of which even more complicated areas could be computed. "Let's see that little Monsieur Descartes pull *that* off!"

These rants promptly got their hearers thinking about how excited Mersenne would be to hear this gossip; and then about how excited *Descartes* would be when he heard what Roberval was saying about him.

Alas, they were wrong.

"Eh. Like two or three flies buzzing around my ear," Descartes commented when told of the remarks, "before I swat them away."

But Roberval was not so easily swatted away. He attended the weekly *soirées* through January of 1627—until Mersenne finally banned him—taking every opportunity to attack Descartes. Descartes perhaps had moments where he regretted canceling his planned "break," but he didn't show it. Instead he might coolly respond to Roberval's attacks by saying, "The man is so lacking in credibility that if he said the Chinese have two eyes, like us, I would believe that China is a land populated by Cyclops."

"But who *is* this man, really?" Roberval would ask anyone who would listen over the summer of 1627. "He appears from nowhere, a mathematical 'genius' no one had ever seen before. He claims he's a product of La Flèche, but Mersenne has no recollection of him from there. And he arrives in Paris just when everyone knows the Rosicrucians got here. He has not had my training. He does not have my experience. He is nothing."

"Roberval reminds me of the braggart captain in an Italian farce," Descartes might say when Roberval's words got back to him, "who after having had his face slapped with a slipper continues bragging and remains always victorious and invincible, in his own mind."

"And what is that scar on his jaw?" Roberval was saying around the new year of 1628. "He claims he was injured in battle but that is hardly believable. He says he served in Maximilian's army in 1619, but I found someone from that regiment who doesn't remember him. This man also knew Descartes's brother, who told him that Descartes actually fought for the Protestants. He is a fraud!"

"If anything could get me to abandon our religion," Descartes answered Mersenne when the latter reported the comment, "it would be the prospect of running into Roberval at Mass."

"I should hope your faith runs deeper than that," Mersenne objected.

"My faith runs deep, Père, but my aversion to Roberval runs deeper. He is as vain as a woman who ties ribbons in her hair to look pretty but neglects to wash her face. With due respect, Père, please stop sharing his comments with me. We have enough toilet paper around here."

Villebressieu, who was enjoying it all, snorted. Mersenne frowned.

But no one would be snorting a few months later.

Back during the summer of 1627 Roberval's investigation

into Descartes's past wasn't the *only* thing heating up. First Minister Richelieu's migraines were stirring, and so were the Huguenots. The Duke of Buckingham brought eighty ships to the Île de Ré to persuade the Protestants of La Rochelle that they could rebel against King Louis XIII. In preparation for the upcoming siege Richelieu had already settled seven thousand soldiers in the area, and planned to mobilize twenty-five thousand more. Villebressieu was beside himself, walking around the streets of Paris laughing out loud.

"You must come see what we're building," he said to Descartes one day at breakfast (served to Descartes at the monastery at 12:30 PM, to accommodate his insomnia).

"Your descriptions are vivid enough."

"You're too sensitive. That's your problem."

"You are inadequately sensitive. That is yours. I will not go to La Rochelle. Enjoy your siege without me."

In the late fall of 1627 Gérard Desargues finally did arrive in Paris.

"Wonderful news," Mersenne announced over the Minims' Sunday dinner, consisting of soiled greens and stale dark bread. "Desargues can finally join us for a *soirée*."

Descartes suddenly looked about as healthy as the greens on the plate. "Père, I am sorry. That trip I postponed. It is time—"

"To visit your father, perhaps?" Mersenne gazed at Descartes.

"Perhaps, yes."

"Monsieur, you can trust me."

Descartes looked away and didn't answer.

In light of Descartes's absence from town during the weeks that Desargues was there, Mersenne asked the latter to take over Descartes's role at the *soirées*. "Perhaps you might tell me," Mersenne asked Desargues after the first *soirée*, "what is the history between you and Descartes?"

"History?"

"He seems to believe you are on bad terms. Something

from La Flèche, presumably?"

Desargues looked surprised. "I have only vague memories of him there. He was a mathematical prodigy of a sort. I may have challenged him with a problem now and again. But bad terms? I cannot imagine. But now, Père, who is this fellow I'll be conversing with at next week's *soirée*?"

"A bit of a character, I'm afraid. But a promising mathematician. A young fellow named Roberval. Speaking of being on bad terms with Descartes, however."

"Oh?"

"Long story. To keep Descartes happy I've had to ban him from the *soirées*. But with Descartes away I thought this would be a good opportunity to hear what he has been working on. But just one warning."

"Yes?"

"His mathematics is superb. But don't believe anything he says about Descartes."

Roberval's mathematics the following week *were* stunning. But even more stunning was his sudden claim that Descartes had stolen material from him.

"My most important notebook went missing immediately after the—episode," Roberval announced to the shocked crowd, feverishly. "And then after Père Mersenne—requested that I forbear from attending these esteemed *soirées*, I heard that Descartes was presenting equations similar to these."

"Outrageous!" Mersenne rose to his feet.

"It's true! And I found someone who says that at La Flèche there was a boy—"

"Silence! Roberval, out!"

Descartes dropped his head into his hands when Mersenne relayed this information to him some weeks later, after Desargues had departed, Roberval had been re-banned, and Descartes had returned from wherever he had been.

"This is not," Descartes said quietly, "going very well."

"Don't worry, Monsieur. Where there's no truth to the matter there is nothing to fear."

"Who do you think he has been speaking to? About—La Flèche?"

"Perhaps he invented it. He is a young man with a hot head."

"Not to mention a large one," Descartes answered, wishing that Villebressieu were around to hear the coming quip, "but filled with so little sense that he thinks its size is actually an advantage to him."

But Villebressieu was not around, now busy with the ongoing siege of La Rochelle. In the spring of 1628 he was overseeing four thousand workmen as they constructed a sea-wall seven hundred *toise* long to block sea access to the city. He was having the time of his life solving all the engineering problems; so much so that he didn't mind that hardly any of the besieged Huguenots in the city had starved to death yet.

For a while things got quiet.

Mersenne took a hiatus from the *soirées*. Descartes retreated from view and dedicated himself to his work. Roberval himself took a break from maligning Descartes, having run out of new accusations. Anyway the man he had hired to find out more about Descartes's past would soon enough turn up something. And slowly the stomachs in La Rochelle became emptier and the population got lower. It was around this time that they began eating the rats.

But Descartes was having trouble concentrating on his work.

He had been sleeping even more poorly than usual since hearing that Roberval had unearthed details about Maximilian's army back in 1619, and about La Flèche. All Descartes wanted was to quietly go about his work. He was serious now, a new person. But with Roberval's— *slanders* was the word Mersenne used—it was only a matter of time before he was found and found out, by Joachim and Pierre, by his colleagues, by the—authorities. To do his work he needed to stay, to be in Paris. But all he wanted to do was run and hide. If only he could speak openly to Mersenne, to get his help and advice!

But he just couldn't entirely trust him.

But he also couldn't handle this pressure on his own.

One night in late July 1628, an hour after the last bell at the monastery, he slipped out of the building veiled by his cloak and hood. He took a circuitous route along the darkest streets in the Marais. Twenty minutes later the shadowy turrets of the medieval fortress rose before him, silhouetted by the new moon sky. Descartes slinked around to the back, as he had been instructed long ago, and found the door to the second cellar hidden behind some shrubs. He took a deep breath then applied the secret knock. After waiting for twenty seconds he applied the secret follow-up knock.

The back door to the Temple of the Marais swung open.

The leader of the Parisian Brethren of the Rosy Cross stood before him.

"You?" they said simultaneously.

"Why didn't Eudoxus tell me?" they both said next, having entered the building. They were in a small chamber furnished with long tables, wooden chairs, and lit sconces.

"The man always has his reasons," Mersenne answered first.

"But you were so suspicious of me. You are relentless against the Rosicrucians."

"We advance masked," Mersenne smiled. "Isn't that right—Polybius?"

"I suppose so. But wait. What shall I call you?"

"I like Pythagoras. But Père is fine. Or perhaps, if you prefer," he added softly, "Marin?"

They sat for a moment in silence.

"I need your help, Marin."

A few days earlier Roberval had assured someone that Descartes was keeping a secret, something bad, criminal perhaps. Or maybe political views, treasonous. Or maybe religious views, he was almost certainly a secret Huguenot. Maybe all three. "I've been doing some research," Roberval had continued. "My source down south reports that Descartes's father and brother are furious with him. They call him a 'lying wastrel'—exact words. They say he's stolen money from them. He spent those missing years of his on the run from them. And turning into a treasonous heretic with the Rosicrucians. And there's more."

"What?"

"There was some boy he took with him into the army who was never seen again."

"What are you saying?"

"The boy disappears. Descartes disappears for a couple of years, then shows up with a long scar on his jaw. You," Roberval liked to say, "do the math."

"So what are you going to do about it?"

"I've already done it. I've written to his father to let them know he's here."

The interlocutor promptly reported this conversation to Mersenne, who reported it to Descartes.

"Is there anything you might like to tell me now, René?" Mersenne was asking gently.

Descartes looked down. "Marin, it is not what it seems."

"I assume."

"But I prefer not to explain."

"But why not?"

"I prefer not to explain that either."

Mersenne looked at him a moment longer, then his expression relaxed. "All right, then. But I am afraid we must get you out of Paris."

"You think that is necessary?"

"From what I know of your father. And especially of

your brother. Yes."

"But—the *soirée*. With the Cardinal."

Père Pierre de Bérulle, the pointy-chinned former Ambassador to Spain, had been elevated to Cardinal a year earlier. Most of that year he had spent harassing First Minister Richelieu over when his red hat would finally arrive. At some point word of the remarkable M. Descartes had reached his exposed ears. He had thus "kindly requested" that Mersenne set up a *soirée* featuring the mathematical genius in "conversation" with the Sieur de Chandoux, a popular free-spirit who had been tantalizing Paris crowds with his calls to bring the Church out of the Middle Ages. At this *soirée* Descartes would, naturally, expose the man for the charlatan he was. Cardinal Bérulle would return from the siege at La Rochelle to attend.

For a man wanting to be known as the world's greatest mathematician it was an impossible invitation to decline.

"It is two months away," Mersenne countered. "You cannot wait that long."

"You think that Pierre could get to Paris before then?"

"It is surely possible."

"But if he does not then we shall have wasted an extraordinary opportunity."

"And if he does we shall have wasted an extraordinary life."

"Perhaps the Brethren can help. Perhaps they can monitor him. They can track his journey. So we can know when he will arrive."

"And if he is to arrive before the *soirée*?" Mersenne asked.

"I depart."

It was three weeks later when the letter arrived in Bordeaux with a note scrawled atop from Joachim. Pierre Descartes opened it and read it, his fingers tightening on the paper. A week later he had arranged his affairs, had his saddlebags packed, and climbed upon his horse. He checked to see that his sharpened rapier was fastened in its sheath at his side. He felt into the left saddlebag to make sure that his new pistol was secured. He then blew some kisses to his children watching him and headed north.

A moment later the man stationed outside Pierre's house was on his horse and heading north as well.

Things were bad in La Rochelle as the summer of 1628 drew to a close. The rats were all gone, as were the dogs and cats. At the end of August the city leaders requested permission to bring a few corpses out for disposal in the countryside. It turned that by "a few" they meant "a few thousand," including the emaciated bodies of many little children.

Meanwhile quite a scene had developed outside the besieged town.

Sieges were actually kind of boring. No fool would try to escape from a city surrounded by soldiers, and those soldiers weren't fool enough to rush the walls of the city from which many a cauldron of boiling oil had been poured upon a marauder's head. In fact the siege's main achievement as of its first anniversary in August of 1628, besides depleting the population of rats, dogs, cats, and children within, was to have depleted the Royal coffers without. It was Villebressieu who brilliantly devised the idea of marketing La Rochelle as a tourist destination. It was safe for civilians after all, since nothing was happening. And more importantly the engineering feat involved in the siege—*his*—was a marvel to behold. Who *wouldn't* want to see it?

Pamphlets were printed, placards were posted all over Paris; affordable caravans were assembled to facilitate travel. An entire secondary economy sprung up around La Rochelle. People needed lodging, so inns were built. Taverns were established and stocked with merchandise from businessmen like Joachim Descartes. With these came the entertainers, the con men, and the prostitutes, building veritable tent cities among the forts and military structures. By September 1628 the environs of La Rochelle were the place to be if you were interested in the military, in engineering, in a vibrant social scene, or in making, spending, or losing money.

On a balmy evening in the third week of September a man rode into the town outside the town and made his way to one of the makeshift inns. Yes, he wanted to get to Paris to confront that lying thief of a brother of his, but he could not pass up visiting the most exciting place a Catholic zealot could be right now.

"I want your best room," Pierre demanded of the innkeeper. "And your best whore."

When Pierre had settled into his room and into the arms of Collaye—the innkeeper's second-best whore, and also his wife—the innkeeper scrawled a note and flagged the stable boy out back.

"There's a franc if you're back in ten minutes," he said, and sent it on its way to Paris.

"He is on his way. René."

It was just after noon, just after Mass. Mersenne was shaking him awake. Through the streaked window of his cell he could see the early October sunshine of a beautiful Sunday afternoon.

"He has left La Rochelle?" Descartes said groggily.

"Yes, finally. And now you must leave Paris."

"Père. Not yet. The *soirée* is just next week."

"He could be here within the week."

"He will make stops along the way. La Haye. Tours. Perhaps—La Flèche."

"We cannot risk it."

"But we can. Can we—you—not keep a man on him?"

"Of course we can. But the closer he is to Paris the less notice we shall have."

"I will not leave before the *soirée*, Père."

"You can impress the Cardinal some other time. Maybe

publish something."

"No," Descartes shook his head. "I will not miss this opportunity."

Mersenne bit his lip. "He is armed."

"I once was pretty accomplished with a sword myself."

"With a pistol too."

Descartes exhaled. "Villebressieu is due back from La Rochelle tomorrow. He will concoct something for me."

"You," Mersenne muttered, "are stubborn."

At just that moment Pierre was passing La Haye, southwest of Paris, and not stopping.

The people of La Rochelle—those who were left—were too weak to leave their homes inside the town. In contrast the people of Paris were out in abundance on this cool evening of October 18, 1628. Those who were scholars were in the living room of the Papal Nuncio, waiting for the start of the first event of the intellectual season.

The Nuncio did not keep them waiting.

"On behalf of His Holiness Pope Urban VIII," said His Holiness's representative in Paris, "I welcome you this evening!" A throat was cleared in the front row. "And of course also on behalf of His Eminence, Cardinal de Bérulle, whose wonderful idea it was to assemble this evening's program. And last but not least on behalf of Père Mersenne, whose *soirée* season for 1628-29 commences tonight!" He paused to allow Mersenne to nod, who was too nervous and distracted to notice. "Without further ado, then, our first speaker, the renowned Sieur de Chandoux."

The renowned Sieur then stood and launched into an account of the many flaws of the medieval scholastic philosophy that had become the official worldview for Catholicism. His analysis of its errors segued into an account of the virtues of the *new* philosophy, by which he meant his own. He spoke as convincingly as possible for someone who, by year's end, would be hanged for passing false gold.

When he was done speaking, Mersenne stood and—after looking out the window to make sure the two men he had hired were at their posts—then said, "We will now hear from perhaps the world's most preeminent mathematician, Monsieur Descartes."

Descartes rose and started speaking. He too was distracted but forged ahead, delivering a twenty-five-minute oration in which he casually destroyed, first, every proposition endorsed by Chandoux, second, every argument Chandoux made to support those propositions, then third, every inference Chandoux drew from them. When it was over the room was completely silent except for the sounds of Chandoux quietly weeping.

"But surely," Villebressieu jumped in for the entertainment value, "you fail to give our colleague due credit. Perhaps the propositions are dubitable, but his *method* is commendable. The new alchemy he has sketched, with its basis in the empirical, is surely an improvement over the scholastic?"

Descartes sighed impatiently. "The method *is* the problem, my friend. With some simple manipulation it could refute or support any arbitrary proposition you like. Allow me to demonstrate. Will someone please propose some incontestably true proposition?"

There was murmuring before the audience settled on: "An angle is the meeting point of two lines."

"Very well," Descartes said with a glance at Mersenne, who was looking out the window yet again. "On this definition you would say that there exists an angle where the line ab and the line cb meet at point b. But now if you were to intersect angle abc by the line de, you would divide point b into two parts, so that half of it is added to line ab and the other half to line bc. But this, of course, contradicts the definition of a point, which has no size. And so the proposition that an angle is the meeting point of two lines entails the contradiction that a dimensionless point has a dimension. It must therefore be false."

The room was silent again except for Chandoux's sobbing. At the same moment Pierre Descartes's horse was approaching the gate of Saint-Michel on the western side of the city.

"Perhaps you are right, Monsieur," Mersenne now turned to Descartes, "that the method may sometimes refute what we take to be truths. But perhaps it might be useful, in other cases, in establishing, and thereby eliminating, falsehoods?"

"Fair enough, Père. Will someone please propose some incontestably *false* proposition?"

Again some murmuring, until they settled on: "1=2."

"Very well," Descartes said again. Then applying Chandoux's method he proved in three rapid steps that, in fact, 1 *does* equal 2. "An obvious falsehood has been proven true. Thanks to Sieur de Chandoux."

"Remarkable," Cardinal de Bérulle muttered under Chandoux's wailing. "He proves the true false, and the false true." The Cardinal rose and pulled Descartes by the elbow. "Come into the study, my son. Let us speak together in private."

"You have received a gift from God, my son," the Cardinal began once they were seated. "It is our obligation to use your great mind properly, for the benefit of our sorry human race."

This was about the moment when Descartes's great mind wandered to Pierre, whose horse was just then nearing the Marais and stopping before a placard announcing the *soirée*. Certain phrases did puncture Descartes's distraction though, such as "as a good Catholic you obviously will ..." and "I shudder to think what might happen if you *don't* ..." Mersenne stood outside the room nervously watching the clock as the Cardinal spoke of the *Congregatio de Propaganda Fide*, and then the missionary college founded by the Pope last year—which, by the way, could use a mathematician on their faculty. But meanwhile the *Congregatio*, tasked with spreading the faith, could also use someone with a talent for making good arguments (those supporting the true faith) and refuting bad arguments (those supporting any other faith), and not only would the job pay well—eternal salvation was a benefit—but the employee would get to travel, to Holland and England and Sweden and wherever they had strayed from the truth. True it could be risky where they tended to burn Catholics; but then again wouldn't it be riskier *not* to accept the job, what with the certainty of eternal damnation, not to mention the possibility of being burned on a pyre much closer to home?

"So," the Cardinal was saying, peering at him, "how does 'Chief of Propaganda' grab you, my son? I shall train you myself."

Descartes had been thinking about the pistol that Pierre—just now turning down this street—was carrying. "Your Most Reverend Excellence," he forced himself to focus, "I am flattered you would even consider one such as I for this exalted position."

"There is no need for such formality, my son. A simple 'Your Eminence' will suffice."

"Your Eminence, surely your hands must be full, with the siege at La Rochelle. Are you not too busy to undertake such a significant commitment?"

"You fail to flatter *me*, my son, by presuming to advise me on matters of my administration."

"My humblest apologies, Your Eminence," Descartes bowed, wondering if he was supposed to kiss the Cardinal's enormous ring to make amends.

"In any case the siege requires little of my attention. I shall remain in Paris for now, so we may begin immediately. I shall see you at my office at 7 AM sharp tomorrow."

Sounds of shouting, a scuffle, came from outside the study door.

Pierre Descartes was in a bad mood.

It had been a long ride. What he wanted now was a large tankard of beer, a larger prostitute, and a long sleep. But his father had demanded that Pierre get that worthless criminal brother of his back down to Limoges by mid-October, and thanks to his having stopped so often for tankards and prostitutes it was already mid-October and he was just arriving in Paris. He had planned to lodge near the address that that skunk Roberval had provided and deal with the brother the next morning. But when he saw the placard, and thought about confronting the runt in front of a crowd, he couldn't resist.

Still, perhaps he shouldn't have been *quite* so quick with his rapier.

"Let me in, you apes!" he had said to the two large men at the door, right after spearing the arm of one and possibly mortally wounding the other.

The priest on the inside stood his ground longer.

"Where is he?" Pierre demanded, bursting in, his rapier swishing.

The bright lamps inside disoriented him a moment. He could just make out a lot of well-dressed people in the glare.

"On behalf of His Holiness," the man in the humble black cassock said standing before him, "I welcome you to the residence of His Representative in Paris, Monsieur—" the priest was gazing at him, "Descartes. How good it is to see you again."

"Where is he, Père?" Pierre demanded again, too irritated to respond to the reminder that he was dealing with the Pope here.

"No weapons are permitted on the premises, Monsieur."

Pierre pointed his rapier at the closed door at the end of the room. "Is he in there, Père?"

"You may not go in there."

Pierre advanced on the door.

The priest blocked his path. "What, are you going to murder him?"

"I am only authorized to hurt him," Pierre answered, pushing him away as the audience, stunned, all backed away. "Unless, hopefully, he resists."

Pierre flung the door to the study open and rushed inside.

The Cardinal looked up from his desk, where he was writing some notes. "You are really," he said, his eyes narrowing sharply, "most out of order."

The chair opposite him was empty.

"This is pretty comfortable," Descartes said.

"I know. We've just been raking it in," Villebressieu breathed contentedly.

They were several hours south of Paris, in the plush carriage in which Villebressieu, as head engineer and tourism director, was entitled to travel between Paris and La Rochelle. It had been parked outside the rear entrance of the Nuncio's residence that evening. Mersenne had packed it with Descartes's few possessions, his notebook, and his most important papers.

"That was close," Descartes said.

"Yes, your brother seemed like he meant business."

"I meant the Cardinal."

Villebressieu laughed. "Well La Rochelle is the last place he'll think to look when you don't show up tomorrow."

"It is about the last place I would want to be."

"Forget the 'suffering' already. You'll find the place fascinating. The engineering is amazing, if I do say so myself. Now how about we get some shuteye? We're not stopping until dawn."

For the next two hours Descartes stared out the windows at the black forests around them, listening to the wind, the pattering hooves, and the impressive snores of his friend on the seat opposite him. Finally he too drifted off thinking about Pierre, and the Cardinal, and about how to apply mathematics to the relief, rather than cause, of human suffering.

They arrived in La Rochelle on the morning of Friday October 27, 1628. Villebressieu dragged Descartes out to show off the engineering. They toured the military encampments around the town, the infrastructure maintaining thirty thousand troops and their horses and other animals. And, of course, they spent most of their time on the magnificent sea-wall itself, doing a walking inspection, discussing its design, maintenance, and so forth. For an instrument whose main purpose was to inflict extraordinary misery, Descartes admitted, it really was a thing of extraordinary beauty.

There was much to talk about that night in the tavern, and not just the engineering.

Word had just come that La Rochelle was to surrender in the morning.

On Saturday October 28, 1628, at 7 AM sharp, the last major Protestant town in France finally fell.

The fourteen-month siege was over.

Descartes had remained awake all night since that was easier than getting up so early, as Villebressieu confirmed by sleeping through the whole thing. So Descartes was there without his friend when Acting Mayor Guitton—the Mayor had died of starvation several weeks before—opened the gates of the town and allowed His Majesty's generals in.

Descartes was there for this major turning point, downward, for the future of French Protestants. For this downward turning point for personal and religious liberty in France. For this downward turn for the residents of La Rochelle, or those who were left. They began some twenty-seven thousand strong. Fourteen months later maybe two thousand remained.

Descartes entered the town some time after the

generals, when some of the bolder tourists figured it was time to get their money's worth.

Most of the buildings were in ruin, having succumbed to the artillery barrages, been torn apart for firewood during the winter, or just fallen apart during those long fourteen months. Descartes was sickened at the destruction, at the waste of human enterprise, at the futility of building things that were only to be destroyed.

But he was even more deeply sickened by the corpses.

Piles of them, everywhere.

And he was most deeply sickened by the survivors. Hollow-eyed skeletons, sore-infested skins wrapped tightly around the bones, most too weak to move, to stand up, looking like the corpses they were soon to become. With one or two of these living dead he made eye contact, but the suffering he saw therein was so intense that he had to look away. Not a single one was wearing shoes, despite the filth everywhere and the growing chill of the late fall weather.

They had long ago eaten the leather.

He lingered long enough to witness documents being signed to confirm the surrender. He lingered long enough to hear the Royal General proclaim to Acting Mayor Guitton, after the barely living skeleton had signed the document, "Though you no doubt shall soon pass from this earth there is still time to obtain eternal salvation through the true faith. On the authority of His Eminence Cardinal Bérulle, we have sent for the priests for your conversion." He was just leaving the town as the Royal soldiers were entering with horses pulling large carts, ready to begin loading first the corpses of the children for transport to mass burial places.

Descartes did not return to Villebressieu's lovely home that evening.

Instead he spent the night outside the encampments, in the woods, sobbing like a baby. By dawn he had obtained a horse, retrieved his notebook and papers without waking his friend, left a note for him and another to be posted to Mersenne, and set off toward the northeast.

Toward Paris, but not *to* Paris.

He was escaping to the United Provinces, where he was to live for the next twenty years.

32
THURSDAY,
FEBRUARY 14, 1650
STOCKHOLM, SWEDEN

Running, snow, dark, the warren. Baillet stumbling hard through falling flakes, trying to follow the flapping cloak, to keep pace with the long stomping legs of the nervous mathematician.

And with the man's mutterings as well.

"Of course, of course," Roberval was mumbling. In the bobbing lantern light the man's face looked moon-like. "First ship. First ship."

"Control yourself, man!" Baillet exhaled, almost running, breathing hard.

"Danger. You, too, Père. Get out now."

"What are you—"

"The mathematics, you fool!"

"The mathematics?"

"You don't understand. Bramer. The compasses. He stole it from me."

"Now Bramer stole from you too?"

Roberval stopped stomping. In the lantern light his eyes were darting, feverish. Baillet used the pause to gulp in some frozen air.

"Père, listen. Those compasses were based on Cartesian geometry, were they not?"

"I'll say yes?"

"No, Père. *Robervalian* geometry."

"The material Descartes stole from you?"

"Exactly."

"But didn't you say Descartes published that material? With some additions, or something?"

"I did."

"So why couldn't Bramer have gotten it from there?"

Roberval huffed, impatient, nervous, afraid. "Descartes changed the notation. He used an algebraic notation, for no good reason except that it was his own. My work was expressed in a far superior notation. More flexible. Clearer. Mine lays the groundwork for the infinite—"

Two drunken men popped around the corner, singing in slurred Swedish. Roberval's entire body froze, prepared to spring away. But the men stumbled past them, singing, without noticing them.

"So?" Baillet asked, having used the pause to attempt, in vain, to figure out what Roberval was talking about.

"Don't you see?"

"What?"

"*Bramer was using my notation.*"

"So—"

"So he must have known Descartes. They were in on it together!"

"But—in on what? Why?" Baillet's mind was racing. Hadn't Bramer said on the ship that he had never met the philosopher?

The falling snow intensified with Roberval's panic. "I told you Descartes was not what people thought. That he had an affiliation with German mathematics, all makes sense now. Those missing years, between La Flèche and Paris. The Protestant connection too, the Rosicrucian rumors. That his work—*my* work—might be at the base of the most powerful military engineering in history—"

"Professor. I don't quite follow. You are suggesting—"

"We're not safe here, Père," Roberval glanced in all directions before taking off in one of them.

Baillet set after him attempting, again, to keep pace with the man. "But—why?" he said loudly, from behind him. "Even if what you say is true?"

"Someone murdered Descartes on account of the mathematics," Roberval answered without turning around, accelerating. "And his brother. He was looking, too. For the notebook."

"But that isn't right. He was interested in—"

"And Bramer!"

"What?"

"That lecture tonight. That was for my benefit. He knew that only I would understand its meaning. It was a sign. A warning. A—" Roberval stopped for a moment, sweat glistening on his round face despite the cold. "*Trust no one,*" he muttered hoarsely, then turned and disappeared around the corner.

He was gone.

So Bramer knew Descartes, Baillet thought, standing at the corner looking down the deserted snow-filled street, catching his breath. Why would he have lied about that? And his keen interest in Descartes's papers. That had struck Baillet as odd but now perhaps made sense. The missing notebook. With some secret mathematics that somebody desperately wanted to get their hands on.

Enough, possibly, to commit murder.

Two murders.

What role could Bramer have had in any of this?

Bramer, who had told him to disregard Roberval. Who had lied about knowing Descartes. Who wanted Descartes's papers. Who kept popping up wherever Baillet went.

And who was strangely adept with a folding gully.

33

*W*ell that wasn't so hard, Baillet thought. He had just found his way out of the maze behind the Castle and emerged onto the lovely lamp-lit Slottskajen. It suddenly occurred to him that he hadn't seen the vagabond for a while.

He took a breath and turned to look behind him.

Snow, people, the Castle.

All this talk of danger and of murder was rattling his nerves.

He turned back around and made his way onto the Norrbro, headed back to his rooms. Fifteen minutes later he was at the outside door to the rooming house. He tried the handle and was not surprised to find it unlocked. He took a deep breath and climbed the stairs as quietly as he could, avoiding the steps that creaked. At the top he gently touched the doorknob to his flat, gently turned it, without resistance.

He was not surprised that it was unlocked.

Someone was in there.

Again.

Forget the landlady, with her shoulders the breadth of an ox, her rolling pin the size of Schlüter's plank, her mustache comparable to the Ambassador's.

Baillet could handle this himself.

"Sweet Mary," he whispered as he pushed the door open and burst inside.

Dark.

He fumbled with his tinder and flint, lit a candle, a small cone of light.

Nothing.

The sitting room was fine, empty, in order. He walked through the flat, the cooking area, the bedroom. All was fine, empty, quiet.

Hm, he wondered.

Maybe he had left it unlocked. Certainly possible, with all the distractions, the suspicions, the murders.

He was *so* tired. He would worry about it all in the morning. How delicious it was to undress, slip under the quilt. He had been up since four this morning again, on the move, battling the snow, the suspects. Thirty seconds under the quilt and he was drowsy, trying not to think about the wires on the Chancellor's new rack pulling tight, slowly wrenching arms and legs from their sockets with the snap of the tendons ...

He heard a noise out front.

Someone was inside his flat.

Again.

The moments ticked by.

Nothing. Quiet.

The element of surprise, he reminded himself. He slipped out from the quilt, retrieved his tinder and flint, a candle.

Then with a quick breath he opened his bedroom door and burst into the sitting room.

"You again!" he exclaimed when he saw the small boy standing there, dripping from melted snow.

"Message for you, sir," the boy said in that little voice, offering a slip of paper.

"Yes, yes, child—" Baillet started to reach for it, but then his eye fell on a small bundle on the table next to the chair. "Is that for me as well?"

"I wouldn't know, sir."

"All right, child, then, thank you," Baillet took the note from the boy, who immediately dashed out the door.

Baillet gazed at the damp slip of paper in his hand. He sat down in the chair, rested his candle on the table, just as the pendulum clock struck the quarter-hour: 11:15 PM, he realized with regret at the lateness of the hour. Well, at least he was just minutes away from burying himself again beneath his quilt. He brought the note under the candlelight, deciphered the old man's scrawl.

Retrieved information, per your request.

Five bells too dangerous. Come half past four instead. F.

Then: *P.S. Destroy this note immediately!*

Baillet groaned. And then he remembered the bundle on the table. Someone else had been here, he thought, his stomach tightening. It was very light, he realized, picking it up. A piece of cloth, something in it. Small and hard, he felt through the cloth. He brought it next to the candle and unwrapped it. Two, three folds and something small and hard fell from the cloth onto the table.

A human finger, the blood dried around its severed edge.

It was sporting something Baillet instantly recognized. The ring with the patrimonial seal of the family *Descartes* on it.

Pierre's ring.

34
FRIDAY, FEBRUARY 15, 1650

Riddarholm was just ringing the half-hour when an exhausted Baillet knocked on the door of the Royal Library. A horrid (and brief) night suffering a frenetic mix of all his awful dreams. He was in a tunnel, crawling, struggling to breathe when his lantern went out, leaving him in darkness, paralyzed. But then it was a coffin, he was in *the* coffin, stuffed in with another body, when something sharp, a sword, thrust in, between him and the body, just missing. He screamed silently, opened his mouth as to scream, screaming as he did back at La Flèche, when those other boys would beat him and call him names, shaggy-haired gallinipper, sausage muncher, son of a—of a whore. He was *not*—that, he knew that, he knew it in his bones, though he knew nothing of his mother. Rector Charlet had said something once, gently applying warm cataplasms to his bruises, that the boy, Descartes's boy, *was*—that, that the Rector had saved him from that life. But into what? To die at the hands of his master, Descartes? A gentleman bully like the rest of them? In his dream Descartes was beating *him*, beating Baillet, until Rector Charlet burst in to rescue him ...

"Out with it already!" Baillet sputtered once more seated in the Queen's Study. "What did you learn about Père Viogué?"

Freinsheimus sat across gazing at him, meaningfully, a sparkle in his ancient eyes. "I think you'll be *very* pleased, Jesuit. I was researching your man, and then did some more research on my own. *Very* interesting material. *Dangerous* material, Jesuit."

"Just tell me! There's no one here!"

The old man's eyes darted around the empty room. Then he reached beneath his shirt and withdrew a stack of papers.

Baillet reached for them.

"I don't think so," Freinsheimus pulled them back.

"What? Why?"

"The public may only handle materials in Her Majesty's Public Reading Room."

"I can't just read them right here?"

"In the Queen's Study? Ha! Follow me, Jesuit."

Baillet sighed. Freinsheimus led him between some long tall shelves stuffed with yellowed manuscripts, then down another dark corridor to another door. They emerged into a large square room containing nothing except three chairs and a candelabra on a stand.

"Her Majesty's Public Reading Room," Freinsheimus proclaimed.

"Am I supposed to read all those papers here? Can't I take them somewhere more—comfortable?" Not only were there no cushions on the chairs but there was no stove either, and his teeth were already chattering.

"Really, Jesuit, what could be more pleasant than Her Majesty's Public Reading Room? The light here is truly superb."

Baillet looked at the large glass window, outside of which it was entirely dark.

"Once the sun rises," Freinsheimus explained.

Baillet reluctantly sat down in a chair, pulling his greatcoat around him.

He looked at Freinsheimus and opened his hands expectantly.

Freinsheimus gave him a meaningful look. "Are you ready for danger, Jesuit?"

Baillet nodded.

Baillet had been so busy suspecting Bramer the whole past night that he'd completely forgotten about Père Viogué.

The Librarian had done his work well.

There were communiqués from Rome, papal announcements, concerning Père Viogué's career leading up to Stockholm. From his earliest years he was an aggressive member of the Papist Congregation known as "Propaganda of the Faith." He served as a missionary, sent to the New World to convert heathens and all over Europe to convert the Protestants. He became legendary for his success, where success was measured via the ratio between how many souls you saved and how many you had to put to death. There were some setbacks, of course; in one report Viogué complained of ill treatment in the United Provinces at the hands of one miserable wretch of a minister named Voetius, who for some reason kept calling him a "dog." But these were exceptions, and his overall success in converting sovereigns led to his current appointment in Stockholm, as the Apostolic Emissary to the Northern Lands, where the ruling sovereign was rumored to be unsteady in her faith.

Next in the stack were some essays, pamphlets, and sermons that Viogué had composed over the past few years. If the first documents showed that Viogué was a Catholic to be reckoned with, this second set showed something else.

Père Viogué despised René Descartes.

There were attacks on Descartes's "new philosophy"

for its inconsistency with Christian dogma, citing many passages in the philosopher's writings. In one pamphlet Viogué argued that Descartes's obsession with the study of nature amounted to atheism. There was harsh criticism of Descartes's skepticism and emphasis on reason, both of which also suggested the rejection of faith. There was a vicious critique of Descartes's philosophical account of the Eucharist, which Viogué claimed was pure capitulation to Protestant heresy. All this confirmed, Viogué wrote, that Descartes was either an atheist, or, worse, a Protestant. There was a memo Viogué had written to the Chancellor, urging him to rescind Descartes's invitation to Sweden. There was a letter Viogué wrote about how something had affected Descartes's religious outlook during the wars, how Descartes abandoned Catholic France to live in the Protestant United Provinces. Baillet shuffled back to look again at the first sheet of this letter. When he saw the scrawled salutation he gasped.

It was addressed to one miserable wretch of a (former) minister named Voetius.

Viogué and Voetius, Baillet thought, breathing fast. History there.

But more importantly—what must have gone through Viogué's head, when he learned that Her Majesty had invited Descartes to become her philosopher? Not merely would Viogué now be in close contact with a man he had long despised but he must have been alarmed that Descartes—the secret atheist, or perhaps Protestant— would obstruct his mission to convert the Queen.

It was all coming together.

Viogué had lied to him. He had said Descartes's was a pure Catholic soul. That he was unfamiliar with Descartes's writings. That he was glad to hear of Descartes's invitation to Stockholm. That he had— provided Descartes with the last rites, even though Wullens insisted that Viogué refused to.

So Freinsheimus, that fool, had hit on some truth after

all. Someone *was* trying to prevent Descartes's influence on the Queen, but it wasn't a Protestant defending the Queen's Protestantism. It was a Catholic resisting the anti-Catholic philosopher.

A Catholic priest who on two occasions slipped communion wafers into the doomed man's mouth.

Whose name Descartes had whispered to the Ambassador on the last morning of his life.

Baillet leaned his elbows on his knees, on top of the unread papers remaining there, trying to recover his equilibrium. On the floor next to him were the carefully piled papers he had already read. Containing his—case. His stomach was upset, turbulent. He found himself sweating, overheated, despite the chilly draft penetrating the window.

The window outside of which stood a man in the darkness looking in, watching Baillet's every reaction and expression inside.

Baillet sensed a presence and looked up.

Nothing but darkness outside. He was *really* becoming paranoid. He found himself thinking of Descartes's body now under the frozen ground of that little children's cemetery. He wondered how long it took a body to decompose in this frozen wasteland. He thought of the boy, the missing boy, who had left Charlet's home with Descartes all those years ago and vanished, maybe somewhere in Germany in 1619 or 1620. He wondered how long it took for the boy's body to decompose, in whatever ground it had been buried. If it *was* buried. With these thoughts weighing on him he took the letter from Viogué and placed it on the pile of already read documents on the floor beside him.

He turned to the next document on his lap.

The door to the room flew open.

35

Baillet sprinted down the hall, found the door, rushed outside into the pre-dawn darkness. He raced down the path, stumbled in the dark, regained his footing, continued through the snow. At the end of the path he stopped to catch his breath, calm his pounding heart, gaze down at the lamp-lit street. He had a few minutes to recover, he realized. By the time the old man made it all the way back out to pursue him Baillet would be out of range.

His heart didn't quite slow, however, as he caught his breath. He'd never stolen anything before, and he had to admit, it was—exciting. He slipped his hand inside his greatcoat, felt the papers stashed beneath his cassock.

Only what now?

The Librarian had startled him in the Reading Room. But Freinsheimus had given him no choice. Baillet had not yet read all the documents, and he could not wait until tomorrow morning to come back, as the old man insisted. Baillet congratulated himself on slipping the unread papers inside his cassock before leaving the room. He was so busy pulling off his little trick that it hadn't occurred to him to ask what Freinsheimus meant with that mysterious comment: "They really *are* everywhere, are they not?" He was glad to leave the room, however. He had gotten another—*vibe* from the window the moment before, and the place was starting to feel creepy.

But what now?

Walking down Slottskajen he scrounged his brain for somewhere to go. What he needed was somewhere to read through the rest of the stolen papers. Returning to his flat, where little boys broke and entered, where psychotic vagabonds lingered, where severed body parts were left to terrorize him, did not appeal. Try to find Bramer's flat perhaps? No, that was somewhere in the warren behind the Castle. And right—Bramer was no more to be trusted than anyone else here.

He suddenly found himself on the verge of weeping again. He had never exactly had many friends in his life. But now he was stranded in this dreadful place without a single friend and, quite possibly, with a whole host of enemies.

Was that another—crunch in the snow?

He spun around to look down the street back toward the Library. Nothing, nobody.

Père Viogué.

He had to read more.

A safe, quiet place to read.

He stood in the light flurries now falling, beneath a streetlamp light, at the foot of the Norrbro.

He looked around. He turned back to the Norrbro. Then he glanced down to the side, to the dark expanse of Helgeandsholmen below, speckled with a few lights.

The Museum of Curiosities.

There were lights. It was supposed to be open. It was likely to be heated. And at this awful hour it was likely to be relatively deserted.

There *was* another crunch in the snow behind him. But this one Baillet did not hear as he was already bounding down the steps from the Norrbro. The man with the long knife in his pocket waited a few moments before following him.

36

Rudolf II, Holy Roman Emperor until his death in 1612, was sexually attracted to almost everything that came near him. It was this relentless state of desire, he often said, that led him to become a collector. He was drawn to animals exotic and ordinary, flowers, scientific instruments, weapons; he pleasured himself in the presence of instruments of torture. He liked natural philosophy and natural philosophers, filling his court with astronomers, physicians, engineers. On any given day you might find Brahe or Kepler talking shop, Sinapius experimenting with embalming techniques, Bürgi tinkering with a grandfather clock. And then there were the arts, the artists themselves. Rudolf spent vast sums acquiring masterpieces, by Dürer, Brueghel. He could stare for hours at paintings and sculptures, and at the painters and sculptors creating them, who were required by their commissions to do so in the nude. And no, he insisted against the slanders, he was *not* homosexual: he merely liked to look at naked men painting pictures of naked men, and sometimes have intercourse with them.

History would list many achievements after Rudolf's

name. But it was his *Wunderkammer*—his collection of items of natural history and natural philosophy, ethnology, religious and historical relics, antiquities, the occult, jewelry, and art—that caught the attention of Ebba Sparre, whose nightly nudgings in turn caught the attention of Her Majesty Queen Christina, whose inexhaustible need to please her *Belle* then caught the attention of Her Majesty's Chancellor Zolindius.

The Thirty Years War was nearly over by the summer of 1648, but there was one last item of business before the treaties were signed. Under Zolindius's orders the Swedish negotiators dithered while their troops approached Prague, the city that had started it all with the defenestration of 1618. They swiftly collected the Hradčany Castle itself. Rudolf's *Wunderkammer*, stored in the Castle, was already on barges to Sweden when the signatures finally ended the bloodshed.

None of this was on Baillet's mind as he stood before the gargoyled columns at the entrance to the Museum of Curiosities. It was dark and it was cold and Baillet had terror in his heart and a severed finger on his mind. The Museum was indeed open, and appeared to be deserted.

A glance around—he could see no one—and he pulled open the door and went inside.

The first thing he saw in the central foyer was a large statue of two naked men doing something he did not look long enough to figure out. He averted his gaze, chose one of the narrow halls leading from the foyer, plunged down it. It was uncomfortably narrow and dark, lit only by scattered sconces. Baillet felt himself sweating in the tight space. Fortunately the hallway soon led to a medium-sized room; unfortunately from this room departed only more narrow dark hallways. The narrow halls he soon learned led to rooms of various sizes. He also learned that there were *things* everywhere. Objects on the walls, in cases, on stands, or on the floor. The art was mostly erotic, he uneasily observed via sideways glances. There were also many scientific instruments with placards describing them. One small room featured a mechanized globe of some sort. Another contained a glass display case, inside of which was the famous Voynich manuscript, or so said the placard. Baillet might have paused to learn exactly what this was but the small room and dim light were suffocating. Taking a deep breath he plunged down another narrow hallway and finally came into a large room with a window, that was fairly well lit.

It also contained several bodies.

Or parts thereof.

In the center of the room on a pedestal was the jeweled gold crown Rudolf had had made for his reign. Directly beneath the crown was the perfectly preserved head of Emperor Rudolf himself, its heavy-lidded eyes, long nose and lip-licking tongue gazing salaciously to perpetuity thanks to the embalming wizardry of Sinapius.

On one of the walls nearby hung the head of former Swedish Chancellor Axel Oxenstierna. The great diplomat looked almost alive, except for the grossly swollen black tongue that no one could stuff back into his mouth. The placard beside it made no mention of his alleged assassination at the hands of the current Chancellor Zolindius.

Zolindius *was* mentioned, however, on the opposing wall of the room. Here in rows were the heads of the many enemies of state—the traitors, the heretics, the beggars, the Rosicrucians—whose treachery had been terminated by the justice-loving Chancellor. After their brief stint on the Norrbro spikes the most significant of these heads made their way to these prestigious spikes. With a turn of his stomach Baillet saw there were a half-dozen more empty rows beneath these heads, awaiting future occupants.

Catching his breath Baillet looked around. His choices were to plunge down another dark narrow hallway or to stay here. He had wasted enough time already getting himself lost in this place. And at least the room was spacious, and the light was decent.

With a last glance up at the Emperor's crowned head he withdrew the papers from his cassock, sat down and leaned against the pedestal, and began to read.

Freinsheimus *had* done his work well.

These were not more papers of Viogué's, as Baillet had expected. Instead they were documents in French and Latin about the Brotherhood of the Rosy Cross. Had Viogué turned out to be a Rosicrucian? He skimmed through the strange titles. There were primary sources, translations, commentaries, but all were written in allegorical language he could barely make sense of. There was the *Fama Fraternitatis R.C.*, apparently a founding document of the group. There was a copy of *The Chymical Wedding of Christian Rosenkreutz*, which as far as Baillet could see was a poorly-written account of a badly run wedding party. Baillet was just starting to feel frustrated when he came upon a document entitled *Confessio Fraternitatis* and suddenly remembered something.

The word *confessio*.

Something Schlüter had said. Descartes wanting to confess during the week of his illness, but the sick man had muttered in Latin. *Confessio*. It was Viogué who insisted that Descartes was calling for confession. Viogué who apparently had an interest in getting Descartes to take the sacraments, to take communion. But what if—Descartes had been referring to this Rosicrucian text?

Baillet returned to the papers with renewed excitement.

The next sheets seemed to be scientific in character. Skimming through he saw discussions of the laws of nature, of alchemy, and so on. One section called "The Method" caught his eye, recalling Descartes's *Discourse on Method*, which Roberval had claimed was partly stolen from him. There were rules here for how to study nature, how to enter the College of the Invisibles, how to comport oneself. The Brethren were aiming to mathematize their knowledge of nature and design powerful new scientific instruments. They were to abide not only by the *Fama Fraternitatis R.C.* principles of healing the sick and remaining secret, but also to adopt the clothing and customs of the country they inhabited, and to employ the letters R.C. as their seal and mark.

Those letters, Baillet thought.

The first page, the cover page, of Descartes's missing notebook.

Offered afresh to learned men throughout the world and especially to G. F. R. C.

Descartes had spent important time in Germany. Something happened to him there in 1619 or 1620, something that changed him. The Rosicrucians were founded in Germany, before emigrating outward. The most prominent group would have been the German one—the German Fraternity of the Rosy Cross.

G. F. R. C.

The crazy Librarian was right after all, with his obsession with the secret group. Descartes *was* a Rosicrucian. Or at least influenced by them. And if Viogué knew this, then all the greater would be his need to eliminate the philosopher.

Baillet felt light-headed. The exhaustion. The weather. All these embalmed heads staring at him hardly eased his mind either.

But he forced himself to keep reading.

The next pages were filled with mathematical symbols. Baillet skimmed them to get a sense of their significance. He looked at page after page of symbols, foreign, strange. There were apparently connections between mathematics and mystical wisdom, this idea of mathematizing nature had ancient roots, mathematics and religions were not distinct pursuits, but the details, no time now to work them out. He was about to stop when several symbols looked familiar. He had seen them. Recently. The last few days were a blur, but definitely, recently, he had seen these symbols. Maybe it was—

Bramer.

The notation.

That Roberval claimed had been stolen from him by Descartes. That had been used by Bramer in his Gala lecture, just—last night.

Baillet's heart began to pound.

Feverishly he scrolled back through the pages he'd been reading.

To the first page of the essay.

He hadn't even noticed.

The author's name.

He scrolled back through the other documents.

All of them. The translations, the commentaries.

By the same author.

Benjamin Bramer.

Who was clearly then a Rosicrucian.

Who was intimately familiar with Descartes's mathematics and natural philosophy. Who was almost surely, as Roberval alleged, a close acquaintance of Descartes himself.

Who had a thing for severing digits, Baillet recalled the episode on the ship.

And who had repeatedly lied to a naïve novice investigator he pretended to befriend.

Just then Baillet heard a sound down one of the narrow hallways leading to the room.

He stopped breathing. He tried to still the pounding of his heart.

There it was again.

A footstep.

Coming his way.

37

Baillet grabbed his papers then darted down the nearest dark hallway. Then wished he hadn't, because this was the narrowest hallway yet and he felt the panic from the walls closing in build on to the panic from the footsteps. He stopped moving, leaned against the wall, trying to listen. All he could hear was his own rapid breathing, which seemed to be echoing through the building.

Then another quiet footstep somewhere behind him.

He pushed on, his own steps thundering.

He emerged into a room containing alchemical artifacts. There were beakers and flasks and long tubes of glass and devices maybe for heating. A display case with metals in it, lead, silver, gold. There was also a knife of half steel, half gold, with a slightly curved blade attached to a mother of pearl sheath. Wasn't that a—gully, like Bramer's knife?

The steps were coming after him, louder now, quicker.

He darted down another hallway, narrower, darker still. He paused again, leaned against the wall in the shadows, listened. There were five hallways leading from the alchemy room, it seemed wise to remain quiet and see whether his pursuer might take one of the others. His murderer—for surely this was his murderer—had entered the alchemy room. The footsteps paused down there. They slowly started again. His murderer was stopping at the end of each hallway, looking down the darkness, listening for footsteps, for breathing. His murderer was now at the end of *this* hallway, listening for *his* footsteps, his breathing, his pounding heart. Be still, be still, Baillet urged each of these, counting each long moment until his fatal destiny arrived.

But then—his murderer moved on.

Baillet exhaled a sigh of relief.

Mistake. His murderer must have heard it.

He was now coming back to this hallway.

Baillet took off, ran through another room, heard his murderer running behind him. He darted down another hallway, another warren, he realized, he had no idea where he was or how to get out, more panic adding to all the rest. He passed through an enormous room devoted to instruments of torture. There was the large wheel on which the victim would be tied, then spun, as hammers broke all his bones in turn. The curved iron saw, whose ragged metal teeth slowly cut through the skull as it slid back and forth over the victim's head. The Breast Shredder, whose functionality was all too easy to discern. In the center of the room was a rack, a prototype of the new rack the Chancellor had boasted about. Baillet was proud of himself for not vomiting as he dashed through this room though by now he was weeping, giving away his location with each half-stifled sob.

The steps were coming louder, faster, behind him.

There were four hallways leading from this room. He chose one at random and darted down. The narrowest yet. Unlit. He felt his chest constrict as he restrained his weeping and began sliding sideways along the wall to fit through. Maybe ten paces down he came upon a deep narrow depression in the wall. He squeezed into it, realizing that this was both an ideal hiding spot and the smallest space he had ever been crushed into. It was pitch dark. Suffocating. He stopped breathing. He must have, that was the only explanation for his silence. For he surely was not capable of breathing when he felt as if he were buried alive, under the earth, in his own grave.

All was still.

In the silence he heard his murderer again down the hallway, in the torture room. The footsteps were moving, trying to decide which hallway to pursue. Once more they came to the end of his hallway, *his* hallway.

Was that—were those—steps coming this way, down this hallway?

Baillet found himself silently—praying.

The memory, the image, in that closet his mother suffocating him as the soldiers were about to fling open the door—

Then all *was* still.

There were voices.

Familiar voices.

"Would you look at that?" an Italian-accented French proclaimed.

"Magnificent!" another replied.

Baillet slowly emerged from his crevice back into the hallway, allowed himself to breathe a little again, then crept down toward the room.

"It says here," the monocle was reading the placard, "that the point of the spear would be inserted into the anus or vagina, and then they would slowly force the criminal down upon it over the course of many hours or even days. They called it the Judas Cradle."

"Such genius you *rarely* see anymore," the spectacles admired.

"Excuse me," Baillet said as he emerged from the hallway.

"Dear Lord! Don't startle us like that!" the monocle blurted.

"You look like death, my good man!" the spectacles

exclaimed. "Are you all right?"

"I'm sorry," Baillet answered, recovering his breath. "I'm all right, thank you. I'm wondering if you might—do you think you might guide me to the exit?"

"You seem to need help finding your way around a lot, eh, Père?" the spectacles chortled.

"Well," the monocle pointed out, "I suppose it *is* about time for the breakfast. I hear they are serving pasties from the animal combat the other day."

Outside, the freezing air was for once refreshing, after the sweat-producing heat Baillet had just endured. Breakfast didn't interest him, not even the lion pasties his rescuers were so enthused about. "Rescuers," really, he thought as he ascended the steps to the Norrbro. Perhaps that was a little dramatic. He didn't actually know that the person in the Museum was his *murderer*, now did he?

He had to stop letting his imagination get away with him and—

What. Be a *man*.

Maybe he should get a weapon.

Speaking of, this Bramer business.

It was time for decisive action. The Gala was to end tonight, and if he was to resolve anything about this case then the time was now.

It was a little before 7:00 AM. Bramer was an early riser, he knew. He would go find the man's rooms, confront him. Clarify the lies. If he was involved in some way, then find out for sure. If not, then Baillet could use his advice.

And if Bramer were not in his rooms?

Baillet softly smiled. If he were ever going to become a real investigator then now *was* the time. He had already crossed a line by stealing those documents from the Royal Librarian.

Perhaps it was time to do a little breaking and entering of his own.

With a slightly greater skip in his step Baillet turned

right onto Slottskajen in front of the Castle and headed back to the streets behind.

The man with the knife in his pocket, about fifty paces behind him, followed suit.

38

Baillet's gloved hand reached for the doorknob to the building Bramer had pointed out two mornings before. He gripped the knob. It turned. He took another look up and down the street, saw no one. He stepped inside and closed the door behind him.

There was a hallway before him, and at the end a staircase, like his own lodgings. There were doors on opposite sides of the hallway. Baillet tread as softly as his boots on the wood floor would allow.

The board right before the staircase creaked.

Baillet stopped, listened to his heart beating.

Then he began to ascend the staircase.

Creak after creak, each a small stab in his heart.

And then he stood before Bramer's door.

He listened at the door. All he could hear was his own breathing. He briefly thought about retreating, returning to his rooms, maybe for a few days. Then he thought about Descartes being poisoned in his own bed. And the boy who had disappeared with Descartes. And about being a man. He took a quick breath and tapped lightly on the door.

No answer.

He reached for the knob, turned.

It was locked.

Thank you, he whispered.

But then he thought: no. The world had bestowed upon him an opportunity to do something meaningful. Discover the truth. Achieve—justice, maybe.

But what did he know about breaking into flats?

Nobody seemed to have trouble entering *his* rooms, he thought. But then maybe Baillet had neglected to lock his doors, he being that sort. How many times had the Rector reproached him, for leaving the house and leaving the doors unlocked behind him? There was that one time—

No, stay focused.

Keys.

He removed his gloves and felt in his greatcoat pocket. The keys to his flat were there, tangled with the yellow band.

It was absurd to imagine that his key would fit Bramer's door. But then again it was absurd that he was here in the first place. And what was the alternative, he thought as he slipped the key into the hole—that he should try to force the door physically?

It turned.

Shocked, Baillet entered.

Unlike his own rooms Bramer's already appeared well lived in. But that made sense, since Bramer, a member-elect, had come to settle in permanently. Perhaps the Chancellor had furnished the place. Baillet had no idea where to begin searching. In fact he had no idea what he was searching for.

Stay focused, he thought.

Bramer was a Rosicrucian; knew Descartes; mathematics; had been lying to him. Documents maybe, something that would help Baillet understand what Bramer's role in all this was.

Or whether he was on Baillet's side or against it.

He could be working for the Chancellor, could he not? Zolindius wanted to be kept informed about Baillet's investigation, to suppress scandal. Wouldn't it be useful for him to have an inside man to keep track of what was going on?

Must be quick, Baillet thought as he began sorting through some documents on the desk.

But he was not quick enough.

A man with a knife was coming up the stairs.

The man was ascending more quietly than Baillet had, but he had the advantage of already knowing that the third, fourth, and seventh steps creaked. Carefully stepping over them as he climbed, he stood outside the door and listened. He heard the noises that Baillet could not help making inside as he moved around, looked at things, shuffled through papers.

Quietly, carefully, the man removed his gloves. Then he took out his knife, felt its familiar grip in his hand, unsheathed it.

He opened the door.

Baillet's back was turned as he tried to make sense of the papers. Most were filled with mathematical symbols, incomprehensible. He was deliberating whether—now that he was an accomplished thief—he should slip these inside his cassock when a hand clamped over his mouth and something hard pressed into his back.

"Don't move," a voice growled behind him.

Not a problem, Baillet thought, over his pounding heart.

But then he found himself doing something he didn't know he could do, namely to simultaneously bite on the finger which ever so carelessly protruded into his mouth, turn sharply around toward his murderer, and ram his elbow into his attacker's face.

Equally simultaneous were the man's scream, the clattering of his knife to the floor, and his punching Baillet in his own face.

Baillet fell to the ground and the man was on top of him in an instant. Another instant later the man had him flat on his stomach on the floor in a painful headlock, had retrieved his knife, and pressed it into his throat exactly where Baillet's larynx protruded.

"Murder!" Baillet squeaked but this time, as a man, audibly, as he felt the knife pushing into his throat.

39
1629-1640
THE UNITED PROVINCES

The United Provinces had proved hospitable since Descartes's escape from Pierre and from Cardinal Bérulle three years earlier. He didn't completely escape Roberval however, since Mersenne strangely kept updating him on the man's career. But then again that had its advantages. Some well-placed nasty letters from the world's greatest mathematician could easily impede the world's biggest-headed mathematician. When Mersenne wrote in early 1632 that Roberval had unexpectedly been turned down for the prestigious Ramus Chair, in Paris, Descartes wrote back only "unexpected by whom"?

Descartes was not proud of himself; but he felt stung by Roberval's aggression against him, and threatened by the man's near *exposure* of him, and could not help himself. He might have occupied that Ramus Chair himself by now, he knew, but for the fact that he was now making his home one-hundred-and-fifty leagues to the northeast.

"But who needs Paris?" he had thought aloud one

afternoon, shortly after moving into his little house on Kalverstraat. He could do everything here in Amsterdam. He might even publish something. There were printers everywhere, and the censors only occasionally called for your head. He had plenty of money stored away in the Wisselbank, liberated from Joachim. He could move on a whim, whenever he felt restless or threatened. (Over the next two decades he would live in a dozen different towns and residences.) He could communicate with anyone he wished, through Mersenne; and avoid communication with anyone he didn't wish, since only Mersenne knew his address.

And he was doing some wonderful work! His dioptrics, his meteorology, his work on the universal science of nature, all made advances. For his biological research Amsterdam provided plentiful carcasses to dissect and rats and rabbits to vivisect, not to mention the occasional stray dog—though for the latter he had to force himself to ignore their agonized howls as he cut them open, firmly believing by this point that animals are not sentient. And when he was done working—or needed to recover from vivisecting—he would head out into the streets and explore.

The rest of Europe was awash in war but this great city was flourishing. Daily the news came in of the military advances of the Lion of the North, Swedish King Gustavus Adolphus, against the Catholic Empire. This news came in on the ships arriving in Amsterdam's harbor and fueling the city's economic and cultural explosion, which was present everywhere. On the Nieuwe Brug were the prospering bookshops, stationers, and purveyors in nautical goods. At the bustling wharf area Descartes would watch the ships unloading the colorful crates of Malacca pepper and cloves, the sappan wood, the Japanese porcelain. Afterward he might stroll down the Warmoesstraat to the storefronts displaying the fabrics and fine furnishings, the Spanish taffeta, and the Haarlem linen bleached immaculately white.

Not that he wanted any of these things (except perhaps the taffeta, his one weakness). He just liked to look. To look and to think. And then to make his way, early in the evening, back to the small house on the Kalverstraat. He would eat a meal of some root vegetable with a chunk of hard cheese, then light a candle and settle in for another evening of dioptrics or meteorology.

Who needs Paris, he thought, looking around the nearly empty house and wondering what was missing.

They may not be sentient, he thought, but maybe he should get a pet.

For a man who wanted to be alone and well hidden, Descartes did not long remain either.

First he got himself a dog. Though the powerful Dutch preachers were strangely averse to dogs he solved that problem by remaining averse to the preachers. He chose a handsome Kooiker he named Kosmos, a good dog with a loving, happy character whose ability to catch rodents for his master's anatomical studies was a bonus.

And then there were the sentient animals.

He couldn't help himself, dealing with people again. He had tried in Paris, but then failed; perhaps this time, he thought, he could manage not to rub people the wrong way. There were some particular people he hoped to rub the right way. Compared to the cobwebby Catholic French universities the Dutch universities were more or less brand new. They hadn't yet become corrupt, Descartes wrote to Mersenne; there were whispers of the new philosophy, of Bacon, of Galileo, and soon (he hoped) of Descartes. But if that were to happen, he would have to do more than merely scribble his ideas in his notebook with Kosmos at his feet. He would have to get some professors acquainted with them.

That project—and his perpetual sense of threat—kept him moving between various residences. But by the early

1630s he could count several important figures among his acquaintances. Metius, geometer and astronomer at Franeker. Golius, orientalist and mathematician at Leiden. Huygens, poet, composer, and secretary to two successive *stadhouders*.

And Henry Reneri, the philosopher who in early 1632 invited Descartes to Deventer to teach Reneri his physics. The two men had many a pleasant afternoon breakfast that February and March debating motion, the laws of nature, and whether Descartes should violate his diet to taste the remarkable omelettes made by Reneri's servant girl.

"Just a taste, Monsieur," the good-natured Reneri urged. "For science."

"For science?"

"The girl won't tell me how she makes them. I am hoping you can work it out."

"I prefer not to eat flesh."

"But surely one bite won't hurt you. Just taste this." Reneri was holding up a goopy chunk of egg on his fork. "Well? Monsieur?"

For science indeed, Descartes thought. He needed Reneri: the man was enthused about Descartes's physics and preparing to lecture on it next term. Anyway, it *was* just one bite.

But what a bite.

"This *is* remarkable," Descartes said after finally swallowing. He had let the eggs linger on his tongue to study them. "What is that flavor?"

"She won't say."

"She won't say?"

"She snaps at me when I ask."

"You are rather lenient with your—servants, I gather?" For a moment he had an uneasy sensation, recalling his experience at Rector Charlet's all those years before and all that followed.

"Precisely. At least when I wish to keep them. Monsieur, I wonder whether *you* might be able to pry the secret from her?"

"Me? Why would she listen to me?"

"It can't hurt. We already know she does not listen to me."

Descartes was skeptical; but he needed the man.

In the kitchen, a few minutes later, the eighteen-year-old's arms were crossed over a bosom as buoyant as her eggs. "I am sorry, Mynheer, but I cannot say."

"You cannot say?" Descartes peered at her. This required him to look slightly upward, given their respective heights. "But why on earth not?"

"First rule of the kitchen. *De kok* keeps her secrets."

"But it is just a simple omelette!"

"Apparently," the girl said, returning his gaze, looking down at him along the length of her perfectly straight nose, "not, Mynheer."

They were a study in contrast. The girl was wearing a plain white servant's frock with thin stockings while Descartes wore his tailored taffeta suit, with silk hose over the warm wool ones he sported all winter long. His face was puffy, with bad skin and swollen bags under sleepless eyes; her skin was smooth and clean, her nose a perfect specimen, and she had a delicate little chin that seemed defiantly to say, "and you thought the nose was nice!" In short she was perhaps the rosiest-cheeked, blondest, and bounciest Dutch maiden that ever milked a cow, while he was a somber Frenchman in his mid-thirties, nearing the end of the average man's life expectancy.

With what breath still remained in him the Frenchman attempted to summon the anger he knew he was supposed to be feeling. Instead he just stared at her briefly and then made himself retreat. That evening Kosmos's tongue slobbered enthusiastically over the leftover omelette his master had brought him. His master sat gazing at that slobbering tongue a long time, thinking about the mechanical processes of digestion, the way the fine fluids he called *animal spirits* flowed through the nerves into the brain, and about how glad he was that he had held off tasting that omelette until the end of his stay in Deventer. If he weren't heading out to Leiden for the summer, he thought the next day, he wasn't sure he could control himself.

Everyone was busy over the next few years.

The Swedish King Gustavus Adolphus's military victories kept coming. These included the victory at Lützen over the Catholic armies of Wallenstein and Pappenheim, and over Pappenheim personally when a Swedish cannonball traveled directly through his face. King Gustavus celebrated this death for about twenty minutes, when a perfectly aimed Catholic bullet did the same to him. (Or so it was reported by previously unknown Swedish soldier Carolus Zolindius, who discovered the King's body in the woods and retrieved it at the cost of a serious leg injury.) This sudden demise left the monarch's six-year-old sexually ambiguous offspring, Christina, as the new monarch-in-waiting, left his ambitious Chancellor Axel Oxenstierna scheming around the court, and left nobody paying attention to Carolus Zolindius and his intimidating limp rising through the military and political ranks, despite (or perhaps because of) the growing rumors that he had himself assassinated His Majesty. With Sweden reeling, France's Richelieu saw that the anti-Habsburg, anti-Imperial cause needed some help. Once his intestinal tuberculosis was reined in, he planned to send French troops into Germany, or what was left of it after fifteen years of the conflict.

Speaking of Germany, it had been a long time since any letters had arrived from Eudoxus, via Mersenne.

Descartes preferred not to think about why.

What he was thinking about instead was *The World*. In this aptly named work he attempted to show how his mathematics could explain *everything*. He had been working on it for years, tinkering, polishing, thinking about it every time he passed the printers' shops on the Damstraat. Well, they were busy in Italy too, it turned out. Five days before Descartes finally entered a printer's shop with his manuscript in hand, the Inquisition in Rome convicted the great Galileo of promulgating nefarious cosmological beliefs—beliefs just like those defended in Descartes's own manuscript. When the news of Galileo's fate arrived in Amsterdam a week later, a man was seen running in a panic into the shop demanding they stop the presses, literally.

It was not until the fall of 1633 that Descartes was able to visit his friend Reneri again, in Deventer. He was eager to go: there were so many important matters to discuss, what with the devastation across Europe and the devastating news about Galileo.

"That new Hungarian spice that everyone is talking about, the *paparka*?" Descartes asked.

The girl, on her knees scrubbing out the open oven, did not look up. "Never heard of it, Mynheer."

"Sausage, then."

"Did you see any sausage, Mynheer?"

"Ground finely, invisible to the naked eye."

"What are naked eyes?" she asked, rolling her own.

"Never mind. The beating then. You must beat the eggs an exceptionally long time."

"I have no time to waste beating eggs!"

"An exceptionally short time, then."

"Mynheer!"

"What is it? What is the problem?"

"You're standing in soot," she said with irritation, sitting up. "You are going to soil my clean floor."

"Sorry!" Descartes stepped away, promptly planting two sootprints onto the kitchen floor she had just scrubbed. He grimaced. "Sorry!"

The girl looked at him, this strange little man with the ill-fitting green suit, his hose sporting two or three holes. "Perhaps you could wait in the parlor until my master returns, Mynheer?"

Descartes didn't move. His eyes wandered around the kitchen. Shelves lined with pots, pans, dishes along one wall, jars of jams, pastes, pickled vegetables, leading to the open doorway of the larder. From a circular rack on the ceiling hung a half-dozen geese and hares, waiting to be plucked or skinned for some university feast Reneri was about to host. The hatchet in the woodblock in the corner awaited some animal's head to detach. Two platters of herring were waiting to be fried.

On another long shelf were some books.

"*De Verstandige Kok of Zorgvuldige Huyshouder,*" Descartes read aloud. "*Schat der Gezontheyt.* Are these cookbooks? I am sorry, did you just laugh at me?"

"The way you speak, Mynheer. It is most amusing." The girl had returned to her oven on realizing the annoying Frenchman was not leaving.

"I apologize for my imperfect accent," Descartes answered stiffly.

"It isn't your accent, Mynheer. It is—the way you speak." There was something odd about it: so formal, those gently rolled r's.

"It is not the way one speaks. It is what one says that matters."

"What you say is amusing too."

"I am sorry?"

"*Are these cookbooks?*" she imitated.

"That is amusing?"

"No normal person could not know what these books are. Next you will be asking if *Het Leerzaam Huisraad* believes that Dutch women should keep their houses clean."

"Does *Het Leerzaam Huisraad,*" Descartes asked quietly, "believe that Dutch women should keep their houses clean?"

The girl stopped scrubbing. She looked at this funny little man again. According to her master he was a brilliant mathematician, decoding the secrets of the universe. But it looked to her, rather, that he could use some help getting dressed in the morning. His wig was not on straight, she noticed. And his complexion—what was that on his cheek?

She found herself feeling sorry for him.

"This is about the omelettes," she said.

He nodded.

"You really need to know?"

"If you would only be so kind," he whispered.

"All right, then. It's the eggs. They must be brooded either eight or ten days."

"Eight or ten?" he perked up. "Are you being precise, or just estimating?"

"Oh, very precise, Mynheer."

"But why not nine days?"

"God, no, Mynheer! Now go. My master wants this oven clean."

"But wait."

"What *is* it?"

"What," Descartes hesitated, "is your name?"

"My name?"

Descartes nodded, pale again.

The girl frowned. "Helena."

He looked at her a moment, then bowed and departed.

The plague wasn't *all* bad.

Between 1633 and 1635 the disease made several circuits around the Provinces. The obvious downside included all the suffering and death. But as it departed in early 1636 there was an unexpected upside: the resulting shortage of labor caused a dramatic increase in real wages. Suddenly nearly everyone had cash to spare and could get in on the blossoming tulip craze. Even the common Witte Croonen bulb might rise in price a dozen times a day, allowing a man to start the day a cutthroat, purchase a trade apprenticeship by noon, become a banker by supper, and retire for life before bed. That is to say nothing of the exotic bulbs, the Generalissimo, the Semper Augustus, which soon were worth more than there was minted money to actually buy them. The new economy needed new economics. New technologies were developed, in agriculture and horticulture. Dutch painters became *very* good at their craft at this time. There were just so many wealthy people to buy the paintings.

But not everyone enjoyed the party.

The *predikanten* could be a downer with their nasty sermons, their threatening placards, and the reproving looks they cast at everyone passing their way. But fortunately they were too busy arguing with each other to hamper the new economy. The Orthodox Calvinists and the more liberal Remonstrants were constantly at each other's throats. In the early 1630s the Orthodox leadership passed to Heusden *predikant* and definite party-pooper Gisbertus Voetius. Voetius was very excited to begin casting aspersions from his new position as Professor of Theology at the nascent University of Utrecht. This delightful, sharp-tongued man moved to Utrecht over the summer of 1634.

Also moving to Utrecht that summer was Descartes's friend Reneri, who was to become Professor of Philosophy at the new university. On hearing the news, Descartes made plans for he and Kosmos to move there, too, for a few months themselves.

"But why were you so keen to come?" Reneri asked him on his arrival, at the start of September.

"The astrologers are predicting a cold winter," Descartes explained, his eyes lowered, "and Utrecht should offer fine conditions for studying the formation of snow. For the essay on meteorology I am thinking of appending to my *Discourse*. When I finally publish."

"But you reject astrology."

"They still get it right sometimes."

"Ha! Then there is the matter of my disseminating your philosophy."

"That as well," Descartes said agreeably.

"Did you hear I had to dismiss my servant girl, Monsieur? For insolence. She apparently revealed the secret to her omelettes to one of my guests yet refused to tell me!"

Descartes suddenly flushed. "But, Reneri, I wonder whether that was perhaps—hasty."

"But you yourself criticized her disrespect, I recall."

"Yes, but that was before—"

"Before what?"

"Before I badgered her into revealing the secret to me."

"Not unlike the way that I," Reneri started to laugh, "have badgered you into revealing your secret to *me*, Monsieur?"

"My secret?" Descartes's flushed skin became pale.

"Your defense of a servant girl is quite gallant," Reneri was still laughing.

"Well," Descartes relaxed a bit, "it *was* for science, after all. I have spent the past year experimenting in chicken embryology."

"And?"

"My manservant's omelettes still stink. You did not really dismiss her, did you, Reneri?"

"Are you out of your mind? Of course not, Monsieur."

Then Descartes started to laugh, a hearty laugh in that thin chest of his. This was a lot for a man whose main joy in life was to think and who had spent nearly half of the now nearly forty years of that life being torn apart by his conflicting needs. And in fact he smiled often that fall, especially when he was at Reneri's house discussing natural philosophy, and *especially* when he was undertaking his side project of educating the servant girl, Helena Jans, a project Reneri proposed and Descartes was quick to accept. The twenty-year-old was bright, Reneri said, and she deserved better than to have to castrate roosters so he could enjoy his favorite trussed capon stuffed with chestnuts.

"She can't stand for them to suffer," Reneri explained.

"Is that right?" Descartes said thoughtfully.

"Would I lie to you?" Reneri burst back into laughter.

"You know," Descartes said one mid-September afternoon of 1634, after Reneri excused himself to prepare a lecture on Descartes's laws of motion, "that animals lack souls, Juffrouw."

They were seated at the kitchen table. The iron pots for the mutton *hutsepot* she had served her master for dinner were already washed, and drying on the rack. The smaller pot in which she had prepared her master's guest's version—substituting Edammer cheese for the mutton— was drying beside them. They were drinking tea spiced with clove. They had begun talking about some elementary geometry but had digressed to the topic of rooster squawking.

"But our religion teaches that, Mynheer," the girl replied.

"Yes but without souls they also lack sentience."

"What does that mean?"

"They do not think. They do not feel. They are merely complicated machines that respond mechanically to certain stimuli. The squawking means nothing."

"But I think. And I think they do. You can hardly have lived with a dog and believe that."

"Juffrouw, you cannot trust your immediate experience. You must contemplate all the facts and reason about them. The fact, for example, that no animal is capable of speaking a language. Why should that be, if animals are endowed with minds similar in nature to our own?"

"But animals do speak, Mynheer. We merely fail to understand them."

"That is preposterous."

"So you say, Mynheer. But perhaps you are so busy reasoning about your facts that you simply fail to observe other ones. The ones that are very clear. To the 'naked eye.' For example."

"For example?"

The girl hesitated. "Why do you keep coming here, Mynheer?"

"Why, Juffrouw?" Descartes answered as indignantly as he could. "To teach your master my physics!"

"But why do you really keep coming here, Mynheer?"

"Why?" he added with less bluster, "to teach *you* my physics, Juffrouw."

"But why do you *really* keep coming here?"

"Because," he answered softly, slowly, "you ask very good questions."

She stared back at him. "Perhaps you could even learn something from a mindless animal, if you paid the right attention. Mynheer."

"Frankly, Juffrouw, if you told me that the Chinese are born with only one eye I would believe that China is a land of Cyclops."

"I've known that for some time now. Mynheer. Ever since you believed that story about the eggs brooded for eight or ten days."

"I still believe it, Juffrouw, even though I have since refuted it a dozen times over in my laboratory."

"You flatter me. Mynheer."

"I have enough good sense, at least, to do that."

"But why? Mynheer."

"Because I must," Descartes answered. "Helena."

There was a long moment of silence, except for the part where Descartes began weeping.

"It is the tea," Helena said gently. "You should not have had the second cup."

"No," Descartes shook his head.

"Bontekoe says that too much tea can make you emotional," Helena pointed to her bookshelf. "It can also make your joints rattle. How do your joints feel?"

"Lousy."

"See!"

"But not because of the tea. Helena. Listen to me."

"No, thank you. You listen to me."

"What?"

"Are you done weeping?"

"For now." Descartes wiped his nose on a napkin.

"It is pickled whale's eye."

"What is?"

She stood up and grabbed an oversized jar from the shelf. "This is."

He could just make out a part of the enormous retina staring at him through the brine.

"You keep your ears open at the market," she continued. "When a whale washes up somewhere you move fast."

"You are talking about the omelettes?"

"I am, Mynheer. You won't start weeping again on me, will you?"

"You are mocking me."

"You do a fine job of that yourself, Mynheer."

There was another long silence as they looked at each other.

"Just to be clear," Descartes finally said. "Are you mocking my manner, or are you mocking me about the pickled whale's eye as well?"

"Only your manner, Mynheer. I am giving you the secret ingredient for my omelettes. Are you—weeping again?"

Descartes nodded.

"But I don't understand. Have I not given you what you want? Mynheer?"

"No, Helena, you haven't," he said, looking at her with the saddest eyes she had ever seen. Eyes of such intensity and longing and regret that she could not help herself from reaching up with her hand, the same hand that minced pickled whale's eye into omelettes and melted Edammer cheeses into *hutsepots* and stewed a parsnip and prune soup that could cure whatever ailed you, and maybe even whatever ailed Descartes. She reached up with that hand and found herself unacceptably, outrageously, impossibly stroking that strange long scar that ran along the sad man's jaw.

"René," she said softly.

In all the years since—the woods, he realized, not a single woman had called him by that name.

Perhaps it was understandable then that he was having trouble concentrating lately. Forget the work for now. Even the correspondence was too much to keep up with. (Still nothing from Eudoxus; war was still raging, he reminded himself anxiously.) Mersenne for some reason kept forwarding nasty notes from Roberval, the "You stole my geometry!"s and "You sabotaged the Ramus Chair!"s and the "When I get my hands on you ..."s. Descartes would stare at the letters and simply not feel like responding. Nor did he feel like responding to the news that after six years Pierre had been released from the Bastille for his assault on the guards at the Papal Nuncio's that night Descartes fled. Pierre celebrated his release by publicly renewing his vow to destroy his worthless younger brother one day. "But don't worry," Mersenne concluded the report, "I have not revealed your address to anyone."

Descartes was not worried. In fact he didn't care at all about it. Nor about Mersenne's information that Joachim Descartes apparently was becoming frail and seeking to make amends with his younger son before he died.

Descartes stared at the letter awhile then put it aside.

He had more important things to think about.

"But why not?" he pleaded.

"I neither need nor want to be married," she said.

"Is it me?"

"Is what you?"

"Is it specifically me that you neither need nor want to be married to?"

"Of course it is you! Who else?"

"No! Do you have a principle against marriage? Or is it just me?" He hesitated. "My appearance? Am I too—short?"

"Don't be foolish."

"I can grow a beard to cover the scar."

"Stop."

"I can start smoking a pipe, as you Dutch do. Bontekoe says it is good for the skin. I have been reading. He says that tobacco also prevents scurvy, gout, and worms."

"René, you don't have any of those problems."

"And I shan't, if I start smoking."

"It is a dirty habit," she said. "And it does nothing that my parsnip prune soup cannot."

"But Van Diemerbroek claims it protects against the plague. And Blankaart says it is a sedative. For curing my insomnia perhaps."

"So, fine! Why don't you try it, then?"

"It is a dirty habit," he concurred. "But I promise not to pick it up, Helena, if you will marry me."

"René," she sighed. "It just could not work."

"Why not?"

"For one," she said, pulling away from him. "You are a gentleman, and I am a servant."

"The difference is smaller than you think."

"You are a mathematician and I make omelettes."

"It is clear that yours is the nobler pursuit."

"That's my point," she smiled.

"I am sure that is amusing," he said without smiling.

"You are still annoyed about the pickling!"

"Of course I am still annoyed. I have wasted weeks experimenting now."

Helena had refused to tell him the secret ingredient in her pickling recipe. "I am just trying to stay interesting to you, René."

"You don't have to worry about that, Helena."

She studied his face a long time.

"People would disapprove," she said softly.

"People can go suck a nine-day-old egg."

"My master would not let me go."

"I would not let him see my manuscript." Descartes was referring to the first draft of *The Discourse on Method*, which Reneri had been begging to see for weeks.

"René," Helena said. "You would have to convert."

"Where do I sign?"

"You can't be serious." She wasn't sure whether his willingness to abandon his religion for her drew her to him or repulsed her. "You don't give up the religion of your childhood just like that."

"The differences between them are also smaller than you think," he said.

"Professor Voetius better not hear you speak like that."

"I have escaped the clutches of a Cardinal. I am not afraid of a theology professor."

"It isn't about you, René."

"Then what?"

She gazed at him beside her. "It's about your work. If you abandon Catholicism to marry a Protestant servant girl then no one will ever read anything you write."

There was the briefest hesitation. "That's all right."

"It is *not* all right."

"You do not understand, Helena."

"No I don't, René. Because you won't tell me. Your secret. But it doesn't matter. Your work is more important than anything. Than me."

"But I am willing to give up everything for you."

"And I am not willing for you to do so. René." She said this with the determination of a woman who had preserved her own secret omelette against nearly three years of relentless prying. "For your sake. You don't reveal yourself. You don't know yourself."

"But what about—" Descartes ignored this with a new angle, "the child?"

"What child?"

He pointed at her tummy.

"There is no child," she answered, understanding. "I took precautions."

They were in his bedroom, in the house he was renting on Westerkerkstraat in Utrecht, several blocks from Reneri's to keep their relationship discreet. His experiments in human anatomy, he had explained to her, would not be complete without certain observations he *badly* needed to make. The experiment had not gone smoothly, but it had gone. It was only when this mysteriously troubled man had immediately after climbed back into his taffeta suit then gotten back into bed beside her still naked body and started talking about marriage that it occurred to her to ask, hesitantly, "Could this—have been *your* first time?"

He remained silent, thinking of those nocturnal trips to Luché-Pringé at La Flèche, the whoring in Breda, the festivities in Frankfurt; thinking of these and feeling sick to his stomach.

"This is—*new*," he murmured and began to weep.

"Just tell me," she whispered, caressing him as he continued weeping.

It was Sunday, October 15, 1634. Later that night Descartes scribbled that date in his notebook, noting that on this day he believed both that he had made his first child and that he had begun convincing one perfectly maddening absolutely perfect Helena Jans to marry him.

One out of two wasn't bad.

During the winter of 1634-35 Reneri introduced the first Utrecht students to the natural philosophy of René Descartes, including some of his medical ideas about prolonging human life. These remarks caught the attention of Henricus Regius, the cosmopolitan town physician of Utrecht. Regius was angling for a professorship at Utrecht, and thought that knowing the secrets of longevity might do the trick. He spent several months hanging around campus hoping to bump into Descartes, not realizing that

Descartes spent all his time hidden either at his home, Reneri's home, or sneaking the back alleys between them. Finally he gave up and wrote several fawning letters to the master.

Descartes might have read them, too, if he weren't so busy figuring out how to obtain marzipan when the *predikants* were closing down the sweet shops, or where he might find some blooming aster this late in the season.

"But Mynheer," his manservant said, "whatever for?"

"You make a tonic from it, Willem, that reduces the hiccups."

"And the rose-hip syrup?"

"For her mood."

"And the beer?"

"For my mood."

Helena was sure it was going to be a girl.

But then again, Descartes pointed out to her, she was also sure that the charm around her neck—the walnut shell full of spiders' heads she bought from that strange old woman at the market—warded off fevers. "But you have a slight fever right now," he said ever so triumphantly.

"But it might have been worse without the charm," Helena said from the bed, her bloated belly a mound under the blanket. "Is there any more marzipan?"

The pregnancy soon became difficult, mainly for Reneri and Descartes who by the fifth month were deprived of Helena's talents keeping Reneri's house clean and by the sixth month, worse, of her cooking. But she was often ill, and the many books on pregnancy and childbirth she had been reading agreed that she must remain in bed as much as possible. Reneri and Descartes discussed hiring another girl, but the need to keep the relationship and now the child secret overruled it. So they had to make do in Reneri's dirty house, eating the jarred victuals Helena had thoughtfully stored away for them early on.

"I had Willem make inquiries in Deventer," Descartes

353

said to her one morning in early April 1635, as he rubbed her swollen feet. "He has found a cottage for us. It overlooks a canal, and is very private."

"But René—"

"I want you to live with me, Helena. You and Francine. Since you insist on being discreet we can tell the landlady that you are my servant and that Francine—"

"Fine! Whatever you need, René. But three things now."

"What?"

"It says here," she pointed to a passage in Blankaart's *Verhandelinge van de Ziekten der Kinderen*, "that cool, wet foods increase the chances of a girl."

"So from now on you want your stewed apples cooled?"

"Exactly. And listen to this." She flipped to another volume on the bed. "*Het Leerzaam Huisraad* has some good tips here: treat fevers with tinctures of rose water and vinegar on the child's brow, and belly pains with chicory root and honey. Can you make a list for Willem, please? We need to stock up."

Descartes sighed. "But doesn't your Van Beverwijk recommend violet syrup instead?"

"No, that was the *Kleyn Vroetwyfs-boeck*. I think." She began flipping through pages.

Descartes awaited further instruction. When none was forthcoming he said, "I believe you said there were three things."

"What?"

"Three things?"

"Oh, right. We are not naming her Francine."

"François will do, if it is a boy."

"I want something Dutch. Something traditional. Annetje, maybe. Tryntje. Pieter, maybe, if the cold stewed apples don't work."

"But Helena—"

"Blankaart says not to argue with a pregnant woman."

"Common sense says not to argue with a pregnant woman! Nevertheless I insist on Francine. Or François."

"But René," Helena said more gently, laboriously turning on her side on the bed, "You yourself have said you will never return there."

"That is right."

"So perhaps it is time to let go. To let *it* go. A little."

"She will know where she came from," he said firmly. "And where I am—exiled from."

But even with all the good advice from Blankaart and Van Beverwijk things began to go downhill as the weather warmed and the day approached.

There was no time to open those letters from Mersenne. No time to read about Joachim's apparent desire to reconcile, about geometry and Roberval. No time for the news about central Germany, how many had died. No time to work on his *Discourse*, to decide about publishing. No time to interpret the look Helena gave him when she found the little recipe booklet Kunigunda had made for him, stashed away in a drawer, a mix of pain and hurt and love with her eyes welled up with tears. For there was only one thing to think about now, and that was the incredible pain Helena was in during those sticky hot days of mid-July 1635.

She was moaning in her bedroom in the back.

"Van Roonhuysen is on his way," Reneri said to Descartes at the kitchen table, biting his lip as the moans got louder. He had also sent Willem to fetch Utrecht's semi-official midwife, since Helena had made him swear not to let her go into labor without the woman there.

"Mmm," Descartes answered absently.

Nor did he have more to say when Utrecht's pompous obstetrician arrived with his assistant carrying a birthing stool and a heavy bag filled with levers for expanding the birth passage, shears for cord-cutting or limb-amputating, hooks to turn the infant *in utero* or extract it, dead, *ex utero*, and so on. The *vroemeester* first demanded his deposit, then stormed off into the birthing room.

Moments later the moans became screams.

"Mmm," Descartes said, his face as white as it had been in his youth.

At one point Reneri reached out and held his hand.

Two hours later there was quiet back there.

"Mmm," Descartes said at the kitchen table.

Van Roonhuysen emerged splattered with blood and clearly concerned about earning his full fee. "The child is not yet born," he said evenly, "but it is already dead. I shall have to extract it to save the life of the mother."

"Extract it?" Reneri asked weakly.

"It is lodged in the passage. We must amputate the arms and legs to pull it out."

The assistant, now emerged as well, held up the large hook and shears as if to illustrate.

"Mmm," Descartes dropped his eyes.

"And—the mother?" Reneri asked weakly.

"High risk of fatality. But it is the only chance. Have we your permission to proceed?"

After all those hours of moans and screams there was an almost unearthly silence in the house. This was now broken by the sound of the front door crashing open.

"The midwife!" Reneri exclaimed as Willem shepherded in the famous Catharina Schrader carrying her own black bag of supplies.

"You!" the *vroemeester* and the midwife said to each other simultaneously.

"The child is already dead," the *vroemeester* snapped.

"Then return your deposit to this poor man and leave," the midwife pushed him aside. "Willem, grind some bloodstone and prepare a saffron broth immediately. And bring me fresh sheets." She disappeared into the back room.

"We shall stay," Van Roonhuysen said haughtily. "Our assistance may be necessary for saving the mother." And, he was thinking, for salvaging his fee.

"Mmm," Descartes said, his eyes still toward the floor.

A few minutes later Willem emerged from the room with the broth he had brought to the midwife. "She said it is for you, Mynheer," he explained, placing it before Descartes, who didn't move.

Always the good host, Reneri offered some broth to the *vroemeester*'s assistant, who was clearly eyeing it. "Thank you," the young man replied. "I haven't eaten a thing all day."

The *vroemeester* glared but accepted a bowl for himself.

Within the hour the bedroom door swung open and out came Vrouw Schrader, carrying, wrapped in a bloodied sheet, the body of a very small person.

She stood before the kitchen table.

She frowned.

She poked the sheet.

A very small baby cry emerged.

"Here is your dead child," she said to Descartes, Reneri, and especially to *Vroemeester* Van Roonhuysen. "Two arms, two legs."

There was shocked silence except for the sounds of the baby crying, Van Roonhuysen harrumphing, and his assistant slurping the broth.

Vrouw Schrader handed the wrapped child to Descartes, who, unlike his newborn, had not resumed breathing. He took it in his stiff, inexperienced arms. Then he looked up at the midwife imploringly, with watery eyes.

The midwife returned his gaze for a long moment.

"She says you can call her 'Francine,'" she said.

Descartes began to breathe.

"Although why you couldn't choose a nice normal name like Annetje or Tryntje is beyond me," she added.

But Descartes didn't hear this last remark, too busy clutching his little Francine to his chest and sobbing.

On August 7, 1635, the baptismal register of the Orthodox

Church in Deventer was inscribed:

> Vader Rener Jochems
> Moeder Helena Jans
> Kint Fransintge

The marriage register in the same church did not mention any nuptials between *vader* and *moeder*. Descartes did not convert to Calvinism and did not marry Helena. But for the sake of his child he insisted on officially declaring himself the little girl's father, and managed to win one other argument with the little girl's mother: they would come live with him if he would keep their existence secret, for his own sake.

For the next few years they lived as if on the lam. Descartes with his "servant and niece" moved between residences in Deventer and Leiden, on the coast in Egmond, and country houses near Santpoort and Amersfoort. With the exception of Reneri, the pastor who performed the baptism, and the devoted Willem and Kosmos, no one knew the truth. Not Mersenne, not Regius (whom Descartes finally agreed to meet in 1638, in Utrecht, since the newly appointed Professor of Medicine and Botany had promise as a useful disciple), and not, Descartes occasionally thought, Joachim Descartes, the man whose liberated money made their life possible.

The old man was sick and begging to make amends, Mersenne reported in 1638, but Descartes couldn't bring himself to respond, not even with the news of the new little girl.

"But he is old, and he is dying," Helena probed one evening after their daughter was in bed.

"My illegitimate offspring with a Protestant Dutch servant girl? The news would kill him. I do him a kindness by not responding."

"She is *not* illegitimate," Helena reminded him. Under Dutch law, Descartes's name on the baptismal register gave the child the same legitimacy as marriage. "Are you—

weeping again?"

He *was* rather inclined to weeping lately.

Maybe it was because he was now in his forties, the often last stage of human life (at least until he deciphered the secret to longevity). Maybe it was because it was so exhausting keeping his life with this wonderful woman and child a permanent secret.

Or maybe it was just because he was—*happy*.

He slept late each day. Helena arose earlier with Francine, fed her, dressed her; then when 11:30 AM came they were permitted to awaken him, which they did either by bringing him a secretly-pickled-whale's-eye-omelette or jumping into bed with him in a fit of giggles. The afternoons he often spent with Francine in the garden; and then he would sit on a stool in the kitchen while Helena prepared supper, Francine helping by making as much of a mess as possible. After supper he and Helena put Francine to bed together. He would make up a story for her, they kissed her forehead and blew out the candle and sat beside her for the few seconds it took her to fall asleep. Then he and Helena spent some time together before Helena followed their daughter's example and fell asleep. He would kiss *her* forehead and head down to his study to work until dawn, before climbing into bed next to Helena's gently breathing body an hour before Helena would awaken with Francine to start all over again.

Speaking of work, Descartes's *Discourse on Method* had finally appeared in 1637, through Mersenne's mediation. It spelled out his scientific method and included three groundbreaking essays applying that method in geometry, optics, and meteorology. "Send copies to every mathematician in France," Descartes wrote Mersenne, "with the exception of Roberval—to whom send only a copy of this note." Although he had been rather famous for over a decade already, it was actually the recently forty-year-old's first publication—and it took that fame to the next level.

But he had more important things on his mind than his own swelling reputation.

Bubbles.

Francine loved bubbles.

A scallop shell filled with soap solution, on a nearby hillside or beach. Descartes would wave the shell just so, the wind would skim the solution's surface and a bubble would magically appear. Iridescent, evanescent, the wind lifted the ephemeral orb and sent it spinning, spiraling, on its way. Francine giggling, Kosmos barking, in furious chase—"look, papa, papa, look!"—laughing when she caught it, popped it, laughing when it got away and kept going until out of sight. Descartes watched the perfect spheres floating upward, their surface tension holding them together yet rippling in the wind, he stared at the sunlight refracted through the soap, the liquid rainbow in its brief burst of color before evaporating. Francine was not good at making the bubbles herself, she wasn't patient enough to find the right angle or breeze. So one summer afternoon Descartes stepped into a tavern near their house. The good Dutchmen inside were downing tankards and smoking pipes. The smoke reminded Descartes of the bubbles, the way it drifted lazily up for a moment then was gone forever. Levity and gravity, at the same time. A few coins later and he was the proud owner of a Govert Cinq pipe, with the famously long stem. If his Francine was to have a pipe for blowing bubbles, it might as well be the best.

And how adorable she was puffing, the little bubbles popping out! No matter that the fun was as short-lived as the bubbles. Two days later the anti-smoking Helena found the pipe in Francine's toy chest among the knucklebones, and snapped it in two.

Then there were the echoes.

He was thinking about the transmission of sound one afternoon in the garden when he accidently dropped a clay

pot on a stone. To his surprise—and to Francine's, just
three then—the shattering sound reverberated back from
an overgrown corner of the garden, with a slightly higher
pitch. Francine ran off to that corner as if to find what had
shattered there. Finding nothing, she ran back to him. "I
then clapped," he wrote Mersenne late that summer of
1638, "and the sound came back from that same spot, a
sharp retort but elevated in tone as if the cry of a bird."
What he didn't mention was how giggling Francine ran off
to find the mysterious bird in that overgrown spot and
giggled even harder when there was nothing there to be
found. That he clapped again and she cried, "come back,
echo, come back!" and ran off to look again. That again
and again he clapped and she looked, she found nothing,
she giggled, she came back.

And of course there were the bugs.

Oh how they loved their hours in the garden!
Especially the one around their house in Amersfoort
where they spent the next summer, with its blooms and
cherry trees and pears. Francine loved to kneel beside him
picking weeds, Kosmos asleep in the nearby shade. She
loved to haul the pail up from the well and water the
herbs, especially since that required splashing him. He
would try to be furious with her until she began to giggle
and her sheer joy in her little trick took all the air out of his
anger. The same thing would happen when she dropped a
bug down the back of his shirt, he rising in mock fury until
she began to giggle, unaware that he had conveniently
kneeled in the first place to put his collar within her reach.

"What are you two laughing about?" Helena might ask,
bringing a tray of lemonade out for her two hard-working
gardeners.

"Oh, just *this*," Descartes pulled some juicy beetle or
long-legged spider from the back of his shirt and thrust it
before her.

"Uck!" Helena exclaimed, leaving the tray and her
giggling four-year-old and husband out in the garden while

she retreated into the house for safety.

"*Erucarum ortus*," Descartes said softly, his little Francine on his lap in the garden, "the wondrous transformation of caterpillars. Look at this here."

On the cabbage leaf in his hand was a small naked caterpillar, crawling and nibbling, oblivious to being in the center of attention of the world's greatest natural philosopher and his daughter.

"What's it called, papa?" she asked.

He hesitated a moment, remembering that room at the Rector's, back behind the kitchen, all those jars, that notebook with the drawings; wondered what had become of all that as he suppressed the uneasy feelings in the pit of his stomach. "A colewort," he answered. "Or whatever you like, really." He tickled her and she giggled. "He doesn't care what we call him. He'll just keep on eating until he's ready to make himself a little house and take a nice nap inside. Then, presto!" He snapped his fingers. "A week or two later, he's a butterfly!"

"Presto!" she echoed him and tried, unsuccessfully, to snap her fingers.

He smiled. "It's called metamorphosis. A change of shape. He goes in one way, hides for a bit, and comes out different."

"I'm sad," Francine suddenly said.

"What? Why?" Descartes asked, stroking her.

"For the caterpillar."

"It's true he isn't around very long," he said quietly, "but then he becomes a beautiful butterfly."

Which also isn't around long, he did not add.

But she had moved on. "Papa, look at this!" she exclaimed, jumping from his lap and running after some other bubble, echo, or bug.

In the late 1630s the world was abuzz about Descartes, but Descartes was hidden from the world. His Helena and his Francine, and his Kosmos, were world enough for him.

He began to remember.

The days of dreaming, those vivid dreams now two decades before. The vision, that vision, about the mathematical foundations of nature. He dug out the notes he'd scribbled after. With the *Discourse* now on its way and university doors opening to him it was time to step back, to the beginning, to the foundations. There was still something missing, the final thread tying the pieces together, some basic equation or equations. He had felt so close to it, to *IT*, when working on *The World*, and earlier when working on the geometry that Roberval was always harping about. Maybe the missing piece was there, all the way back there, in that stove-heated room where he had had those dreams. He began reviewing, rethinking, meditating.

In the spring of 1639 Helena turned twenty-five. Descartes surprised her by getting up early—10:30 AM—and insisting on making her an omelette for breakfast (or lunch, for her). "How hard can it be?" he said in response to her protests. Forty minutes later he called to her to bring Francine out to the table in the garden. He had laid the table beautifully with their china and the golden linen napkins.

"Muffins!" Francine squealed and set upon hers immediately.

"What happened to the omelette?" Helena asked as she sat down.

"Harder than I thought. I found the muffins in the larder. Also this."

He pulled out a small box wrapped in brown paper, with a broad yellow silk ribbon knotted around it, and set it before her.

"Can I open it?" Francine abandoned her muffin and grabbed. "Can I have the ribbon?"

Helena frowned. "I don't need a present."

"All the more reason for giving you one. Open it."

Helena frowningly obliged. And then frowned more

when she found the string of pearls inside.

"Strung with genuine English wire, drawn in Tintern," Descartes said proudly. "I had it ordered in from Amsterdam. Don't—don't you like it?"

"It's lovely. Almost as—"

"What?"

"As lovely as the fact that you are more interested in the wire than the pearls."

"Look, papa, look!" Francine was squealing. She had laid the ribbon out on the table, roughly in the shape of a large butterfly. "*Eru-crum orts!*" she said haltingly, trying to remember the phrase.

It was later that summer of 1639, that beautiful summer at Amersfoort when Francine turned four. Father and daughter were in the garden. For her birthday entertainment Descartes was making up stories about animals and manipulating the yellow ribbon into the corresponding animal shapes as he did so. But this was not quite the same yellow ribbon, for he had since improved it. The ribbon being too flimsy to shape precisely, he had cut long pieces from the extra Tintern wire he had bought, twisted them together and pressed them flat, then had Helena fold the silk over and sew the wires inside, leaving some grooves exposed on one end and tips of wire on the other so you could fasten the ends and make a loop. Now firm but flexible the ribbon—the band—could be shaped almost any way one pleased, whatever got Francine to giggle.

"And the Leviathan swallowed him up!" he exclaimed, swooping the now-shaped-like-a-two-headed-sea-monster band onto the squealing Francine's neck, as if to swallow her up.

"What's a lah-vie-than?" Francine giggled.

"The biggest, meanest creature of the ocean. With enormous horns. He's so huge he eats whales for breakfast. Only one thing can challenge him."

"What, papa? What?"

Descartes retwisted the band into a long narrow filament. "One tiny, almost invisible creature. No bigger than the tip of one of the Leviathan's horns. But they could swarm into its gills and suffocate him."

"What are they, papa?!"

He held up the filament and smiled. "The kilbit, my little France. A tiny sea worm. Haven't I told you there's nothing bugs cannot do?"

"Now the dog story!" Francine begged, her attention span now satisfied with the Leviathan.

"Fine, fine. Remind me how it starts?"

"The dog came in the kitchen ..." Francine giggled.

"Right. The dog came in the kitchen," Descartes began, now twisting the band into a canine shape. But then he stopped and started untwisting the band.

"Don't stop, papa!" Francine demanded. "He stole a crust of bread."

"Right," he answered, distracted. "Then cook came with a ladle, and—"

"Don't stop!" Francine said again.

He didn't respond.

He had been manipulating the band. While beginning the refrain he had twisted one end of the band, flipping it over, and brought it to meet the other end and inserted it. He held up the now looped band and gazed through the loop at the beaming face of his daughter.

Look at that, he thought to himself as he looked at the band, and looked at her, and looked at the band, and no longer heard her imploring voice.

That night he made a simple entry in his notebook: *At last*.

The next day he began writing the work he was to call *Meditations on First Philosophy*.

The wars continued to rage across Europe during the winter of 1639-40. The deceased Swedish King Gustavus Adolphus's heart continued to rot inside the little box carried now seven years by his mentally unbalanced widow. Their daughter, thirteen-year-old monarch-in-waiting Christina, took the advice of her language tutor, the same Carolus Zolindius who had returned a wounded hero from the wars and was now teaching her every European language. "Your mother might be more comfortable in Gripsholm, Your Majesty," he murmured with a deep bow, naming the remote castle prison with the thick walls from which no one had ever escaped. Meanwhile Joachim Descartes declined rapidly that winter, leading him to write one last pleading letter to Mersenne in Paris attempting to contact his prodigal son, even reinserting him back into his will.

The prodigal son was himself quite busy that winter. He sent a draft of *Meditations* to Mersenne to forward to other scholars for comments which he might then include, with his replies, when it came time to publish. He mourned the unexpected death of his good friend Henri Reneri. And he began to cultivate the relationship with Utrecht Professor Henricus Regius. In the late spring of 1640 Descartes, aiming to reinsert his work into the University now that Reneri was gone, spent a month in Utrecht and invited Regius out to his country house for ripe cherries and pears. He knew this would be a challenge, now that anti-everything Gisbertus Voetius had become the leading Orthodox Calvinist in Utrecht, serving both as Professor of Theology and Rector at the University.

If Descartes had escaped his troubles in France by exile to the United Provinces, this invitation for fresh fruit would soon have him searching for a fresh exile.

It was an extraordinary summer for pears, at least, which made it all the more difficult for Descartes to leave his quiet world in Santpoort at the end of August. Mersenne had returned a half-dozen sets of comments to his *Meditations* and Descartes had prepared his replies, and it was time to proceed to publication—which required a journey to Leiden.

"Three weeks," he said to Helena, embracing her. "Four at the most. And you—" he turned to snatch Francine, who was wriggling away and giggling, "be good."

"No, papa!" she giggled.

But he was not gone even one week.

Just five days after his arrival in Leiden a messenger came informing him that his daughter was ill and that he should return to Santpoort immediately. He left everything with the printer and rode home without resting.

The five-year-old girl was in her bedroom next to their bedroom.

She was lying on her back on top of the bedcovers. A spotty reddish-purple rash was all over her face and neck. The rash had also spread down her chest and back and begun to streak around her underarms. Her tongue was as bright red as the fresh strawberries they had been enjoying with their pears all summer.

And she was burning with fever.

"Scarlatina," the local Santpoort physician said.

This was not useful, since the diagnosis was obvious.

"Get out," Descartes hissed.

The man backed out past the weeping Helena at the door.

"You've already tried rose water and vinegar?" Descartes murmured to Helena, who nodded. "All right then. Fetch some cold wet cloths."

He turned back to his daughter and saw that the yellow band next to her bed was still shaped into the twisted loop, as he had left it.

He bit his lip and whispered to her, *come back*.

They watched all night and morning. They tried cool cloths, tinctures, recipes, charms. He snapped at Helena several times, who merely stood beside him weeping. He was sick in his heart as her fever continued, enraged at himself for having suspended his medical studies over the past few years to focus on his metaphysics. And now he had it, he had solved it, he understood, *everything*. But for what? For whom? The one man who would appreciate it, Eudoxus, was gone. And the world wasn't ready for it. It would have to remain secret until things had changed, until the world had changed. And even then it would be appreciated only by those so absorbed in the life of the mind that they lost sight of life itself, period. He had lost focus. He should have remained focused. He had obtained the secret of the universe but not the secret of how to treat the fever.

It went higher.

And higher again.

He who understood everything could do no more than hold her hand and wipe her burning forehead with a cool wet cloth, whispering *come back come back* while his— Helena wept on the bed beside her, clinging to her little five-year-old's purple body.

The girl's breathing became labored in the early morning hours of September 7, 1640.

And then it stopped.

40
FRIDAY, FEBRUARY 15, 1650
STOCKHOLM, SWEDEN

*"M*urder!" Baillet squeaked but this time, as a man, audibly, as he felt the knife pushing into his throat.

The man released the knife.

"Adrien," he said, letting Baillet go.

Baillet rolled over and looked at his would-be murderer. "Benjamin?"

"You surprise me, Adrien."

"I could say the same thing," Baillet sat up.

"What the hell has gotten into you?"

"More importantly—Benjamin—where did you learn to fight like that? An old man like you. You never did tell me. On the ship."

"No, I did not, Adrien. But perhaps it is my place to be asking the questions." Bramer studied Baillet, sitting next to him on the floor. "Are you investigating *me* now?"

Baillet forced himself to return the gaze. The lying Rosicrucian who was awfully strong for an old man, and who carried a sharp knife. Better not to confront him just

369

yet about the lies. A good investigator does not reveal his hand.

"I came by to see if you wanted to get some breakfast," Baillet congratulated himself on thinking this up, then instantly regretted not having thought about what should come next.

"And then you broke in?"

"The door—" Baillet began to lie but then thought better of it. "Sorry."

Bramer examined his face a long moment. "All right, then. I'm actually glad to see you, anyway. I wanted to speak with you after my lecture last night, but you disappeared. With our friend Roberval."

Baillet had to say *something*, otherwise why had he allegedly come to have breakfast with Bramer? But again, it was better not to confront the man, not yet. Better to distract him.

And perhaps get his advice.

"You were right," Baillet said, "about the priest."

"Viogué?"

"Turns out that he did not care much for Descartes. He's written at length against him. Believes he was secretly a Protestant. Perhaps even—a Rosicrucian."

"So Viogué wanted to stop Descartes from hindering his effort to convert the Queen."

"Exactly. Viogué gave Descartes communion. At the beginning, and—"

"At the end," Bramer said, almost—Baillet thought—sadly. "When it looked like he would survive the first dose."

Baillet nodded.

There was a long silence.

For a moment Bramer looked like the old man he was, Baillet thought, a far cry from the powerful murderer a moment ago. "Let me ask you—Benjamin. You suggested we would have to solve the mystery of his life to solve the mystery of his death. You dismissed the Rosicrucian angle,

I know, but still: might he have been a secret Protestant?"

"Adrien," Bramer answered slowly. "I don't know whether Descartes converted. And despite the evidence I do not know for certain that the priest did this. You're going to have to confront him directly, I'm afraid. It is the only way to be sure. But there is one thing I do know."

"What?"

"There must have been some papers. A notebook."

"Again, Benjamin, I've already told you—"

"I know what you told me, Adrien. But I also *know* there was a notebook. And you either have it and are keeping it from me or it has gone missing. Which is it?"

Trust no one, Baillet reminded himself. Especially those who have lied to you repeatedly. "Benjamin, there was no notebook."

"You wouldn't lie to me, Adrien, would you?"

"I could ask the same of you, Benjamin."

"You needn't be so dramatic, Adrien. I just want his mathematics, as I told you. But I am also trying to help you. The mystery of Descartes's life, as you just put it, is going to be related to his mathematics. There may be a connection to the religious issues, too, as you have suggested. But I am certain that whoever killed him did so because of his mathematics."

"Murder over mathematics? How is that possible?"

"You would have to learn the mathematics to understand, Adrien. I'm afraid you'll have to trust me on this one."

"What makes you think his work is in a notebook, anyway? Not just—sheets of paper?"

"Adrien, please. Do you have the notebook? Have you seen it?"

Baillet had largely forgotten about the notebook. And of course it must be relevant, part of the answer. Both Roberval and Bramer were keen on finding it, and since neither had it, someone else was eager for it as well. And from what Baillet had seen—the dedication, the cryptic

"*He* is here"—it was obviously important. Père Viogué may have been involved, but that theory made no mention of the mathematics. The mystery of Descartes's life—and death—might well depend on it after all.

"I'm sorry, Benjamin. You'll just have to trust *me* on this one."

He was sorry indeed. He was going to have to find the notebook, and do so without any help from his formerly trustworthy advisor Bramer.

The two men sat a few moments longer on the floor.

"All right, then, Adrien," Bramer conceded. "Confront your suspect. See if you can get the priest to talk. And then we can talk. Oh, and by the way: how *did* you get in here? The door did not look forced."

Baillet reflected quickly. He had not confronted *this* suspect, he thought. To the contrary he had said too much, perhaps, to this man he did not trust. But at least doing so had diverted them from the uncomfortable question of why Baillet had broken into the flat.

"My method is a secret," he forced a smile.

"Did your own key fit? Is that it?"

"I didn't say it was a *good* secret."

"Very amusing, Père. While you're confronting the priest I'll go have my lock changed."

41

Baillet tried not to think about the fact that he was kneeling, his mouth open, waiting for the man to place that thin wafer on his extended tongue. The same man who had six days earlier placed a similar wafer onto another man's tongue, sprinkled with arsenic.

His eyes closed, Baillet accepted the wafer from Père Viogué. Did he really have any other choice, he thought as it dissolved on his tongue.

He hesitated, then swallowed.

All right. Still here.

So far.

Baillet loved the Mass. The beauty, the solemnity, the glimpse of infinity and eternity. During those years at La Flèche he had attended Mass often, for there he could sometimes forget that he belonged nowhere and to no one. His mind might sometimes wander to Descartes and the boy, his predecessors at the Rector's home, and marvel that despite differences in class, wealth, education, despite never having met them, he somehow felt connected to both. Descartes was one of *them*, of course, those gentlemen's sons, but at the same time he wasn't, he lived apart, didn't fit. The boy was—well, the boy was also him, Baillet, living outside, lacking status, bound with Descartes but then disappearing. And now here Baillet was trying to determine what had happened. Solving the mystery of his own life, he thought, while trying to solve Descartes's.

When the ceremony was over Père Viogué led him back to the tiny study. Baillet firmly refused to look at the excruciating crucifix over the door as he wondered whether arsenic dissolved in hot chocolate. "Thank you, Père," he said, reluctantly accepting the drink.

Viogué just sat there, waiting.

"You may recall, Père," Baillet finally cleared his throat, "that there were some discrepancies. You said that the Monsieur looked ill before communion on Candlemas, Saturday the 2nd. The valet had said he did not become ill until the next morning. Well, I have since—I now believe that the Monsieur first in fact felt ill shortly after taking communion that morning."

Baillet paused, uncomfortable. Viogué remained silent, waiting.

"All right, then. There was some question about who initiated the second communion, on the next Saturday, the 9th. You said that the Monsieur called for it, as he began to feel better. But the valet said—he thought that you, rather, insisted on it. After which the Monsieur became—even more ill."

Again Baillet paused, forcing himself to breathe. Viogué said nothing.

"Then at the end, I now believe that Descartes was largely—incapable of speaking from Sunday morning onward. And that it was not you who suggested the last rites, but in fact you—"

"What, Adrien?"

"Refused them, Père."

There was a long silence while the gaze of the senior cleric shot daggers into Baillet's eyes.

"You accuse me, then, of murdering Descartes,"

Viogué said coldly.

"No, of course not, Père," Baillet stammered.

"Oh, but you do. You are suggesting that I have lied to you. That his illness began after I performed the sacrament, and renewed itself after I insisted on performing it again. And you clearly believe there is some great clue in the matter of the last rites."

"Well, Père, when you—"

"How dare you accuse me of such a crime!"

"Père," Baillet said gingerly, thinking fast. "I do not—could not—suspect a fellow—a Catholic, a priest—*you*—of such an action. But please, put yourself in my position for a moment. All I have to work with are the testimonies of the witnesses. And these conflict."

"You take the word of a *servant* over that of the most senior Catholic in this land?"

"There is also the physician, Père. He concurs. That you—"

"A Protestant!"

"But Père. You also said that you thought Descartes's soul was pure. And that you hadn't read any of his controversial writings. But I found—" with a dramatic flair Baillet pulled out the documents he had stolen from the Library.

"And these are ...?" Viogué glimpsed the mathematical symbols.

"Sorry," Baillet stuffed them back in. In the excitement he had forgotten that he had read Viogué's writings in the Library and stolen Bramer's. "I meant to say that I spent this morning in the Royal Library. Reading some of *your* writings."

Viogué's face softened.

"Then perhaps you can appreciate my position, Père?"

Viogué hesitated. "All right, Adrien. I suppose I should tell you the truth."

Well *that* was easier than expected, Baillet thought. Unless the priest were merely waiting for the arsenic in the chocolate to work its magic.

"I despised Descartes," Viogué said bluntly. "As any good Catholic should, yourself included. I stand by every word I wrote. The man was a *free thinker*. He was at war with our faith. At times he was an atheist. Other times a Protestant. Whatever suited his purposes. He spent formative years in Germany during the Rosicrucian movement, surely participating in it. He worked hard to spread those heresies through all of Europe. And his personal vices! Voetius—you have spoken with him?"

"Unfortunately not," Baillet answered, as the cleric had avoided the Ecumenical Breakfast..

"The man is a miserable wretch, but a useful source of information. He had Descartes's personal life investigated. Your Monsieur produced illegitimate children. Then abandoned them. He was a beast."

Baillet nodded, though he found himself feeling defensive of Descartes. Still, could it be true—Descartes with a—family?

"I was not going to allow him to disseminate his *filth* here. To hinder my important work."

"To influence Her Majesty ..."

"Of course."

Baillet's mind and heart were racing equally fast. He was hearing his first murder confession and didn't know whether to be excited or terrified or both. "So you—put an end to it."

Viogué gave him a strange look. "I did everything in my power to prevent his coming here. When I heard that the Chancellor was keen on inviting him I let His Excellence know my opinion immediately."

"The Chancellor? I thought it was the Queen?"

"They are essentially the same."

"And then," Baillet was suddenly eager to get to the confession, "after he arrived?"

"I shall be honest with you, Adrien. Descartes was not as objectionable as I had imagined."

"What?"

"He seemed so sad, or defeated even, right from the start. Something weighing on him. After my years of despising him he just seemed like a melancholy aging man. Almost hard to ..."

"What?" Baillet was not prepared for this turn of the conversation.

"Believe he was a threat, I suppose. We began a ... sort of friendship. Perhaps that is too strong a word. But a reconciliation of sorts. He came to see me a few times. He came to services sometimes. He confided in me. To a degree."

"Confessed?"

Viogué shook his head.

"Not even at the end, as you claimed?"

Viogué shook his head again. "He had a secret, Adrien. A deep secret, that went a long way back, that had plagued him nearly his whole life, he said. It tormented him in Germany. It drove him from France. It nearly destroyed him in Deventer, he said. In the Provinces."

"What does that mean?"

"That is all he would say, Adrien."

"The secret Protestantism, maybe? The Rosicrucianism?"

"Perhaps."

"The secret family?"

"He refused to share his burden, Adrien. I felt ... sorry for him."

Baillet was unsure how to process this information but realized they were getting off track. "But Père, what about your—lies? The communions? The last rites?"

"I could not bring myself to perform the last rites, in the end. My beliefs about him, his apostasy, were too strong. I remain convinced that he was not, in the end, a ... Catholic."

"And the rest?"

"Given the almost ... affection ... I found myself feeling

377

toward him, once I saw how *broken* he seemed, I thought that there was still perhaps something I might do for him. If not rehabilitate him, as it were, then the next best thing. Rehabilitate his reputation."

"As a—pure Catholic soul?"

Viogué nodded. "I am sorry, Adrien, that I lied to you."

"He was not in fact able to speak about spiritual matters on that final day, was he?"

"It was I who spoke to *him*, while he lay ... delirious. About immortality and resurrection. Hoping something might ... sink in."

"He didn't say those beautiful things about his soul departing at the end?"

"No ... Or not exactly. He said that other thing. Right at the end. It seemed to ... imply his belief in the eternal soul. I thought perhaps my remarks had affected him."

"Was that the—returning to France comment?"

"Precisely. About going back to his little France."

"His 'little France'? What did he say? Exactly?"

Viogué reflected. "Something like ... '*reviens* ... *ma petite France.*'"

"'I return'? 'My little France'? He was suddenly—patriotic?"

"I do not know, Adrien. But the returning, the coming back. I thought it something that one who believed in an eternal soul might say. And then a moment later the others were back in the room and it was—all over."

Baillet again felt confused, off track. "And—the communion? The second Saturday? He didn't request it after all, did he?"

"Actually, Adrien, he did."

"He did?"

"I was as surprised as you. But he was feeling better, and asked for communion. And I was certainly not going to deny him."

"But Wullens said that you insisted on the communion."

"Of course I did, because Descartes had requested it. Whispered to me."

Baillet was resisting fluster. This was a bit of a twist from his earlier understanding, but nothing that affected his overall theory. "So, Père, that's—how you did it."

"Did what?"

"Um—murdered him?"

"I did no such thing."

"I don't understand. Aren't you in the process of telling me both why and how you murdered him?"

"Adrien, I am torn by my guilt. In lying about this case to you. But I am not a murderer."

"But you lied about the onset of the illness. You said it was before that communion on Candlemas."

"I did not lie. He *did* look unwell, when he arrived for Candlemas. I asked him half-jokingly if he had seen a ghost and he just stared blankly at me."

"But you—gave him the two communions."

"Of course I did. To save his soul, as any priest would."

"You poisoned him," Baillet felt himself flailing. "On Candlemas. And again on the following Saturday. You poisoned the wafers and you placed them directly in his mouth."

"I did no such thing!" Viogué exclaimed. Then he suddenly turned pale. "Adrien!"

"What?" Baillet asked, miserable.

"The wafers."

"What?"

"I did not provide them."

"What?"

"The valet brought them. To Descartes's bedroom."

"Schlüter."

Viogué nodded.

"But—" Baillet's entire theory of the crime was falling to pieces, "Candlemas? Wasn't that here? In the chapel?"

"Of course it was. But Adrien. They were late. They were always late, when they came to Mass. Everything was put away. I was happy to accommodate Descartes's request for communion, but ..."

Baillet understood. "Schlüter was ready with the wafers."

Viogué's eyes filled with tears. "What have I done ... Adrien, what have I done?"

But there was no time for Baillet to react to this, to decide whether he was more disappointed in losing his murder confession or pleased to have—now—arrived at the correct theory of the crime. The door to the priest's study flew open and his servant came rushing in.

"What is the meaning of this?!" Viogué stood up abruptly.

"Message from the Ambassador, sir," the boy trembled, handing over a note.

Viogué grabbed the paper. "There has been an arrest, Adrien. In the murder case."

"What?" Baillet exclaimed. "They know who murdered him?"

"Not *him*, Adrien. The other one."

"Which other one?"

"The brother. Pierre Descartes."

42

"Confound this traffic!" the Ambassador exclaimed.

The crowds were swarming on the Norrbro. Baillet grimaced when he saw three men wearing only crowns of thorns and loincloths carrying enormous wooden crosses on which, possibly, they were soon to be crucified.

"Just some theater," Chanut chimed in, "one hopes."

Despite their being late Baillet was glad to have a few moments to think. Now that he had solved the mystery of who murdered Descartes—the philosopher, not the brother—he was feeling gripped by the other mystery, that of Descartes's life. The poor man knew he'd been poisoned, had tried desperately to expel the poison via the wine sop, then, in his last moments, had said something to the priest about returning to his little France. Surely those words were some clue, but what could they mean?

"Ask the valet. A loyal valet always knows his master's secrets," Chanut suggested when they'd boarded his carriage.

The *not*-so-loyal valet, rather, with the poisoned wafers. Baillet would go find the man—whose ship should not yet have departed—right after this meeting with the

Chancellor. He wanted to confirm his solution of the crime, but there were also some questions about the details. The motive: possibly financial, but given Descartes's circumstances that wasn't certain. And where had Schlüter obtained the poison for the wafers? And the—parsnip soup. That hadn't yet been resolved. The second poisoning could just as well have been the soup as the wafer, really; that Descartes requested the second communion suggested he at least did not suspect the wafers. And then there was the issue whether the servant had acted alone. If he were working for somebody else, then the pool of suspects instantly expanded again to include pretty much *everyone*.

These weren't just details, Baillet realized with a sigh. Maybe he *hadn't* yet solved the crime after all.

"Let us hope, eh, Père, that our tardiness," Chanut said cheerfully as they stood before the Chancellor's desk, waiting for His Excellency, "does not move the Chancellor to have our heads join theirs."

Baillet instinctively turned, and groaned.

It wasn't merely that these four heads were different yet again from the last time.

One of the heads was the vagabond's.

"What?" Chanut turned around.

"The one on the left. The vagabond. 'Sully.'"

"Well," Chanut stroked his goatee thoughtfully, "he had a good run."

Just then the door swung open. Baillet stiffened and faced the empty desk, gazing forward. He could hear the footsteps entering the room, slowly, the one step just heavier than the other.

"You may relax, gentlemen," His Excellency said, taking his chair before them.

Neither gentleman complied.

The Chancellor spoke after a long moment of stillness. "We have made an arrest in the murder of the Monsieur's brother. May we assume your discretion, gentlemen?"

"Of course, Your Excellence," Chanut proclaimed.

"Père?"

Baillet was fiddling with the yellow band in his pocket, thinking that Schlüter had seemed rather fond of Descartes, when Chanut elbowed him. "Ah, yes, of course, Your Excellence."

Zolindius's eyes lingered on Baillet before he picked up a sheet on his desk. "I have in my hand the confession of someone you know. Fortunately he yielded to our—" the strange half-smile appeared, "methods of interrogation. Gentlemen, it is my somber duty to inform you that the murderer of Monsieur—" Zolindius paused, then seemed almost to spit out the word, "*Pierre* Descartes is—"

Baillet's stomach churned as he stared at the Chancellor's lips. Baillet was also aware of the Ambassador's round body swaying beside him, leaning against him, until he realized that in fact it was he himself who was swaying against his compatriot.

"Your Excellence?" Chanut prodded gently, as the Chancellor had fallen silent, staring at Baillet.

"Is it not always the valet, gentlemen?"

"But Pierre Descartes did not have a valet," Baillet objected.

"I think he means the Monsieur's valet, Père," Chanut explained.

"Schlüter?"

"I am afraid so, Père," Zolindius answered.

There was a long silence. Nobody spoke. Not the one at the desk, the two before the desk, the four on the wall behind them.

"But *why*?" Baillet exclaimed.

"The criminal element always has but one motive, Père," Zolindius answered. "Our interrogations have exposed his disreputable background. It seems he misrepresented his previous employment. Spent several years in prison, in Amsterdam."

Baillet's mind was racing. "And that motive?"

"Why, money, of course. Surely you are aware, Père," Zolindius said deliberately, "that the Descartes family was possessed of lands, posts, and titles. The Monsieur— Pierre—himself held lands in the southern region of your great country." Zolindius paused, then added with an almost angry edge in his voice, "They were moneyed. To say the least."

"A robbery, then," Chanut summarized quickly, alarmed about the Chancellor's tone.

"But that makes no sense," Baillet interjected without thinking, "Monsieur Pierre had lost the money. And his clothing, all tattered. He did not give off the—air of a wealthy—"

"'Airs' aside, Père," Zolindius interrupted, "I go by what the criminal himself has written in his confession." He waved the sheet of paper. "I am afraid you overlook the matter of the inheritance, Père."

"Sir?"

"The Monsieur—the younger—left half his estate to the valet. Unaware of his criminal background, naturally. The valet admits his concern that the arrival of Monsieur Descartes—the elder—meant he would contest the will. And so it was necessary to eliminate him. That answers your point about the Monsieur's 'air,' does it not, Père?"

"Yes, sir," Baillet conceded, thinking, as he fingered the yellow band, that Schlüter had said that Descartes's estate was meager. Surely not enough to be grounds for murder. Especially one as vicious as this one, he thought, recalling the butchered body. And if there wasn't adequate motive for the valet to murder Pierre, there wouldn't have been adequate motive to murder René either. "I suppose if Schlüter could hide his past from your vetting process he could hide it from the Monsieur."

There were two audible gasps from Chanut, who could not believe first that Baillet had just charged the Chancellor with incompetence, and second, that the Chancellor did not immediately order a fifth spike installed on the wall behind them.

"Turning to the other matter," Zolindius instead just stared coldly at Baillet, "Père, may I ask if you have completed your report? On the—*natural* death of Monsieur, the junior?"

"Nearly, Your Excellence," Baillet answered, aware of how easily lies were coming to him now. "But might I— would it be possible for me—to speak with Schlüter, sir? There are—I still have a few questions about the Monsieur. Loose ends."

"Have you not already spoken to him twice?"

The Chancellor, Baillet thought uneasily, was aware of *everything*. "Some questions have arisen since, Your Excellence."

"What questions?"

Baillet made a snap judgment. "Descartes's final words, for one."

The Chancellor sat still, waiting.

"...*reviens ... ma petite France*," Baillet elaborated.

"And the significance of those words, Père?"

"I was hoping Schlüter might know."

"And what other questions?"

Baillet made another snap judgment. "This will sound odd. I was just wondering who provided—the groceries, the food. For Descartes."

"Why?"

Baillet was about to explain, but then made an even snappier judgment. "It's nothing, really. Just details. I mainly wanted to speak with Schlüter about the Monsieur's last words."

"I see." Was that a *spark* in the Chancellor's eyes? Almost playful, the way the cat played with the mouse before biting its head off? "Well, I am afraid the criminal is in transit, Père. To Gripsholm."

The Ambassador gasped a third time.

"Ambassador?" Baillet asked.

"You remember what I told you about Långholmen

prison, Père?" Chanut asked, breathless.

Baillet nodded, recalling the Ambassador's description of the dreadful place.

"Well Långholmen is where prisoners in Gripsholm *wish* they were. At least for the brief period until they—" Chanut searched for the appropriate words, "are broken."

"The criminal will be out of commission," Zolindius continued, "long beyond your concern, Père. The Gala concludes this evening, as you know."

"Yes, sir," Baillet lied again, realizing he had completely lost track of the week. It felt like he had arrived a year ago rather than a mere four days.

"May I expect your report no later than tomorrow evening, Père?"

"Death by natural causes," Baillet nodded agreeably. "Inflammation of the lung."

"May the relations between our two great nations remain forever strong," Chanut added.

There was another silence. From outside a strong gust of wind could be heard.

Zolindius stood. "Now, gentlemen, I am sure you are both eager to prepare for tonight's events. We will be seeing you this evening, will we not?"

"The ballet, Your Excellence," said the Ambassador with a bow, "I should not miss it for the world."

43

*T*hey shook hands and parted as the sky grew darker and the snow picked up. Baillet left the Ambassador at the rear gate of the Castle to go write up his report. But he had a lot on his mind as he set off into the streets. How could he be so foolish, he wondered, as to ask the Chancellor to speak to the valet? Zolindius did not want him stirring up trouble. What Zolindius wanted was what he was going to have: a French report confirming that René Descartes had died of natural causes, and the discreet resolution of the murder of Pierre Descartes. The facts all fit nicely enough. The valet murdered René via the poisoned communion wafers, then murdered Pierre: one murderer for the two crimes. If it was good enough for the Chancellor, it should be good enough for him.

Of course the most important question remained unanswered, for both murders: *Why?*

Baillet simply did not accept the money motive. Schlüter knew that René was broke. And the same applied to Pierre, who also stood to gain little from the will.

If there were money in it for Schlüter, Baillet thought as the snow transitioned from showers to storm, then he must have been hired for the job. The valet would be the perfect hired assassin: no intrinsic loyalty to René, he would know that René received private communions, he could provide the wafers when the time was right. And once he'd murdered René he might have a motive to murder Pierre—who, for all he knew, would want to avenge his younger brother's death.

Or a motive, Baillet thought, suddenly feeling the chill—to murder *him*.

Oh, right: Schlüter was en route to Gripsholm.

Unless he weren't the murderer. Or the person who *hired* the murderer.

Who was still out there.

Baillet made a sharp right down a narrow street for no reason other than that the snow piled ahead seemed slightly higher than that on the street to the right. And while this turn took him into the roughest section of the city—near where Pierre had been butchered—it at least lost the two men who were following him. Or briefly lost them, for as the men arrived at the corner they just caught a glimpse of his greatcoat disappearing around the bend down the street.

Baillet was oblivious to them, too busy thinking that Schlüter would have known that Pierre, rather than avenging his brother's murder, would have liked to carry it out himself. Pierre had tried to see René, and Schlüter had fended him off, so he knew about their hostility. Unless, of course, *Pierre* paid Schlüter to murder René? And then Schlüter killed Pierre to cover his tracks?

No. Pierre had no money.

And really, how could the Chancellor not have known that Schlüter was a thug? The arms on that fellow. His facility with a plank.

Hey, Baillet wondered, halting: when did this storm become a blizzard?

Standing in snow above his knees he peered up and down the street. It was only around noon but it was dark from the heavy clouds, and with the swirling snow visibility was minimal. Cold wet flakes assaulted his face as he tried to make out where he was. This quickly being pointless he returned to his trudging and to his thoughts. What made the most sense was indeed the one murderer theory: whoever murdered René also murdered Pierre.

But it did not make much sense that Schlüter was that one.

Wait—it was undeniable now that Schlüter murdered René, by providing the poisoned wafers.

Unless—had he done so—*unknowingly*?

Was that possible?

But then if Schlüter wasn't behind it all, then whoever it was, *was* still at large ....

Baillet stopped, looked around, tried to see through the dark and snow. He noticed the same tavern he had seen a short while ago, realized that he was moving in circles mentally and physically. That's when he realized that he had absolutely, completely no idea where he was, other than in the middle of one hell of a freezing blizzard somewhere in that God-awful city of Stockholm.

Attempting to quell his panic he turned around to look down the snow-filled street he had just been through, for some reason thinking this might orient him. That was when he saw the two men coming toward him. He had no idea who they were but with his recent thoughts and cresting panic he had no intention of finding out.

He started to run. Or rather to *try* to run, for actual running wasn't possible through the snowdrifts of a bona fide Swedish blizzard.

The two men had the advantage.

They were used to drifts and blizzards. They also knew where they were and where they were going. Nor did the cold bother them one bit. In fact they had already removed their gloves so as to have better grips on their preferred weapons: for the one it was a razor-sharp knife he had pulled from his mother's corpse, for the other it was a heavy iron hammer he had lifted from the first man he had murdered, using his best friend's razor-sharp knife.

Baillet looked back once more. The men were gaining on him. He trudged, breathing hard, his heart pounding, he looked back again, realized that the time it took to turn and look allowed the men to gain on him further. The glimpse he caught of the weapons in their hands might have accelerated his pace if not for the near stoppage of his heart that cancelled it out. One more look and they were just a dozen paces behind him. In a swirl of confusion he made a last-ditch effort to lose them, by dropping into a ditch and lying down, hoping they might not see him in the snow. When that didn't work—he heard some sarcastic snorts in Swedish—he went to his backup plan, which was to begin praying for a miracle to get out of this alive. But as the two men came upon him, with weapons bared, he understood that any so-called miracle would have to be his own doing.

His heart pounding so hard he was no longer aware of his panic he clambered to his feet—not easy from the depths of a snowy ditch—and put up his gloved hands ready to fight. A strange calm came over him. His sudden martial pose, and poise, were impressive enough that his two murderers hesitated before him to absorb it.

In that moment Baillet found himself remembering the attack on the ship on the way here, how helpless he had felt before Bramer's rescue, how resolved he had since become to take care of himself.

He clenched both fists and prepared to inflict pain.

He was a *man*, he thought.

That's when someone tackled him from behind.

44

*B*aillet was outside himself, floating, looking down, looking at himself lying in the snow.

He could see himself curled up beneath these three men, enormous in their greatcoats. There were blows raining down as time seemed to slow and he suddenly remembered being curled up beneath all the beatings at La Flèche as well. Ah but back then there were just fists and knees; now there were glints of metal, knives clanging—a hammer, clanging against knife! Yet these three murdering Swedes seemed as far away as the bullies at La Flèche, he could hear their voices in the distance screaming in Swedish; and he could hear his own cries, his groans, his feverish prayers as he began reverting to his original backup plan, the prayer for a miracle.

That's when he understood that some kind of miracle in fact was underway. The men were not attacking him, he realized.

They were fighting *each other*.

Glints of metal and clanging knives but none directed at him. The voices screaming in Swedish were not all alike: one was barking commands, the others were resisting.

Then there was a shredding sound, a scream. Baillet was back in his body beneath the pile, aware of hot wet liquid spraying. There was another scream—*not* his own—then two of the men were gone, running, yes they could run, these Swedish hoodlums, even through a blizzard, they were running away, disappearing into the snow from which they had emerged.

The third man remained standing over him, holding a long curved knife with something fleshy and red dangling from its point, a knife with which Baillet was all too familiar.

"You," Bramer muttered as he helped Baillet up from the snow, "are a hard person to keep an eye on. Why must you constantly wander through these absurd streets?"

A short while later they were seated in their tavern. Baillet realized he was famished enough to eat the entire plate of rooster testicles before him.

"They did a number on you, my friend," Bramer gazed at him. "Those are some nasty scrapes."

Baillet touched his face, winced. "It's mid-day. Isn't there some Gala event you should be at?"

"Yes. But I've got more important things to do."

"Following me?"

"Protecting you, you idiot. You're not going to thank me for saving you out there?"

"That depends."

"On what?"

"On what *you* plan to do to me now."

"What does that mean?"

"You with your 'diverse experiences,' your murder-quality knife, and your habit of showing up wherever I am, are also one rather accomplished liar. Who knows what you're up to?"

"I'll remind you that it was *you* who broke into *my* rooms this morning. And wait a minute—who are you calling a liar?"

"Only the great Rosicrucian Benjamin Bramer."

"Ah!"

"Is that all you have to say?"

"No. I'll add that you are a fool in addition to being an idiot."

"Excuse *me*, you big liar."

"Adrien, drink your cider. And then when your brain has returned to normal operating temperature I will explain something to you."

Baillet started to protest but then realized what he really needed right now was a hot drink and a good explanation.

"I want his mathematics," Bramer said quietly a moment later. "Adrien. Really."

"The Rosicrucians?"

"That is all nonsense."

"But I've seen your writings."

"If you had bothered *reading* them you would never have gotten yourself all confused about this."

"I *am* rather busy with a murder investigation, you know."

"Fair enough."

"So?"

"So," Bramer said with a deep breath. "In the early '20s there *was* a group that called itself the Brotherhood of the Rosy Cross. Most of its members were more interested in dressing up and adopting secret names than in doing any real work. But there was a serious motivation for the group originally. And some of us were quite serious about it."

"So you *are* a Rosicrucian?"

"That depends what you mean, Adrien. The group existed for several years, but except for myself and a few others we couldn't generate enough serious members to keep going. Meanwhile legends started spreading about us all through Europe. That we were infiltrating the continent. That we were arch Protestants out to destroy the Church. That we were invisible, even."

"That wasn't true? The Church part?"

"Not a word. A few of us lived in some different cities, but that was it. There didn't seem much point to trying to counter the legends. They were sort of amusing, really."

"All right. But then why not just say you were, but are no longer, a Rosicrucian?"

"Because what we were in no way corresponded to what people meant by the name. *Those* Rosicrucians truly never existed."

"So—what were you, then?"

"Mathematicians. Natural philosophers. Mathematicians who believed that natural philosophy *was* mathematics."

"Listen, you're speaking to someone who didn't pay attention in school."

Bramer smiled. "It's simple enough, Adrien. We believed that everything in the natural world can be explained in mathematical terms. That if you could only discover the correct equations you would understand the cosmos on its deepest level, its organizing principles. You would then be able to solve more or less all problems: cure illness, improve human welfare, establish religious tolerance, that sort of thing."

"I suppose," Baillet got the main drift, "you conceived of God as a mathematician as well."

"I suppose we did, Adrien."

"And I don't suppose the authorities thought too highly of that."

"Exactly. Hence the secrecy, and the code names. Mine was Eudoxus, for example. After an important ancient Greek mathematician."

That strange name seemed familiar to Baillet, but he couldn't place it. "And? Did you succeed? Or give up?"

"If you are asking whether I still believe in the basic goal, the answer is yes. But did we discover the correct equations?" Bramer's voice became softer. "Some of us may have."

There was a moment of silence.

"René," Baillet said.

Bramer nodded.

"You knew him, after all."

Bramer nodded again.

"You used his notation at your lecture the other day— or Roberval's notation, according to him, stolen by René. And when you used it that confirmed for him that you and René knew each other."

"He's right about the latter, but only by luck. René stole nothing from that man."

"But how do you know?"

"Because he and I developed it together."

Baillet paused to process this. But then he gave up. "All right—Benjamin. Take me through this please."

"Roberval may well have had his own little notebook back in the '20s, in Paris," Bramer began. "And maybe Roberval discovered something, or maybe not; and maybe his notebook was stolen, or lost; I don't know. But he and René did not get along, and at some point he began spreading this story about René stealing his notebook and the nonsense about the notation. But it was all just slander."

"You know this for certain."

"I do."

"And how?"

"Because I am the one who gave René the notebook in question. Long before Roberval came into the picture."

"You," Baillet said after draining his flagon, "are just full of surprises today. You might have told me some of this earlier on, don't you think?"

"No, I don't. How could I know whether you could be trusted? When we met you told me you were from La Flèche. You were wearing that costume of yours. For all I knew you were a scheming, conniving Jesuit priest perpetrating one of your schemes."

"Was it a scheming, conniving Jesuit priest off whom

you took your folding gully?"

"Unfortunately not. Just one of his henchmen. The priest got away."

There was a long silence. Baillet was feeling uneasy, and not merely because of the rooster testicles in his stomach. Something ... familiar ... Nervously his hand slipped into his cassock pocket and began fiddling with the yellow band. "So what makes you so sure *now* that I'm not a Jesuit priest perpetrating some conniving scheme?"

"I've seen you in action."

Baillet felt himself getting red. "All right, fine. I see your point. So: Roberval, notation, notebooks. Now that my incompetence has earned your trust, Benjamin, perhaps you can continue?"

Bramer gazed at him with some warmth. "Roberval is a buffoon, but an intelligent buffoon, and his dispute with René proved crucial. Simply put, Roberval developed techniques for solving certain kinds of problems individually. But René sought to discover general methods, that would solve every problem of the same kind. And in that original dispute with Roberval, he found it. The next step was to continue to generalize so that more and more kinds of problems would be solvable the same way."

"The Rosicrucian thing. Some basic equations explaining—everything."

"Exactly."

"And then what?"

"*Continue* to generalize. To search for the most general method. The single method, the single equation, that could describe everything."

"'*The* Equation,'" Baillet proposed.

"The Equation, Adrien. A single expression that contains every possibility. The infinite captured in a finite form. The essential unity of nature." Bramer paused. "That's what René was working on."

"How do you know that? How do—did—" Baillet corrected himself, "you know *René?*"

A trace of sadness appeared in the older man's eyes. "I trained him, Adrien. When I met him it was immediately clear that his was an exceptional mathematical mind. But he had had almost no formal training. So I provided it."

"But he studied mathematics at La Flèche. When did you meet him? Where did this training occur? You said this was *before* Roberval?"

"Good, my friend. Let me take your questions in reverse order. Yes, before Roberval. René and I worked together in the early '20s, in Kassel, in Germany—"

"I thought you were from Rotenburg."

"Originally Kassel. I was forced to move several times. From the wars. From the end of 1620 until early 1623 we were in Kassel. In the first half I taught him everything I knew about mathematics. In the second half he began teaching me. That's when I realized he needed to move on. So I sent him away."

"And you? How did he—come to you?"

If Baillet asked this question hesitantly then Bramer answered it even more so. "He just showed up one night. It was right after White Mountain. With his brilliant mathematical mind and his dearth of formal training, and of course without that boy of Charlet's. Though he had rescued the—"

Bramer stopped speaking as a strange look crossed his face.

"What is it, Benjamin?"

"It's nothing. I'm sorry. He just showed up."

"But—" Baillet felt flustered by the way Bramer was staring at him. "What?"

"That's all I know," Bramer dropped his eyes.

"What about La Flèche? His training there?"

"He would only reveal fragments about his past. Nothing about where he had been, what he was—well, running from. He said it didn't matter. *René*, he once reminded me, 'reborn.' He had been reborn. Started afresh."

"A lazy, cheating wastrel—to quote his brother—decides to become a—"

"Serious world-class mathematician."

"So," Baillet said, observing the sad look in Bramer's eyes, "you did not come to Sweden to murder him."

"No, Adrien, I did not. We corresponded for some years as we worked on the search for The Equation, as you put it. He would consult with me on his major life decisions. What to publish, and when. What moves to make, and when. It was me who sent him to Paris, to make himself known to the mathematical world. And then ..."

"What?"

"He disappeared. For a long time. Around the early '30s."

"What happened?"

"I don't know. The post was completely destroyed in Germany, from the wars. And of course I had to move several times. I worried he had died, perhaps from the plague in the United Provinces. You can imagine my shock when after fifteen years of silence the letter arrived from Stockholm—" Bramer was trying to maintain his composure.

"From René."

"Yes. Informing me he was here to be the Queen's philosopher. To write the statutes for the Academy. That he had seen my name on the list of inductees and my current address. And that—"

This time Bramer was less successful. Baillet waited for the man to recover before probing further. "Did he say anything? About those missing years?"

Bramer shook his head. "He told me about his problems with Voetius. He made references to Deventer, in the Provinces, something happened there as well. But he never explained."

"The mystery of his life," Baillet echoed their earlier conversation.

"I didn't come to murder him, Adrien. He was almost

... a son to me."

Baillet touched Bramer's shoulder. "I'm sorry, Benjamin."

Bramer took a breath. "I had lost my wife and two of my children when he arrived in Kassel. He was about the same age as my son would have been. It was a natural substitution, I suppose. And then my remaining daughter ... My Kunigunda. I found myself hoping that perhaps she and Polybius might, perhaps, be together. At any rate she died a couple of years later herself."

"I'm so sorry," Baillet touched the older man's arm on the table as the latter suppressed tears. Poor, poor Benjamin, he thought. And that name, too, was familiar— Kunigunda. Odd. And Polybius, from the notebook, suddenly very familiar ...

"Anyway, Adrien," Bramer continued, so focused on controlling himself that he didn't notice Baillet's distraction, "René also wrote that he had something extremely important to show me. The second of the two 'great truths' he had discovered in Deventer, he said. But he did not think it safe to put it in the post."

"The 'second'?" Baillet asked, still thinking about the names.

"The first was that I was right, he said. But about what, I have no idea. As for the second ..."

Baillet understood. "The Equation."

"One must assume. I booked the first ship to Stockholm. That infernal fluit."

"I wondered why you were on that ship. It was awfully last minute for an inductee."

"I wasn't planning to come until that letter arrived. All I could think on the way over was that I would see him again, after all these years. My protégé. My—"

Bramer looked away. Baillet thought about what Bramer must have been feeling at that moment their ship arrived in Stockholm, expecting to see René but instead receiving the news of his death just hours earlier.

They remained silent a while.

Polybius. "Your interest in his notebook," Baillet said when it clicked in his mind. "The Equation."

"Exactly, Adrien."

"Polybius's notebook. The Cosmopolitan. Offered to learned men, and especially to G. F. R. C.?"

"*Germania Fraternitatis Roseae Crucis*," Bramer's eyes opened wide. "I knew it. You *do* have it."

"I am so sorry, Benjamin. I—lost it."

"You lost it?"

"I found it hidden in his study. I quickly skimmed it. Lots of mathematics. Obviously. Lots of drawings of *bugs*, for some reason. Nothing I could understand or tell you about, I'm sorry. But there were also some—personal things."

"Personal? Recent?"

"The day before he fell ill. He wrote '*He* is here.'"

"Who?"

"Didn't say."

"Then what happened?"

Baillet explained how he had taken the notebook to examine later, and how when he returned home after the banquet his flat had been ransacked by two or three different people, and that the notebook had been missing since.

"Two or three people?" Bramer asked.

"Pierre claimed that Roberval was there when he arrived. Roberval claimed that the room had already been ransacked before he arrived."

"So someone else knew that you had the notebook."

"Apparently. But how—" Baillet froze. "Benjamin. I never closed up the wall. The hiding space. I was in such a hurry to get the notebook to my rooms that I completely forgot. So—"

"Schlüter knew you had found something. And retrieved it from your rooms when he knew you'd be out. So we need to go speak to the man. Right now."

Baillet grimaced, and caught Bramer up since their last conversation. Schlüter *was* the main suspect, but lacking any direct motive it was likely he was working for someone. And unfortunately he was not available for questioning, being if not already dead at Gripsholm then wishing he were. Bramer had the wench refill their flagons as Baillet went back over everything from the top, focused now on who might have engaged Schlüter. The Chancellor had originally hired him of course, but his being involved in Descartes's murder made no sense at all. Zolindius was eager to bring Descartes there to establish the Academy, and doubly eager to suppress scandal during the Gala. And what could be his motive? Descartes's influence on the Queen's faith? Zolindius had never expressed any interest in religious matters beyond those relevant for state affairs; if anything, maintaining the alliance between Sweden and France should mean that he was committed to Descartes's well-being.

It made more sense to imagine that someone else paid Schlüter to remove the philosopher. And then the philosopher's brother, to protect himself. And that Zolindius had Schlüter arrested to suppress the case quickly.

"But you've left out the most important part, Adrien," Bramer objected.

"Who paid Schlüter. And why. I know."

"I'm telling you. It's the mathematics."

"The notebook."

"Exactly."

"So what's next? We can't speak to Schlüter."

"His last words," Bramer suddenly said. "What did the priest say they were again?"

"'...*Reviens ... Ma petite France.*' 'I return to my little France'?"

"Oh. I heard it differently. Not as an abbreviated 'I return', but as a command: 'Come back, return, my little France.'"

"So any idea what that means?"

"No, but I was just thinking. About the empty spaces. In Descartes's life. The late '30s. You said that both Viogué and Voetius were spreading rumors of René's having a secret family?"

"Yes?"

"Well when two bitterly opposed ideologues agree on something, it's probably worth investigating."

"So in the late 1630s René was with—woman and child?"

"Or children, perhaps."

"Let me guess. In Deventer."

"Maybe those words are somehow a reference to his ... family."

"Or to the first 'great truth' he discovered there."

"Or both. Adrien." Bramer was staring at him in a strange way again. "How old are you? Your early thirties, or so? I am just curious."

"I'm not entirely sure. They didn't know how old I was when I was delivered to Charlet. How old are *you*—" Baillet asked with an awkward smile, "Eudoxus? Eudoxus?"

Bramer's attention had wandered. "Sorry. I was just thinking about how I'm going to send you to Deventer. I'm seventy-two years old, Adrien."

"I'm sorry? You're sending me to Deventer?"

"We're at a dead end here. Deventer is the next step. Find out what happened there. Find out about his family. Find out," Bramer paused, "what I was right about."

"Why can't you go?"

"Well, let us see. One of us is being inducted into the Royal Academy of Sweden, this very evening. The other has no particular obligations to Sweden after tomorrow. In fact the other has no obligations anywhere, as he was raised in a Jesuit college to which he developed no attachment and which, he tells me, developed no attachment to *him*. He was then dispatched to this frozen wasteland where, if he stays, he will surely soon lose his head by antagonizing a head-hungry Chancellor." Bramer was gazing at Baillet in an almost—fatherly way.

"You want me to get back on a ship again? Don't you remember—"

Bramer held up his hand. "We'll find you an overland route. Or mostly overland, anyway."

"But—I don't have funds. Said Jesuits only gave me— one-way passage here. I—"

"Adrien. Stop."

"What?"

"I'll take care of you. Listen." What was it with this gaze of Bramer's? This wiry old man with the secret strength was melting in front of Baillet's eyes. "Mathematics has been good to me. My compasses, you recall. In great demand throughout the wars. And now I've got the Academy. I'll take care of you."

"I'm not taking your money, Benjamin."

"Adrien. Listen. I have no wife. No children. Anymore. I'll take care of *you*."

"But Benjamin—"

"And I want the truth. I want to know what happened. Here in Stockholm and there, and then. In Deventer. If he had a family I want to know about it. And I want to know what happened before 1620."

Baillet softened. "And of course there's The Equation."

"That would be nice, too, Adrien. But I am obligated to remain here. You," he paused, "are all I have. So let me take care of you."

Perhaps triggered by Bramer's reference Baillet suddenly thought of his arrival at La Flèche all those years earlier. Most of the details were fuzzy—he was so little— but he recalled traveling overnight, all night, in a carriage, freezing, it was spring he thought but felt like winter. He was wrapped in a blanket, covered up, as usual couldn't breathe, the carriage was being drawn at top speed over bumpy roads. Once or twice men shouted but he couldn't understand them, it was a foreign language. And then—it stopped. They were there. It was dawn, maybe. So quiet suddenly. He remembered rough hands pulling him out of the carriage, unwrapping him from the blanket, this little sleepless frightened boy who didn't understand what they were saying and didn't know where he was or why he was there. And there was Rector Charlet, standing there, waiting for him, to receive him. Gazing at him with almost the same expression, Baillet thought, that this old German mathematician was directing toward him now.

Eudoxus, Baillet thought. Kunigunda.

Polybius. "I completely forgot about this," Baillet's mind clicked. "In René's drawer."

He pulled the yellow band from his pocket and placed it on the table.

Bramer picked up the band, looked at it, examined it.

"I think it's a child's plaything," Baillet said. "It obviously meant something to him."

Bramer was running his finger over the surface, looping around. The soft expression on his face was gone, now, replaced by, what—a mathematical one. He ran his finger around the band one more time, slowly, thought a moment, then handed it back to Baillet. "See what you can find out about it, while you're at it."

There was a long moment of silence while both men gazed at each other. An old man staring in a strange way at a young man, who stared the same strange way back.

45

*H*is Excellence limped up to the podium in a way commanding instant silence from the room. He then stood without saying a word, just staring for long painful minutes, his sharp beard silently reminding you of his skill with a razor. It seemed fitting, Baillet found himself thinking, that the Chancellor's remarks at the Closing Banquet would consist entirely of silence. An eternity of silence, he thought, before the Chancellor limped away and the meal was begun. Once more one of the Chancellor's favorites: sheep stuffed with pig stuffed with rat.

The man liked his meat.

"You could come with me," Baillet had suggested to Bramer at the tavern.

"You're ready for this, Adrien."

"But you of all people should know better. You've seen me in action, as you said."

"Yes, but the last thing I saw was you standing your ground with your fists up, ready to defend yourself against those hoodlums."

"Right before I was tackled from behind by an old man."

Bramer smiled. "At any rate you'll have this."

He pulled out his folding gully and pushed it across the table.

"Benjamin," Baillet began to object.

"Let me take care of you, Adrien. By helping you take care of yourself."

"But you—don't you need it?"

"The only threat I face here would be from the Chancellor. And I'm afraid that if he should want my head, my gully would be useless to preserve it. And anyway—"

"What?"

"I told you I took it from a Jesuit. It somehow feels right to return it to a Jesuit. You can do this, Adrien."

On leaving they embraced, an embrace lasting long enough for Baillet to realize he had never been embraced this way before. It wasn't until he reached into his greatcoat pocket for his limericks a few minutes later that he found that Bramer had slipped something in there: Baillet's own deck of playing cards, the one Bramer had won from him on the ship. There was also a note: "In case you encounter an even worse card player than you along the way. Safe journey, B."

It was this greatcoat that Baillet wore over his official costume as he arrived at the Closing Banquet. He'd had a productive afternoon. A stop at the Ambassador's Residence to inquire about overland travel back to the continent; he casually made up a story about an urgent message from his superiors requiring his immediate return to La Flèche. The lovely round Marguerite—after expressing concern for his facial bruises, from his "slipping on the ice"—assured him the Ambassador would make the arrangements. Then he returned to his flat and easily composed his report for the Ambassador. All he had to do was give brief summaries of his conversations, then echo the Royal Physician's conclusion that Descartes had died of inflammation of the lung.

"Thank you, Ambassador," Baillet said at the banquet

table after Chanut passed over some travel documents, starting with a reservation on a sleigh departing Stockholm at eleven the next day. Baillet then withdrew some papers from his robe. "So perhaps I should give you this now."

"Your official report, Père?" Chanut took them.

"Yes, sir."

"Natural causes?"

"Of course, sir."

"Very good, Père. His Excellence must have been pleased."

"He hasn't seen it yet, Ambassador. I thought I'd give it to you first."

The Ambassador thrust the papers back into Baillet's hands with alarm. "God, no! The last thing we need now is to insult His Excellence's sense of priority. I can have a copy made later for His Majesty."

"But I depart at eleven tomorrow. I have no time to—"

"We'll get you in first thing in the morning. Now hush. The benedictions are about to begin."

Before long the dishes had been cleared away, the speeches were over, the *brännvin* had been refilled one last time. Baillet had been unable to concentrate on the speeches, or the speakers, or the inaugural members of the Academy. He surely would be unable to concentrate on the ballet, to be performed shortly in the Royal Theater. What he was thinking instead was how tired he was, and how wonderful it would be if he could just close his eyes for a minute ...

The next thing he knew he was being prodded awake.

Standing in front of him, poking him in the belly with a long bony finger, was the Royal Librarian.

"Down here, you thieving Jesuit!"

"Yes, yes," Baillet sputtered groggily. "You can stop poking me now!"

"I think not!" Freinsheimus exclaimed with a final poke. "Where are they?"

"What are you talking about?"

"My documents, damn you!"

"Ah," Baillet said. In all the excitement of this long day he had forgotten that he had indeed become a thief. "Sir, I—"

"Hand them over! Now, before I poke you again!"

The old man's finger aimed menacingly at his belly.

"Look, I am sorry. But—" Baillet observed himself so easily lying, "I needed them because I have developed—" Baillet dropped his voice, "a new theory. I need to speak to you about. Thanks to your documents, sir, I now believe that—there are dark—and dangerous—secrets in Monsieur Descartes's past. Darker, more dangerous than—the Brethren."

"Oh?"

"A *sex* scandal."

"Details, Jesuit!"

"Shh! Not here. It isn't safe." Bramer glanced around furtively.

"Of course it isn't! I cannot *believe* you even brought it up here."

"Listen, Herr Freinsheimus," Baillet locked his eyes on the old man's. "I need some information from you. *Very* delicate information. Perhaps we can meet in the morning. At the Library. When I'll return what I've—borrowed. All right?"

"All right, then, Jesuit. I will see you at—"

"Not half past four again," Baillet interrupted.

"You're right. Too sensitive. Make it four bells even."

46

SATURDAY,
FEBRUARY 16, 1650

*I*t was René that Baillet was thinking about at that absurdly early hour while the Librarian ranted at him for removing the documents, for having doubted his opinions about the Brethren. René reappearing in Benjamin's life after many years' absence. His discovering The Equation on his own, writing it in that notebook. Waiting alone in Stockholm for Benjamin to arrive, waiting to see him again, to share the incredible news. Yet also worried about *something* ... The fear, the terror in those final words "*He* is here ..." Had Baillet himself actually glimpsed The Equation without knowing, in that glance into the notebook before it disappeared?

"Fine. Now," the Librarian, done ranting for the moment, glared at Baillet, "for your scandal, Jesuit?"

"Of course, Herr Freinsheimus. As I said last night, thanks to your—*outstanding*—work, I now believe Descartes kept a dangerous secret. Involving ..." he dropped his voice, "a secret family. Perhaps one arranged by—*the Brethren.*"

"Obviously," Freinsheimus snorted.

"Indeed. Likely in the late 1630s or so. Very likely in Deventer, in the United Provinces."

"Illegitimate family, I assume."

"One assumes. Can you help me find any further information, do you think? Precise dates, locations, and—names, if possible? And you understand—"

"Absolutely confidential. Please, Jesuit. Who do you think you're talking to?"

Baillet nodded respectfully.

"Very good, then," Freinsheimus said, a glint in his ancient eye. "I will let you know tonight what I find out. I'll send the boy."

Baillet grimaced. "I should have mentioned. I depart today. At eleven."

"Ah? So soon?"

"I've been recalled. To La Flèche."

"Yes you *should* have mentioned. Give me a few hours then. I'll send the boy to your flat. By ten bells, shall we say?"

After Baillet departed, the Librarian walked quickly—for him—to his desk in the main hall. Lighting a candle he sat down and withdrew some stationery from the drawer. How he loved that letterhead, the bold letters declaring that the missive was "From the Office of the Royal Librarian." This was an important moment, he knew, his chance to reclaim the favor that had been stolen from him over the past few years. His Excellence had never respected him, ever since taking over his job as the Queen's foreign language tutor. Well here was a chance to prove his value, and he was not going to waste it.

Freinsheimus dipped his quill and wrote a few very important sentences. Then he slipped the letter into an official envelope and stamped his official seal. Then he walked quickly—for him—and retrieved his greatcoat from the Coat Hook of the Royal Librarian.

His Excellence, he knew, was an early riser.

47

Stockholm was already retreating into the distance, disappearing into the gray haze of snow through the sleigh window. From here Baillet could still make out the spire of Riddarholm Church, the towers of Tre Kronor Castle. Somewhere in there were Her Majesty, Her Royal Consort, Her Royal Chancellor; Baillet had dropped in for a visit but this world was where they would remain, where they belonged. Benjamin too, he thought, with a sad twinge. Baillet himself, he didn't belong anywhere. Not there in Stockholm, not where he was going in Deventer, not back at La Flèche. Not even in this sleigh the Ambassador had arranged for him, which, with its fancy built-in stove, was designated for dignitaries such as the three Danes already slumped over asleep around him.

With a last glance and with a heavy sigh he saw the city evaporate from view.

His companions snoring, he withdrew the envelope he had found in his rooms just before departing. He slowly pulled out the yellowing sheet within. The old man hadn't enclosed any note. But then again he hadn't had to.

It was a sheet from a baptismal registry.

About two thirds of the way down, under the date of 7 August 1635, there it was:

> Vader Rener Jochems
> Moeder Helena Jans
> Kint Fransintge

Ma petite France was his first thought on seeing the little girl's name. *Come back*. But he hadn't had time to reflect on this because his eyes had promptly descended to the next line, revealing the location.

Little Francine had been baptized at the Reformed Church in Deventer.

He returned the sheet into the envelope, and the envelope to his pocket. Then slipped his hand into his other pocket, next to the deck of cards and yellow band. The handle of the gully was for some reason warm to the touch.

48
1640-49
THE UNITED PROVINCES

Descartes did not remain in Leiden for long. After making arrangements with the printer to bring out a new edition of *Meditations* he moved to a small cottage in Endegeest, outside town. This would be a quiet place to begin work on his planned textbook and to continue his work on the physiological basis of fevers. It would be good for his undernourished Kooiker too, Monsieur Grat, who would no longer have to contend with the cruel street urchins from whom Descartes had rescued him. They would live quietly here, alone, man and beast, sharing cold suppers of hard cheese and stale bread.

The news from Mersenne that Joachim had passed away a year ago, in October of 1640, barely touched him. The letter from Pierre that Mersenne forwarded shortly after, in which Pierre threatened to kill him if ever he should find him—"After defrauding our father you worthless pig turd, I shall make sure that not one franc of

Father's estate gets to you. When I get my hands on you ..."—he simply turned over to use for some calculations. Mersenne sent more news that Roberval was writing mathematicians all over Europe charging that Descartes had stolen his geometry. He, too, threatened to kill Descartes should the worthless pig turd ever show his face in France again. Descartes sighed and turned this one over, also, for some calculations.

Over the next few years the world outside continued to turn, and to burn.

First Minister Richelieu finally stopped complaining about his health in December of 1642, when he died. Five months later King Louis XIII followed suit, somehow never having noticed that his five-year-old son with wife Anne of Austria, now boy-King Louis XIV, bore an uncanny resemblance to his First Minister.

Meanwhile Christina of Sweden reached her majority and her monarch-hood, in 1644, and brought her sort-of-womanly touch to the ongoing conflict across Europe. With the German campaign now under her name the Swedish army slaughtered thousands of Imperial soldiers, raped and plundered everywhere they arrived then burned everything when they left. If peace were ever to come to Europe again, it was clear, it would have to be by mollifying Sweden. The only thing slowing the Lutheran powerhouse was the growing conflict between Christina and her Chancellor, Oxenstierna. The word on the cobblestone was that her personal advisor Zolindius was personally advising her to give up Axel, preferably in some fatal way.

But these things were all far away, comparatively speaking. Compared, that is, to what was about to happen right there in the United Provinces, beginning in the fall of 1641.

The exotic spices from the East Indies, beguiling men away from virtuous home cooking. The sauces dressing honest meat the way cosmetics made decent women into whores. The sugar from Brazil destroying the otherwise pure souls of waffles, pancakes, and *poffertjes*. Alcohol, obviously; smoking, like the hellish vapors of so many Sodoms and Gomorrahs; women, women, and women. But also those filthy dogs, whom people seemed to care more about than human souls. And those *humanists* who cared only about studying human anatomy and learning how to prolong our worthless human life. Probably secret *Rosicrucians*, all of them.

Welcome to the mind of Gisbertus Voetius, Chief Pastor of Utrecht, Professor of Theology and Rector at the University of Utrecht. A man whose brow was furrowed into a permanent scowl, who loudly proclaimed "No!" then asked what your request was, the sort of man who counted no one amongst his friends unless they were the sort of man he was.

"No!" he proclaimed before Regius had explained what he was asking.

They were in Voetius's office, in the high tower at the center of campus from whose window Voetius could glower down upon everyone.

"But, sir, I am perfectly positioned to do this," Regius replied, trying not to notice Voetius's eyes beneath that scowling brow.

"You believe that your training in medicine and botany prepares you to sponsor a disputation in natural philosophy?"

"I do. Sir. You are perhaps aware, sir, that I have been working with—Monsieur Descartes."

He might as well have confessed that he'd been eating sugared *poffertjes* in the company of loose women and dogs. But one consequence of Voetius's face being locked into its scowl was that he was not capable of looking any angrier than he already looked. There was a long silence as Voetius absorbed this confirmation that Regius had been consorting with the notorious philosopher.

"This man is not of our faith," Voetius said tersely. "It is not clear that this man is of *any* faith."

"But, sir, it *is* clear. He believes in our Lord. He has written as much."

"My son, do not be fooled by superficial remarks. It is well-known that this man stresses the power of human reason to understand God's ways. That he believes sincere faith allows anyone to obtain salvation. To the contrary we believe in the inherently sinful nature of man and that pretty much no one will obtain salvation. We do believe that, do we not?"

"Of course we do, sir. But Monsieur Descartes is perhaps the most eminent mathematician and natural philosopher alive. My proposal is merely to present some of his work, and my own ideas, to our students and to whoever else chooses to attend."

Voetius was not happy about this but also understood that he was ultimately powerless to stop the process. Better to restrain it, at least, if he could not suppress it altogether.

"You will, then," he conceded, glowering, "restrict yourself to matters of natural philosophy. You may make no mention of any matters pertaining to the faith. Above all you may not mention the name of that man. Is that clear?"

"Of course, sir," Regius nodded. "You have my word."

A week later Regius arrived at the room on Maliebaan that Descartes leased for whenever he made the long day's journey from Endegeest. Regius was, as always, struck by how spare his mentor's lodgings were. And of course that mangy dog that was his constant companion. The candle stub burning on the little table only emphasized the oddness of meeting at one in the morning, his mentor's preferred time.

"A disputation on natural philosophy," Regius said. "You have read what I sent you, Monsieur?"

Descartes nodded.

"And?"

Descartes hesitated. "Your exposition of my account of motion is adequate, Regius, and you rightly explain my rejection of scholastic forms in the etiology of fevers. But there are several points of concern. For one, your problematic doctrine on the soul."

"But—Monsieur, I present persuasive arguments on its behalf!"

"My concern is the practical question. Our mutual friends will not approve your suggestion that a person is an accidental union of the body and soul."

"But you must say that, once you reject scholastic forms."

"It is not the content of your doctrine to which I am objecting, just its mode of presentation. You must not reject scholastic forms explicitly. You must simply ignore them as you present your natural philosophy. And the same," Descartes added quickly, "must be said concerning the motion of the earth around the sun."

"But these questions must be addressed, Monsieur!"

"Regius, there will be no one present who does not know that you are presenting my own philosophy, or theories derived from it. Is that not so?"

"It is, Monsieur."

"Then I must insist you make the changes I require. I have written up some of the specific details." Descartes gestured toward one of the stacks of paper on the table. "Regius."

"Yes, Monsieur?"

"I have been making great progress on my *Principles of Philosophy*. I have also made strides in—personal matters. What I need is solitude and serenity."

"Monsieur?"

Descartes stood and picked up the papers, extended them to his disciple. "If you insist on this disputation then you must give me your word that you will restrict yourself to matters of natural philosophy. That you will make no mention of any matters pertaining to the faith. Above all that my name will not be mentioned. That you will—" he paused, then concluded softly, "leave me out of it. Is that clear?"

"Of course, Monsieur," Regius nodded. "You have my word."

"You gave me your word," Descartes moaned two weeks later.

"I'm sorry, Monsieur. It just spilled out."

Descartes remained silent, his head still in his hands. The one-in-the-morning candlelight reflected the gray strands in his wig. When he finally looked up his face looked thin and tired. "He will not allow this to stand."

"Indeed he will not, Monsieur." Regius produced a broadsheet, copies of which had been posted all over town. "I pulled this down outside the *Rasphuis*."

The *Rasphuis*, or "Sawhouse," was Utrecht's notorious house of correction, so nicknamed since its sinful inmates spent fourteen hours a day working saws back and forth through thick logs, powdering brazilwood for dyes. That the Rector had posted his broadsheet there was an ominous sign.

"The devil has arrived,'" began the broadsheet, "and its name is 'the new philosophy.'" The "accidental union" of the soul and body? Then each could exist without the other, contradicting the necessity of resurrection for salvation! Copernicanism? That directly contradicts scripture! And imagine the chaos, the sin, if people were to believe the cosmos was centered around the sun instead. A return to sun-worship, paganism! And to reject Aristotle's forms? Only skepticism could follow, as the infamous father of the new philosophy, a certain Frenchman, made clear in his scandalous work recently appearing in that immoral city of Paris. And from skepticism, irreligion comes next. The broadsheet ended with a fervent call to remove the devilish elements from their midst.

"I did not want this, Monsieur Grat," Descartes moaned, rubbing the sleeping dog's head.

"What should we do, Monsieur?" Regius asked.

"Perhaps we can ignore it."

"I'm afraid you underestimate the Rector, Monsieur. If we fail to respond then everyone will think that we have been defeated. That will only encourage him."

"I prefer to stay out of this, Regius."

"But you are already in it!"

"Nevertheless. I am just—"

"What, Monsieur?"

"Too old for this. I need—serenity, Regius. I must ask you to let it pass. Let it blow over. Do you think you can do that?"

"Of course, Monsieur. You have my word."

Several weeks later, in February of 1642, Regius posted his own broadsheet anyway. Bolstered by arguments borrowed directly from his mentor, it savagely attacked the application of Aristotelian forms to the soul. The following month the Academic Senate at the University, overseen by Voetius himself, banned Regius from teaching natural philosophy. The Utrecht *Vroedschap*, or Town Council, followed by issuing an official condemnation of Cartesian philosophy.

"My dear Rector," his colleague Professor Wittewrongel said upon noticing Voetius's scowl after these important victories for the Rector, "I should think you would be smiling now."

"But my dear Wittewrongel," Voetius replied with an unchanging expression, "I am."

Descartes could not help himself either.

The second edition of *Meditations* was about to go to press augmented with some new material. There was just enough time for Descartes to incorporate into this material some remarks about the recent matter with Voetius. No mention was made of Regius, since Descartes was no longer on speaking terms with his former disciple.

Descartes employed a few particularly choice phrases. The Rector was a "quarrelsome pedant," an "enemy of the truth," his fulminations being "a combination of the ridiculous, the vicious, and the false," and so on. When the new edition of *Meditations* came out later in 1642 it became quickly clear to all that Descartes was the world's greatest thinker. What wasn't clear was *what* he was thinking when he included this material in the volume. For he was a foreigner in this country, a Catholic, a layman, unaffiliated with the University; and here he was he was publishing a nasty personal attack on the distinguished Orthodox Dutch Calvinist minister who was also Rector of the University of Utrecht.

If one were looking for peace and quiet then one would *not* find it here.

"My dear Rector," Professor Wittewrongel said upon noticing Voetius's merely ordinary scowl after Descartes's attack came out, "I should think you would be feeling *extraordinary* anger right now."

"But my dear Wittewrongel," Voetius replied with an unchanging expression, "I am."

Descartes tried to return to his *Principles of Philosophy*, but there was so much to distract him.

To distance himself from Utrecht and conserve his funds he moved to an even smaller cottage in Egmond aan den Hoef, up the coast from Haarlem. He found himself spending more time here having one-way conversations with Monsieur Grat than working on the *Principles*. Lately the pour hound had been suffering from gum problems, so he also spent long hours mashing his food for him. At Mersenne's prodding he accepted some correspondence with Princess Elizabeth of Bohemia, who was curious about the relationship between the mind and the body, as well as about the human passions.

"Anything, it seems, my dear friend," the retreating

philosopher whispered to a snoozing Monsieur Grat late one night, "to keep from working on my *Principles*."

Anything, including responding to the new manifesto—sarcastically called *The Admirable Philosophical Method of René Descartes*—that appeared in 1643. Replying to Descartes's attack it was authored by young Martinus Schoock, who had been wisely impressed by Voetius's threat to excommunicate him if he refused to put his own name on Voetius's document. It was bad enough that Descartes was a Catholic, the manifesto asserted; but he was also somehow a skeptical atheist at the same time, not to mention a Rosicrucian for good measure. And then there was that inexplicable affection for that filthy canine of his. The true believer could only fantasize about what awful sinful things went on in that hovel of his.

With that filthy *male* canine, by the way, which was even worse.

"It was one thing to attack my character," Descartes wrote to Mersenne, "but to attack Monsieur Grat? That was too far."

He couldn't help himself.

He abandoned his physics and returned his attention to the Rector, resulting in his *Letter to Voetius* appearing later in 1643. In two hundred thorough pages he demonstrated precisely why Voetius's manifesto was cruel, slanderous, libelous, impudent, insolent, evil, and prosecutable. Once these charges were proven he called on Utrecht's Academic Senate to punish the man for corrupting the young students they were paying him to teach. He followed this up with an open letter to the Utrecht *Vroedschap* explaining why censuring Voetius would be for the good of the town as a whole.

Also, he said, tell him to leave the dog out of it.

That's when the lawyers got involved.

Speaking of Princess Elizabeth of Bohemia, the troubles that her father, the "Winter King," had helped start were slowly, finally, winding down, just as Descartes's troubles were heating up. After two-and-a-half decades of everyone killing everyone, there were whispers of peace in the air.

It helped that France was getting busy with internal problems again. To pay for all the warring, Richelieu's successor Cardinal Mazarin was now taxing not merely the peasants but the nobles too. Irritated, they demanded that the new four-year-old boy-King, Louis XIV, respect their long-established privilege of not paying for anything. They began slinging rocks and the rebellion known as the *Fronde*, the "sling," was under way.

Meanwhile the more mature nineteen-year-old Swedish Queen Christina grasped that France's retreat made it the ideal time to consolidate her gains and orchestrate a general peace. Unfortunately her stubborn Chancellor Oxenstierna disagreed, wanting to continue warring until Sweden had crushed every country around the Baltic. Unfortunately for him it would be he who was crushed first. Moments after watching the ship bearing his son to the 1645 Peace Congresses in Osnabrück and Münster disappear from Stockholm's harbor, he began to feel ill. He was dead before he made it home, crumpled outside his own front door. True he was an old man at sixty-two, but there was something about his death that wasn't right; that grossly swollen black tongue, for example. Rumors swirled about his assassination but nothing was ever proven. The subject of those rumors—the Queen's personal advisor with the intimidating limp, Zolindius—was sent to the Peace Congress to replace Oxenstierna's son, immediately after replacing Oxenstierna himself as Chancellor.

But none of this mattered to the lawyers busy in the United Provinces.

Voetius sued Descartes first, for libel. "I am neither impudent nor insolent," huffed Voetius in a broadsheet about his suit, "although I admit I can be cruel—in prosecuting the evil in our midst. Guilty there as charged!"

Descartes, having finally sent his overdue *Principles of*

Philosophy to the printer, promptly countersued for libel from the claims laid in Schoock-Voetius's earlier manifesto *The Admiral Method*. "A certain Reverend," Descartes wrote in a broadsheet after filing the countersuit, "dares to question my faith. Dares to question my—*proclivities*. Well I can assure you that were I ever to engage in such activities with a canine—and I admit *nothing*—it would be a female."

From here the dispute only degenerated. Voetius responded by filing a further suit, against the material Descartes appended to the *Meditations* in 1642.

"A 'quarrelsome pedant'? 'Enemy of the truth'? 'Ridiculous, vicious, and false?'" Voetius wrote in a broadsheet. "I grant only that I am ridiculously vicious in correcting the false, quarrelsome with evil, and enemy of all who are enemies of the faith." Further, "I do not know what he does with that filthy dog of his. I do not want to know. But I do know that the man is a threat to all that is right and true. A man who consorts with women outside of matrimony. Who you may be certain has produced illegitimate children. Such a man judges me!"

This countersuit left Descartes *very* uneasy.

First, what was it with that preacher and Monsieur Grat? The poor dog, who could barely gnaw the mashed beef tips that Descartes painstakingly prepared for him? But more importantly, had Voetius somehow learned something about his past? Voetius did not have the facts quite right, but did he actually know anything or was he just rumor-mongering? Descartes was feeling dizzy from all the countersuing. He was a man who could do a half-dozen calculations in his head simultaneously but he had not yet mastered how to navigate a world filled with actual human beings.

Dizzy or not, Descartes prepared to file two more lawsuits. The first would target Voetius's original broadsheet back in early 1642. The second would target the most recent countersuit claims about the illegitimate children. It was a risky move, he knew. But not to take the risk when he had challenged all of Voetius's other claims would be perceived as an admission.

He would file the suits next week.

First he needed to make a journey back to Deventer.

One can imagine how he felt. Breaking into the Orthodox Church by cover of night. Carrying a lantern into the office in the rear. Finding the large baptismal register displayed on its stand. Flipping back a decade, finding, then carefully removing, a certain incriminating page. Torn, while tearing, between destroying it and preserving it. The wisest thing would be to destroy it, he knew. But then he knew that the wisest thing wasn't possible for him. He would slip it into his pocket, take it home, slip it into his notebook.

He hesitated in that office, thought about this, wept.

Alone.

By mid-1646 Descartes was running out of money. He moved to an even smaller cottage in Egmond-binnen, a short distance further south from Egmond aan den Hoef. Then he had to move again when the landlord, of the same cheery brand of Calvinism as the Rector, realized Descartes had a dog. Descartes and Monsieur Grat found themselves in a modest unheated cottage behind the dunes about halfway between the two Egmonds. "Modest" was Descartes's euphemism for "uninhabitable," but at least the cottage compensated for its modesty in its isolation and affordability. The sound of the wind whipping in from the North Sea he found sometimes soothing.

In response to Descartes's plea Mersenne wrote, "I am working on collecting your bequest from your father, but that will take time. And I struggle to make sense of your circumstances. I understand that you enjoyed a sizable inheritance from your Grandmère, which you supplemented with funds from your father. Could all these funds already be exhausted, with your simple, solitary lifestyle?"

Warming his fingers over the candle Descartes read this letter and prepared to respond. More than ever he wanted to open up, to be honest; if not with Mersenne, then with whom? To have engaged with the cosmos so deeply, to have *conquered* it with his mathematics—and yet to feel always, at all times, defeated by it at the same time. Alone. Alone with the secret of the universe. Alone with *his* secrets. He realized that he had not merely been thinking these thoughts in this little room, at maybe three in the morning, but speaking them aloud. Monsieur Grat contentedly gnawed in his sleep, undisturbed by his master's thoughts. To be undisturbed; he was envious. Not just of the sleep but of the lack of sentience. He loved this dog, he realized. It was not sentient and even if it were, it mostly slept anyway.

But he loved it.

Had he just said that aloud too?

He could not bring himself to explain to Mersenne where the money went. Where the money was going. Where it all would go.

He put down his quill.

Voetius smelled blood.

It helped that his was the home turf. He had little trouble whipping up frenzies among his colleagues. Over the next couple of years a half-dozen Calvinist professors published tracts condemning Cartesian philosophy. Teaching it was banned in Utrecht, Leiden, and Groningen, restricted elsewhere. More than a few *vroedschaps* even banned its being discussed within their town limits.

Voetius was also helped by his knowledge of the Bible. Over the course of the lawsuits he quoted almost every single thing the Bible condemned then claimed that Descartes was guilty of that thing. He was not merely a bestial homosexual but had committed incest, a kind of adultery (he'd been unfaithful to his unmarried consort), and had worn garments mixing wool and linen. When it was pointed out that mixing these fabrics was a prohibition only for Jews, Voetius's eyes narrowed and he said, "He is a *Jew*, too." The way Voetius hissed made it clear that this was as heinous as any of his many sins.

As heinous as his having sired illegitimate children. As his being a Catholic Rosicrucian. As his having a brother back in France who was apparently very interested in getting his hands on him.

As his very possibly having committed murder some decades before.

"This is really bad," Descartes muttered to Monsieur Grat, sharing a pre-dawn blanket with the snoozing dog to ward off the October chill. "He may just be making every accusation he can think of. But what if—he knows something?"

Monsieur Grat responded with a moist snore.

"You are right," Descartes replied. "I got myself dragged into this, and now I am in over my head. I need help."

As he settled under the too-thin blanket he looked at it more closely. It was made of wool and linen.

He sighed.

The next evening Monsieur Grat had the brilliant idea of writing the French Ambassador, the Marquis Gaspard de la Thuillerie.

"Why did I not think of that?" Descartes said, spooning beef pap into the ailing dog's mouth. "I am a French gentleman. The honor of France itself is at stake."

"So what would you like me to do, Monsieur?" the Ambassador Marquis asked when Descartes had been seated in his office in The Hague. The Ambassador looked curiously but kindly upon the tattered suit the famous thinker was wearing, his gray wig. He was also surprised by how small the fellow was.

"Perhaps, Ambassador, you might write to the

magistrates assigned to the lawsuits. I believe it imperative to establish that—"

There was a knock on the door. The Ambassador's secretary stuck his head in. "Forgive the intrusion, Ambassador, but Monsieur Chanut has just arrived and insisted upon conveying his—"

"Gaspard! You old frog!"

The dapper Hector-Pierre Chanut rolled in, his fancy top hat atop his head, his perfect mustache perfectly waxed and his perfect goatee perfectly trimmed, his impeccable suit impeccably pressed, and his straight white teeth straight and white. In a roly-poly round body with happy red cheeks he instantly brightened the room, embracing his old friend before the Ambassador could pull away and make the introductions.

"Monsieur Resident, I present to you the esteemed Monsieur René Descartes. Monsieur Descartes is an accomplished mathematician—"

"What, Gaspard!" Chanut exclaimed, moving past the Ambassador to vigorously shake hands with Descartes. "Do you think I would not know of France's most famous philosopher? What a pleasure to meet you, Monsieur! And most fortuitous timing, as well!"

"You honor me," Descartes said, awkwardly trying to remove his hand from Chanut's.

"I do! Ten more shakes and I shall let you go. There!"

"Monsieur Chanut is the honorable French Resident in the Swedish Court," the Ambassador explained as Chanut took the seat beside Descartes and reached out to shake his hand again. "And no doubt soon to be Ambassador. An extremely important diplomatic position these days, indeed."

"Indeed, Gaspar. I am just en route to Paris from the peace negotiations in Osnabrück, and I can tell you that Her Majesty Queen Christina will soon be the most powerful monarch in Europe."

"And you Ambassador to her court! How did you pull

that one off, Chanut?"

"Easy, my friend! You learn how to lie continuously and to maintain inconsistent sets of false beliefs in at least a half-dozen interacting people at once," Chanut chortled. "But enough about me. Tell me what I have interrupted here. What has brought my distinguished philosopher friend into the office of my distinguished diplomat friend?"

"Monsieur Descartes has got himself in some trouble, I'm afraid," the Ambassador answered.

"Ah!" Chanut exclaimed. "I'm sure it's nothing that a few well-placed lies cannot fix—especially when told by the soon-to-be-Ambassador to the most powerful monarch in Europe!"

After an almost uncomfortably long silence Descartes began to speak.

The Queen of Sweden was herself a collector.

As a young girl she collected lead soldiers. As she grew up she became fond of weapons, and of hunting gear, and of wearing men's breeches. She liked shooting muskets and riding horses and soon owned dozens of each. She collected languages and under her advisor's tutelage became master of most major European ones. She had a taste for swear words and bawdy jokes, and she liked to share these with attractive young women whose embarrassed blushes she found appealing, so she collected plenty of such women in her court. As she became more powerful she collected territories and indemnities. She *loved* military booty, and giggled the whole summer of 1648 as Sweden retook the city of Prague where it had all started thirty years before. The best part, just as Chancellor Zolindius had promised, was the Hradčany Castle and its treasures from the former Emperor Rudolf II's own glorious collection. By late summer of 1648 Christina had shipped back to Stockholm its many "curiosities": paintings, statues, scientific instruments, coins, medallions, manuscripts and books, and one solitary live lion found roaming the Castle's abandoned halls. It would take months to catalogue all these things, not to mention figure out what to do with the lion.

"But that isn't all," Chanut exhaled with a chortle. "She is collecting scholars too!"

"As 'curiosities'?" Descartes said skeptically.

"That's rich! But who cares, as long as she pays? She plans to found an Academy. Like our *Académie Française*, you know. Something befitting her status as the new Queen of Europe. Her man Zolindius has already established a Royal Library to lay the foundations. And she has begun inviting famous scholars to her court. She is planning some Gala to inaugurate it, once the treaties are signed."

"And you believe that I might be part of this?"

"Not just I, my friend. The Queen herself believes it!"

"What, she needs a librarian?"

Chanut chortled, but stopped when he saw that Descartes was not smiling. "She has bigger plans for you, my friend. Chancellor Zolindius pulled me aside just last week at the Congress. He asked me to convey Her Majesty's request to you—should I be able to find you— that you come and oversee the founding of her Academy. To write its statutes, be its First Philosopher, that sort of thing. And what luck for me, to find you here!"

"I do not understand."

"What isn't to understand? They say you are not only the First Philosopher but the First Mathematician as well. Why shouldn't you found an Academy for the First Monarch?" He paused to let this sink in. "And there's one more thing. Her Majesty wants you to tutor her personally in your philosophy."

"Pardon?"

"She is a scholar herself, you know. She has a thing for languages. Has glimpsed at classics, literature, that sort of thing. She has read your *Meditations*. She dabbles."

"I suppose that means I would have to travel there."

"That would help, surely!" Chanut chortled.

"They call it the land of ice and bears," Descartes said resignedly.

"And now lions," Ambassador Thuillerie added cheerfully.

"Descartes, listen," Chanut clapped the back of his new best friend. "This is a wonderful opportunity for you, *and* for France. Here you are, practically heckled out of this lovely land of milk and cheese by this crazy *predikant*. You will forgive my saying this but you have obviously," he gestured to Descartes's worn clothing, "fallen on hard times, shall we say. And here comes the wealthiest monarch in Europe who wants to dump money on you and take you away!"

"I seek—serenity," Descartes answered. "I do not relish the attention."

"It appears too late for that, Monsieur," Ambassador Thuillerie interjected not unkindly. "The attention seems to relish *you*."

Descartes lowered his eyes. "And for France, you said?"

"Descartes," Chanut dropped his voice. "Listen to me. There are rumors."

"What rumors?"

"The Queen is secure in her power," Chanut whispered, "but not, perhaps, in her faith."

"I do not understand."

"All I am saying is that it would be much in the interest of our beloved France—our beloved *Catholic* France—to have a, shall we say, *representative*, who has the ear of this powerful Lutheran lady."

"Monsieur Chanut—"

"Eh!" Chanut waved his hand. "I am just saying. Do with that information what you will."

"I am inclined to ignore it."

"Anything but that."

"It is not really my—thing," Descartes said, whose need to remain hidden suddenly felt overwhelming.

"Is being scandalized by this Calvinist *predikant* more your thing? Or perhaps starving to death in the land of milk and cheese?"

Descartes stared at the highest-ranking French official at the Court of Queen Christina, noted his gaze darting from Descartes's eyes to the pustule now flaring up on his cheek, and then to the scar on his jaw. "May I think about it awhile?"

"Of course!" Chanut chortled, returning to his earlier demeanor. "You're a philosopher, are you not? Think all you like!"

"And it is true, what you said—that the Queen is interested in learning my philosophy?"

"Would I lie to you?" Chanut said cheerfully, clapping him on the back again. "Now, let us put our heads together and think what we might do about this little— what was his name—this despicable Voetius fellow?"

Descartes returned to his cottage behind the dunes to think it over.

"I feel," he wrote to Mersenne late one night, "I have become twenty years older in the past year alone. Like Monsieur Grat, who can no longer walk any distance, I am more feeble, in greater need of my repose than previously. It is hard to imagine my surviving the journey to this land of ice and bears. And impossible for Monsieur Grat."

Wait—what was that sound? Just the wind outside? It sounded like whispering. "But who would be whispering out here?" he asked Monsieur Grat, who kept on snoring. He found himself wondering again what had happened to Eudoxus. The wars ravaging that land were drawing to a close. The treaties were soon to be signed at Westphalia. Too late no doubt for his former mentor. Too many years having heard nothing. Descartes could only hope his death had been an easier one. That perhaps he had joined his beloved daughter—Descartes hesitated, not remembering her name. Some time back he had burned that little recipe book she gave him. He was so cold, needed the kindling—Kunigunda.

In his *Discourse* he had written that once you make a decision you should not re-think it, not question yourself. In *The Passions of the Soul*, which he was attempting to finish, he criticized remorse, the feeling of regret over how things might have been, over what is now irreversible. But all he could feel now, on another lonely late night in the dunes, the cold North Sea crashing nearby, was the weight of those two points. It was imperative to make the right decision because once made there was no turning back, not practically, not emotionally. There were many techniques for mastering one's emotions. He was developing these in his work on the passions. The problem was that he hadn't yet mastered any of them himself.

Was that a footstep outside? No, it couldn't be. There was no one around here, not at this time of night. "I fear from your silence," he wrote again to Mersenne on another lonely late night in the dunes. "It has been many weeks now since I have had word from you. I am in *dire* need of the funds you were attempting to acquire for me. But more importantly I am worried about you. Please write directly to assure me of your good health."

He paused to listen to the sounds outside again. The caw of a nocturnal seagull sounded almost like that of a child calling, lost in the wind. His heart pounded at the thought. He looked under the table at his dog. He wished Monsieur Grat could really speak. Not just in his master's imagination. It *was* just his imagination, he thought.

"I do not seek any position," he continued writing, "that would remove my leisure to cultivate my mind, even if came with honor and profit. Tutoring a Queen may well come with conditions. Obligations at the court. Dealings with other scholars. It might be unbearable. As you well know, my friend, I cherish serenity above all. Nor do I wish to entangle myself in the intrigues of Monsieur Chanut. And yet here I am. Perhaps if the funds in question were to arrive that would free me from having to accept this offer. Please send word immediately, dear friend. Chanut has written again seeking my reply. He seems determined to ensnare me."

Determined, indeed, was a good word to describe Hector-Pierre Chanut, the newly named French Ambassador to the Court of Queen Christina. There were reasons he had risen so quickly in the diplomatic ranks. He was the sort of man who figured out what was best for himself, or those he represented, then figured out how to get that thing done.

For example, that despicable Voetius fellow.

The fall of 1648 was an extraordinary time.

On October 24 the Treaties of Münster and of Osnabrück were signed between the Holy Roman Empire, France, Sweden, and sundry allies. This "Peace of Westphalia" marked the end both of the Eighty Years War between Spain and the Dutch Republic and the Thirty Years War between absolutely everybody. Queen Christina celebrated Sweden's new status as the Most Powerful Nation in Europe by officially announcing the founding of the Swedish Royal Academy and the Gala to inaugurate it. The Germanic regions, which had the most to gain from ending the wars, also had the fewest people to appreciate it. Perhaps only thirty percent of the population survived the devastation, the famines, and the pestilence. Most of these would die shortly after the peace, of famine or pestilence.

The next several months saw celebrations throughout the newly independent United Provinces too. Fireworks, drinking, festivals in every town and village, now that they were free of those awful Spanish. A glorious Christmas had come and gone and it was going to be a glorious new year for all of them.

Or all of them except Rector Voetius.

Voetius, that is, who could have no idea how eager the highest judicial authorities in the Provinces were, post-Westphalia, to earn the favor of the mighty Queen of Sweden; nor how grateful they were to Ambassador Chanut for enlightening them how they might do so.

"The Rector's behavior in these matters," the letter began, copies of which Voetius and Descartes received simultaneously in their large office at Utrecht and their decrepit shack respectively, "is not in keeping with the strict moral standards required by our Orthodox faith. We find that the libel suits filed by the Rector are as without merit as those filed by Monsieur Descartes are replete with it."

Descartes and Voetius both stopped breathing at this point as well.

The letter continued.

"In addition we find the Rector's personal attacks to be reprehensible. A Professor of Theology, and all the more so a *Rector*, at any University of the United Provinces, must be a man of only the purest integrity. Heer Voetius must be stripped of these and related titles."

And *that* was not all.

"We hereby recommend to the Utrecht *Vroedschap* and to the Ordination Council of the Orthodox Church that Heer Voetius no longer serve as Chief Pastor of that great town, nor as pastor anywhere at all. We further recommend the Right Reverend Swartenius to serve as his replacement in Utrecht. Signed on this day of our Lord ..."

The fireworks exploding outside Voetius's office could not match the fireworks in his soul.

He stared at the page through the narrowly slitted eyes of his deepest scowl.

Twenty-five leagues to the northwest in his shack Descartes stared at those same words and felt nothing. But what he was thinking was that Voetius was not the sort of man who would take this result lying down.

"No good will come of this," he wrote to Mersenne late that night. "I should not have let myself become involved. I seem unable to manage with—people. I am afraid even to go to Egmond tomorrow, to post this letter. Already when in the village to purchase my bread and scraps for Monsieur Grat I see that people are looking at me. Whispering about me. Following me. I am thinking of accepting the Queen's invitation. A word from you, dear friend, is desperately needed. It is now months since your last letter. I am at wit's end with worry."

The next afternoon Descartes did make the journey into Egmond to post the letter. It was a wet, gray, cold February day. A solitary seagull accompanied him overhead as he walked along the sand. The several people he passed all seemed to stare at him, he thought, before looking away when he met their gaze.

There was a letter waiting for him.

It looked important, with its impressive royal seal.

He slipped it into the pocket of his frayed greatcoat and took it home to read later.

Ambassador Chanut was pleased to inform him about the Peace of Westphalia. "And I stress," he wrote, "that Her Majesty Queen Christina is now planning her Academy and Gala. For February of next year." Meanwhile Descartes may also have heard "of the untimely passing of Père Mersenne, several months ago. He was fifty-nine they tell me, when he died in his cell. I understand you were once close to the good man. You have my condolences. But I am confident—" and here Chanut referred to their earlier conversation, "that Père Mersenne would have been enthusiastic about the assignment you are about to undertake."

It was on receiving this news, Descartes thought long after, that he had made that internal transition. For years he had sought to master nature so as to be able to prolong human life. But now he realized there was a far wiser strategy. It was better to learn, simply, not to fear death.

He himself was in his early fifties. That is what he was thinking as he read the Ambassador's letter a dozen times that long night, the wintry wind whipping around the dunes outside, almost like someone whistling out there. It was nearly impossible to imagine that Mersenne was gone.

Mersenne was gone.

Gone with him was any hope of acquiring those desperately needed funds.

Not to mention nearly every connection Descartes had to other human beings.

He pulled the thin blanket closer, sure he heard something at the window. He went over to the dirt-smeared pane of glass. Pitch dark outside, of course. He wouldn't be able to see anything even if there were something to see.

This was why he did not see what *was* there.

The young man who a moment before had been standing at that window, looking into the gloomy room lit by that candle already burned nearly to the bottom. Who was staring into that window at the dog sleeping under the table and fingering, in his pocket, a small packet of dry powder. Who was not happy about *his* assignment, about coming out to this cold forlorn place, but who was even less happy about the alternative.

The young man who the next afternoon would watch Descartes bundle himself up and take his daily now solitary walk along those lonely dunes. Who would then slip over to the cottage, force open the door, and say quietly, "Here, boy. I have something for you."

It was too cold. His greatcoat was too thin. His beaver hat was nearly useless for warmth. The North Sea waves seemed especially unfriendly today, angry. Threatening him, even. He kept his distance from the water as he walked. He thought he heard whispering in the wind then realized that he did: he was whispering to himself.

He decided to cut short his walk and head home.

The door to the cottage was open.

He didn't think he had left it that way.

His heart was in his throat as he entered.

Monsieur Grat was gone.

He ran back outside and looked up and down the dunes. There was nothing to see but gray empty sand and the angry endless waves. If there had been footprints they were already erased by the wind.

He looked up and down the dunes.

He looked up and down.

He looked down.

He was not one of those who held that tears were appropriate only for women, he had written to the now departed Mersenne long ago.

No he was not indeed.

The weeks passed. The weather did not. It remained cold and wet and gray. He slept a lot. He went into town as infrequently as possible. He did not like the way people looked at him. He must have looked terrible. He didn't know because he had first turned his mirror around to face the wall and then just thrown it into the sea. He grew a beard, not deliberately but by omitting to shave, which seemed advisable given what he had done with his mirror. The beard did not grow in evenly. Patches of white and gray on his rough skin. Without Monsieur Grat to care for he mostly didn't know what to do with himself. He slept a lot. He ate hard cheese and stale bread when he felt like eating. After a while he returned to his manuscript on the passions, perhaps because he was, lately, alternating between feeling them so intensely and not feeling them at all. The weather remained cold. He ate some bread and cheese. He slept a lot.

In March or April a man came by. He pounded on the wooden door for a long time before Descartes finally woke up. It may have been mid-afternoon. It may have been spring.

"Who, now?" Descartes asked, groggy and trying to understand the man's incompetent French.

The man claimed to be from Sweden. The navy. "Flemming" may have been his name.

"Where is your uniform?" Descartes asked skeptically since the man was dressed as an ordinary Dutchman. But the man did not understand Descartes's question and Descartes did not understand his answer. Nor could Descartes understand the document the man kept thrusting into his face. The document might have been written in Swedish, and it might have been Swedish he was speaking.

But then again he might just be an assassin, Descartes thought suddenly.

He slammed the door in the man's face.

He went back to sleep.

Some time later there was more knocking on his door, which soon became pounding. Descartes lifted his head from his mattress, then placed it back down. After a few moments the pounding stopped.

Then the window of the cottage was shattered as a stone hurtled through.

Descartes jumped out of bed to see the red puffy face of Ambassador Chanut peering in the window.

"Open this door this instant, you maniac!" Chanut puffed.

Descartes obliged.

Chanut stormed in, then stopped in his tracks.

"My God, this place is not fit for a dog!" Chanut exclaimed, looking around the hovel.

"It was," Descartes answered quietly.

"When was the last time you even left here?!" Chanut stared in disbelief at the piles of trash around the little dark room.

"What is ... today?"

"Wednesday."

"No, I mean what season."

"My God! Look at you!"

Descartes frowned, unable to figure out how to comply.

"This will not do. Not at all. Listen, Descartes. Step outside. Into the light. And air, for that matter."

Descartes again obliged, and squinted against the glare on the beach. The sea waters were calm, the ocean sky was blue, the salty air was warm. "Ambassador—" he began to say.

"Don't talk. Just listen. What the hell were you thinking with Admiral Fleming? Answer me!"

"You said not to talk."

"After you answer me!"

"Who is Admiral Fleming?"

"Who is Admiral Fleming? In charge of the Swedish Royal Fleet, that's who. Queen Christina sent him to Holland a couple months back to pick up some scholar's library she had bought."

"What has that to do with me?"

"And to pick *you* up personally and take you to Stockholm. He says you screamed at him like a crazy man and slammed the door in his face."

"That sounds vaguely familiar."

"Why didn't you go with him?"

"I did not know who he was."

"But I wrote you he was coming for you."

Descartes stared at the Ambassador without comprehending.

Chanut sighed. "You didn't read my letters."

"I—have not been to town in a while."

"Since when?"

"What season did you say it was?"

"Oh for the love of Mary! You nearly single-handedly destroyed the alliance Richelieu and Mazarin have spent decades developing. I hope you are happy."

"I am not," Descartes answered.

"All right, then, listen." Chanut stared at this strange little man with the long patchy gray beard, the wild hair, shreds of clothing. So this is what genius looks like, he thought. "We shall start all over. Chancellor Zolindius informs me that the Admiral will be in Amsterdam again at the end of the summer. When he returns to Stockholm the Chancellor wants you to be on that ship with him. This will give you time to settle in, begin tutoring Her Majesty, and prepare for Her Highness's 'Birth of Peace' Gala in February. Have you finished your piece on the passions, by the way?"

"I have," Descartes answered, having forgotten how Chanut knew of it.

"The Chancellor wants it as soon as possible. Her Majesty is eager to read it before your arrival."

"I am not sure I—"

"Monsieur," Chanut interrupted sharply. "Chancellor Zolindius is frankly a very intimidating fellow who represents the most powerful monarch in Europe. It does not matter what you are, or are not, sure about, I'm afraid. And listen."

Descartes did.

"They are going to take care of you. They will be sending you some new clothes, materials for your work. And some help, too. A valet."

"A valet?"

"You may have forgotten, but a gentleman requires a valet. The next time someone knocks on your door, will you do me a favor?"

"What?"

"Open it. All right?"

Descartes gazed at him a moment then nodded.

Ice and bears, Descartes thought to himself (or whispered aloud) much later that night while the summer sea breezes swirled around outside. But to be of service to the Queen. Unless she only wanted him as a curiosity, like an exotic animal to show at court. Like her lion. But she seemed serious. She was collecting scholars. Collecting books, sending her Admiral to collect entire libraries for her own Royal Library. Chanut had left him with the name of the Queen's librarian, a Freinsheimus, said he should write to request the Royal Library acquire any particular volumes. But then what need had *he* of other men's writings, he who had generated science from its foundations, who had deciphered the cosmos—even if the secret was his alone, no one to share it with, the world not safe enough for it? Still, it might be worth writing Freinsheimus to test the waters. What other scholars had Her Majesty collected so far? How many enemies would Descartes find on his arrival? Petty minds jealous of his accomplishments, stinging at him like angry horseflies. It would be better not to go. But to stay here, in this shack, with the sand and sea and gulls. He was out of money now. His clothes were unwearable, his shack uninhabitable. The Queen would take care of him. He could continue to work. A valet, even. Rather ironic, that, in a way. But it would be nice.

Ice and bears.

But here.

This lonely stretch of sand. Chased here by the strange hostility that always seemed to find him wherever he went, whatever he did. Most recently Voetius's rage. Regius stopped speaking to him. Villebressieu broke off with him, so long ago. That Cardinal, Bérulle, threatening him. Roberval.

And *him*.

In those woods.

He took a deep breath.

He remembered Sully, back at La Flèche.

How did he get dragged into all this.

"René Descartes is not," Descartes said aloud softly, to the empty spot under the table, "a good fit."

Perhaps there had been a few. Mersenne. Reneri. Eudoxus. Monsieur Grat. Kosmos—

He couldn't continue the list.

All gone.

He had been chased out of France by the Catholics and now out of the Provinces by the Calvinists.

Maybe it was time to try the Lutherans.

On September 1, 1649, René Descartes boarded a ship in Amsterdam belonging to the Swedish Royal Fleet. For the occasion he was wearing his new green silk suit with its stiff white collar, his lace-spangled snow-white gloves, his crescent-pointed boots, and his extra-curly wig sprinkled with gray hairs. Two steps behind him was his German valet, Schlüter, dressed far more sensibly for the voyage than his master. All around the harbor people were going about their business, unaware that the world's most famous philosopher was in their midst and embarking on the final, brief, stage of his life.

49
FRIDAY, APRIL 1, 1650 (GREGORIAN)
DEVENTER, THE UNITED PROVINCES

$\int$pring was everywhere.

It was in the earth, in the crocuses opening, the daffodils stretching, the tulips for which the United Provinces were so infamous. Spring was in the air, in the warming temperatures, the clamorings of partridges and grebes. It was in the fire, the fires in the hearts of the men and women surviving another demanding winter. And it was in the water, the seasonal rains, the melting lakes, and the surging canals criss-crossing the cities and towns.

There was one such canal nearly surrounding Deventer. From the center of town the main street led all the way out then over the small bridge over that canal. Continuing another two leagues the road became a mostly muddy path; another two leagues further was a cluster of small farms. Here they raised mostly roots and tubers, a few beans, some chickens, eggs. It was a decent hardworking life, where the men and the women and the children each had their designated chores.

At least if there *were* children.

For one of the households had not been so blessed, and given the age of the woman, at thirty-six, they had nearly given up hope. Nevertheless this man and this woman were not unhappy on their small farm. They worked hard and prospered adequately, thanks especially to the woman's magic touch in the kitchen and her uncanny grasp of the therapeutic properties of every possible food, flower, fruit, or herb. Indeed they supplemented their income nicely by selling her preparations in the Apeldoorn market each Saturday. The man would pack the goods early Friday afternoon along with their farm's produce for the week. They would linger in their embrace before he set off on the five-league journey along that difficult muddy road. Her cousins in Apeldoorn put him up overnight, and he would be home before sundown the next day.

And so it was about 1 PM on that Friday, the first of April, a mild moist early afternoon simply bursting with spring, that the man began his embrace of the woman. He was running late, but was in no hurry with his embrace. Maybe it was the warm spring air, maybe it was the potion of pomegranate and pears his wife had made for him last night, but his blood was still rushing and his mind was still racing with thoughts of *last*-night's embrace. "My love, it's time to go," she whispered in his ear, pulling away from him at last. "You'll be back tomorrow afternoon."

She knew that he could and would satisfy his urges then; and hers too. But she knew something else, she felt it, that she did not yet share. That inside her something was forming, something was growing. She could not, would not yet say it. She had her superstitions, she had had her bad luck, her heart broken too many times to say anything prematurely. She would wait until it was a little more certain. Just another day or two.

She watched him walk off into the mist, taking a last glance back at her, then prodding the lazy mule pulling the cart beside him. She watched him for a minute longer, then turned and took her thickening womb back into the house so she could scrub the kitchen. Her husband would be back tomorrow afternoon and their modest home would be clean and waiting for him.

But she was not the only one watching him walk away.

There was a man in the copse just outside the farmhouse.

Unlike the couple he was not in a pleasant mood.

He had arrived down that awful muddy road several hours earlier, his clothes now soaked and soiled. And he had started out from Amsterdam already irritated, not at all interested in this job but recognizing he had no choice. The money was attractive, but remaining alive even more so: his employer had this way of making people turn up dead all over Europe. But maybe this would be the end of it, he could free himself of this entanglement at last. And at least he'd had a few days to formulate a little plan to turn things more to his advantage. Early that morning, on arriving, he had hidden himself near the house. He had seen the woman through the window working in the kitchen, had watched the husband loading the cart. The woman was not bad-looking, he thought. A little older than he liked, but not at all bad. That thought engendered an idea. He would have to keep it in mind as events unfolded. Maybe this would be worth his while after all. He saw the woman pulling away from her husband, saw that the man was leaving and would be gone—for a while. With a cart loaded like that he was heading at least into Deventer, and probably on to that other town. Bare minimum he would be gone for hours.

And that, the man hidden in the copse thought to himself—feeling the smooth bone handle of the new steel blade he had recently bought with his earnings—would give him all the time he'd need.

And then some, for a little fun.

The woman in the kitchen, he could see, with her back

to him, was busy doing something. With steps as unhurried as the couple's embrace had been, the man came out from the copse and made his way through the fresh warm drizzle to the farmhouse door. He removed his hand from his pocket, from the smooth bone handle, placed it on the doorknob and turned.

50
WEDNESDAY, APRIL 6, 1650

*F*ive-and-a-half weeks out of frozen Stockholm, Baillet was now a solitary mule rider splashing his way through the continuous bog that was the United Provinces in spring. Along the journey he'd had lots of time to think about the mystery. He was no closer to solving it but he was now closer to obtaining the next piece of information. The secret woman and child in René's life, he was almost there.

By early afternoon he was in Deventer. He stopped at the first tavern. His incompetent Dutch did not obtain any information about Descartes, though it did obtain a flask of *jenever*, which he downed quickly. Hesitantly he withdrew the sheet from the baptismal registry, and showed it. Very strange looks, serious looks, were exchanged when the local men saw this. Baillet was not surprised—here was a stranger showing up with a document illicitly removed from the local Church—but he was unnerved by the alarm he detected in the Dutch muttering that ensued. Finally one of the men pointed at him, then pointed at the registry sheet, then pointed at himself.

Baillet handed it over.

There was a silence, more strange somber looks. The kinds of silence and looks that locals might direct at the second of two strangers to appear in a tavern within a few days of each other seeking the same destination.

Especially after what had happened after the first one.

And then the man mumbled a few words. When Baillet failed to understand he made a gesture, guessing that Baillet might have writing materials. The man took Baillet's quill and scribbled a rough map on the sheet, with one X indicating the tavern they were in and another X indicating the destination. Next to the destination he scrawled a word, which Baillet now realized was one of the words they had been saying to him: "Bloemaert."

Baillet accepted the sheet, took back his quill, nodded to express his gratitude.

The men watched him as he left the tavern and climbed back onto his mule.

The rain was picking up.

51

After an absolute downpour lasting sixty seconds the sun was now shining on a glistening spring day. Baillet was too distracted by the men's reaction in the tavern, though, to appreciate the weather. Those somber stares really rattled him. The kind of stare you might get, he thought, if you wandered into a funeral and unwittingly asked to speak with the deceased.

Well, it would be resolved soon. As the muddy road made a slight bend a modest farmhouse came into view. It was a well-maintained property, a barn, some chickens. A peaceful scene of domestic bliss, he imagined, for some happy family. The only thing missing were the children running around after the chickens.

Oh, and one more thing was out of place, Baillet thought as he approached. The man sitting on the step outside the farmhouse door, head in hands, sobbing.

With a sinking feeling Baillet dismounted and waited until the man finally looked up.

"Good morning," Baillet said in French, tipping his hat.

The man wiped his eyes with his hands, both of which Baillet noticed had scratches and cuts on them. His weeping now under control he stared at Baillet without answering, waiting.

"I am looking for the—possibly former wife of—René Descartes," Baillet explained haltingly. "By the name of—possibly—Helena Jans. Or perhaps a—maiden by the name of—Francine."

The man's swollen red eyes gazed at Baillet, who found himself wondering whether he had just asked to speak with the deceased at a funeral. The man then said something in Dutch which Baillet didn't understand. The only thing Baillet did catch, however, was the word "Bloemaert."

"Monsieur Bloemaert?" Baillet asked, pointing at him.

The man nodded. Then he called out in Dutch, addressing someone inside the house. A moment later a lovely woman about Baillet's age wearing a country dress and white bonnet emerged, wiping her hands on her apron. Baillet couldn't help but notice her rosy cheeks, her blonde hair slipping out from under her bonnet, her delicate nose and chin. He had never thought much about women—there didn't seem much point—but he found himself thinking about this woman. Baillet bowed awkwardly to her and introduced himself.

"My name is Baillet," he said in French.

"I am Vrouw Bloemaert," she answered in serviceable French, giving him a surprised look, "and this is my husband Heer Jacob Bloemaert."

"Please, Vrouw Bloemaert, call me Adrien. I am sorry to disturb you but I have traveled a great distance to speak to—"

"We were expecting you, Adrien."

"You were? But—"

"Please come in. I have a *hutsepot* on the fire. And my husband can loan you some dry clothes, I am sure."

"But—Vrouw Bloemaert—I don't understand. How can you have been expecting me?"

"Come inside and warm up, Adrien, and I'll explain. And please," she said, taking his soaking coat from him, "call me Helena."

52

"René is—dead," Baillet said as gently as he could.

Helena did not flinch. Her light blue eyes gazed ahead. Was her expression one of spite or hatred? Or—sadness? Baillet watched her closely as she translated for her husband beside her at the kitchen table, who then put his hand on her arm.

"I suspected as much," she said quietly. "When?"

"February. In Stockholm."

"The circumstances?"

"He got sick. The weather. Inflammation of the lung."

"You are kind, Adrien," Helena rested her other hand on her husband's. "But that isn't possible. René was meticulous about his health." Her warm gaze focused on Baillet's eyes. "René had many enemies, Adrien. You can be honest with me."

Baillet hesitated. "There is talk of poison," he admitted, his heart fluttering under her gaze. "That is why I am here. With some questions about his life. I'm sorry."

Again she did not flinch.

She translated for her husband, then fell silent.

Then her husband put his arm around her and she

began to weep.

"You loved him, then?" Baillet asked when the weeping began to subside.

She turned to her husband to say a few words. Bloemaert stood, his own eyes welling, bowed to Baillet and left the room.

"Please excuse Jacob, Adrien. There are chores to do. And you and I have much to discuss."

"Of course, Helena. But is everything all right? I noticed your husband was—upset. Outside, when I arrived. I don't want to intrude, if he was recently—or this is a bad time—"

"You misunderstand, Adrien," she answered with a small smile. "In fact it's a good time. Bittersweet, with your news. But a good time. We have prayed for a child for many years. And just when we had given up hope ... I told Jacob this morning that I am with child. His tears outside were of joy."

"Ah! That *is* wonderful news."

"But you have not come all this way to learn about our tiny lives. You have questions about René. Please, Adrien. Feel ... comfortable."

Baillet's gaze wandered around the kitchen. For a modest farmhouse kitchen it was well stocked, filled with hanging cookware and shelves packed with bottles and jars and books and pamphlets. The stew she had been preparing now lay untouched on the table between them.

"Thank you, Helena," he began slowly. "You and René were—together?"

"Yes," she said simply.

Baillet hesitated. "Married?"

"No, Adrien. Just together. About six years."

Baillet found himself feeling anger at Descartes for taking advantage of this woman. "And he just left?"

She shrugged, tears appearing again.

"I'm sorry," Baillet said, wanting to—touch her arm himself. "I would think—imagine you might feel bitterness. And yet—"

"There's a lot you don't understand, Adrien."

"Regrettably that isn't unusual."

"I am truly, deeply happy now. Jacob is a wonderful man. Who weeps with joy at the news of a child. Who is probably this minute heading into town to order his paternity bonnet rather than taking care of the chores. Who loves me more deeply than I could possibly deserve. And who lets me love *him*." She paused. "René made our life possible, Adrien."

"By—leaving you?"

"No. I mean yes, obviously. But no. After he left he sent money. Never a letter, no words, just a few notes wrapped in paper, every few months. That money allowed me to manage, those first years. I moved here, to this farm, to keep it going. It was very small then. And then when Jacob and I met ..."

"May I ask when that was?"

"The summer of 1642. No one here would ... talk to me, in those days. Jacob wanted to do nothing other than talk to me. He asked me to marry him within the week. But of course, it wasn't possible."

"Why wouldn't anyone speak to you? Was it your— relationship with—René?"

Helena nodded.

"And why couldn't you marry Jacob? If René hadn't—" again Baillet felt that surge of anger, "married you?"

"We didn't have enough money, Adrien. Jacob had not a guilder to his name. I had enough to manage for myself, from René. But to start a ... family ..."

Baillet gestured to indicate the farmhouse and surrounding fields. "You have managed well, you and Jacob."

"Yes, and no. This would not have been possible without René. He continued to send money. He had one or two other properties he sold off, sent the proceeds. I wrote that I was fine, I had more than enough, but he was

... stubborn. Disencumbering himself, I suppose. And then I thought ... Well, I would hold onto it, if perhaps, some day ..."

Her voice trailed off. Baillet waited for her to resume.

"Anyway," she continued with evident determination, "I wrote to him to tell him that I had met someone and that we would eventually marry. And that I was ... happy."

"You must forgive me, Helena," Baillet felt himself blushing, "I am not very familiar with—romantic matters. But is it the usual course—after someone has left you—to write—so warmly?"

"This was not a usual matter, Adrien."

"Please?"

"Two weeks later René sent me four thousand guilders. With a note, the only words he ever wrote after leaving, words I have repeated to myself a thousand times since: 'May you, who deserves it most, know bliss, my beloved Helena.' With that money he allowed us to purchase this land and have our life." She paused and then touched her belly. "And at last this baby ..."

Helena resumed weeping. Baillet thought about that enormous quantity of money, and about what Ambassador Chanut had said—that by the end of the 1640s René was living in a decrepit shack by the sea, and that he had come to Sweden because he had run out of money. And now Baillet understood that he had run out of money, had been driven to his murder, because he had—given it all away.

"He loved you," Baillet whispered when the weeping had slowed.

Helena nodded.

"But he wouldn't—marry you?"

"To the contrary, Adrien. He wanted desperately to marry me. He was ready to give up everything, his work, his ... everything. It was I who ..."

"I'm so sorry. I don't understand."

"I couldn't let him do it, Adrien. I knew him better than he knew himself, in some ways. He wanted desperately to be known. Just slightly more desperately than he wanted to remain hidden. If we had married it would have destroyed his career. At the time we thought ... it seemed that we could just keep our secret. He trusted me, Adrien. He felt safe with me. I should have ... If I had only ... Perhaps he would have ..."

Baillet waited again while she wept. Perhaps René would forgive him, he thought, for having thought ill of him a few minutes ago.

"Something happened to him, Helena," Baillet probed gently. "Something. I don't know exactly when, or where. It was perhaps 1618, 1619. After he left La Flèche but before he resurfaced. In Germany. In 1620. This was before he knew you. Obviously."

Helena's expression became tense.

"You know, don't you?" Baillet asked.

She did not answer.

"He is gone now, Helena. By a strange chain of circumstances I have been charged with the task of understanding why. What I can promise you, Helena, is this: I am a friend. I am his friend. And I am your friend."

Baillet couldn't recall precisely when understanding this man's life and death had become the most important aspect of his own life.

"He trusted me, Adrien. Only me. But even that wasn't enough."

"Trust me now, Helena," Baillet whispered.

"You mentioned Germany. It was in the Black Forest. In Ulm. And it was on November 10, 1619. René told me that on that night, in that place, he became *rené*. Reborn."

Baillet waited, breath suspended.

"That's it," she said.

"That's it?"

"That's it."

"What happened?"

"He wouldn't say."

"He was 'reborn'? What does that mean?"

"I don't know what it means, Adrien."

"And he wouldn't say?"

"He wouldn't say."

Baillet gazed at her. "Helena, there was a boy with him, back then. From La Flèche. Who disappeared. Could it have been—could that be it? Did he ...?"

"He said nothing of that."

Baillet stared into her eyes, read them.

"All right," he continued gently. "René wanted to remain hidden. He was not the person he appeared to be. He had a secret. An important, bad secret."

Helena returned his gaze but said nothing.

"He felt safe with you. He shared that secret with you. Only you."

She still said nothing.

"Because of that secret, somehow, you felt you couldn't marry him. But you loved him anyway, Helena. Helena," Baillet said suddenly, not noticing her expression, "who else—did anyone else know that you knew his secret?"

"Adrien, stop," she said, looking away.

The stew on the table was cold, thick, coagulated.

What a lucky man Jacob was, Baillet found himself thinking.

"There was a child," he continued, knowing their time, his time, was short.

Helena nodded, looking down.

"What happened?"

"She—died."

"May I ask ...?"

"A fever. She turned purple and died. She was five."

"When ..."

"In September of 1640."

"And then—"

"He left."

Reviens, Baillet thought.

"I am so sorry," he whispered.

He wanted to leave, to leave her alone, in peace. No, to

leave *with* her, to console her, to care for her, then he caught himself, stopped himself.

He forced himself on.

He reached into his pocket and withdrew the yellow band. "This was hers?"

Helena covered her mouth with her hand. "Did he have it ...?"

"I am so sorry," Baillet whispered, nodding. "What—is it?"

"It was a toy. For our ... daughter. They played with it endlessly, twisting it into shapes, animal shapes." She closed her eyes a moment, then reopened them. "May I?"

She examined the band briefly, found a certain spot on it, then pulled. The band opened up, revealing several wires protruding from one of the separated ends. She twisted that end once and reinserted it back into the other end. "There's this trick. It now has only one side."

"I'm sorry?"

"Run your finger along it."

Baillet discovered he could slide his finger along the band, over what appeared to be its front and back sides, and return his finger to its starting point without removing it from the surface.

It *was*, somehow, one-sided.

"René was excited about it," she explained. "Something mathematical. I don't know. He said it was some kind of wonderful discovery."

Baillet stared at it, committing the mechanism, the twist, to memory, to share with Benjamin later.

It didn't need to be said that he was leaving the band with her.

"Helena," Baillet continued after a moment, "you said you were expecting me."

Helena took a breath, then reached over to open a drawer. She pulled out an envelope and handed it to him. "A man came a few days ago and left this for you."

"A man?" Baillet asked, taking it.

On the front he saw, in large block letters, "Baillet."

"He wouldn't say who he was. He walked right in the door. He had a ... I thought he was about to attack me. But then he seemed to change his mind. All he said was that you would be arriving soon and that I should give you this. And then he ran off when he heard my husband coming back into the yard." What she didn't mention was that Jacob had returned because he needed one more "snuggle" before his journey to Apeldoorn.

Baillet was staring at the envelope, at his name.

Slowly he opened it and withdrew two sheets of paper.

On the first were the same large block letters: "If you want the rest then bring three hundred guilders to ..." A barely legible Amsterdam address was scrawled there.

In different handwriting, on a yellowing piece of parchment, were scribbled tightly woven series of mathematical symbols. Mathematics crammed in, every space on the page, both sides, except for one little part on one side in French that Baillet was just able to decipher. At the bottom of that side there was the date, August 15, 1639. And there were the words: *At last*.

It was a sheet from Descartes's notebook.

53
SATURDAY, APRIL 9, 1650
AMSTERDAM, THE UNITED PROVINCES

*B*aillet stood at the door of the flat on Kalverstraat.

The last few days were a blur. The wonderful supper with the Bloemaerts, Helena's omelettes, the *jenever*, and the overall good company left Baillet seriously regretting having spent his adult life stashed away in La Flèche. With a long embrace he had left Helena the next morning, Jacob accompanying him as far as Apeldoorn to help him negotiate for a coach. Baillet had no idea how his investigation would end but one thing was clear: he was not going back to La Flèche. And one other thing: the day's ride on the coach from Amersfoort to Amsterdam was not long enough to absorb the image of the sad philosopher playing the echo game in the garden with his poor little daughter. Or the image of beautiful Helena sobbing after she told him about it.

Come back my little France, Baillet was thinking over and over as his coach entered Amsterdam, bumped down the Rokin, where the coffeeshops were packed with investors,

459

speculators, messengers, spies, ministers, and whores. He found his way to his inn near the Wisselbank, where Benjamin had deposited funds for him. A sleepless night. Dreams of Stockholm, winter, the heads on Zolindius's wall. Of Helena, René, Francine. *Come back my little France* ...

And now here he was at the flat on Kalverstraat.

The sun was beating down. He was perspiring.

He stood at the door, staring at it, hesitating.

He felt in his pocket, for the purse stuffed with notes.

To think how close he was to the notebook.

But then again he was also close to somebody who had probably paid Schlüter to murder René, murder Pierre, and steal the notebook. Somebody who might either be interested in selling the notebook now to Baillet, or in luring Baillet here to murder him too. Baillet felt in his other pocket for the gully he was now very glad Benjamin had given him. It occurred to him that he should switch the blade and the purse, so his weapon would be ready to his right hand.

Then it occurred to him simply to have the weapon *in* his right hand.

Baillet knocked.

54

*T*here was no answer.

He knocked again, waited.

He tried the knob. Locked. He glanced up and down the street. It was thick with people minding their own business. He bent down to examine the mechanism. The keyhole was large and, peering in, he could make out the latch mechanism. With another glance up and down the street he slipped his gully's pointed end just far enough in to jiggle the mechanism.

After a moment of this he heard the click.

He opened the door, and slipped inside.

The door had just closed behind him when he realized he had merely assumed the murderer wasn't home. But what if he were waiting inside *pretending* not to be at home, to lure Baillet in?

His heart wasn't even pounding, he realized.

The room he had entered was spacious though dark, the windows facing the street having their blinds drawn. If Baillet had examined the room closely he would have seen that it was nicely furnished, that some of its pieces were high quality, and even familiar to him.

But there wasn't time to look closely.

For he was very distracted by the stench and by the flies. But at least the mystery about what was causing that stench was more quickly solved than the mysteries of Descartes's life and death. For it was hard not to notice the dead body crumpled up in the puddle of blood before him.

Baillet covered his mouth with one hand and approached the body, waving away the flies with the other. Gently he reached out to turn the body over, to have a look. It was remarkable how heavy a dead body was, he thought as he exerted himself. Why exactly the fact that it was a familiar face somehow made it worse he could not understand—he would reflect later—since the face was only that of an acquaintance, someone he even believed to be a criminal and a murderer.

Perhaps it was because, with one eye frozen open and the other having been carved out of its socket, it looked almost like Schlüter was winking at him.

55

Baillet hadn't the slightest idea how Schlüter could be lying dead here in Amsterdam rather than lying dead back in Gripsholm prison.

But Schlüter *was* here. The notebook was here, or had been till recently.

Baillet began searching the room.

Although it felt like an eternity it probably took no more than ten minutes to search the drawers, open the cabinets, feel around the mattress, look under the bed. He was about to leave when his eye fell on the one painting on the wall, which looked familiar: some young men and women playing dice. Baillet remembered where he had seen it: on the wall of René's study, covering the notebook's original hiding place. Feeling clever he lifted the painting and felt around, pushed, prodded. Feeling much less clever he returned the painting to the wall and took a last look around the room.

Nothing.

He had looked everywhere.

Except—the body.

Once more he approached the thing, waving away the flies.

Again he pushed as hard as he could to turn the body over a little. But at last the body turned again, a little but just enough, to give Baillet another look at that gaping bloody eye socket—and access.

He felt around the man's body, in the pants pockets, outer coat pockets.

Nothing.

Inside the man's clothes, he thought with a grimace.

He slipped his hand inside the man's coat.

There was an envelope in the inside pocket.

He pulled it out. It was covered in blood. There was a rip through the envelope where one of many knife wounds had landed.

But on the back was something still recognizable.

There was the hardened seal wax, imprinted with the Swedish Royal Coat of Arms, the yellow lions and crowns against the blue background. Beneath them were the letters H. M. C.

And beneath those, the initials C. Z.

Her Majesty's Chancellor.

Carolus Zolindius.

56

Baillet had no idea how he returned to his room at the inn. His mind had been running as quickly as his body, too quickly to pay attention to streets and passersby curious at the sight of this man dashing through them. Freinsheimus, that old goat, must have snitched. For other than Benjamin, only Freinsheimus could have suspected Baillet was going to Deventer. And so Freinsheimus must have told Zolindius, who must have then written to Schlüter. Schlüter, who wasn't in Gripsholm. Who could not possibly have escaped. So he must have been let out.

Or never sent there in the first place.

The words on the letter in Schlüter's pocket were chilling:

> Our clever friend is en route. Take care of the woman and we shall take care of you.

Baillet shuddered as he ran through the market at Warmoesstraat, thinking about what might have befallen Helena, not even noticing the older man walking slowly the opposite direction and casting him a bemused glance ...

And Schlüter, well, he was now confirmed to be in Zolindius's employ, so Baillet could keep his theory that Schlüter had been paid to murder René and likely also Pierre. He could add to it Schlüter's being commissioned to "take care of" Helena as well.

And add one more thing: Zolindius, the man writing the check for all of this. The man who probably then paid someone else to "take care of" the man he'd paid to murder the previous victims.

The only thing missing from Baillet's theory of the crime was, of course, everything.

Why?

Baillet suddenly stopped running at the market gate, sensing somebody watching him. He turned around quickly.

Nothing. Just busy Amsterdammers doing Easter market things.

Baillet took a breath and resumed running again.

Why?

Surely it went beyond Zolindius's alleged interest in suppressing scandal. Someone responsible for three murders and an attempted fourth was not moved by keeping anything quiet.

It must somehow be personal.

Why Helena? Perhaps if she knew René's secret, whatever happened in Ulm in November of 1619 ... And if she knew it then maybe Pierre knew it too, which might explain why he was murdered. But whatever Helena might know she hadn't shared. And she hadn't been murdered. She was alive and Schlüter was dead and Baillet did not know why.

The mathematics.

The notebook.

That sheet excised from the notebook must have come from Schlüter. But the rest of the notebook was not in Schlüter's flat.

So whoever murdered Schlüter must have taken it.

So Zolindius must have wanted that notebook.

Or maybe wanted it *back*. Maybe Schlüter had stolen it from *him*. Maybe that was why Zolindius had Schlüter eliminated: the man had stolen the notebook, was running his own operation with Baillet to make money from it.

What he needed was a plan, he thought as he entered his room at the inn. Benjamin would be handy right now. But Benjamin was weeks away by coach. Returning to Stockholm seemed an awful ordeal, but it wasn't as if he had anywhere else he needed to go, or anyone else who— needed him to be somewhere. Seated on the bed, preoccupied with these thoughts, it took several minutes before Baillet even glanced down on the bed to notice what he surely ought to have noticed sooner, given that it was right next to him and covered with blood.

He gazed at it a moment, letting it register, realizing it must have been left here within the past hour. He took another moment to realize how surprisingly calm he was, given the circumstances. For some reason, Schlüter's bloody detached eyeball was barely even making him queasy.

He took another moment, still, before he realized just what it was that the moist orb was resting on. It was a notebook.

The notebook.

57

*W*ell *that* was unexpected, Baillet thought, impressed at how calm he felt.

After nudging the eyeball aside Baillet had seen that there was a sheet of paper slipped into the cover of the notebook. In now familiar handwriting was a short message:

> For Père Adrien Baillet, Sleuth Extraordinaire. With
> warmest regards, H. M. C., C. Z.

So, he thought, now unpacking the supplies he had gone out to pick up: a large block of hard cheese, a larger loaf of harder black bread, and a dozen candles for what would be a long night ahead.

Zolindius. Behind it all. Now leaving him the notebook.

But why?

Because he wasn't threatened by it, that's why. Baillet applauded himself for this excellent thought, until he had the next thought.

Or because Zolindius was trapping him somehow.

Really, that made more sense. Zolindius had gone to great lengths to obtain and keep the notebook. Even murdering Schlüter to get it back. The notebook must have meant something to him, to do all that. But then it must also mean something that he was now dumping it on Baillet. And the idea that a three-time murderer might be up to something sneaky might be that very thing.

Or—thinking of himself—maybe four-time murderer.

Who had perhaps been in this very room just several hours before.

Baillet calmly sat at the table, took out a knife and sliced the cheese, making a tall stack of slices. He then did the same with the bread. He pulled out a flask of *jenever*, took a swig then placed it next to the stack of bread slices. He lit two candles, briefly gazed at their lovely flames.

He thought about René, he thought about Helena. He thought about Benjamin.

Then he opened the notebook and began to read.

58
SUNDAY, APRIL 10, 1650

*I*n the distance Baillet heard churchbells chiming five. Dawn had arrived without his noticing. He rubbed his eyes, glanced at the candle stubs, continued not to notice the stacks of bread and cheese that he hadn't noticed all night long, then closed the notebook.

For a moment he felt nothing, thought nothing.

And then it began, *he* began, to review, to process, to analyze.

A mysterious life, in bits and pieces.

The *Mathematical Treasure of Polybius the Cosmopolitan.* The dream in November of 1619, then the "beginning" of the grasp of a "miraculous discovery." Resolving to live hidden, advance masked. Mathematics, symbols, equations, drawings. Bugs, carefully drawn, remarkably and repulsively lifelike, though Baillet now noticed how many of these sketches were surrounded by mathematics too.

Then there were the scattered personal remarks. Admiration for Eudoxus—Benjamin. (Eudoxus, Eudoxus, Baillet thought.) Missed rendezvous with Galileo, in 1623.

A cryptic remark from July 1625: *Tonight the sun went down and shall never rise again.* Observations about health and medicine throughout the 1620s and 1630s: advantages of fruits and vegetables, the claim that the human lifespan should extend to one hundred years. In the late 1630s René wrote that he had not been sick for thirty years, that with his research he felt he would live to one hundred. A decade later he wrote that it was wiser to focus on learning not to fear death.

Going back again, comments about Paris in the late 1620s, warm remarks about Mersenne (his "truest" friend), remarks about Villebressieu, a comment about how hard it was to be understood when one had to live "in secret." A rude caricature of Roberval and a sketch of a melon bug; rough calculations of the volumes of melons. Then a note of alarm that Roberval was digging into his past. Then the words "La Rochelle, October 1628," followed by a long blank space.

The next entry was four years later, anatomical sketches of animals that Descartes had been dissecting in his laboratory in Amsterdam. *What I want, what I crave, is to be left alone. I fear fame and reputation more than I desire it.* This followed soon after by *There are whispers, here, of the new philosophy, of* my *philosophy.* The terrible contradiction between wanting to be known yet remain hidden. Sketches of chicken embryos at different stages of development, surrounded by mathematics. The letter "H" appearing once or twice, then frequently. There were no dates for many entries here but Descartes had begun to think about the passions, felt he was beginning to understand the causes and nature of laughter. Some sketches of—bubbles, surrounded by mathematics. Caterpillars and butterflies. The handwriting became small and frenzied, and familiar. Just then it struck Baillet. He found the sheet of the notebook that Schlüter had left with Helena. Looking closely he saw the nearly straight line the razor had made along its edge, saw that it fit the ragged edges at that spot in the notebook. Carefully he returned the excised sheet to its place; completing the circle, he thought with some satisfaction.

Turning the page gently he saw on the bottom the date and cryptic words again: "August 15, 1639, At last." But now he could see at the top of the next page that there was a sketch of the yellow band. With lines indicating the twist that Helena demonstrated for him. Surrounded by dense mathematics, and then a single long series of strange symbols with a thick box drawn around them. And then once more the same words though now in capital letters:

AT LAST.

Baillet knew he was staring at The Equation.
What he didn't know was what any of it meant.
Benjamin.
Eudoxus.
Kunigunda.
Baillet was beginning to understand his *own* miraculous discovery.

The next page of the notebook was blank. Deliberately blank. Baillet thought *ma petite France*, thought of losing a child, of losing one's parents, of finding and of losing. The next entry was dated merely *1647: They are all trying to destroy me.* There were only a few entries over the next couple of years, and more mathematics. Somehow less intense than before. Then the date "November 10, 1619" and the name "Ulm-Jungingen." This anachronism and geographical anomaly confused Baillet until he saw them repeated down the page, and again on the next page. René wasn't dating and locating these entries but thinking about that date and place repeatedly. The November when he'd had the dream about his future path in life. The night that he had been "reborn." Very much on his mind apparently, in his last years.

His last years indeed. In 1648 there was a mention of a

"Monsieur Grat." Then a mention of Stockholm, followed by "ice and bears." And then he became almost verbose toward the end, the last months. In precisely dated entries from October 1649 onward there were:

> I fear this experiment has been a terrible mistake.

And

> No one speaks to me. The Queen can barely be troubled to meet with me, and only at the impossible hour of five bells; and the Chancellor is so preoccupied with the Gala that I have not yet seen his face.

On 15th January, 1650, René wrote:

> The winter is so cold in this place that men's thoughts freeze, like the water.

On 20th January:

> I am not in my element here.

And then on Thursday, 31st January:

> Word has come that I am to deliver my statutes and verses directly to the Chancellor himself tomorrow morning. At last I will meet this man who is responsible for my exile in this frozen land.

Baillet's already pounding heart squeezed in an extra beat as he turned the page, to the very last page of the notebook, already knowing, remembering, precisely what he would read there:

> Friday, 1st February, 1650
> *He* is here.

Baillet stared at that tense, trembling handwriting.

The sun was coming up and it was all becoming clear.

Or almost all.

Something happened to René long ago. Something that made him the man he became, the man who was to revolutionize mathematics and natural philosophy, who discovered The Equation that—explained *everything*, who was as widely known in intellectual circles as he was hidden in every private one, and who was to be murdered by one equally mysterious Chancellor named Carolus Zolindius.

Zolindius was who René was shocked to find there in Stockholm.

Zolindius, who apparently had something personal against him.

Who was apparently as interested in René's secret as Baillet was.

Who had brought René to Sweden, to murder him.

Who had read this very notebook and therefore knew precisely what Baillet himself now knew. Who had left the notebook for Baillet, *wanting* him to know it.

Namely that anyone who wanted to learn René's secret was going to have to make his way to a little village somewhere in the Black Forest.

59
MAY 13, 1650 (JULIAN)
ULM, GERMANY

"*W*hat are you drinking, pal?" he said in that thick southern accent.

The emaciated tavern owner with the pock-marked nose had approached the table carrying the long axe he kept behind the counter. When new people arrived trouble usually followed, and you couldn't be too careful. Ulm had not fared well during the wars, after all. Almost all the buildings were destroyed or badly damaged. Even the *Ulmer Münster* had been ransacked by both Protestants and Catholics at different times, and once by both simultaneously. Not that there were many people left to care. Most of those who hadn't been massacred or succumbed to famine or pestilence had chosen, at various points over the past three decades, to move away to some other village to be massacred or succumb there.

Ah, how Baillet had enjoyed hearing the lovely German tongue these past weeks, even despite its Bavarian contortions. These comfortable sounds were the perfect accompaniment to his ongoing ruminations, during his journey, over the remarkable news he had learned just as he was departing Amsterdam en route to the southern German lands. Incredible, scandalous, stunning. Two days after the Gala, the Swedish Queen Christina had announced that she was going to become a man; and worse, as far as her countrymen were concerned, that she would also become a Catholic. The clergy squealed, the nobility was up in arms, even the peasants were about to revolt when the Queen nipped them in the bud by nipping a few of their heads in the bud. This she had to arrange herself, since her usual head-nipping Chancellor Zolindius himself had resigned in protest the day of Her Majesty's— or rather, His Majesty's—announcement. Turns out the man had "principles," or so he claimed in his resignation, shortly before completely disappearing from Stockholm. The man's infamous rise through the ranks to the highest administrative position in Sweden had ended just like that.

Now he was nipping a few of his own heads down here on the continent, Baillet was thinking for the hundredth time since Amsterdam as the tavern owner arrived to the table with the schnapps. Having nothing else to do, the man treated himself to a stein and joined Baillet at the table.

Fifteen minutes later Baillet had learned what he expected to learn.

"Two weeks ago, *ja*," Reinke said, having already refreshed their schnapps after returning his axe behind the counter.

"He just showed up, just like that?"

"*Ja*. Moved right back onto the old Rausche farm."

"The Rausche farm?"

"Grandpa Rausche. Built the whole place himself."

"And he's ...?"

"Dead. Many years. A few years after the wars started." Reinke belched, showing his five remaining teeth. "They say he killed more than a dozen of those bastards before they got him. They cut his schlong off and made him eat it before they cut his heart out and made him eat that too."

Baillet grimaced. "Did you say the man moved *back* onto the Rausche farm?"

"*Ja*, he used to live there. Long time ago."

"I'm sorry?"

"I don't think he was their son. Or maybe he was. No one is left around here who remembers."

"I am very confused. He lived here? When?"

Reinke shrugged. "Long time ago, pal. In the '20s. I don't remember. I was a kid."

"How old are you?" Baillet asked, surprised.

"Thirty-two, pal. Look pretty good, don't I?"

Baillet nodded, having thought he was in his fifties. Not that he was thinking much about Reinke at the moment. No one in Stockholm had been able to say exactly where Zolindius had come from. He had appeared on the battlefield in the early '30s, retrieved King Adolphus's body from the woods, worked his way into the young Queen's confidences ... His impeccable Swedish had raised no doubts in anyone's mind that he was a native Swede.

But apparently Zolindius was German.

"You can tell me how to get there?" Baillet asked quietly.

Once there had been a road there, back when there was traffic between Ulm-Jungingen and Ulm itself. Now there was just an overgrown tangle of brambles and weeds, a barely discernible path, along which Baillet's horse plodded slowly. But the gentle pace was fine as neither the horse nor rider were keen to rush the journey. There would be time enough soon for whatever was next. Clarification, at least. Confrontation? Likely. He had his gully, had been practicing unsheathing it, stabbing, hacking mostly fruits and vegetables along the way. He was ready. He was not the least bit afraid, for some reason. He was on a roll, really. All of his theories lately had been correct. Zolindius had come here to the Black Forest, as Baillet surmised; had come *back*. Baillet was now sure that Zolindius had been here when René had his—experience, whatever it was. They likely knew each other, after all. So whatever that experience was, it had given Zolindius some personal motive against René.

And now he was getting close.

To *understanding*.

And should he survive it, he thought with a smile, he would settle back up—well, maybe even in Stockholm so he could tell Benjamin all about it.

There was a clearing, right where Reinke said there would be.

And then there was the farmhouse.

Appearing just over a hillside it loomed, once formidable but now a mere reflection of its former glory. Some broken timbers, a hole in the roof covered with makeshift thatch, two windows boarded up; but the scattered tools, the ladder against the wall, suggested that repairs were underway. The surrounding fields were mostly overgrown too, Baillet observed as he approached, but one area had recently been plowed and sown. Zolindius had returned—home—to exchange the life of the most powerful Chancellor in Europe for that of a small village farmer.

Baillet tied his horse to a tree, then crept up on foot to look around. There seemed to be no one in the vicinity, in the adjacent fields. He looked carefully around, then approached the house and peered in one of the windows.

An empty sitting room. Sparsely furnished, a couple of simple chairs, a small table missing a leg. Almost hard to believe that someone was living here. But that was much easier to believe when there was a noise behind him and he felt the sharp point of a rapier pressing into his throat.

"*Ich fürchete, dass du nicht kommen würdest, Vater,*" a familiar deep voice said in perfect German. "I was afraid you weren't coming, Father."

60

"Your Excellence," Baillet said from force of habit.

"You may turn around, Vater," the man said, withdrawing the rapier.

Baillet stared at him uncomprehendingly.

"I know. It is disorienting," the man said without moving a muscle.

"I have never known a beard to make such a difference."

"I did not believe that this—" the man gestured to the scar along his now shaved jawline, "was appropriate for a man of my position. Or rather my *former* position."

"The injury must have been very painful."

"Indeed it was. I lost the use of my facial muscles on that side as a result." Zolindius—or whatever his actual name was—stared at him, then broke into his half-smile. "But *very* good, Vater. I would have wagered a large sum that you would not find me here."

"And yet you smile?"

"I like being proven wrong. It increases the thrill. Now—" the half-smile faded, "where *is* my hospitality? After your long journey you must require some refreshment."

479

It didn't seem wise to Baillet to decline an invitation from a man with a rapier in his hand. "Your name is not Zolindius obviously," he said, preceding the man's rapier into the farmhouse.

"Obviously. Step to your left, please."

Baillet entered the room, sat in the indicated chair. "By what name shall I call you, then?"

"Your weapon please, Vater."

"Your name, please, Your Excellence." Baillet was briefly impressed with his own courage, before wondering why he wasn't *un*impressed with his stupidity in coming here.

"In due course. I won't ask again for your weapon, Vater."

Baillet removed the gully from his pocket and placed it on the table.

So much for all that practice.

"Now, please, Vater, let us get your strength up. A hearty Bavarian meal, some fresh chopped offal with *Knödel*. Then afterward we can engage."

Baillet was starting to see a pattern here. This man liked to entertain his guests lavishly—he had brought René all the way to Stockholm with expenses paid—before murdering them. But now why was he concerned that Baillet should get his strength up?

Weaponless, however, Baillet decided not to ask. The meal was happily non-fatal, passed in silence. Baillet tried not to stare at that face, at that missing beard, at that frightening long scar.

"Are you adequately refreshed now, Vater?" Zolindius asked.

"That depends on for what, I suppose."

"Shall we take a walk?"

As they went out the door Zolindius stepped back in for a moment, then returned holding two rapiers but without a word of explanation. It was a sunny mid-afternoon now, a perfectly wonderful day to be murdered in the beautiful Black Forest, Baillet thought as he walked in front obeying Zolindius's directions through the woods, Zolindius limping behind him. The woods gradually became denser, though after perhaps twenty-five minutes they entered a relative clearing. Baillet could not understand why he was not nervous, nor afraid. Here he was defenseless in this deserted place, and yet he somehow felt—confident. Maybe it was the fact that Zolindius hadn't killed him yet. Why would he have waited, after all, if that were his intention?

Then again there were the two rapiers to think about.

"Here we are," Zolindius said as they entered the clearing.

"And where," Baillet turned to him, "is here?"

"Where your man gave me *this*, and *this*," Zolindius pointed one of the rapiers to his jaw and the other to the limping foot.

"And why would Descartes have done that?"

"Descartes," Zolindius practically spat the name.

"I'm sorry?"

"Vater, do you fence? You're a Jesuit so I assume the answer must be yes."

Baillet recalled his work as a target dummy at La Flèche. Well, all that time being poked had allowed him to pick up a move or two, he thought; or hoped. "I suppose the answer *is* yes."

"That will do," Zolindius tossed him one of the rapiers. "I'm a bit rusty myself."

"You're giving me this?"

"It would not be interesting unless I gave you some chance, yes, Vater?"

So that explains the meal, Baillet thought. "*En garde*!" he exclaimed, surprising himself at his readiness.

Zolindius's half-smile faded as they began tapping swords, gently at first, loosening up.

And Zolindius began talking.

"Your *Descartes*," he said scornfully, "indeed gave me

481

Andrew Pessin

these injuries thirty years ago. He left me for dead in the snow, in this very spot."

"And so you—"

"Returned the favor, in a sense, yes," Zolindius parried, not particularly inhibited by his limp.

"So you are the boy?" Baillet said with a thrust. "From La Flèche?"

Zolindius gave him a strange look, then smirked. "The boy. Yes. You've become quite the sleuth, Vater."

"You took your time. With your revenge."

"It took me half a decade just to recover from my wounds. I was most fortunate to have been found, and taken in by, the man who built the house you were just in."

"Grandpa Rausche," Baillet stepped aside to avoid a jab intended for his body. They were no longer warming up.

"Very good, Vater," Zolindius acknowledged either Baillet's information or his fencing.

"And after recovering you—"

"Joined in with some passing Swedes and became Chancellor of Sweden, yes. That took a while too." Zolindius stepped away from Baillet's own jab. "But I'm afraid that we do not have the time for all the details. More precisely, *you* do not."

Zolindius landed a blow on Baillet's forearm. The first trickles of blood made Baillet feel woozy.

"You left me the notebook," Baillet forced himself to stand straighter.

"A nice touch, yes?"

"But why?"

"I was curious whether you could piece it together."

Baillet found himself puffing his chest up proudly, that he *had* pieced it together; but realized his mistake when Zolindius's rapier came within a half-inch of his puffed-up chest. He de-puffed and went on the offensive.

"But why did you take the notebook in the first place?" Baillet attacked. "Was it the mathematics?"

"What would I care about mathematics?" Zolindius

482

defended quietly.

"You didn't help Descartes with his mathematics? At La Flèche?"

That smirk again. "You and your sleuthing, Vater."

"Then why take the notebook?"

"I didn't. That fool Schlüter took it and gave it to me. Listen, Vater," Zolindius had pushed Baillet's rapier almost out of his hand, "you might want to try the Italian grip."

"I thought this *was* the Italian grip."

"No, this way," Zolindius shifted his wrist to demonstrate, then continued as Baillet pushed his rapier back. "As for giving you the notebook, my task was accomplished. It was no longer useful to me. Or a threat."

Baillet remembered its last entry. "Descartes must have known. What was happening."

"Descartes," Zolindius spat again. "But ah, the look on that man's face when he showed up in my office that day. You cannot imagine how hard it was to avoid him for three months. Until I was ready."

No wonder Descartes looked like he had just seen a ghost when arriving for Candlemas, Baillet thought, recalling what Viogué had said. He *had*.

And his murderer.

"You paid Schlüter to murder him," Baillet thrusted. "Through Père Viogué."

"In a sense," Zolindius stepped aside.

"In a sense? He worked for you. He provided the poisoned wafers, at your command."

"Let me give you a hint, Vater. Unlike you, the man was not very bright. Shall I give you a minute to think about it?"

They paused their contest. Baillet noticed that Zolindius was perspiring and out of breath. For a man in his fifties and with a limp he was an excellent fencer; but he *was* in his fifties with a limp, while what Baillet lacked in training he at least made up for in age and endurance. With a small boost of confidence Baillet realized that the break was for Zolindius's sake, to recover.

"Well, what is your theory, Vater? Or must I do all your thinking for you?"

Some pieces fell into place. "Schlüter didn't know he was poisoning Descartes, did he?"

"Not bad, Vater."

A detail that had been bothering Baillet now made sense. Schlüter insisted Descartes only fell ill after that first communion, but why would he have done so if he himself were guilty of poisoning him at that communion?

"The parsnip soup," Baillet continued. "It wasn't anything special that it had been delivered. Your office routinely delivered the groceries, didn't it? Including the wafers Descartes occasionally consumed. And *only* he consumed. He was always late to Mass, when he went at all. Schlüter always brought the wafers."

"Convenient that, yes, Vater?"

"And the second poisoning. The same wafers were already there, at hand."

"Yes," that half-smile crossed Zolindius's face. "Schlüter was very annoyed about all that."

"Annoyed? But wasn't he a murderer? What he did to Descartes's brother?"

Zolindius stared at him. One thing remained from his earlier appearance: those penetrating eyes. "He let himself become fond of your man, apparently. And as for Descartes's *brother*, that was my doing. You cannot imagine the lovely look on *his* face when he saw me."

Baillet could, unfortunately. "And then you killed Schlüter."

"He irritated me."

"He stole a page of the notebook from you."

"The fool. And besides, he was weak. He couldn't even take care of a *woman*."

"And why," Baillet whispered, cringing, "was it necessary to send him after her?"

"She had her value, Vater. In any case, who am I to

dispute the roll of the dice?"

"What?"

Zolindius pulled some dice from his pocket. "I prefer to let chance make decisions for me. Minor ones such as who shall live, who shall die, that sort of thing. The arbitrariness of it, I find thrilling. Unfortunately that little lady had an unlucky number the day I wrote to Schlüter. Fortunately for her, her luck was better the day he showed up."

"You are evil," Baillet said flatly.

"Not at all. Just indifferent. Even your man, your Descartes. He was lucky that day, on this spot, and I was not. Later on I was lucky and he was not. Isn't that how it is, Vater?"

"So you murdered him just *because*."

"You make that sound so dirty, Vater."

Baillet grimaced. "In a sense, you said."

"You've done so well so far, Vater. Did you not read the notebook?"

Then Baillet understood. "He *did* know what was happening."

"Of course he did. He was a liar, a fraud, and a murderer, or attempted murderer anyway, but unlike his valet he was no fool. Even I must grant him that."

Liar and fraud? Baillet wanted to rethink these, but then refocused on those final notebook entries. The man's unhappiness, despair. The emptiness after the loss of his child. "He wanted to die."

"Let us just say that he did not put up much resistance."

"He asked for the second dose," Baillet remembered Viogué's testimony, feeling the weight of the poor victim's sadness.

René had had—*enough*.

"The first dose did not work out. I had not calculated for his unusual constitution. That strange diet of his. I did not know whether to be glad he finished the job for me or furious. That he took his own life and deprived me of the pleasure."

"But he asked for an emetic, at the end. To get rid of the poison."

"And why might that be, Vater?"

Baillet's felt sick. "A moment of weakness. Perhaps he—became afraid."

"As so many men do, Vater, when death confronts them." Zolindius tapped Baillet's foot with the tip of his rapier. "I must say I underestimated you, Vater. I would have wagered half the Swedish treasury you would not have made it this far, yet here you are. But now speaking of death, are you rested enough, now, to re-engage?"

Baillet immediately noted two things. First, that it was Zolindius who was now rested and ready to re-engage. And second, that the former Chancellor had just transferred his rapier into his left hand.

He had only been toying with Baillet so far.

"Aren't you going to roll the dice," Baillet tightened his grip on his weapon, "to give me a chance here?"

"I don't think so, Vater."

"But why not?"

"Just," Zolindius said with an aggressive thrust, "*because.*"

Baillet fought it off, realizing that he hadn't yet asked the most important question. "But why," he asked, pushing his rapier back against his adversary's, staring into eyes that had become as gray and cold as steel, "were you and Descartes fighting here in the first place?"

Zolindius merely began slashing his rapier through the air. He landed a blow on Baillet's other arm, drawing more blood. Baillet backed away. Zolindius advanced, limping, slashed Baillet's left calf. Baillet backed away further, toward the edge of the clearing, now in defensive mode. Nothing but woods behind as Zolindius advanced, the rapier swishing. It was beyond formality, decorum, gentlemen's rules. Baillet had vivid images of his time as a target dummy but for some reason he was not afraid, not at all. Zolindius advanced, was now directly in front of him, as Baillet raised his rapier into his best defensive posture.

Zolindius with one quick swish knocked the metal stick out of Baillet's bleeding hand.

"Really, Vater," he signed, "I was hoping for more of a challenge. The Jesuit training seems to have declined since my days."

Zolindius's rapier was back where it started earlier that day, on Baillet's throat. Only now its sharpened point was poking just underneath his larynx.

Baillet's eyes were locked with Zolindius's.

"Your Excellence," Baillet whispered with strange calm. "Is this really necessary?"

Zolindius paused a moment, reflected.

"No," he shrugged.

He began to push.

61

You don't often get to look into the eyes of your murderer as he slowly begins your murder. Even less frequently do you get to see the look in those eyes suddenly change as the murderer changes his mind.

Both of these happened to Baillet.

But it wasn't that Zolindius changed his mind, Baillet realized. Something had happened to him. Something sharp, and in his back.

Zolindius groaned and turned, fell to one knee. Protruding from the former Chancellor's right shoulder was the handle of the folding gully, its blade embedded in the shoulder.

Just beyond the wounded man was seventy-two-year-old Benjamin Bramer, rubbing his own right shoulder with his left hand.

"I am getting too old for this," he muttered. "I think I pulled a muscle."

"Benjamin," Baillet whispered hoarsely, falling to his own knees, the enormity of what had almost happened just hitting him, "left-handed."

It was too late. Zolindius had sprung back up, the knife

in his shoulder slowing him but not affecting his left-hand grip on his rapier. "You should have stayed in Stockholm, you fool," he approached Bramer. "That would have improved your chances of surviving one more day."

"Perhaps," Bramer stepped back. "But it's quality of life that matters to me. Not quantity."

"Regrettably you are short on both, I am afraid." Zolindius emphasized this point by spearing Bramer just beneath the right shoulder. "How is that shoulder now, old man?"

A growing circle of blood appeared.

"Been better," Bramer groaned, falling to his knees.

"I know what you mean. But at least I—" Zolindius grimaced from pain, "have only *one* shoulder injury." With that he speared Bramer just beneath the left shoulder, producing another circle of blood. "Ah! The symmetry! I am sure the mathematician in you appreciates it."

Bramer's face contorted in pain.

"Come on, old man," Zolindius stood over Bramer and pointed the rapier directly between the latter's eyes. "Some final words from an inaugural member of the Swedish Royal Academy? Something brilliant to remember you by?"

The old man stared up at him, thinking that you don't often get to look into the eyes of your murderer as the murdering begins. Even less frequently, he thought, do you see the look in those eyes suddenly change as the murderer changes his mind.

Zolindius screamed, falling on his side, dropping his rapier.

Behind him stood Baillet, who had used the preceding sixty seconds to retrieve his rapier, creep up behind Zolindius, then thrust the rapier into the man's back hoping to poke something thick and sticky.

Mission accomplished.

"I suppose my own experiences," Baillet remarked, "are now diverse."

"Welcome to the club," Bramer said weakly as Baillet helped him up.

"You all right?" Baillet pointed to the large bloody circles on Bramer's chest.

"Been better. As has he."

Bramer pointed to the man bleeding on the ground, moaning.

"What do we do with him?" Baillet asked.

Bramer looked around the clearing, absorbing the utter isolation of the spot. How many tens of thousands of people had been murdered or left to die in this region over the past several decades? One more could hardly make a difference.

Especially one who as Chancellor of Sweden was responsible for his share of that general carnage, and who as individual was responsible for more than his share of particular carnage.

Bramer picked up Zolindius's dropped rapier. "Well, Vater, I suppose we can do whatever we like."

"I would still like the answers to two questions, actually."

Bramer jabbed Zolindius with the rapier. "Are you still with us, Your Excellency?"

"Unfortunately," Zolindius barely whispered.

"Would you roll over please?" Bramer jabbed him again.

Zolindius groaned and obliged. The puddle of blood framing his body was expanding.

"You're sure this is him?" Bramer asked Baillet, staring at the man's face.

"I know," Baillet answered. "Without the beard—"

"That is some scar," Bramer observed. "I would say it's unique, except ..." His voice trailed off as he now noticed all the blood. "Adrien, you'd better ask your questions."

Baillet took a deep breath, resisting the undeserved compassion he was beginning to feel for the man suffering on the ground. "Your name, first. And second, if you please, what were you fighting about with Descartes here in these woods, thirty years ago?"

"I believe those amount to the same question, Adrien," Bramer interjected.

"I'm sorry?"

"You, there," Bramer kicked the man on the ground. "Open your mouth."

Zolindius glared at him, as fiercely as one whose blood was draining away could glare.

"Shall I open it for you?" Bramer pointed the tip of the rapier between the man's lips.

Zolindius opened.

"Out with it!" Bramer shouted.

Zolindius glared.

"Cut it out! Or do you want *me* to cut it out?" Bramer pulled the rapier along the man's lips, drawing blood.

Zolindius stuck out his tongue.

"What?" Baillet asked, confused.

"Look closely, Vater," Bramer said.

Baillet did as instructed. "I—don't understand."

"Will you explain, *Monsieur*," Bramer said sharply, gently scratching the extended organ with the blade, "or shall I?"

The tongue was withdrawn with a grimace, the blood draining from Zolindius's body now draining from his face. "He stole my goddamn life," he whispered hoarsely.

"I believe he felt the same of you," Bramer said.

"Descartes...?" Baillet started to ask.

"Vater," Bramer said, "the boy."

"Who disappeared. Yes I know."

"But there's something you don't know," Bramer stared down at Zolindius. "There was another baby after René, a boy. Given away shortly after its birth, to a wet nurse with a reputation for losing her charges. It was a difficult delivery, and it—caused their mother's death. At least," he added, with a glance at Baillet, "according to the old timers in La Haye to whom Rector Charlet directed me."

"Sign of the devil," Zolindius whispered, fading.

491

"Perhaps ... they were right."

"Brothers," Baillet continued Bramer's account, beginning to understand. "The wet nurse raised the boy instead. He ended up with the Rector, at La Flèche. Like ... me," Baillet turned to Zolindius, struggling hard to resist his compassion. "You fought in these woods. A dispossessed brother. He attempted to murder you. Left you for dead."

Zolindius may have been nodding, or falling unconscious.

"He," Bramer continued, "showed up a year later in Germany, a new person, as he said. At least when hinting at his secret. And a good thing, too, for mathematics and natural philosophy."

"Benjamin!" Baillet suddenly remembered. "The Equation. The notebook. I've got it!"

Bramer looked at him, nodded. "And Pierre?" he said, directing the question at Baillet rather than the man on the ground.

"Pierre would have recognized him. Had to be eliminated."

"And Helena?"

"He suspected she might know the secret as well," Baillet answered in a whisper. That amazing woman who preserved her man's secret for a decade and clearly would have preserved it even when facing death.

"And now I ask *you*, Vater," Bramer said. "What should we do with him?"

Baillet looked down at the dying man. He was no longer the dangerously powerful commander of the rampaging Swedish armies. He no longer looked much like a murdering villain.

He was a badly damaged human being, in great pain.

"He was a liar and a fraud," Baillet summarized softly.

The man on the ground gave a low moan.

"A would-be murderer," Baillet said, "who stole your life."

An even lower moan, in agony.

"The world's greatest philosopher," Baillet concluded.

There was no sound but the man's eyes were open, alert, locked onto Baillet's.

"Adrien," Bramer whispered.

Baillet realized he was running out of time.

"And you," Baillet said softly to the man on the ground. Without taking his eyes from the man's he moved the tip of his rapier directly over the man's heart.

Slayer, he thought to himself, and of himself, with very mixed emotions; then staring down, down, at the man beneath him, he added: *and slain*.

And he thrust the rapier once, hard, and this time fatally, into the chest of René Descartes.

EPILOGUE

JUNE 21, 1650 (GREGORIAN)
AMSTERDAM, THE UNITED PROVINCES

The bright sun in the clear blue sky, the shimmering water, the ships with their white riggings and sails billowing in the breeze, everything full of warmth and color and life. Activity everywhere, arriving and departing, loading, unloading. From their outside table along the harbor they could take it all in, they could watch the loads of jewels, fabrics, breathe in the spices, tobacco, the scent of decaying fish and brine. Baillet had no idea exactly what day it was, having once more transitioned between calendars. What he did know was that they were here in Amsterdam, the center of worlds both new and old.

Beyond that, he knew nothing.

"Just think about it, Adrien," Bramer urged.

"That isn't the problem, Benjamin."

"Then what is?"

"That I have so many other possibilities to think about too."

The man came to refill their glasses with *jenever*; Bramer held out two travel flasks for filling as well.

"Look, Adrien," Bramer continued when he had gone. "We have about an hour before my ship departs. Let's go through them. Methodically."

"Fine. Stockholm."

"Pro's: You'll be with me. We shall study the notebook together. You shall participate in some of the most important mathematics in history."

"Tempting, but con: I know nothing of mathematics."

"Pro: You shall have me to teach you. And anyway," Bramer referred to an earlier conversation, "it's in your blood."

"Con. Stockholm. Frozen. Dark."

"Pro: If you accept my affiliation with the Academy you can use the private tunnels."

"Con: I hate tunnels. Tight spaces. Badly ventilated."

"All right, but pro: Chancellor Sparre. She'll find a position for you, I'm sure. Perhaps you might take over at the Royal Library when Freinsheimus retires."

Baillet briefly thought about the beautiful Chancellor, wondered what it might be like to—work with Her Excellence. "Con. Can't get there without boarding a ship once or twice."

Bramer smiled and withdrew a package from his bag. "This prevents seasickness. Works beautifully. My daughter developed the formula years ago. You can go anywhere you like with this."

"But you saw how sick I was! On the journey to Stockholm! You didn't think to offer it to me then?"

"Of course I did. I decided actively not to."

"Oh?"

"I told you then. I don't like Jesuits."

Baillet was about to answer angrily but Bramer's smile stopped him. "All right, I'm just being difficult, Benjamin. The opportunities are appealing. I would love to learn with you. And now I suppose I can handle the journey. But there's also Deventer."

"Con. Deventer is not where I will be."

"Yes, but they could use me." With an active farm and a baby on the way, Helena and Jacob were in need of some help.

"Sounds quiet, Adrien. You may as well return to La Flèche."

"That I won't do that is the one thing I *do* know."

"Well then you don't strike me as the farming type."

"I don't strike myself as *any* type, Benjamin. And besides it might not be so quiet. There are—" Baillet was about to mention Helena's comment that there were lots of lovely Dutch girls around; then realized how out of place that would sound—coming from him.

"What?" Bramer asked.

"Nothing. Maybe I'll work with them a little while. Help them, save up some money. I would like to travel perhaps." How strange to hear himself say this, too, after his years being fearful of venturing outside La Flèche.

"Don't be silly. You don't need to save anything. The money is yours. Legitimately yours."

"I don't know, Benjamin."

"I have no use for it, Adrien. Especially not now, with the notebook." Bramer paused, then smiled. "Besides I owe it to you, thanks to His Majesty."

Baillet smiled too, remembering their wager, but didn't say anything. There was a long silence, just the gentle sea breeze, the squawks of the gulls. Both men were thinking the same thoughts, each knowing the other was doing the same.

"You'll never find her, Adrien," Bramer said again softly. "It's so incredibly unlikely."

"So was all this," Baillet raised his hands, referring to all of it, everything, the past six months.

"Where would you even start?"

"Here. Anywhere. Everywhere," Baillet repeated the gesture.

"Come with me. If only to study their works. That old fool Freinsheimus is annoying but he is also thorough with his obsessions. He probably has everything they ever wrote."

It was so tempting, Baillet thought.

Stockholm would give him resources, materials, time. Maybe he would write something himself. Maybe write up the story of—well, "Descartes" was the only name available, they had no other, and it was what they were used to. He could write up the whole thing, the life and the death, the history and the mystery of it. Along the way writing his own story too, as he finally *had* a story, with names and dates and facts, all intertwined with that of Descartes's. Incredibly unlikely, he thought again, that Bramer had known his parents. His father a master instrument maker, inventor of clocks, the "cross-beat escapement" and "remontoire" Bramer said, whatever those were. That mechanized globe in Her Majesty's Museum of Curiosities, his father had created it for Emperor Rudolf! And his mother a mathematician too, they had all worked together in Kassel on the theory underlying those compasses that Bramer and Descartes later perfected. The money from those compasses was Baillet's rightful inheritance, Bramer insisted. Ah, and his father was Swiss, his mother German, of course, no wonder German came so easily to him when no other language did. Diophantus, Hypatia, they were working in Prague then, in November of 1620, when the Imperial Army and the Catholic League stormed the city. If not for—Descartes, studying with them, his mother, Baillet's mother, wrapping her terrified children in blankets in the closet, he pulled them out when the screaming outside was done and the house was burning and wrapped them into that box, two bodies in that box, that coffin, to smuggle them past the soldiers ...

Them.

A sister.

Baillet gazed at Bramer, remembering, vaguely remembering, the kind and gentle Eudoxus, the wonderful warm Kunigunda, was it five months Bramer said they stayed with him until—well, until Bramer took the gully off the henchman while the priest got away.

With the boy.

Who eventually grew up at La Flèche and nearly never left.

Baillet looked at the old man's soft sad eyes, awaiting the younger man's reply.

It was incredibly unlikely. That she might have survived. That he could find her. Where would he begin. His own eyes roamed the busy harbor, gazed at all the ships departing for destinations near and far, the desire to go *somewhere*, or *everywhere*, gripped his heart almost as powerfully as did Bramer and Her Excellence and Helena and Deventer. The world was overflowing with possibility and he wanted just to drink it all in.

Maybe he should just choose some place at random.

As he thought this he slipped his hand into his pocket. Beside Benjamin's seasickness potion (which he'd quietly pocketed) he felt the pair of dice he had, well, *inherited* from Zolindius. They were right next to the gully he had removed from the man's shoulder, which Bramer had insisted he keep.

But now Baillet withdrew the blade from his pocket and put it on the table.

"Hold this for me, Benjamin," he pushed it across. "For now."

Bramer looked at the gully, then pushed it back across. "I don't want the gully, Adrien. I want you."

Baillet swallowed, wondering how such a big ball of tears could have made its way into his narrow throat. Blocking all possibility of speaking.

Almost.

"Soon, Benjamin," Baillet squeaked out.

"All right, Adrien," Bramer said, standing up. "Soon. You may be sure I will hold you to it. If you even consider not making it back to Stockholm I will personally make sure you'll need that gully."

Benjamin was gone.

On a ship, gone.

The sun was sinking, it was well along its long slow downward summer arc, and Baillet sat alone at the table with the gully and the *jenever* and the harbor and his thoughts. Watching, thinking, feeling, remembering. The warm breeze, the ships coming, the ships going, and he was thinking, wondering, imagining that this is how it happened.

The philosopher's daughter would have been about fourteen.

She would have been a beautiful young woman, he knew it. Someone so full of the living spirit could not be anything other than beautiful.

And how she would have loved the idea of going to Sweden! Ever since she was a little girl she loved to hear fairy tales and stories about princesses, and now imagine the news, her father was to be philosopher to the Queen! She would have chattered away nonstop about living at court, playing around the castle, dressing up in her beautiful dresses ...

Had she lived, that is ... Her father must have thought about that a thousand times, maybe while looking at the yellow band he made for her, saved, kept, carried, treasured ... But then had she lived, he might have thought, everything would have been different. He might not have done the work he did do, might not have caught the attention of the Queen, they might not have gone to Sweden after all.

They might have just been happy.

The three of them.

Together.

Sitting in their garden on a beautiful afternoon so long ago. Her father began twisting the band, entertaining the little girl by manipulating it into interesting shapes, then untwisting it and giving it to her to imitate the shape he had just made. She was good at it for a small child, she always came close, she had a remarkable sense of, or for— topography, that was the word. With such a natural inclination for shapes, he thought, she was almost certain also to share her father's natural mathematical talent.

At least the geometry part, to be sure. Whether she would share his analytical ability as well—the ability to describe the shapes in equations—well, with a lifetime of personal instruction by the world's greatest mathematician ahead of her, who could say what great things she was going to achieve, this little girl in her sweet green dress in this beautiful rainbow garden?

As her father was thinking these wonderful thoughts he suddenly also thought of a new way of shaping her band. He gently pulled it apart at the nearly invisible seam, twisted one end over, then reinserted the wires to make it one again, a continuous closed loop with the twist within. As soon as he had done this, the little girl squealed with delight, running her finger over it, feeling the smooth yellow silk. Her father watched, and saw, and did it himself, seeing that he could slide his finger from one point on the band all the way around and return to the starting point, without ever taking his finger off. With the twist within, he saw, the band amounted to a single side that looped upon itself. He stared a long time at the band, thinking, realizing you could travel infinitely on such a surface without ever reaching an ending point, because what might otherwise be its ending point was in fact identical with its starting point.

A kind of infinity captured within the finite loop.

You could go as far as you wanted—but then you always came back.

You always came back.

ACKNOWLEDGEMENTS

Though a work of fiction, this book is based closely on the sad life, and tragic death, of the famous philosopher and mathematician René Descartes. While the novelist's liberties were taken throughout, many of the events and characters depicted in Descartes's life and many of the historical events are indeed real. Much inspiration (and the name for a major character) was drawn in particular from the very first biography of Descartes, the 1691 two-volume adulatory *The Life of Monsieur Descartes*, by Adrien Baillet (1649-1706).

Three centuries later there are now many fine biographies of Descartes, but none quite so exquisite as Richard Watson's *Cogito, Ergo Sum: The Life of René Descartes* (David Godine, 2007). It was this literary masterpiece that convinced me that a novel based on Descartes's remarkable life was necessary, and it was specifically on page 189 that it convinced me, in its heartwrenching description of the "echo" game. (*The Irrationalist* has borrowed from Watson's description of the game, as well as his page 170 description of a key character, with the author's permission and with my deep gratitude.)

It is one thing to decide that a novel based on that life

was necessary; the next question was just which novel? The answer was inspired by Theodor Ebert's important 2009 book, *The Mysterious Death of René Descartes* (Alibri Verlag). Descartes's death indeed was mysterious, and since he had many enemies, very credible rumors swirled at the time that it was no mere case of pneumonia. Ebert argues compellingly that those rumors weren't merely credible but actually true. Though *The Irrationalist* diverges greatly from the specific conclusions in Ebert's book, I acknowledge with gratitude its inspiration.

And, finally, I acknowledge my wife Gaby, who responded to my innumerable requests for guidance while writing this novel by innumerably asking, 'Must I do all your thinking for you?' To which the answer was, and always is: Yes, please.